Origin of The Maker

Sharon K. Angelici

Copyright © 2022

Write with Light Publications
Colorado, USA

ISBN: 9798806348839
ISBN: 978-1-7378158-2-2
ISBN: 978-1-970289-07-7
Library of Congress Number: 2022932781

Dedication

For my husband, my daughter, and my son: you inspire me, and I'm grateful for the minutes, days, and years of living this adventure called life. I adore you. I'm glad you are mine and that my rainbow heart is free to be.

To Taylor, thank you for getting Wildwood and Shay!

For my Aussie family, my Minnesotans, my rainbow support team: thank you for every mile traveled and every celebratory cheer. Three and on to four!

To Hillary, you get it when very few can.

Kathy and Kelly, thanks for your creativity and enthusiasm and all the extras you bring.

To Dad, I love you, and I'm so happy you get to hold my stories in your hands and actually read them.

For Mom, my witchy inspiration. I wish you'd have known my queerness. This world of Bannock begins and ends because you inspired me to be myself. You make me believe. If wishes were reality, this book would be in your beautiful hands.

●

CHAPTER I

DETONATE

"Shay!" I yelled as I stared at the limp body on the concrete floor. As a blacksmith, my hands were steady. They had to be. I controlled every aspect of forging with the precise swing of my hammer. Today, that precision had blown up in my face.

The Peace Prize namesake, Alfred Nobel, invented a helpful explosive in the 1860s. His quest to stabilize the volatile liquid of nitroglycerin led to the blending of sand from the German moorlands to create a kneadable paste; it was the power behind his creation, dynamite, named for Dynamis, the Greek god.

I'd never witnessed the force of the explosive's power, almost as old as the building around me, but standing in the workshop of my carriage house, I was sure I felt Dymanis' influence in the room. For all of the power that the Greek god commanded, he was no match for the life force surge of the goddess Brigid and the hammer that dangled from my anvil. I felt the vitality of the Maker move through me. The Maker, one of the ethereal forces in this tiny ghost town, meant to save us all. When I set my Maker's mark into the head of the hammer, the goddess of the forge became my grounded power–the power that just moved through me and out of me and into my companions.

Dexter, our morphing half-dragon, half-dog, whipped his articulated tail around to shove his snout closer to my girlfriend,

Shay, the woman who lay unconscious on the floor. I dropped everything and crawled to her side.

"Shay!" My hands wrapped around her shoulders to shake her pale, limp body. "Shay, baby. Wake up." I brushed the damp tangles of red hair clinging to the side of her face. Dexter, in dragon form, was breathing over my neck, the force of my Maker power surge changing him from his furry German Shepherd self.

"Maybe you should kiss her." I didn't recognize the voice coming from the shadows of my workshop, but it was as annoying as the grumbling sound of gravel tumbling in a glass.

I looked up to see who or what it was. "Who the hell are you?" I asked as I scooted my knees under Shay's head to draw her up into my lap.

I was surprised to see a quite small, solidly built fairy had landed on my girlfriend's prone body. His round face was pinched with curiosity, and he adjusted the leather belt around his plump belly. Dexter leaned in, snorting hard enough to tumble the small creature off Shay's body and onto the floor.

"Call off fire-face, will ya?" The fairy brushed the dirt from their body. "That's embarrassing."

"Who are you?" I asked again, a little more forcefully. I was losing my patience, and fighting with this irritating creature was keeping me from helping Shay.

"Who *I* am is irrelevant now that I know who you are." The fairy strolled up Shay's body as if she wasn't an unconscious human being. "The Maker. Finally!"

I felt Shay's arm flex as the mini-winged creature walked over the scars on her hand. "Shay?" I called her name again.

Her arm lifted to cover her face as if a bright light was shining in her eyes. "What the hell was that?" she asked as she tried to get up. I gripped her under her shoulders to help her sit.

"My mark." The explanation came out of my mouth, unfiltered. "When I set my mark in the hammer, the room exploded."

The stubby, winged creature flittered above us, and for a moment, I was intrigued by the not-so-delicate features that seemed to match the not-so-delicate sound of their voice. There was nothing graceful about this fairy in front of us.

"That was more than the mark of the Maker, kid. That was the power of the goddess staking a claim."

Shay rubbed balled fists over her eyes and pushed up to sit beside me. "Who the hell are you?"

I could tell from the moment they heard Shay's voice that they were smitten. The fairy dropped down onto Shay's knee for a grand introduction. "I'm Omatarius Fiddlegliph Sotious, the thirty-fifth of my line. But to make life easier, you can call me Stout. My pronouns are he/him, and I serve the Maker. Although…if I'd known the Magick was so gorgeous, maybe I'd have switched teams."

Shay placed her open hand close enough for him to step on her palm. I grabbed her wrist and pulled it back. "Oh, hell no! There's no way he's touching you."

I felt Shay's body move away as she stood from her prone position on the floor. The sudden adjustment of her posture caused her to sway, and I noticed her rubbing the back of her head.

I jumped up to help her, worried she was injured. "Sweetheart, are you alright?"

"Fine." She waved off my question as she walked closer to the anvil. "I think we did it. . . finally." Her hand came up to the back of her neck, and I could see blood on her fingertips when she pulled it away.

"You're not okay," I said. I grabbed her shoulder to turn her toward me. "What's your name?" I gave her body a little shake.

Her hands came up to cover my own. "Are you serious?" she asked as she pushed back.

"Look at me."

My face must have looked a mess. I'd spent most of the day in the workshop scraping the decomposed remains of a demon from the head of Brigid's hammer. I could feel the loose strands of my black hair sticking to the sweat on my forehead. The grime on my hands and face was lost in the tone of my skin. I was a sight, but right now, I just needed to know if the woman in my arms was alright.

She reached forward to push the hair from my face, and her cheeks pressed up with a smile. The green of her eyes was bright, and the shine told me she was my Shay, but I had to focus and not get lost in those eyes.

"You look so good." Her fingers drifted over the fine hairs on the back of my neck.

My hand brushed hers away. "No, I'm not kidding. What's your name?"

She held my fingers and kissed each one on the tip. "Shay Pierce."

The tenderness of her affection was a distraction, and I shook my head to clear my thoughts before asking, "What do you do?" I held tight to her hand.

"Are we seriously going to play fifty questions right now?" Her fingers tangled in my own, but the straight line of my lips told her I was serious. "Fine! I'm a police officer in charge of the K-9 unit for the Bannock Police department."

So far, she was passing the test. "Who am *I*?" I pointed to my chest.

Her lips curled up in a smile. "You? You, with those beautiful brown eyes and those kissable lips and this adorable little scar?" She touched the faded slice on my cheek. My first encounter with a demon and a taser had left a mark on my face. "You are the love of my life, Wildwood Blackstone." Her hand fell to my hip, and she pulled me close. "It would take a thousand celestial explosions for me to forget you." She touched her lips to mine.

My forehead rested against hers. "That's very good." My lips parted as I drew a long breath. Exhaling, I said. "That's very, very good to know."

"I'm glad you got that out of the way." Stout's gruff voice broke through our conversation. He landed on top of the anvil, not far from the teetering hammer.

"Hey! Don't touch that." I grabbed the handle and held it to my chest. I didn't like the way this guy assumed himself to be at home here.

"Sweetheart." Shay's arm came around my waist, her soothing voice reminding me she was always a cop, a keeper of the peace. Something I was not. "It's okay," Shay whispered.

"Okay?" I didn't see the "okay" in the room. "Setting my maker's mark made the workshop explode!"

Stout crossed his arms over his chest. "The mark didn't do it; you did."

I reached to grab the obnoxious fairy, but Shay held my hand. "Wait, just stop, both of you." She rubbed her forehead. "Give me a second to think."

"Yeah, let her think, Woodwild." The mispronunciation of my name was meant to annoy me, and it worked, but two could play that game.

"It's Wild—wood, Obnoxious."

"It's Omatarius."

"I like Obnoxious better," I spat back before he could say anything else, then asked, "What are you even doing here?"

"More importantly, how are you here?" Shay interrupted. "You shouldn't even be here." She turned around, walking to the sacred circle on the carriage house floor. She'd buried a Gatekeeper demon beneath the ring months ago. That ritual was meant to keep all forms of magickal beings from entering, but somehow Stout was here.

"That's not much of a welcome," he grumbled. I could hear the flittering buzz of his wings, similar to a plastic card shoved in the spoke of a bicycle tire. It was not a pleasant sound. He landed just outside the ring. "I'm here. I've always been here. You just didn't notice."

"How?" Shay and I asked in unison.

"Wait, just wait." I held up a hand. "What do you mean, you've been here the whole time?"

His knees bent deep as he pushed off the floor and launched into the air. He flew over to the table and forced a pair of blacksmith tongs to the floor. As he hopped over the chair, the draft from his wings sorted the note pages into a pile. He was a mischief-maker–and a rather good one.

This little fairy was the sound I'd heard the first day I was alone in the carriage house. He was the reason I'd called the police, thinking I had a squatter. I looked at the redhead standing beside me. "Shay?"

The thought must have hit her at the same time because she said, "He's the squatter, isn't he?"

He twirled in the air and gave a bow. "That was me."

Shay was standing next to the table, turning notes into a pile. She picked up a page and pointed it at Stout. "She sent you, didn't she?"

I stepped closer to see what Shay was holding in her hand. I knew the creases on the page. There were tear stains on the corner of the paper. It was the letter from Benton, the last words of Shay's mentor and friend.

Stout held out his hands. Maybe he thought Shay would pound him, but if he did, he didn't know my lady at all. "Regina sent me here the day you picked up your keys, Woo… Wildwood."

"Sent you here for me?" I pointed at myself. "Why? Why not Shay?"

Shay dropped into the workshop chair. Her head fell back against the sliding barnwood door, and I could see that the entire exchange hurt. Those brilliant green eyes closed for a long moment and I waited, wondering what memories she was reliving.

"Because she already knew me," Shay answered for Stout. "She knew everything about me, but you . . ." Shay pointed her letter-filled hand directly at me. "She didn't know anything about you."

"So you're some kind of spy?" I watched Shay struggle to stand. "Hey, you're not okay."

I took the paper from her hand and tossed it on the table. She threw her arm around my shoulder, and we walked to the stairs together. It was rare for Shay to need help, and the way she willingly relaxed her weight against my body meant that she was definitely struggling from the blow to her head.

Her feet hit the bottom step, and she used the handrail to climb to the top. I crossed the room and picked up Brigid's hammer; I wasn't about to leave that with our new friend. I turned around to see the miniature, fluttering man walk across the letter from Benton. He flopped down on her signature at the bottom of the page.

Stout.

What were we going to do with the mysterious fairy named Stout?

CHAPTER II

BOUND

"Shay?"

She was sitting at the kitchen table when I reached the top of the stairs. The apartment's open space made it easy to move from the shelves of books we used for research to the couch and kitchen space that held most of the history of our small town of Bannock and the powers of magick Shay and I possessed.

I had found most of my furniture in the apartment, often rescued from the curb or a dumpster. Turning old and abandoned into luxurious and comfortable resulted from my life as a foster care child. I liked the threadbare couch. Shay and I fit on it well. The kitchen table supporting my girlfriend right now was the only piece of furniture that came assembled when I'd taken ownership of this building.

Everyone and everything in this space felt like home. Brigid's hammer was in my hand. I held hope that we could decipher the Pictish writing that stenciled the edges and interpret the masterfully etched images on the sides.

"Shay?" I asked again.

She was half-holding her head in her hand as I set the hammer on the table in front of her. "We have a personal fairy named Stout." Shay looked up at me as if I hadn't just put an enchanted block of metal in front of her.

"It appears that we do," I said. There was a duffle bag beside the couch, and I could see Shay's body armor lying on top. She'd been in a hurry when she'd come home from work today, excited to stamp my Maker's mark on the hammer. I could see that tonight's research would be more complicated than we'd anticipated. Maybe we needed to pause our plans. "You must be hungry?"

"I am. Dani grabbed something for me at lunch, but that seems like ages ago."

Officer Danielle Forrest was a good friend to Shay and was also part of the demon-hunting side of the Bannock police force. She was good in a fight, and she and Shay took care of one another. That knowledge made it easier for me to watch Shay go out the door every day.

"I think I can whip up a salad." I opened the freezer door. "Oh, how about–"

She interrupted me, saying, "Nothing fancy. I just need some energy, and maybe if you can come over here, I could use a bit of you." She was rubbing the back of her head, and her posture reminded me that the explosion had thrown her across the room.

Two quick steps brought me around the table and beside Shay. "How's your head?"

She turned sideways on the chair and spread her legs far enough to pull me in between her thighs. Her arms wrapped around my waist, and the desperation of her embrace was an answer. Shay was hurting, and she needed me.

"How are you feeling?" I asked.

"I think I'm fine. I just needed to hold you, to be sure."

"And your head?" My hands trailed over the back of her neck, and in response, her body started shaking. "Shay?"

She looked up at me, and I could see the pain in the tiny creases that should be smile lines around her eyes. "I'm drained, Wil."

The clock on the wall said 5:18 p.m. We had hours of research ahead of us. "How about I make you a bath so that you can soak, and we can talk?"

"That would work." She didn't move from my arms, and I was content to hold her just a little longer.

I kissed the top of her head. "Let me go fill the tub." Her arms squeezed me tight before falling away. She looked up at me, and I touched her chin. "I love you."

"I love you too."

She stretched to kiss me, and I could feel her exhaustion as her shoulder slumped against the side of the chair. I didn't want to leave her, but I also knew a bath would ease the ache of being tossed against the workshop's stone wall. The thought seemed too impossible to be real.

I picked up Shay's duffle bag and Kevlar vest and carried them to our bedroom. Her police uniform lay draped over the chair, and her boots, kicked off in haste about an hour ago, were on the floor beneath it. She'd been excited to hurry down to the workshop and mark Brigid's hammer with me, so much so that she hadn't tidied up.

The oversized claw-foot tub looked inviting. I stopped the drain and sprinkled a few drops of lavender oil on the surface. A folded towel beside the ledge was the final touch as I lit the taper candle.

"Wildwood." Her voice was just above a whisper, but I still jumped as she spoke.

Shay stood naked, eyeing me up and down as I did the same to her in return. Her legs were crossed at the ankles as her shoulder rested against the frame of the bathroom door. Something was reassuring about the ease of her posture, and I couldn't believe that this was the same woman who wouldn't let me touch her all those months ago. It was impossible to hide the crisscrossed stab wound scars on her arms, so she didn't. But until I'd moved to town, she'd chosen a solitary life to keep the wounds on her back and torso a secret. Every scar was just another part of her beauty, and I knew that the way we looked at each other right now was the reason she was comfortable in front of me. I made an obvious scan over her broad shoulders, muscular arms, full breasts, defined torso, and…a bag of peas?

"That's kinda perfect." She pointed to my bathtub arrangement.

"I think you're kinda perfect," I said as I raised an eyebrow at the plastic bag in her hand.

"For the swelling." She shook the frozen bag at me as she pushed off the door and walked to the bath. "You getting in, too?" Shay sat on the rim of the tub and wriggled her fingers through the shallow water to test the temperature.

I looked down at my hands and arms. "First, I need to wash off."

"You're going to wash off *before* getting in the bath?"

"You make it sound weird."

"That's because it is." She swiveled over the rim of the tub and lowered herself into the water. It wasn't deep enough to cover her thighs, but she leaned back, sandwiching the peas between her head and the basin, waiting for the water to rise.

I rinsed my arms under the sink's tap and lathered them with soap. "I've been working on the hammer all day, and I'm covered in rehydrated demon sludge. Do you really want to soak with me and *this*?" I turned around to show her my dripping arms.

"Probably not."

"Good! Now, while you're in there and I'm over here, why don't you tell me what we need to do next?" I turned toward the sink and talked to her through the reflection in the mirror.

Her head dropped to the back of the tub as she blew out a breath from her puffed cheeks. "I need to translate the Pictish, and you need to use that hammer."

They seemed like simple tasks to accomplish. Shay spoke at least three languages and read a half dozen more, while I was very good with a hammer. Despite our skills, however, she was planning to decipher a lost language, and I was about to use the many hundreds of years old hammer we'd just found–a hammer charged with the power of a goddess that had just exploded in my workshop. Easy enough, right?

"And what about your new best friend?" The warm water washed over my arms and face, and I reached for the towel to dry them. I turned around to see the curious crinkle of Shay's forehead.

"My new what?" she asked.

"Stout," I explained. "Your new fairy buddy."

Shay was quiet for a heartbeat, and I wondered what she was thinking. I didn't have to wait long before she stood up from the water and climbed out of the bath, leaving a floating bag of peas behind. She grabbed the towel and wrapped it around her torso before marching to the bedroom. I didn't know where she was going, so I turned off the water and followed. She rubbed the towel over her chest and back and threw it on the bed. Her movements were sharp as her head popped through a t-shirt and her legs kicked into a pair of athletic shorts. She pushed her feet into slippers and walked to the stairs. She was on a mission, and I wanted to know what it was.

I waited on the last stair when I saw Shay poking at Stout. "Revoke it!" she yelled, roughing up all six inches of the fairy on the table.

"*She* has to ask me to do that." His little body pitched forward to push back against Shay.

Shay looked at me and, without explanation, yelled across the room, "Tell him to revoke it!"

"Revoke what?" I didn't understand what was happening. My gorgeous, half-dressed girlfriend was shaking a finger at the tiniest, seemingly defenseless fairy.

Shay pointed at Stout. "You told him your name. You never tell the people of the fae your name. It gives them power over you."

"Power over…" I was confused. Only a few weeks before, we'd met an adorable little sprite. That exchange was entirely different from our current situation.

"Yes, power over you." Shay pointed at me for emphasis. "Once a fairy tricks you into sharing your name, you're easy to manipulate."

The fairy interrupted. "I didn't trick her. She just did it." Stout had a powerful voice for his size, and it was odd to hear it coming from such a compact being.

"I don't care what she did. Revoke it. Now!"

"If you know the rules of the fae and the laws about taking names, you also know that you shouldn't piss—a—fairy—off!" He crossed his arms and stomped a foot; his voice was loud enough to get our K-9's attention. Our miniature dragon was less intimidating in dog form, but when his upper lip lifted, revealing sharp canine teeth, the guttural rumble of his growl made even *me* question my safety.

Shay slapped both hands on the table. "And you should know…" She raised her right palm, holding it inches from his body. "*Ignis.*" Her vocalization of the Latin word summoned the flickering blue flame to her hand. Stout backed off, using his wings to hover away from the heat. "Don't—*mess*—with the Magick."

Shay pounded her *ignis* fire down on the table, and blue flame spattered like puckering lava. I'd never witnessed Shay use such force. Sure, I'd watched her slash at an attacking demon, but going after a fairy that would fit inside a pickle jar seemed a little aggressive. It was clear I did not know how dangerous the situation was.

Stout landed on the opposite side of the table. "Fine!" He waved his hand in surrender. "I revoke the name of Wildwood and release her from my bond of servitude." He spoke the words without emotion and with a sing-song delivery.

"Forever!" Shay yelled at him. "Do it, forever."

"Fine!" His wings flittered, and I wondered if they would always be so loud. "I revoke the name of Wildwood and release her from my bond of servitude, forever."

"Good! Now, what else did you do when I wasn't altogether here?" Shay asked. Her voice was still loud, but she wasn't quite as intimidating in her shorts and t-shirt.

"Nothing. I did nothing but try to explain why I'm here."

Shay leaned against the workshop table and crossed her arms over her chest. Stout was about to feel the full power of

Shay's questioning, and I was interested to watch. "Benton sent you here. Why?"

"You sure you want to know? You might not be ready for the answer." He floated away from the table and landed on the rack of blacksmithing tools.

"We're more than ready for answers," I said before Shay could. "We need to know."

"Benton sent me here to get the ball rolling," he explained. Whether or not he intended it, his answer seemed evasive as he kept space between us, flying from the tool shelf to the tabletop.

"What do you mean, 'get the ball rolling'?" I asked.

Stout's explanation gave us very little information. "The two of you, all the pining and longing and sad stories of being apart. You were so busy falling in love that you almost missed that you were supposed to become the most powerful force ever to fight evil."

"We are more than capable of doing both," Shay spat back as her palms slapped against the tabletop again.

"Not from where I was standing." Stout's attitude was curious, and I had to give him credit; he was holding his own against my girlfriend's best intimidation tactics.

"That brings up another question." Shay twirled her finger in the air, pointing around the carriage house workshop. "Where exactly have you been standing?"

Shay's question was odd at first, but then I thought about what she'd said. Stout had been coming and going from the carriage house. He was a secret witness to private moments, intimate moments, and…

"Did you see us?" I asked him, looking at Shay. "We do things in here. Together. Private things."

Stout pushed off the table and hovered in front of me. "I don't stick around for all your sex, if that's what you're asking. I'm a fairy, not a pig. Although you've got some moves, superhero." He flew close enough to Shay's face to wink at her, and I swatted at him for using the playful nickname.

Shay nodded. "You have boundaries. If Benton sent you, I know you were constrained by an agreement."

I didn't know what Shay was talking about, and I was sure I would have to read a few books about not getting tricked by Stout again.

"You're a smart one; I'll give you that," he said.

The sound of his wing-flutter was annoying, and I was sure I'd heard it before, but I couldn't place why it was so familiar. Shay reached up to rub the back of her head. Amid everything else, my girl was also still recovering from the explosion.

"Do you think we can go sit down?" I asked Shay. "You should get off your feet and maybe put those peas back on your head."

"What are your boundaries?" Shay persisted.

Stout held up his hand in front of us, pointing at his fingers as he counted the boundaries off. "I'm supposed to guide and not interfere. I'm supposed to help you the same way I helped Regina. But most importantly, I'm not to follow the code of the fae and..."

"What?" Shay asked. "You just said you aren't supposed to follow the code?"

"I said a lot of things, Red."

"Don't call me that." Shay's voice was loud again. "Look at me, Stout."

Watching the two of them was entertaining, and I felt a little guilty finding pleasure in their exchange.

"I don't want to." He kicked his foot and tried to hide his face.

She held out her hand. "Did Regina tell you to take care of us?"

The fight was over; I could see it in the fairy's eyes. Stout hovered above Shay's palm, staring at the place where her *ignis* flame emerged. "You aren't going to barbecue me, are you?" he asked.

"That depends. Are you here to be my enemy or my friend?"

"I'm here because I loved Regina. I'm here because she loved you, and she didn't want you to make the same mistakes that she did."

His answer seemed to satisfy Shay. "Fine. So let's start again. What do you know about who we are?" Shay asked.

"Whoo, that's a great, big, giant question. Maybe we can take a smaller bite of the apple." He landed in Shay's hand and sat down on the longest scar in her palm. "These are quite beautiful." He rubbed across the old wound.

Shay popped Stout off and pulled her hand to her chest. "Don't."

Stout tumbled in the air before righting himself and flying back in front of us. "I didn't mean that in a bad way, Red."

"What *did* you mean?" I asked, pushing Shay behind me. It wasn't often that I put myself between the cop and any kind of danger. I didn't know if this six-inch creature could do as much damage as an 8-foot tall demon, but I wasn't taking any chances.

Stout held up his hands in surrender. "It's not like that. It's just that the Magick has survived thousands of battles for hundreds of years. Battle scars are like ceremonial garments. The fae world holds you in high regard, Red."

"You have to stop calling me that." Shay pulled out the chair and dropped into it. "What are you talking about? I've heard nothing about scars and garments."

He flew to the tabletop in front of Shay, landing on the letter from Benton. "When did you learn about who Regina was?" He laid on the signature at the bottom of the page.

"After she was gone."

"Do you know why Regina did that?" he asked.

"Because she wanted me to perform the invocation spell." Shay's voice was a whisper. "She wanted me to become the Magick."

"The scars on your hands are a lot like the scars Regina had," he explained. "Every Magick before you suffered terrible cruelty. Regina knew it the first day she met you. Oh, and you translated the Latin riddle. That was another step."

Shay got up from the table and walked up the stairs. She didn't say another word to me or the fairy sitting on Benton's signature. I waited to see if she returned, but she didn't. I lingered as long as I could until I ran up the stairs, skipping every other step until I reached the top. Shay was on the couch, holding her tattered Latin dictionary. She looked up at me, and I froze in the entryway. Her eyes were glassy with tears, and I wondered if the absence of Benton would ever stop breaking her heart.

"It was never really a choice at all?" She looked up at me, holding the cover of the book so I could see it. "They groomed me to become this." Shay was the Magick of Bannock. So far, it felt like a wild ride of mystical powers, but I'd always seen Shay as a perfectly rounded individual. I never doubted she could carry the powers.

"Is it so terrible?" I asked.

I wasn't a complex person. Blacksmithing and welding don't create any amount of conflict. The most adventure I'd experienced in my life had happened after turning the key in the lock of this old carriage house building.

"I don't know how terrible it's going to get. Not yet, anyway."

I walked across the room to sit beside her. She made space for me as I took the book from her hand. "You're an intelligent woman, and you're very good at your job. You'll be great at being the Magick of Bannock, too."

Shay fumbled for my hand. "You carry the hammer made by the Goddess of Creation. You're not even a little freaked out by that?"

I thought about what she'd said. I carried the Hammer of Creation? Me? Why? What was I meant to create? How would I balance my simple life with the mantle of Brigid's fire? "Well, it didn't freak me out, not until just now." I fell against the cushion beside her. The book dropped from my hand, and I pulled Shay into my lap.

As her head fell against my shoulder, she whispered. "I didn't mean to make you anxious."

"It's probably not good for the Magick and Maker balance if both of us are anxious about our powers."

Her body shook against mine, and I worried she was crying. I pushed her away, just enough to see the smile on her face. "Shay, love...we're going to be okay."

She nuzzled into my neck. "We don't have any other choice. I don't want this life if you aren't a part of it."

I thought about our history and then about the complications of the Maker and Magick's relationship. How could anyone balance such powers without very intimate connections? "It must have been hard for Benton."

"To be alone?" she asked.

"Yes, but not just that." I ran my finger along the length of her knee. "We have something that Benton and Jacob didn't."

"I guess we do." She stopped my hand and turned the palm over. She touched the blood-pact scar made by my tiny pocket knife almost fifteen years ago. "I'd do anything to keep us together."

Our fingertips steepled as our palms came together. "And I would too."

"So, we can do this," she said as she sat up. "Now, we need to figure out how Stout fits into our life."

"I didn't know about the fairy folk," I said, feeling rather ignorant about their existence.

Shay's feet dropped to the floor, and she tried to leave my lap. "It's okay, Wil. Why would you think that you'd need to know about the fae?"

"Before now, I wouldn't." I tugged her hip, and she turned around, kneeling to straddle my lap as I looked into her eyes. "I think reading is going to become my newest and least favorite hobby."

"Probably a good choice." Shay's fingers combed through my hair. "Something tells me that Benton and Stout were more than casual friends."

I held her waist, pulling her into me. "I guess that means we need to talk to our fairy friend."

"Mm-hmm." Her hips pressed a little closer. "I feel like we need to do a lot of things."

"Shay, baby. You and I, like this, it's always perfect, but we've got a fairy named Stout downstairs weeping on a letter from Benton."

She arched away, pushing my shoulders against the couch. Those green eyes were like a shard to the heart. "Spoilsport."

"Maybe, but I'm positive that I don't want our little friend to see any more action."

Shay kissed me. "So practical," she whispered as she climbed off my lap.

"I know. You're usually the practical one in this relationship." I snagged the bottom of her shirt with my finger to stop her from walking away. "You're okay?"

"I'm better than okay," she said.

"Should I go get Stout?" I pushed off the cushion, knocking the Latin dictionary to the floor.

"Yes, get him and maybe bring Dex up. I want to make sure he's all right." She picked up the book and carried it to the table.

"What are you going to do?" I asked.

"I'm going to sharpen a few pencils. I think my new friend has much to say about a lot of things." Her cheek lifted, and tiny lines wrinkled around her eyes as she smiled. I'd do anything to keep that expression on her face.

"I'll be right back." Two steps at a time brought me to the bottom of the stairs. I expected to see Stout on the table where we'd left him. Instead, he was standing outside our sacred circle on the floor. Dexter was snorting at him, sending puffs of smoke out his nose.

"You put your mark here?" he asked. His steps were deliberate as he moved around the edge.

"I did," I confirmed, dropping to one knee to get closer to the symbol I'd etched on the concrete.

"You know that's a powerful symbol."

"I know that it's my maker's mark." I ran my finger around the symbol, tracing the circle and lines until I'd cleaned out the dust. The Norse-style hammer was clear to see. "What makes it so powerful?"

"It's the Mark of the Maker." He jumped up, and before he could fall, his wings fluttered. "You shouldn't have put it here. Not over this."

"Dex," I called the dog, and he sat up from the circle. "Go see Shay, Dex." He was up on all fours, his hand-sized paws thumping as he ran to the apartment above us. "Why? What's wrong with the mark being here?"

"There's a Gatekeeper under there. Why would you mark it?"

"I didn't do it to mark the demon. It was just to mark the cement of my carriage house." I wondered how he knew what we had buried beneath the solid ground.

"Red should have known better." He flew over to the anvil, avoiding the sacred circle.

"You really should stop calling her that. She doesn't like it at all."

"What she doesn't hear can't hurt her." He landed on the anvil, bending down to swipe his hand across the bits of scale collected on the surface. He rubbed it over his arms. His wings folded around his body, and he swooshed the dust all over them.

I was curious. "What are you doing?"

"It's been a long time since I've had demon sift. I'm just using a little."

"Demon sift?" I asked.

"I think you've been calling it demon anvil dust. We call it sift. It doesn't matter what you call it. This is powerful magick, and you should not leave it lying around on the floor. Things will come for it."

"Things?"

"Maybe you should call Red down here so she can hear this, too."

The short-handled corn broom was hanging on the wall, and I used it to clean the anvil and the surrounding floor. I collected more than I expected. "I can't get over how much is here."

"It's lucky for you Red is an excellent spell caster, or you'd be crawling with magick folk right now."

"So my anvil dust...I mean, demon sift is in demand?"

"It is." He scratched his head. "You've used it a few times out there." He pointed to the door of the carriage house.

"We have, yes. Shay got hurt a few times."

"How sick did she get?" he asked.

"Sick?"

"The sift of a demon takes a toll on an injured user. The period of adjustment can be difficult." He flew to the bottom of the stairs. "I'm sure she was out for days."

"She wasn't. We just used it yesterday."

He looked up at the light coming from the apartment. "That's not possible. The first time Regina used it, she was unconscious for three days. Jacob was worried and half out of his mind."

"Shay was fighting demons a few hours later," I explained with an inflated sense of pride.

"What are you doing down there?" Shay yelled from the top of the stairs, kicking a foot over the step.

"You should talk to Shay." I jerked a thumb at the staircase.

"I can't go up there."

"What do you mean?" I asked.

He looked up at Shay. "The Magick. Now that we've made that pact, she has to let me up there."

"Why?" It was frustrating. Why was this fairy so tight-lipped with information? If Benton sent him, why wouldn't he just tell me what was going on?

"It's a fail-safe. Regina made me promise to give Red one place. The carriage house is her home, and now that we've made an agreement, I'm not allowed to enter unless she says so."

"What if I say so? It's my house, too."

"Regina set the boundaries, and when she died...Let's just say that Red is the only one that can set the boundaries now."

Shay listened to every word, watching us, waiting for a chance to speak. "If I let you up here, are you going to tell us about the circle and Regina and the Magick?"

"I took an oath to serve the Magick."

Shay sat down on the top step. "I give you permission to enter, but there are a few rules."

His wings made a horrible whirring sound as he swept up the staircase. "What are the rules, Red?"

She shook her head at the use of the nickname. "You may enter with permission only."

"Every time?" he asked.

"Every time until I say otherwise."

He hovered above her knees. "Fine, what else?"

"I don't know yet, so I'm leaving it open. You'll just have to give us time to figure it out."

"Is that another rule?"

"Yes." She held out her hand to him. "Come into the apartment."

He flew into her open palm. "Can you do that *ignis* flame with both hands?"

Shay turned around with Stout in her palm. "Yes, so don't break the rules."

"Got it."

"You coming up, sweetheart?" Shay yelled down at me.

I was flipping the switch for the workshop lights at the bottom stair. "I'm right behind you."

CHAPTER III

ANCESTRY

Dexter lay curled up on his bed in the corner, licking clean every crack and crevice of his paws. Stout didn't waste a minute, making himself comfortable as he sat on the edge of the kitchen table. Bubbles of foam were thick at the top of the glass of beer Shay was pouring. She set it down on the table, and the fairy was fast to his feet.

"You should pour one for me, too." Stout pressed his face to the side of the glass, the prism effect distorting his face as he circled the amber liquid.

"A fairy that drinks beer?" I laughed at Stout's obvious excitement. How much could the little sprite consume? "One for me too, please?" I asked.

Shay opened another bottle and poured half into a glass. Stout flew around her hand and pushed the bottom of the bottle, tipping the entire contents into his glass. "Don't be stingy. It's going to be a long night."

Shay grabbed a beer for me, and I sat down at the table, waiting for whatever was coming next.

"Tell me, Stout, how did you end up here?" Shay wasn't wasting any time looking for the answers that I was trying to sort out on my own.

He flew over to the cabinet and pulled a drinking straw from the top shelf. His little hands peeled away the paper wrapper, and he used the force of his fairy lungs to blow the rest off the straw. The paper ribbon shot in a zig-zag path toward the sink. "Oh, you're eco-friendly paper straw people." He launched it like a javelin into the center of his glass. "These don't last as long as bamboo. You should get some bamboo."

"You're lucky we have them at all." Shay passed my bottle across the table, and we sat down to listen to our beer-drinking fairy.

"You were about to tell us how you gained access to the carriage house." Shay leaned back in her chair and took a sip of her drink.

We watched as Stout wrapped his hands around the end of the straw and sucked down a quarter of the glass. "You see," he began, licking his lips, "Regina had this plan." He slurped down another quarter portion of his beer and wiped his arm across his face. "I was supposed to come in and watch for demon sift, and when I saw it, I was supposed to report back to her."

Shay held up a finger. "Wait, what? What is demon sift?"

"We've been calling it demon anvil dust." I explained. "It's like otherworldly penicillin mixed with superglue."

"From my experience, it works like that and more," Shay said while I tried to block out the memory of her demon fight in the mine and the wounds inflicted upon her body. Without the demon sift, Shay would be recovering in bed, or worse, in a hospital.

"It's powerful stuff, and Regina wanted it. To be honest, all of us want it." He took another drink from his beer. "As soon as she knew you were going to become the Maker, she sent me here for you." He flew in front of us and jabbed at my chest.

I wrinkled my nose. "For me? Why?"

"The daggers," he explained. "She knew that her time as the Magick was about to end, and she wanted to make sure that I was here, visible to you when she was gone."

My thoughts tuned out the conversation as I remembered my first days in the carriage house. The unsettling whispered sounds that I couldn't explain. The bumping and banging of tools falling to the floor. The salt-ringed sacred circle wrecked by my inexperienced shovel and broom. Perhaps it wasn't my ignorance of magick, but a perfectly placed fairy on a mission. "Did you help me damage the barrier and release the Gatekeeper demon?" I interrupted.

He dropped to the table and walked across the notebooks. "I didn't do it on my own, no. I just made sure when you finished sweeping that the circle was very broken."

Shay's elbows rested on the table, and she leaned closer to Stout. "Do you realize how dangerous that was?" She picked up the notebook Stout was standing on. "Wildwood knew nothing about Bannock and the history of demons. You put her life in danger."

Shay was right. When I moved to this town, I came in a car filled with tools. No magick tomes. No dreams of pagan rituals and nothing resembling the forgeable demon material Benton left behind.

"If you remember, she made most of that danger all on her own, Red." Stout was sharing the facts, with no emotion, and no investment in the players, but Shay and I had lived those moments, and they'd almost kept us apart.

I scooted my chair closer to Shay. "That attack is impossible to forget." I took the book from her hand and set it beside us.

Stout walked off to suck down the last sips of beer in his glass. He fluttered around the rim, maneuvering the end of the straw to slurp every drop.

Shay dismissed the comment. "But how are you here? How are you breaking the spell of protection?"

"Oh, that's so easy." He huffed against the knuckles of his hand and rubbed them across his tiny chest, pleased with himself. "How does the rabbit jump the fence?"

I looked at Shay, and she looked at me, and I was sure that Stout was feeling the effects of that beer. "Is this like the chicken crossing the road?" I asked.

Shay's forehead dropped to the table. Her voice was muffled as it vibrated against her arms. "What is wrong with you two?"

Stout tapped Shay's fingers. "You asked me how I got in. I got in because I never got out. That's how the rabbit jumps the fence. He was in it when you built it." Stout jumped up and twirled in the air. "I was in the carriage house when you cast the protection spell. Benton put me here, and ever since, I've been part of everything."

"Everything?" I asked, remembering the reunion between Shay and me. Those first evenings as we'd relived our last years in foster care. The secrets about magick and her scars and the fears of intimacy she'd shared in her most vulnerable moments. Those sensitive conversations were private, and his secret presence felt like an invasion of our most intimate moments.

He held up his hands in defense. "Not everything." He leaned against his empty glass. "As I said before, there were boundaries, and they will remain until you decide if I stay or go."

"What else did you do here?" Shay asked, ignoring his not-so-subtle request to stay.

What was Stout's goal I wondered? What did he do when he was in the building? Why didn't we know he was here? "Yes, what else?" I asked.

He jumped into the air and flew to the stack of cardboard boxes, then climbed through the handle hole and flipped the lid to the floor. Pages of documents tipped up as Stout pushed through the pile inside. His head popped up, and he sniffed the air before flying to the next box. He was searching for something, and it took three boxes until a thick book fell over the box edge, followed by our fairy. His feet clenched the sides of the book as he carried it to the table. Stout's strength was impressive.

"I did this." He dropped it in front of us.

"*Book of Ceremonial Magic*," Shay read, drawing a finger over the title on the spine.

"Chapter Two." He pushed the cover, walking over the first page to open the book.

Shay flipped through the table of contents. "Ceremonial rites and rituals, page 122." Shay was a fast and thorough reader. She had an incredible memory, and I wondered why she didn't know this book. She turned to the chapter. "This is unbelievable," Shay said.

"What is it?" I asked.

Shay picked up our carriage house notebook and thumbed to a page. The pencil scribbles represented the runes on the wall downstairs, the writing surrounding the map of our town. It was the information written in the blood of a demon. We'd always thought that Jacob was the scribe, but it was Stout.

Her eyes were wide. "*You* painted the wall in the carriage house?" It wasn't a question as much as an overwhelming realization.

"It was Regina." He flew to the corner of the kitchen, far enough away from Shay to maybe avoid a blast of the *ignis* flame.

"Benton sent you here to—what did you call it?" The tone of Shay's voice was like a needle scratching across a long-playing record.

He rotated his arms like a wheel spinning in front of his belly. "Get the ball rolling." He was repeating the response from our conversation downstairs.

"How could you do that?" Shay yelled. "How could you set things in motion that would kill her?"

Stout's body flexed stiff as a board, and he dropped to the floor like a rock. I heard him hit hard and ran around the table to pick him up. Maybe it was too much beer, or perhaps Shay's accusation was more than his fairy ears could process.

I poked him with my finger. "Do you think he fainted?" I looked at Shay. "Do you know fairy CPR?"

"There's no such thing as fairy CPR."

Shay removed the straw from his cup to siphon beer from her glass. She waved it over his face like smelling salts. Stout's head popped up, and like a baby to a bottle, he grabbed the straw with both hands. Shay lifted her fingertip, and the fairy guzzled the contents.

He pushed the straw away from his face, stood from my hand and flew in front of Shay. "I loved Regina. I knew nothing about her death."

"Benton died when I became the Magick." Shay stumbled over the words, and I knew where her heart was. It came back to this. Shay would always carry guilt over the transfer of power. "How did you not know?"

"For the same reason that you didn't." He hovered in front of Shay, and I could see the exchange of understanding pass between them.

"You wouldn't have done it either?" Shay whispered.

"Exactly." He slapped his hands together before flying to sit on the highest ledge of the bookshelf. Benton's funeral flag was resting on top, held in a triangle-shaped frame. Stout pressed his fairy hands to the wood. "I loved Regina."

Was it possible to feel heartache for a fairy suffering from heartbreak? Shay sat on the couch and tucked her feet under her thighs. Perhaps they loved her equally, and they didn't have to prove it to each other. I held Shay's hand and watched as the two of them mourned the betrayal in silence.

My shoulder touched hers as I leaned in to whisper. "The two of you have a lot in common."

Shay looked up at the triangle folded flag that once covered her friend's coffin. "I guess we do."

"Maybe he can be part of our team?"

She tugged my hand into her lap. "I guess maybe he should. It's what Reg wanted."

I looked at the pile of paper on the table, the books and notes documenting a life lived and a future unknown. Shay and I longed for a family, for people we could trust when life was too much to do on our own. Bannock was giving the gift of family to us. Benton, Dani, Amelia, and now, Stout. This found family could fill a void, and all we had to do was let it.

"So, what do we do now?" I asked.

Shay pushed off the couch and walked to the table, then pulled off the towel covering Brigid's hammer. "We know a bit about the Magick of Bannock and my spellcasting. What about the powers of the Maker and this?" She tapped the table in front of the handle.

Stout heard the noise and leaned over to look at us. "The power in that hammer is strong. You should be careful with it."

Shay looked up at him. "Will you come down here and tell us what you know?"

He dangled his legs over the side of the bookcase, kicking his feet. "Will you pour me another beer?"

I looked at his empty glass and mine, which sat half full beside Shay's with only a sip gone, wondering if his relationship with Benton had anything to do with the accessibility of beer. I opened the refrigerator and handed Shay another bottle. She poured it in the glass, and by the time the bottle tipped empty, Stout was putting his mouth to the straw again.

Shay covered the straw with her finger. "Nope, let's talk about the hammer first."

He sat on the slope in the straw. "You negotiate hard, don't you, Red?"

"We need answers, Stout." Shay pulled the glass away, forcing Stout to hover in the air.

"I'll give you answers, but it's been a long time since I've had a beer. Regina was in the hospital, and I was locked up with you. You never leave empty bottles in the workshop, not even a drop in a glass. The two of you are too neat."

Shay set the glass on the table. "Hammer first."

He sat on the rim of the glass, pointing his toes to touch the foam at the top. He waved his arms in the air, making a dramatic gesture. "It's the Hammer of the Goddess." Maybe he expected thunder to erupt and lightning to strike, but the room remained silent.

"We already know *that*," I said. I gripped the handle in my hand, bouncing the weight with quick swings. "What does all the writing mean?" I ran my finger over the artwork on the side, tipping the face so the fairy could see it.

The top of the hammer turned toward Stout, exposing the entire silhouette of the goddess. He fell to one knee in mid-air and floated to the table. "Goddess, protect us." Until this moment, I'd perceived the flying man to be without reverence for anything or anyone but Benton. His prayerful slow descent was the first glimpse of respectful behavior from the fairy.

Shay set the glass on the table and sat in the chair beside me. "Goddess, protect us," she whispered.

What was I meant to say? I was holding the hammer in my hands. "Goddess, protect us?"

Stout jumped to his feet and flew in front of me. "You're holding the Hammer of the Goddess. Don't you know what that means?" That he had to ask me the question clarified that I did not know what it meant.

"I don't know what any of this means." I set the chunk of metal on the tabletop and dropped to sit in the chair beside Shay.

Stout noticed the abandoned glass of beer and flew to take a quick sip from his straw. He stood on the rim of the glass. "The power of the Goddess is in the hammer," he said as his chin touched the straw. " If you hold the hammer, the power is in you."

"It can't be that simple," Shay told him.

"Well, obviously, I dumbed it down because it's never that simple." He dangled from the end of the straw, taking another sip of his beer. His wings fluttered out of control before he dropped to the table. He picked up Shay's pencil and scribbled symbols on a blank page. "So Red, you know the runic alphabet. What do you know about Pictish or Pecti-Wita?" He didn't stop writing as he copied the symbols etched on the surface of my hammer.

"I know it exists," she said, "but other than that, I'd need a few books for reference."

Shay got up from the table, walked to the bedroom and came back carrying her duffle bag. Stout dropped his pencil, flew to the top shelf, and pushed a book at Shay, followed by two more. Shay caught all three, and the fairy flew back to the paper and pencil.

"You know my bookshelf well," Shay said as she crossed the room. "Maybe too well."

"I read almost as much as you do. Plus, Regina knew what should be on your shelves. Every book smells different based on the magicks inside." He looked at Shay. "Regina had more than a dozen different references to Pecti-Wita and spoke it—well, she kinda spoke it."

I was trying to process the idea of book smells and their relationship to magick. "The two of you just lost me," I admitted. "What are you talking about?"

"The Goddess. She's inside of you now, Wildwood," Stout explained. "No one else could have heard the call, and no one else could have removed the stains of the demon world." He walked across the table and rubbed his hand over my elbow. There was a smear, remnants of the demon sludge I'd cleaned from the head of the hammer. He held his hand up to show me. "Brigid called, and you answered. There's no going back."

"What if I'm not ready?" I asked. "What if–"

Shay looked up from the book, about to answer when Stout interjected. "You're ready!" He climbed down my elbow and jumped to the Dagger of Doom, which was buckled to my waist. "The first time you transformed a demon into this dagger, you were ready. Benton knew it; I knew it. But most of all, the Goddess knew it."

How was it possible that everyone knew better than me? Blacksmithing was my only passion before Shay, but I never saw it as a destiny. I'm an artist, a creative who turns rusty metal into treasure. There was purpose in putting a hammer to hot steel, and now I'm the Maker, but the Maker for what?

"What am I meant to do?" I asked, trying to hide my sweaty palms and the pulsing rate of my heart. "What if I'm not good at forging with the Hammer of the Goddess?"

"Well, that's the hard part." He flew up to the table.

"As if any of the rest was easy," I whispered under my breath.

He pulled the corner of the paper close so I could see it. "It's not complicated."

I was looking at the most complicated "not complicated" diagram of shapes and symbols I'd ever seen. Pictish looked like a kindergarten penmanship assignment gone wrong, with strokes and slashes meant to represent letters. The only thing missing was a streak of blue crayon.

"What am I looking at?" I turned to Shay as she fanned through a book on ancient inscriptions. I wondered if any of it made sense to her.

"Rules, maybe? Or instructions?" Shay turned the page to Stout.

"Nice one, Red!" He held up a hand for a high five, but Shay was not amused.

"Are you going to continue calling me that?" Shay asked sternly. "I don't like it."

His flat palm was still up in the air, waiting for her to slap it back. "I could call you Ginger. Would you like that instead?" He high-fived his own hand in celebration of the new nickname.

"Hells Bells!" she yelled at him. "No!"

I'd never heard anyone or anything rile Shay so fast. I didn't have a nickname for her, only terms of endearment, but Stout seemed to enjoy poking fun at my girlfriend.

"Red it is." He walked across the page and stopped at the first transcription. "This group here. You should read it as a warning."

"That'll be new for us, 'ey?" I said as I bumped my shoulder against Shay's.

"Yes, that's true. We usually understand the results only *after* the invocation of a spell knocks us on our asses."

She wasn't wrong. We'd come into our powers while fumbling through the buildings of Bannock. Without knowing, Shay had read a spell that invoked the Maker magick. Similarly, I'd felt the pull of the earth's energy, which had led me to invoke the power of the Magick in Shay.

"This is bigger than the two of you," Stout insisted. "To call forth this spell is an absolute never."

"Never what?" I asked, turning the hammer over to look at the back.

"Never release the power trapped inside." Stout stared at the two of us like a disapproving school teacher. "This." He pointed at the back of the hammer. "This looks ornamental, but it's not. It's the evil Brigid destroyed. It's that thing we fear in our dreams."

"What?" I pulled my hand away and dropped the hammer on the table. "I'm not forging with a demon hammer."

"You're not listening. It's—Brigid's—hammer." He was waving his arms, emphasizing the words. "She made it from conquering pure evil. Forced it to be part of the whole, to become the balance of good and evil. That is pure power, and that is the goddess divine."

"Your dramatic explanation is a bit much, don't you think?" I wouldn't hear his words or let them settle in my heart. How could I handle the pure power of Brigid? "Maybe that's a lot to ask of me? You ever think about that?"

"It isn't only you." Stout pushed at the handle of the hammer to roll the head over. He couldn't move it, so I adjusted the angle to show the other side. "It's the Magick's responsibility to maintain balance. To keep the hammer safe for the Maker."

Shay laid her hand over mine. "As I promised, baby, I'll protect you."

"And this." Stout crawled under the handle and placed his open hand near my Maker's mark. "When you struck the hammer today. The power of Brigid didn't just stay in you."

"It flowed through her into me, didn't it?" Shay turned her hand over, and I reached to hold it.

"It threw you, is more like it." I tugged her hand into my lap. "It picked you up like a rag doll and tossed you into the wall."

"That part makes little sense." Stout rolled the pencil back and forth under his foot. "The power should have stayed with the Maker."

Shay stood up and walked across the kitchen, leaning against the countertop. She was thinking, counting something on the tips of her fingers, and like so many moments before this one, I wanted to be inside her head. "So, what makes us so special?" Shay asked.

"I don't have any idea. There hasn't been a transfer of power at this level for hundreds of years. So many generations have searched for Brigid's hammer, and you're the one who found it."

I looked at Shay as she stepped closer, silently touching the Pictish letters on the paper in front of her. She opened a book and compared the symbols to Stout's writing. Shay didn't say anything, not even a whisper, and I was stuck wondering what was turning in her mind.

Then she looked up at Stout. "Is it because we're lovers?"

He stood still for a moment. "You got the ancestry scroll?"

"Ancestry scroll?" I asked.

Shay put her hand on my shoulder, and I looked up at her. "The scroll with the bone," she explained.

"Oh, gross." I got up and went down to the workshop office. The scroll lay tucked inside the backpack Benton had left for us. I pinched the knuckle between two fingers, still grossed out that this was a scavenged remnant of some monster, the bone of something that once was alive. I carried it like a contaminated bag of rotten apples and dropped it on the table.

"You should have let me go," Shay said as she picked it up.

"It's always going to be just a little gross. I mean it–"

Stout interrupted. "You want to know where that comes from?"

I looked at Shay, then back at the fairy. "No, I don't think that I do. You're probably going to tell me it came from an angry, possessed giant or something."

"Close, he wasn't a giant, but he had a big heart. It was pretty big when the demon held it in his hand." Stout raised his tiny fingers, pulsing them open and closed to imitate a pumping heart.

My gasp was loud, and I covered my mouth to catch the bile gurgling in the back of my throat.

"You really shouldn't do that," Shay scolded Stout as she rubbed my back. "Sweetheart, it isn't human. I'm pretty sure it's from an animal–elk or, maybe, deer."

"Ha, clever." Stout clapped his hands. "It is, in fact, from the Cervidae family. More precisely, it is the leg-bone of a Whitetail Deer."

"Not so gross?" Shay asked as she continued rubbing my back.

"Not so gross." I let out a breath. "I handle animal bones all the time, but human or demon, I don't know why that doubled the grossness level."

Shay made space on the table, stacking the notes and files to the side. She anchored one end of the scroll with a book and rolled the parchment across the top before standing back to get a look.

"What do you see?" Stout asked. He flew to the glass of beer and sucked it empty, swiveling the straw around to get the last few drops.

I was hesitant to answer, wondering exactly how much Stout could see. Shay hesitated, too, and I had to guess if she was thinking the same.

"Why don't you tell me what you see?" Shay asked him.

"You know this is the lineage of the Magick and the Maker, right?" He flew over and landed on the aged paper. His hand touched the name of Regina Benton, written in ink that only Shay and I were supposed to be able to see. Well, that's what Benton's letter led us to believe, at least. "You can see it, right?" he asked.

"We can see a lot of things, Stout, but Benton gave us a warning, and I think we should heed it." Shay watched him and his reaction to the warning of mistrust.

"Regina trusted me. I had to earn it all those years ago, and I'll earn it again from you." He flew off down the stairs. I felt a rush of energy as his wings flittered by my ear. There was a lot of magick in our new friend.

"Where'd he go?" I asked as Shay turned to follow him. I grabbed her wrist, tugging her back to me. "Stay here, please."

Her hands came around to hold me. "I'm not leaving; I just want to see what he's going to do."

"I don't think he's leaving either," I said. I could hear his wings, even though I couldn't see him. "Can't you hear him flying around down there?"

"No." She squeezed me tighter. "You can hear his wings?"

"Yeah, I can, and sometimes it's so loud." I pushed out of her arms to cover my ears. "Like right now, he's coming back."

Stout returned, carrying a canvas satchel clenched in his feet. The bag hit the table with a thud, landing on our open ancestry scroll. Stout climbed into the bag and dragged out a bottle of liquid and a stubby, tattered, and very well-worn brush. It looked like someone could use it for painting, but the bristles were bent off in every direction.

He leveraged the bottle upright. "You know what this is?"

Shay picked it up and turned it in her hand. It fascinated me that she didn't shake it or jostle the liquid inside. She held it up to the light, and I leaned in to look through it with her.

"Is it blue?" I asked.

"It is." She set it down on the table.

I thought about the scroll and the writing and everything we knew from Benton. It hit me all at once, and the words burst from my mouth. "It's the demon ink!"

"*Sanquis Caeden,*" Shay said, calling it by name.

"Benton gave this to me," Stout said. "She told me–made me promise–I would only share it with the Magick."

"So you're a fairy scribe?" Shay raised an eyebrow.

"I am your scribe, if that's what you choose."

"Why should we trust you?" Shay picked up the bottle and pulled the cork from the top.

"Be careful." I grabbed her hand. "What if this isn't what he says?"

"I know."

Stout flew up in front of Shay's face. "What can I do to convince you?"

"Tell me what Benton said?" Shay held out her hand, and Stout flew up to land in her palm. "She told me something in the letter. It made little sense until now, but she said something only the two of us would know. If you can answer that, I will believe that Benton sent you to help us."

Stout flew off Shay's hand and landed atop the bookcase near the funeral flag. He paced back and forth, and I worried what it meant that he was taking so long.

"There was a message?" I leaned in to whisper in Shay's ear.

"I'll tell you everything, but Benton knew. Damn, she really knew what was going to happen." Shay leaned against the table and picked up a folder.

"She didn't know about Brigid's siren call," Stout yelled down at us. "About the pull of the hammer. She never planned that you'd find it. Especially not so fast." He didn't leave his perch atop the bookshelf as he added, "A lot of lives changed when Jacob started looking."

I tried to remember the letter. What wisdom Benton had left behind as guidance for Shay and me. I couldn't recall anything about fairies, and I wanted to charge down the stairs to retrieve the letter. Stout's flapping wings broke the silence before I saw him land on the table.

"She told you," he said. *"When the time is right, you'll see everything as I have."* He quoted the letter word for word. "That's what she wrote. She wanted you to know I was the messenger. I was your friend."

"She was clever," Shay said. "And so are you."

"Does that mean you trust me?" he asked.

"It means Benton trusted you, and *that* means everything." She held a finger out to Stout, and he laid his hand against it. "Swear an oath."

"To you?" he asked.

"To both of us," she answered as she held my hand. "Swear fealty to the Magick and the Maker." She raised our clasped fingers in front of the fairy.

"Wait!" I thought about our family. About the trio that made up our home. "And to Dexter. Swear to help him, too."

"You want me to swear undying loyalty to that dog?" He eyed the furry animal in the corner.

"And to the dragon," I added. "We're a family. If you want to be part of it, swear loyalty to us all."

"Dexter!" Shay called to him, and his head popped up to look at her. "Come here, buddy."

The German Shepherd rolled to his side and stretched his legs straight out. His paws were the size of my hand, and when he rambled to my side, his shoulders were well past my waist. He put his nose against our hands, and Stout moved in to touch us all.

"I swear my oath of loyalty to you, as I did to Regina. I will now serve the Magick and the Maker." He paused, and I cleared my throat to draw attention to the dog. "And Dexter. The Magick, the Maker, and Dexter."

"So mote it be." Shay squeezed my hand as she accepted the vow with her blessing.

Stout pushed away, his gravelly voice breaking the moment. "Now, are you going to tell me what you see in the ancestry scroll?"

"We can see the lines of history going back generations," she explained.

"That's very good." He looked up at Shay. "Will you put your hands on it?"

I sat down beside Shay, and Dexter rested his head in my lap. "Hi, buddy. You slept through all the excitement."

"He probably has a hangover." Stout leaned closer to Dexter's nose. "He reeks of the suth."

"Suth?" I asked. "What is that?"

"Babies?" Shay said. "It's Gaelic."

I was horrified. As I held Dexter's face, I asked, "Are you eating babies?"

He sniffed and snorted in my face. I hadn't a clue what he meant, but Stout was there to clear it up.

"I wasn't calling you a baby eater." He was looking at Dexter as he spoke.

I turned toward Shay, who was watching an unbelievable conversation between Dexter the dog and Stout the fairy.

"Wait, are you talking to each other?" Shay asked.

"He's mad that I accused him of eating babies. They're just demons."

"Wait, what?" I put my face closer to Dexter to sniff his fur. "He smells like Dexter and maybe river water and a hint of something else."

"Suth," Stout repeated. "The embryo of the Gatekeeper line. It would appear that your dragon finds them tasty." Dexter snorted at the fairy. "Sorry, *delicious*. I stand corrected. Dexter finds them *delicious*."

Shay looked down at her dog. "So eating them makes him, what? Drunk?"

"More like high. Do you know that old song about dragons and smoke? That's how it affects him."

"I hope your dog doesn't have to pass a drug test," I joked.

Shay let out a quick laugh. "I'm not sure what it would show up as." It occurred to me that, although it was odd that Dexter enjoyed the taste of Gatekeeper embryos, it was more intriguing that Stout could communicate that information to us.

"Wait, how are you talking to Dex?" I asked.

"I'm a fairy." He tapped his chest and pushed off the table into the air. "I can communicate with just about every otherworldly creature. Humans, too, if I feel like it."

"You can talk to Dexter?" Shay dropped into the chair. "You can talk to Dexter." I found it interesting that of all the information shared around this table, Dexter talking to Stout was the one that would knock Shay off her feet.

"I can." He held up a hand to Shay. "But we should talk about the lineage, and the Maker should get to making."

I picked up the hammer. "What can I do with this?" I knew the question was vague, but I wondered what it meant to wield the power of a goddess and transform metal through her.

Stout hovered in front of my face. "You are a blacksmith, aren't you? You should already know what to do with a fancy hammer like that."

CHAPTER IV

INTUITION

"Not ten minutes ago, you called this the Hammer of Creation. That's a little intimidating, even for me." The tool in my hand was extraordinary, but how was it possible that something so beautiful could belong to me, a simple blacksmith and welder? I repaired farm equipment and learned to weld by building frames for bicycles. I looked at Stout, nervous about confronting my destiny.

"The Goddess has been singing her song for the Maker since that hammer disappeared." Stout flew off the table and landed on my arm. "Before you found the hammer, you could hear her calling you, right?"

How did he know about Brigid's call? "It was like nothing I'd ever experienced. I couldn't control myself."

Dexter puffed his nose at me, and the air blasted our fairy friend. "Dexter says he had to work hard to keep up with you in the tunnels."

The thought that our dragon-dog had been chasing after me made me laugh. "I think you're telling that story backward, Dex." I fluffed his head and scratched behind his ears. The dog leaned into the head rub, and I didn't stop. "You're saying that I should go test the hammer?"

"That's exactly what I'm suggesting," Stout said.

I looked at Shay. "You should go put on real clothes."

Shay looked down at what she was wearing. "This too dressy for you?"

"Let's go for less flammable, less skin, and put on that vest just in case." I hooked my arm around her waist as she turned toward the bedroom. "How's your head?"

"I'm fine. I'll be fine." She patted my cheek before pecking a quick kiss on my lips. "I'll meet you in the workshop." She walked to the bedroom.

Both Dexter and Stout stayed upstairs in the apartment, and I was glad to keep the fairy out of my workspace as I figured out Brigid's power. I turned the valve for the gas to the forge and sparked a flame with the igniter. The sound and the spark's reaction to it were the only predictable parts of blacksmithing. I slipped my apron over my head and clipped it in place around my waist. The scorched leather reminded me that this was not my first experiment in magickal blacksmithing.

I was eighteen years old when I met my first professional blacksmith at a trade school open house. The moment his hammer hit hot steel, I knew that's what I wanted to do. I didn't know that I would also be very good at it–reading angles and learning how to strike is the finesse most people don't take time to see. It was a three-dimensional experience for me. It always has been.

I stood in front of my anvil, admiring the hammer of Brigid. She was the Goddess of Flame and Mother to the Smith. I never really had a mother. But from that day forward, she was the one I didn't know I wanted. My heart was racing, maybe with excitement, but mostly from fear.

"Hey." Warm arms wrapped around me, and I felt Shay's body press against my back. "What are you thinking?" she whispered in my ear as her chin rested on my shoulder.

"True confession. I'm kinda afraid to use this hammer." I ran my finger across the handle I'd carved from a piece of hickory. It was smooth to the touch but rough enough that it wouldn't slip from my hand.

"Are you afraid of your powers?" She pulled me close, and I could feel the plate of demon metal fitted over her heart, pushing into my back.

"I'm afraid I'll hurt you again." I hugged her tighter against me.

Shay kissed me just below the ear, and I closed my eyes. She whispered again, her warm breath on my ear creating a supreme sense of calm, "It'll be okay. The Maker and the Magick, remember. Our powers will protect us." She knew me so well.

I already felt the steady confidence only Shay could give to me. "I know it's been a minute, but you should know that I love you so damn much."

"I know. Never worry that I don't know." Her arms moved higher, closer to my heart.

My hands came up to hold her wrist, and I touched the cuff wrapped around it. "You wearing the dagger too?" I asked.

Shay kicked her foot high enough to show me the wrap near her ankle. "I brought the arsenal. I'm ready this time."

"Baby, that is so hot, and I'm glad that at least one of us is ready."

Shay stepped around the anvil. "Look at me."

It was no chore to comply because Shay was easy on the eyes. She'd tied her gorgeous red hair in a tight ponytail. Her skin was pale and beautiful, like porcelain, and the smile on her face almost made me forget my fear. Almost. I really was frightened to wield the full power of the Maker.

"You know, that's not really helping," I said.

"What if you tell me something else? What if you tell me what you're going to make?" Her right hand rested on the horn of the anvil, and her left covered the hardy and curled around the hanging end. The Hammer of Brigid rested between us.

"I thought maybe I would do what I do best."

"I thought we were talking about blacksmithing." She winked at me before pushing back. Shay knew precisely what she was doing. She had a way of turning an emotional storm into a calming breeze. She sure as hell had a way with me.

"I was talking about a knife. My love."

"Were you really?" Shay walked across the room and picked up a chair. She carried it closer so she could watch me work, twirling it around and kicking over to straddle it backward. "Show me what you got." Her forearms dropped over the backrest, and suddenly it felt like a regular night in front of the forge.

But the massive hammer was daunting.

Choosing material was another dilemma. Should I forge with standard knife steel, or should I pick from the collection Benton had willed to us when she passed? I went to the office and returned with a piece of each. "What do you think: demon or not demon?" I held them up for her to make a selection.

"Go with what you know?" she suggested, as confident in my abilities as ever.

I tossed the demon steel on the table and pushed my high-carbon steel into the forge. "Design is next. How about a chopper to go with the axe?"

"Finely diced demon? Is that what we're shooting for?" Shay was playful and calm and exactly what I'd need for the next few hours.

I grabbed my sketchbook and started flipping through the pages. "Or maybe something to counter-strike with once you whip my axe away."

"Why don't you just make a second axe?" Shay suggested. "One for me and one for you."

I grinned at how perfect that was. "That sounds like a good idea."

I ran up to the apartment to grab the axe. Shay used it more often than I did, and each time it flew true for her. She was also pretty good at throwing. I'd proven on more than one occasion that I was a complete flop. Shay was waiting as I took my time navigating the stairs.

"What do you think?" she asked, still perched on her chair.

"I think the design is great for throwing, and since you've proven it can kill a demon, I'm going to stick close to this style." I laid it on the anvil and traced the outline with a piece of soapstone.

"Will the marks stay there when it gets hot?" Shay asked, looking at my rough, sketched lines.

I adjusted the forge's flame to keep the temperature just below 2000 degrees. "It'll stay for a while, but I'll trace it again so that they're a matched set." I used my tongs to grab the metal from the forge. The hammer felt perfect as it hovered over the bright orange steel. I waited, hesitating until the metal cooled, then put it back into the heat.

"What's the matter?" Shay asked. I laid the hammer on the face of the anvil and stepped closer to Shay. "It's okay to be afraid, you know. But I'm here, and if something goes wrong, we'll figure it out."

"Maybe we should put on more than safety glasses?" I suggested as I opened the cabinet and removed ear protection. I passed a pair of mufflers to Shay.

"Even if we surround ourselves in bubble wrap and stand behind a bulletproof shield, it might not protect us at all." She pulled on a pair of gloves and put the ear coverings back on the shelf.

I didn't want to hear the words coming out of her mouth. "Why would you say that?"

"I take risks every day. You've used your power to heal me. I've spent most of my life understanding magick. I trust the goddess wouldn't give you powers that would hurt you." Shay held my hand to her heart, tugging me so I would look into her eyes. "You are the Maker. I believe that whatever happens in the next few minutes, the goddess wanted it that way."

"So mote it be?" I asked. It seemed the perfect thing to say at the moment.

Her smile was better than magick because it lit up her eyes and flushed her cheeks a rosy pink. "So mote it be."

"I can do this," I repeated as I tugged my gloves on. "I can do this."

By the time I settled back in front of the forge, I almost believed that I could. I used the tongs to remove the metal and pivoted back to the anvil. I picked up the hammer, took a deep breath, raised it for a full swing, and before doubt could settle in, I struck the blaze-orange piece of steel.

Three things happened. The first and most expected was the flattening of steel. Every blacksmith knows that any kind of hammer will move hot metal, but the second, and most enchanting, reaction was the illumination of the Pictish letters and scrolling artwork on the hammer's sides. It was breathtaking, each nuanced detail shining through the density of the steel. But the last reaction, the most magickal and unexpected, was the infusion of Brigid's power and energy exchange I felt in the palm of my hand. Shay stepped closer for a better look as I laid the hammer on the face of my anvil. Seconds later, the illumination faded.

"Hit it again!" Shay's voice was loud, her excitement impossible to hide.

I clenched my fingers into a fist, looking closely at my gloved hand. The sensation wasn't numbness but something similar. I picked up the hammer and struck the metal again, over and over, until the steel lost its flaming orange color. The temperature wasn't right to strike, so I moved the metal back into the forge.

I laid the hammer down, and the two of us watched as the intricate artwork shone like the Nordic runes painted on the carriage house walls.

"It's unbelievable," I said, more fascinated by the reaction of the hammer than by the results. Why would the Pictish text illuminate? What was the cause? Did the power of the Maker breathe life into the hammer of the goddess? Why could I feel it in the palm of my hand?

"Tell me what you feel," Shay said as I opened and closed my fist.

"Every time I hit the metal, I feel this explosion of energy. I don't know if it's inside of me trying to escape or if it's the hammer trying to give power to me."

"Does it hurt?" Shay reached for my hand, pulling off my glove, massaging the palm, and rolling each finger between her own.

"It's not pain; it's more like the energy I feel when I'm laying hands on the earth." I knew she would understand this explanation, as that same connection to Mother Earth had bonded Shay and me as teenagers.

"Do you think you should stop?" She tugged my hand as she asked.

"No, I want to keep going." I turned to check the forge. "Sit back down and enjoy the show." I gave her a quick kiss.

Shay settled in her chair. "Happily."

I laid the hot steel on the face of the anvil and worked it with the hammer. Each strike continued to illuminate the Pictish text and the etched symbols. I transferred back and forth, in the forge and out again, to shape the axe head. After a few minutes, I paused. Shay was staring at me. "What?" I asked.

"You look so happy." Her chin dropped to rest on her hands, still gripping the backrest of the chair.

"Blacksmithing makes me that way." I smiled at her. "So does a particular redhead."

"Sweet-talker." She blew me a kiss. "The reaction of the hammer isn't too much?"

"Not at all. I've never felt better."

I was telling the truth. Each time my hammer touched the project, I could feel the power surge inside me. I was meant to work life into my creations. My tongs gripped the newly formed axe head. I laid it on the anvil again. With each strike, I thought about balance. I wanted this to fly straight and devastate a target. If I ever had to use it to protect Shay, I wanted it to dig deep and incapacitate an attacker. I wasn't thinking about anything else as I worked, just the power to defend and an aim that was true.

Close to finishing the project, I set the axe head in the forge again. I traced the original axe on the face of the anvil to check the dimensions. When I pulled out my new axe head, it looked like a twin to the first.

Shay came closer for a better look. "That's almost as perfectly matched as the punch daggers."

"Not bad, right?"

"I'd say your work is amazing."

"Thank you."

"So, what comes next?" Shay asked as she stood beside me.

"One more heat to strike my mark and another to quench it." I put the axe in the forge.

"You're nearly finished?" Shay was almost as excited as I was to hold this in her hands.

"With the forging part, but I still need to make the handle."

"What are you planning?"

The handle was the last thing on my mind. I'd focused too much on the hammer and its reaction that I didn't have a plan for the handle material. "I'm not sure, but it should be close to the original, since we plan to use them the same way."

"Demon hunting," Shay answered. "And maybe kindling for a riverside fire. Speaking of riverside fires, where are Dex and Stout?"

I wasn't sure where our sidekicks were, but I had a guess. "Up in the apartment, maybe? They're not in the circle, so Stout must be learning a bit about your dragon-dog."

"That would make sense. They've both got a lot to share."

I put the axe head back into the forge and walked to the office. The shelf was stacked full of scrap wood, and I picked a piece of hickory for the handle, setting it on the table in the workshop. "This will do."

"Nothing fancy?" Shay asked.

"I'm not going to waste a lot of time on the handle since we plan to throw it more than anything else," I explained. I watched the axe head's color change and readied my Maker's mark. Brigid's Hammer was glowing, and I set it beside me as I grabbed a battered striking hammer and laid it on the anvil.

"You're going to stamp it?"

I thought about this next step. The last time I'd used my maker's mark, it threw Shay against the wall. "You should come and stand behind me. Just to be safe."

Her hands pushed off the backrest as she threw her leg over the chair. "Yes, ma'am."

I reached for the axe head, pinching it tight with my tongs. I laid it on the anvil and held the tongs to Shay. "Hold, please."

Her hand came up to take them, and I centered my mark over the collar of my axe. Pounding hard with the old hammer, I struck my signature into the piece. The vibration of the strike was strong, much like the blow of Brigid's Hammer, and I pulled the stamp away to see the flawless display of the mark of this Maker.

"Perfect."

Shay leaned closer, holding the tongs away from her face. "It really is."

"One more heat, a quench, and then we sharpen."

The time-intensive part of blacksmithing was the heating and hammering, back and forth, between the anvil and the forge, but that was only half of the work. I pushed the blade into the forge and readied the quenching oil to harden the axe.

Shay went back to her chair. "You feel safe now?" she asked.

"I feel pretty darn good," I admitted. The galvanized basin filled with quenching oil was ready, and I tugged my gloves off to put on a heavier pair.

Shay grabbed my hand, turning it up. "What the heck is that?"

The palm of my hand was glowing, much like the Pictish lettering and decoration on the Hammer of the Goddess. "I don't know."

Shay ran her finger over the symbol. I could tell she was thinking, but I was also wondering how and why and what the heck?

"Do you recognize it?" I asked.

"Maybe."

"What do you mean, maybe?" My voice squeaked.

"Does it hurt?" Shay asked, still holding my hand.

"I felt the energy when I was hammering, but it never hurt. No. I just thought it was a transfer of power, not another divine tattoo."

Shay and I had experience with weird symbols showing up on our skin. During the ritual to access our powers, Shay had been covered in scribbles that led us through the Magick's ritual. My disappearing symbols had brought us to Brigid and to the power locked inside my hammer. My blacksmithing abilities were growing beyond common hammers to steel.

"Can you still activate your flame?" she asked.

"*Ignis*," I whispered, and the orange fire popped up in my palm. Shay didn't let go but leaned in closer to look.

"It might be a sigil. Can you see the way your flame travels through like a moat filling with water?"

My imagination manifested a tiny castle with a ring around the outside, filling up with fire instead of water. What was the purpose? "I have a fiery palm moat?"

"Don't be so literal. It's the *ignis* flame but more."

The thought of our flame reminded me of the axe in the forge. It was close to temperature for hardening, and I pushed my hands inside the heavier gloves. "Palm moats later. We need to finish the axe, and you should take a step back for this."

Shay walked around the anvil, putting it between the quench oil basin and her safety. I squeezed the long-handled tongs tight, gripping the axe head, and moved from the forge to the quench basin in one sweeping motion. Flames burst from the oil, and I waited until I was certain the science of tempering had occurred. I pulled it from the basin, and specks of oil flashed with fire as they hit the air. I laid it on the anvil to get my first look.

"It's still got little flames on it," Shay said, watching the tiny fires change to puffs of smoke.

"It'll cool off." I flipped it over so I could see the mark. "Goddess, this looks so good." I left it on the anvil and walked away.

"You're done?"

I shook my head. "With that part, yes, but I still have a handle to fit."

"And an axe to grind," Shay said with a mischievous giggle.

"Oh, that's just…" I shook my finger at her. "No, and then yes. I will be grinding that axe."

"Funny, right?" She winked.

"So hilarious. Are you going to stand over there and be a comedian, or are you going to come over here and learn something?" I covered the quench basin and rolled it back under the table, then threw my gloves on top and stared down at my hand. What did the image burned into my skin mean?

"Are you worried about the sigil in your palm?" Shay asked.

"Not until I have to be."

"I'll do a little research when we finish the axe."

Despite my nod of acknowledgement, I was trying not to think about what it meant that the hammer marked my palm. Was I branded? Did Brigid claim my Maker powers? It was too much to think about right now.

Shay followed me to the table. "Are you going to teach me?"

"Yep." I set the block of wood in front of her. "Hickory for the handle."

"Strong but flexible," Shay said.

"You know your wood." I smiled at her.

"I know trees." She held the piece in her hand. "Hickory is feminine, inherently divine, and charged with the element of air."

"That's very good for an axe forged from the energy of the Goddess of Fire."

"It's kinda idyllic, don't you think? Fire and air are symbiotic."

"The perfect things to bring our magnificent project together."

Shay flipped the stick in the air and caught it. "So, what's the first step?"

"General shape." I carried the hickory to the forge and laid it so the barrel of the axe head could burn a circular impression into the top of the wood. I held it up for Shay to see. "General shape, we start here." We moved into the workshop office, away from the fiery part of the shop. I drew a pencil line on the block of wood as a guide. The woodworking tools were primitive, and I set to work carving and scraping and gouging the shape of our handle.

"Would you like to try?" I asked as I clamped the hickory into the vise.

"Sure." I handed the ultra-thin Royba saw blade to her. "This is…?" she asked as she flipped her wrist to wobble the blade in front of her.

"It's a saw. We're going to cut some vertical stop lines," I explained. "When we chisel the shape, these lines will prevent us from taking off too much material." I made a few pencil marks and wrapped my hands around Shay's. "It's a slow, gentle movement." I pulled the saw toward us and pushed it away, doing it a few more times until Shay recognized the motion. "You got it?" I turned to look at her and almost forgot why we were there.

"Oh, I've got it, alright."

I stepped back. "Do that to all the rest of the horizontal lines." I watched her work as I pulled out a few more tools.

"What's next?" she asked as the saw slipped off the handle.

I gave her a hammer and chisel. "Next, we knock off the big chunks and round the edges."

"Sounds easy," Shay said, brushing the sweat from her forehead with the back of her glove.

"I'm glad you think so."

We spent the next half hour chipping away all the extra material until we had a contoured shape for a classic throwing axe. Shay gripped it with her hands and passed it to me.

"This feels a little rough on the knob," I said. The handle's rounded end prevented the axe from slipping out of our hands too soon. "Here's a piece of sandpaper. Just feel the edges and knock the rough parts off."

Shay worked for a few minutes, focused, tuning me out. She picked up the handle one more time and turned it in her palm. "I like this. It feels good." She held it out to me, and I gave it a wave in the air.

"It's perfect," I said, beaming. "Now we fit the head."

The head of the axe was cold on the anvil, but I still checked for heat with the back of my fingers. The eye of the axe head was tight around the tapered wood. I adjusted it before Shay worked the handle too much. A slip of the chisel and all of her work would have been a waste.

"So, what keeps the axe head from flying off the handle?" She asked all the right questions, making her an excellent blacksmithing partner.

"We're going to split the top of the handle and put in a wedge. That will keep it tight until the handle breaks."

"You're planning to break it?"

I tapped the knob of the handle on the table, forcing the head into its last position. "They all break, eventually."

"Is that why you're so good at making your own?" Shay came to stand beside me for a better view.

"It is, but mostly I enjoy repurposing and scrapping." I shaved down a piece of scrap wood to make a wedge and smeared some wood glue on each side before pounding it into the gap at the top of the handle. "There's a bit of pride in it, too."

"So that's it?" Shay asked.

I pointed to the machine in the corner, which was currently underneath a white tarp. "You remember your old pal?"

She smiled. "The grinder. Do I get to do it?"

I was happy to stand back and watch Shay run the axe against the grinder. "Let me show you, and then you can have at it." I ran the cutting edge against the belt, and sparks flew toward the ground. It seemed ordinary, which was a little disappointing. Shay watched, and after I made a few more passes, she was ready. "You want to try?" I asked.

She pulled the wrists of her gloves and pressed the axe against the belt of the sander as I stood back to supervise. After a few swipes, she would wipe it over a damp rag to cool it down. Back and forth, grind and spark, until the cutting edge had a wide-angled bevel. She was pretty proud of herself, and I was proud of her, too.

"That looks like a match." I held up the old demon axe beside the new one.

Shay took one handle in each hand. "Can we throw 'em?" Her excitement was uncontainable as she danced across the workshop floor.

The target wall was stowed away in the corner, and I raised my hands to pause her enthusiasm. "Let me set the wall up, and you can fire away."

I wiggled the stand into place and ran my hand over the well-worn boards. Testing the demon axe a few weeks prior had left some damage that I didn't have time to repair.

"Did I do all of that?" Shay asked.

Did she do all of that? Shay had knocked chunks out of the target wall the day she heard about Benton's infection and the decision to stop treating the wounds. It made sense that she wouldn't remember how she'd attacked the target, splintering the slatted boards in her frustration. I learned a lot about her that day, and about how the two of us would navigate our future together.

"Yep, you sure did."

The center was still a shredded mess that looked like an accident at a toothpick factory. I got a marking pen and drew a new off-center target. It was a twelve-inch skull and crossbones with tiny lines making a smile.

"That's the new target?" She was already swinging the two blades, twirling and turning her wrists like a trained fighter.

"Yep." I stepped away from the wall, realizing I was more excited about her fighting style than the weapons' performance. "You ready?"

"More than ready," Shay replied as she tinged the butted ends together.

"Go, baby." I waved for her to throw.

Shay moved backward before stepping forward, and without hesitation, she launched the demon axe from her left hand; with the next step, she launched the new axe from her right. I heard the steel cutting the air in the room before two solid thuds from the axes' impact on the wall. It wasn't a surprise when Shay pierced each of the eyes in the skull face.

"That is unbelievable." Shay ran to the wall, kicked her foot against the base for support, and leveraged the axes out. She sandwiched the blades together and carried them back in one hand. The joy in her eyes made the entire project worth it. She squeezed the axe heads as she passed them to me. "Your turn." The handles pointed near my ribs, and I reached to grab them.

"I'll go once because I'm not sure I can deal with the embarrassment." For all the talent Shay possessed with weapons and self-defense, I had zero ability to throw an axe and make it stick in a target. Axes aren't made to bounce and, truth be told, my weapons perform better in Shay's hands.

There was no chance that I could attempt the single-step double-throw I'd just witnessed, so I settled for a simple two-step toss. I started with the original demon axe, performing my best imitation of a battle-ready warrior. I focused my aim on the target, staring it dead in the eyes. One deep cleansing breath, one short stutter step, my tongue half tucked in my teeth for focus, a half-foot drag, and I launched the axe. The bounce back was the humbling experience I had expected.

"I still don't have it."

Her smile was encouraging as I turned to look at her, so I reset my stance to throw the new axe. The handle felt warm in my hand, and I could see the glow of the illuminated sigil in my palm underneath. I took a deep breath and visualized the axe sinking between the eyes of my skull and crossbones. My feet shuffled forward, and as I stepped, the axe released from my hand. I didn't close my eyes as much as I blinked in surprise to see the head buried between the eyes of the pirate-styled artwork.

"I hit it!" I jumped around in a circle, celebrating as Shay wrapped her arms around me.

"You sure as hell did. You've been slow playing, haven't you?"

My hand came up in defense. "I swear. I just saw the axe hitting the target, and it hit."

Shay thought for a moment and said, "Intuitive reflection." Her cheek raised with an approving half-smile. "What were you thinking about as you were forging the axe?" she asked.

"You, mostly. I was thinking about protecting you and finally making an axe that I could hit something with."

She hooked the loop on the shoulder of my apron and tugged me closer. "You hit it, alright." She pointed to the wall where my axe was sticking out.

"I really did." I stepped toward the target wall and had to use a bit of force to wiggle the toe of the head free. "Maybe I should try it again. Make sure it wasn't a fluke."

"Yes, maybe you should." Shay stood behind me, watching as I took aim and launched the axe again. It hit the target close to where the first one did.

"This is incredible!" The rush of excitement invigorated me, and I wondered if Shay felt like this every time she hit the center of a target.

"It's so good. You've got it," Shay said.

"It's the axe and Brigid." I held my palm open to Shay.

"I think it's the Maker and her predestined powers."

"Maybe it's all of it together." I looked at the hammer resting on the anvil stand, realizing it was more than a blacksmith's tool. Brigid's Hammer was the pathway to tipping the balance of good and evil and I had to keep it safe. "Do you think I need to worry about hiding Brigid's Hammer?" I asked Shay.

"I think we can officially call it the Maker's Hammer." She patted my shoulder.

My hand came up to hold her fingers. "I guess we should."

"No matter what we call it, we should talk to Stout. He might have some insight into pumping up my protection spell."

"Boost the Magick security system?" My question was playful until I realized Shay wasn't joking.

"Times ten would be good." Shay put her arm around my waist and hooked her thumb on the apron buckle. "We need to be safe here. The carriage house isn't just your workshop. It's also our home."

"Yes, it is," I agreed, looking up at the clock. It was just past midnight. "It's getting kinda late."

"I hadn't noticed." She walked to the target and removed the axe, then bent down to pick the second up from the floor. "I think this one should be yours." She handed the new axe to me.

"It hits the target better than I ever could." I flopped the axe head over and touched my Maker's mark. "Brigid gave me some kind of power." I had meant to say it in a whisper. That's how it sounded in my ears, but Shay heard my proclamation.

"The Maker wields the Hammer of the Goddess. You." She leaned in to kiss me, and my hands fell to my sides. All kinds of magicks were happening inside the carriage house, and just before my new axe hit the floor, I realized which magick was most important.

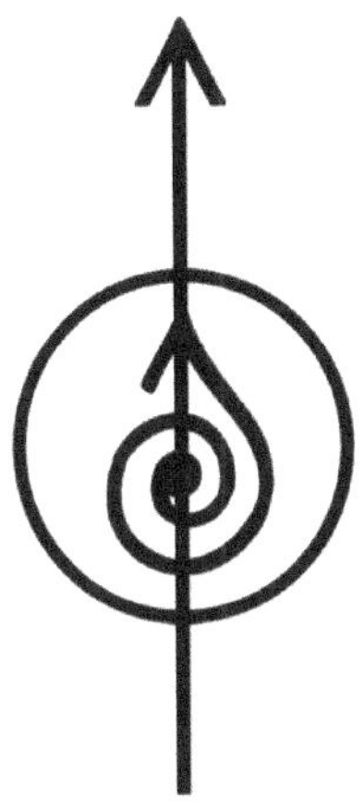

CHAPTER V

PROVIDENCE

"Not yet," I mumbled. 5:30 a.m. came fast. Shay rolled over to slap the alarm clock, and I grabbed her shoulder to pull her back to the bed. I wasn't ready for her to go–not just yet–and I wrapped my leg over her hip so she couldn't move. "Stay, for just a few more minutes."

"You make it hard to say no." She snaked her arm under my ribs to pull me closer.

"Perfect," I said as I rested on her shoulder. "You have a regular work schedule today, right?"

"I do." Her hand came up to hold mine. "I'm thinking I might have lunch with Dani and tell her about the hammer."

My head popped up to look at Shay's face. "Do you think that's a good idea?"

"I think it's necessary."

How could it be necessary? What did Shay think Dani could bring to the table? Then the *who* of the situation hit me. Dani was the daughter of the last Maker. He wasn't the greatest example of a selfless protector. For reasons I didn't know, Jacob Kota had abandoned his commitment to Brigid and his bond with the Magick, Regina Benton. With her history in this town, Dani might have a ton to offer.

"It's necessary because of Jacob?" I asked.

"Yes, her father was the Maker. He had to know about the hammer. And if he knew, then maybe Dani did, too."

I pulled my hand from Shay's and opened my palm to reveal the sigil scorched into my skin. "Dani knew about the tool. Are you saying she might know something about this?"

Shay touched it with her finger. "Yes, and what it might mean for the future of the two of us."

That Dani would know so much about the Maker's history seemed like a significant conclusion to draw, and I wondered how long Shay had been considering her best friend in the equation. "Do you honestly think Dani knows that much?"

"I'm not sure, but I have to ask." Shay hugged me tighter, and I was content to rest on her shoulder. "You know, I should get up."

"I am totally aware that I'm stealing moments, yes." I tucked my hand under her hip to wrap us closer together.

"Sweetheart, that's not going to help." Shay laughed, and I could feel her body angle away from me. She was stronger, and I didn't stand a chance as she folded me across her lap and sat forward. Sitting on her legs wasn't a horrible position, either. "Still not helping," she whispered across my cheek.

"I'm not feeling helpful this morning." I hugged her around the neck and clamped my hands together. I had never felt so out of control of a situation as I did when Shay's legs pushed off the bed, adjusting us sideways as she came to cradle me.

"It'll be kind of complicated to work like this."

My arms fell away in my most impressive imitation of a Rescue Randy practice dummy. Even with my limp body, Shay picked me up and spun me around to drop me on the bed. I stared at her. "Really?" How could she leave me like this?

She crawled over me, hovering above my face. "Yes, really." Her kisses were hard, possessive, almost bruising, and I held my fingers around the back of her neck, opening my mouth to return the kiss. She pushed away, and I stayed, my legs clamped to her hips and arms tight around her body. We were face to face, close, and I could feel her breath as she said, "You've got me. Forever."

I squeezed my legs tighter, and she surrendered. I think I could manage forever.

~~~~~~~~~~

The light over the stove was on, and I could hear the coffee pot popping and sputtering the fresh brew. Dexter lay curled in a ball in the corner with Stout the fairy burrowed into him. I'm sure they were both awake, and I wondered how much of the last hour they'd overheard. I poured a cup of coffee with a splash of milk for Shay and carried it to the bedroom. She was already out of the shower.

"That was quick." I set the mug beside the bed.

"Well, someone wasn't. So, I had to do a suds-'n'-run shower." Shay stopped in her bra and briefs, trying to jump into her pants. Her legs were still damp, and she struggled to pull the uniform slacks to her hips. The blanket and sheets were tangled, and I grabbed her t-shirt from the end of the bed. Shay was already running behind, and I should have been more sensitive, but damn, that uniform did things to me.

"You seem frazzled, superhero." I dangled the t-shirt from my fingertip.

"You try to explain being late when you live four blocks away." Shay reached up, and before I could say a word, she snatched the shirt and popped her head through the collar.

"I work downstairs."

Her lips pecked my cheek as she ran by. "Exactly."

I looked at the clock on the wall, and six forty-five was glowing on its face. She was going to make it. I picked up her mug of coffee and carried it to the kitchen table. The velcro of her vest tore away, and she dropped it over her head. I'd never experienced the gearing-up process on fast forward, but I liked
~~~~~~~~~~

it. Shay buttoned her uniform shirt and tucked it in before cinching the duty belt around her waist.

"Damn." I would not let the moment pass in silence. "You look so good."

Shay held up one finger. "NO!" She unzipped her work duffle. "Stay over there."

"I'm not gonna move." Being wanted, really understanding how it feels to love and have that love reciprocated, was almost better than making love to the woman in front of me.

Almost.

"Good." Dexter's ears perked up at the sound of Shay's raised voice, but responded more to Shay securing her vest to her torso. He was at her side, rubbing her hip for attention. "Hey, buddy." Her fingers dug into the fur between his ears.

"Oh sure, give him all the attention."

Shay smiled at me and held up a finger again. "Behave for the next sixty seconds if you can."

I froze in place, pretending to be a statue as she dropped to one knee to secure the K-9 unit vest around Dexter's torso. The two of them, in full uniform, would always make me smile.

I thought about Dexter in dog form. Was he bullet-proof? Did the dragon inside of him protect the dog on the outside? I had to ask. "Do you think he needs to wear the vest anymore?"

Shay's hands stopped. "You know, I never really thought about it." She stood beside the table, checking the gear in her bag. Satisfied it was all together, she zipped it, and in a quick swoop, the strap came over her shoulder. "Maybe you can talk to the fairy curled up on Dexter's bed?" She pointed at Stout, who lay wrapped in the folds of the dog's blanket.

"Right. Stout." I realized I had my own personal companion now. "Forgot about him."

Shay checked her watch. "Shit, I'm so late." She grabbed the top of her coffee mug and guzzled half of it down.

"No sweat, you've got five minutes."

"Says the woman who is going right back to our bed." Shay tapped Dexter's shoulder, and the dog ran down the stairs.

"Maybe I am."

Shay leaned in to kiss me as her fingers pinched together. "Maybe I'm just a teeny tiny little bit jealous of that bed." Her lips touched mine, and she pulled away fast.

"You know where to find it…and me."

"Woman." She held a hand up, keeping me from stepping closer.

"I love you, too," I said, and she stopped in front of the stairs.

"I love you, and seriously, your love is impossible to miss."

She jogged down the stairs, and I could hear her talking to Dexter as they walked out the door. She had less than five minutes to get to the station—plenty of time. I turned to the empty apartment, but it wasn't empty at all. Stout the fairy was flying around our kitchen.

"You got any more beer?" he asked. "I could use a little sunrise boost."

"It's not even seven in the morning." I picked up Shay's mug, dumped the cold coffee, and filled it to the top.

"Don't judge." He hovered in the steam rising from my mug. "You drink coffee in the morning. I drink beer."

"Yes, but you *only* drink beer." I wanted a piece of toast before going down to the workshop, so I opened the refrigerator and grabbed the bread. Stout dropped to the countertop and ran into my open hand.

"When did you get this?" he asked, pointing to the sigil in my palm.

My hand pulled away, reacting to the fairy's question and his uninvited touch. "It happened last night when we were forging the axe."

"Wait, what?"

"Last night. Shay and I forged this." I turned toward the table, picked up the new axe, and waved it through the air, slicing and slashing at the space in front of me.

"With Brigid's Hammer?" He stared as I laid the axe down for him to inspect. He walked the length of the hickory handle. "You forged an axe, and the sigil burned into the palm of your hand?"

"Yep, that's right." I dropped a slice of bread in the toaster and pushed the handle. I moved around the kitchen, adjusting to my nosy fairy companion's presence, but irritated that his questions never led to answers.

Stout hovered in front of my face. "Did Brigid's Hammer glow when you were using it? Did you see the face of the Goddess on fire?"

"It did, and we did, and if the artwork is a representation of my goddess, she is stunning." The toast popped up, and I laid it on the plate to spread a thick layer of peanut butter across the top.

"We? You said we? Shay was there?"

"Of course, she was there." I sliced the toast in half from corner to corner and turned on the water to rinse my knife. Stout flew into the stream and hovered in the flow.

"Would you make it a little hotter and maybe drip a bit of soap on me?"

It should have been more exciting to see a fairy taking a shower in the tap water in my kitchen. It wasn't. I was thinking about my hammer, and our collaboration the night before. I squeezed the dish soap until a drop fell on his little hands and wondered why Stout didn't remember our blacksmithing last night and why Shay's presence was so amazing.

"You saw us go to the workshop, didn't you?"

"Dexter and I were having a heated debate." He was lathering the suds over his tiny body, and I watched the water beading off his wings like oil in a hot pan.

What could a fairy and a dragon discuss that would keep them engaged while I hammered for hours? "About?"

After shaking the suds from his body, Stout flew out of the water stream. "Survivability."

"Survivability?" This fairy knew how to get my attention. "What do you mean?"

Stout flew from the sink, wiggling drops of water from his body as he drifted to the table. "Dexter is fiercely loyal to Shay. Not like, 'Oh, she's wonderful and has beautiful hair and her scars will make the fairy world swoon.' Not like that. It's more like he would die to save her."

This fairy had a crush on my girlfriend, that's certain, but he also had insight into our dragon-dog that we longed to understand. Stout walked across the table, stopping in front of the ancestry scroll. "I told him it would take something more than a massive demon or terrible evil to kill a dragon."

Stout's comment made sense once you'd seen a dragon in real life. Dexter could expand in ways that seemed to defy physics, and in a heartbeat, he could retract into a fluffy dog. I didn't want to think of a single scenario that would harm him or even consider his death.

"Is that really true?" I sat down at the table and took a bite of my breakfast. "Big like what?"

"Big like ultimate hell-monster big, times one hundred."

"Those things in the tunnels?" I pushed the notebook open to the page about Gatekeeper demons. "Big like these?"

Stout shook his head. "That's not big."

Gatekeepers were the most enormous demons I'd seen with my own eyes. "Where are demons that grow bigger than a Gatekeeper?" I hated to ask, afraid to invite the monsters that made our fairy shiver.

"You don't want to know." Stout had a way of making me fear the shadows. I'd met a demon once or twice, and I didn't feel strong enough to win that fight.

"How do I protect everyone that I love?"

Stout shoved my hand, and I rolled it open. "You keep doing this."

The sigil pattern felt warm in my palm. My skills as a blacksmith suddenly became medievally important. In the era of guns, my forging abilities were the protection Shay and Dexter would need. "That's the plan. The goddess puts two people together as earth and fire, elite warriors who protect each other."

"Yes, but you and Shay? You are something different." He looked at the refrigerator. "How about that beer?" He smacked his lips. "My mouth is getting a little dry."

When I opened the fridge, I counted five bottles. One beer. What could it harm? "You want it in a glass?" When I turned around, the fairy was hovering beside me with a straw, the wrapper floating to the floor.

"The bottle is good." His smile stretched wide enough to squint his eyes.

I held the beer in my hand, and he used his wings to stabilize himself against the bottle's neck. I twisted the top, and Stout speared the straw inside. He didn't take tiny sips. He guzzled it until the slurping sound of an empty drink filled the apartment.

"Were you thirsty?"

His arm dragged over his mouth to wipe away any residue. "You don't know the half of it."

"What's with the beer?" I asked.

He sat on the table beside my plate. "It's a fairy thing."

"I kinda figured that much, but what's it got to do with you, specifically?" The toast on my plate was a little stiff, but I took another bite.

"Not so long ago–like, a few days, actually–you had a supernatural encounter with Shay and an exchange of power. You needed balance for that magick transfer."

I remembered. It was impossible to forget Shay unconscious on the floor, her body depending on my execution of a spell. I'd fumbled through the incantation until I had to trace images on her lodestone. I'd traced those symbols using... "Fairy powder. *You* left us the fairy powder?"

He nodded and tapped the empty bottle. "How about another?"

I got a second bottle, mainly because if he was the source of the powder-filled envelope, he was also the reason Shay was the Magick and why she was alive. I set it in front of Stout and took the empty one to the recycle bin. He'd consumed the fresh bottle by the time I made it back to the table.

"You're going to drink us right out of our home."

He laughed as he slurped the bottom of the bottle. "Why do you think Regina had so many micro-brews on the menu?"

I thought about my first time in the bar and how the list of beer was twice as long as the list of food. "I'm a blacksmith, not a bartender."

"Don't worry, Regina planned everything to perfection." Stout stretched out, leaning against the empty bottle. His wings seemed to wrap around the glass to prop him in place.

"What does that mean?" I asked.

"Regina took care of us. I'm sure Shay will find out soon enough, and I don't want to ruin the surprise."

I picked up my plate and washed it, leaving it to dry on the rack. I finished my cup of coffee and refilled it. "You want another beer before we go down to work?"

He waved his hands, shocked that I would suggest such a thing. "Two's the limit, or I can't fly straight."

"I haven't flown straight in fifteen years."

He laughed at me, although I hadn't meant for it to be a joke. "I like you, Wildwood."

"I guess that's a start," I said as we made our way down to the workshop. The area around the forge was exactly as I'd left it the night before. I swept the wood scrap and shavings left behind from hefting the axe. Stout was standing on the table, walking in circles around the Hammer of Brigid.

"She is so beautiful."

I looked up. "The hammer or the Goddess?"

Stout kept a full fairy body length between himself and the hammer. "They are one and the same now."

His words threw me as they spun around in my head. The hammer was the living goddess, and I was the only one who could use it. The sigil burned into my palm. Why? What did the power of the goddess in me mean for Shay? How would Brigid's Maker energies help the two of us maintain balance? But most importantly… "What did you mean when you said Shay and I were different?"

"Oh, that." He flew closer to me, hovering near my face. "The goddess blesses the two, the Magick and the Maker. Their bond is sacred and must never break. She deems you worthy and ties you together through elemental enchantments we will never understand."

"That makes sense because Shay and I have been able to do a lot when we're together."

"It's more than that," Stout explained. "That's why I wanted to look at the ancestry scroll. I don't think the Magick and the Maker have ever been bonded by emotional and physical love. It's the only thing that makes sense."

He was talking in circles, and it was frustrating. "Makes sense of what?" I asked.

"Using the hammer and lighting the Pictish invokes the power of Brigid, and I'm not sure that the Magick has ever forged with the Maker and not become sick."

Shay and I had worked together at the forge dozens of times. Sharing my passion with others as a blacksmith was a career goal, but working in unison with Shay was a significant part of our relationship. Why did our fairy wait so long to tell me this bit of information?

"What do you mean, sick?" I asked.

"Fire energy, the source of Brigid's power, can be intoxicating. Shay's power comes from all five elements. Every time you use the hammer, you draw fire energy from everything around you, even Shay."

"Are you saying I could have hurt her with this?" I picked up the hammer. The instant my fingers wrapped around the handle, my palm, and the etchings, came to life with a fiery orange glow.

Stout's wings stopped fluttering as he landed on the anvil, and it looked like he was wiping tears from his eyes.

"What's wrong? Are you crying?"

"No, I'm not crying. It's just unbelievable that you're here. It's hard to accept that the Maker has returned to Bannock."

Our fairy friend was overloading me with praise, and I think I liked him better when he was obnoxious. How was I supposed to console a six-inch-tall fairy? "Do the tears mean happiness?"

"They do." He flew up to my arm and wrapped himself around my wrist in a strange hug. I let him stay until it got awkward. I cleared my throat, and he dropped back to the anvil.

"Will you tell me if using this hammer with Shay could hurt her?"

He paced back and forth across the face of the anvil. "It should have, but it didn't." That was a horrible answer. "Shay is the Magick, meant to balance you, but–" He held up a finger to stop me from speaking. "–you also balance her. I don't think that's ever happened before."

"Like *ever*, ever?" I asked.

He jumped off the table and flew to the stairs. "May I go up?" he asked.

Since he'd spent the night in our apartment, I didn't see a threat. "Sure, what for?" I asked.

"To get the ancestry scroll."

I nodded my consent, and he darted up the stairs. He was back in a few seconds with the parchment-wrapped bone clamped in his feet.

"Open this up and let's look back at the history of the Magick and the Maker."

I anchored the flapping end of the scroll on the table with a piece of scrap steel and stretched the parchment across. I could see that my name was written on the bottom, marking my place in the lineage of Bannock's history. Tracing one's ancestry wouldn't have been so important to most, but as a woman with no history of her own, this felt like a first.

"Your name is there, Wildwood." He laid both hands on the letters spelling my name, my Maker's mark now beside it.

"Why can you see it?" I asked.

He sat on the parchment. "Regina did that, too."

"Why?" I asked, curious to understand why Benton would entrust so much knowledge to this fairy.

"Regina wanted me to help you."

"Help me how?"

"Not just you; Shay, too. Regina wanted Shay to be safe, and she didn't want what happened to Jacob's family to happen to you."

What was he saying? So far, his help was like all the help we ever got, one question leading to ten more. "What do you mean? What happened to Jacob's family?"

"It's a long story."

"It always is." I sat down in front of the scroll. My finger trailed over the name Jacob Kota. "I heard he wasn't such a nice guy."

"He was nice enough if you knew him way back, but he lost his wife, and then he lost his only child. That makes a person bitter."

"I saw the report, and I know Jacob didn't get kicked by a horse." I watched Stout react to my comment. "What kind of demon killed him?"

"It was a *Huic Ostiarius*. You're familiar with those, aren't you?"

I was more than familiar with the massive Gatekeeper demons, with their flaming eyes and buckle-tight skin over twisted bone. They were the stars of my nightmares, and he knew it. "I've seen a few, and we buried one right over there." I pointed to the ring burned into the floor of my carriage house.

"I know what's buried beneath the ground there." Stout flew to hover over the circle. "They're nasty to tangle with on a good day, but Jacob, he wasn't having a good day."

"I guess not." I rolled back the scroll. "What about Sabine Althora? What can you tell me about her?"

"I never met her in person." He flew back and landed on the page. "Her mark." He stood on top of the circle with an S and an A. It wasn't a complex mark for a maker, but there wouldn't have been much of a battle between blacksmiths in this frontier setting over a hundred and fifty years ago.

"Was she kind?" I was curious about the people who came before me, about their character and their heritage.

"Sabine was very talented. Any metalwork on the buildings of Bannock probably came from her forge."

"Do you know where her blacksmith shop was?" In some strange way, Sabine Althora felt like a sister, like an extended relative I never knew.

Stout flew up the stairs to the apartment and came down with our pencil-sketched map clutched in his arms. He dropped it on the table in front of me. "There was a building here." He pointed to the map and a square that Shay had made. We didn't know what it represented when she'd sketched the town.

"A blacksmith shop?" I asked.

"It was the home of the Miller." Stout walked across the page. "He gave Sabine a place to live and work. Women, well, they didn't have the advantages you have today."

"Advantages? Oh, you mean prejudice because she was a woman."

In the 21st century world of blacksmithing, I was seen as inferior because of my female identity. Not much has changed, but I am who I am, and I love how I love.

"And because she was mixed race." Stout continued reading through the ancestry scroll as he walked across the names.

"A mixed-race woman on the frontier, working as a blacksmith and a demon hunter." He nodded to confirm my summary. "How did she die?" I asked.

"*Huic Ostiarius.*"

"Gatekeeper demon." I leaned in close enough to see the scroll. The letters were scribbles of Pictish writing. Stout was activating the powers of the *Sanquis Caeden* ink written on the parchment. "Is that how we all die? We get killed by Gatekeepers?"

"Not always. Grab that." Stout pointed to the scrap steel, and I lifted it. He held the loose end of the scroll and tugged it off the edge of the table. "Sometimes death is noble, like Regina's."

I thought about his comment and about Shay. Would Shay see the sacrifice as a noble one? I looked at the anvil stand and Brigid's Hammer resting on top. "Who was the last Maker to use Brigid's Hammer?"

Stout flew off the parchment and landed beside the hammer. He held his hands above the silhouette of the goddess. "Kai." I waited for a second name—some kind of surname to show an origin or skill set. Stout said nothing more.

"Just Kai?" I asked.

He sat on the edge of the anvil. "Not *just*. Kai was a powerful Maker, and her Magick pairing was the stuff of legends." Stout had a way of creating dramatic pauses that were unnecessary.

I looked at the scroll, the nasty bone wrapped in yellow parchment. I picked it up and opened it to the section about Kai.

My text was easy to read, as the only language I knew was English. Kai had no ancestry, like me. She had no family, like me. She heard the call of the Goddess, like me. I felt connected to this stranger who'd walked the grassy fields long before settlers constructed the buildings in Bannock.

"It says nothing about Kai's work or if she was a blacksmith."

"Kai was a solitary practitioner. She followed the laws of the earth and the ether," Stout explained.

"Was she human?" I asked, trying to conjure an image of this legendary Maker. I saw the rough chiseled *K* beside her name. It was a primitive signature, her Maker's mark.

"She was more than just human. She carried the weight of the Magick and the Maker combined."

"How?" I thought about my powers, and I thought about Shay's, remembering the transfer spells that had knocked us unconscious. We were powerful people, but neither of us could contain all that energy alone.

"The goddess willed it, so mote it be." He flew back to the table and fluttered near my ear.

"So mote it be," I whispered in response. "Tell me, what happened to Kai? Wait, please don't say *Huic Ostiarius*."

"It is unfortunate." Stout jumped down to the table. "She died at the hands of a Gatekeeper."

I set the scroll on the table and walked away, feeling like our fate was sealed. How were we going to rewrite the only history of the Magick and the Maker? We would fight the demons living deep in the mine; we would keep them buried in the ground. But ultimately, they would be the death of us.

Defeated, I kicked off my boots and left them by the stairs. I walked to the bedroom and stripped down to a t-shirt and took a deep frustrated breath. The scent of herbs and oils fixed my senses, and I thought about Shay. My arms wrapped around her pillow, clutching it to my chest, and my eyes closed as I tried to dream of a life without hammers, demons, and death.

CHAPTER VI

LEGACY

"Hello, beautiful." A cool hand brushed my cheek, and a light touch trailed over my forehead to push away the hair covering my face. The tenderness was delightful, but I wanted to cling to the mindless state of sleep, void of monster-filled dreams. I felt a hand cup my chin and then heard a voice that made every fear disappear.

"I am the light. She is the light. We are the light."

Her fingertip caressed my cheek, and she was inside me like every intimate moment before. It was comforting to have a love like hers. "Receive light, give light. Receive protection, give protection."

I took a deep breath, and I could smell the lavender on the hand traveling over the bridge of my nose and across my forehead. She was here in our bed with me, and all I wanted to do was stay in this safe place between sleeping and waking. I felt the mattress sag beneath me as her weight tipped my body closer to hers.

"Shay," I whispered her name and felt warm fingers touch my lips.

"Hi, beautiful." Her voice was a caress, and at that moment, she was all I needed to hear. I opened my eyes to see shining green eyes staring back at me. I reached to touch her face and confirm the solid human in front of me.

"Hi, back." My voice was scratchy and low from the deep sleep I'd just enjoyed.

"How was your day?" She propped her head against one hand.

I noticed she wore her uniform shirt buttoned to the neck, and I felt her duty belt as my hand moved to her hip. "Are you going back to work?" I pouted.

Her finger traced my lip. "It's four fifteen in the afternoon, sweetheart. I just got home."

The blush on my cheeks felt warm as I smiled. "That's very good to hear." I threaded my fingers through the hair at the back of her head and pulled the elastic from her ponytail. Her chin tipped as I tugged her hair free. "That's so much better."

"Is it?" She smiled as she asked. I leaned in for a kiss, and her mouth opened to mine. Then she pulled back with a satisfied smile. "Mmm, I think that's the best." I felt safe as I lost myself in the sensation of Shay. "The shop is clean, so I know you weren't in bed all day. Tell me how your day was?"

I was hesitant to talk about the conversation with my fairy friend, the mention of the Gatekeeper demons, and my thoughts about our unpreventable demise at the hands of pure evil. I didn't want to say it out loud, not to her. "Stout and I read through the ancestry scroll." That got her attention.

"You did? That's good." Shay pushed up to sit.

I shook my head and noticed the rain falling against the bedroom window.

"That's not so good?" Shay asked as she slid her sock-covered feet off the bed. She unbuttoned her shirt while she waited for my answer. I know Shay didn't intend to distract me by undressing. I'm sure she just wanted to get comfortable at home, but I wasn't listening anymore. "Wildwood?"

"What? Sorry." I blinked hard, and she knew exactly where my thoughts drifted. I felt her response when a wadded-up uniform shirt landed over my face.

"You are so predictable," she said as the velcro tore away from her vest, and I was quick to pull the fabric from my face to watch her undress.

"You should get used to it." My tongue moved across my lip. "I plan to adore you pretty much every day for the rest of our lives. However long that might be."

"A very long time." She draped her duty belt over the chair, unzipped her pants, and kicked them off before walking to the dresser, pulling out a clean pair of jeans, and sliding into them.

"Yea, I hope it is, but there's a catch."

Shay turned around to look at me. "There is? What's that?" She sat down on the bed beside me.

"We have to not get slaughtered by our Gatekeeper."

Shay didn't say a word as she pulled her BPD t-shirt off. I reached to touch the scar on her back, and she paused, taking a deep breath as I rested my flat palm against the rippled skin. It was a reminder that even with all the magick, the two of us were also human. Shay opened the neck of her clean shirt, and her head popped through the collar. Her silence made me wonder if she'd missed what I said.

"Did you hear me?" I asked.

"I heard you." She tucked her shirt into her pants.

"You don't have a reaction? Nothing? Aren't you even a little bit worried?" The questions circled inside my head and right out of my mouth. She was so calm while I'd spent the last few hours suffering alone with this fear.

"Are you up here sleeping because you're worried about being hurt by a Gatekeeper that's locked in the ground downstairs?"

I hitched my chin to my neck in a half-shrug. "Maybe a little."

"Come here." She rested her back against the headboard of our bed and opened her arms to me. I wiggled in to cuddle up against her. "It's going to be alright. We will figure this out, and I will protect the two of us."

"What if you can't?" I could hear her heartbeat as my head rested against her breast. The sound of mortality was thumping in my ear, and all I could think about was a life without her in it. "What if something happens and we aren't strong enough?"

"We'll make a plan, Wil." Her fingers combed through my hair, twirling the dark strands until they fell away. I don't think she was aware her fingers were moving, but they had a calming effect. I liked her idea of making a plan. Knowing what to do would help.

"Okay," I agreed, "we should make a plan." Shay leaned forward to get up, but I held tight to stay in my place. "I didn't mean right now."

I could feel her body shake as she laughed. "Okay, a few more minutes."

"Yes, a few more." I snaked my hand behind her back.

"Better?" she asked.

"Much." My head snuggled into her shoulder. "How was your day?"

"It was a big day for me. I completed the listing with the realtor, and the house is on the market."

My hands pushed off her shoulder to sit up. "You did?"

"Yep." Shay stood up. She held a hand out and yanked me from the bed. "The realtor's got a little work to do. She's been telling her clients about the place, and it shouldn't take long to sell. It's priced right." She noticed I wasn't wearing more than a t-shirt and enjoyed a long glance at my unshaven legs.

"We're really going to do this?" I asked. "We're going to be a family." I wrapped myself around her. This was perfect, even if I was a little surprised she wanted to go forward with the sale. Shay loved her little two-bedroom house, and I loved it, too. She'd built a cozy, safe space for herself in Bannock.

"I'm tired of living in two places," she explained, "and this building feels like home. I never thought I'd want to sell my house, but being here with you feels right. It's just better."

"And you're sure you're ready to let it go?"

Shay picked up my pants from the floor and handed them to me. "Get dressed. Let's take a walk." She dropped to one knee to slip on her boot and tie it, then tugged up the cuff of her pant leg and tucked the punch dagger into her boot. The way she treasured the blade thrilled me.

I pointed at the water droplets snaking down the glass of the window. "It's raining."

Shay walked to the window and unlatched it before pushing it open and holding her hand outside. "It'll be done soon."

"You're a meteorologist now?"

She closed the window. "Not at all, but I listened to the weather report."

I'd missed quite a bit while I was sleeping. I put on my pants and looped the Dagger of Doom to my waist. "Where are we going?"

"I want to show you something." She stood up and held her hand to me, but I was still upset about my conversation with Stout and all the doubts he'd planted in my mind. Shay's fingers curled around my hand, and the warmth of her magick was soothing.

"What are you going to show me?" I kicked into my boots and tied the laces.

Shay was waiting in the bedroom doorway, her arms up over her head, gripping the trim as she leaned forward to taunt me. "You'll have to wait and see."

I jumped forward and grabbed her waist. "I guess I can be patient."

"You can?"

I squeezed her and walked her backward down the hall. "Not really, but I'll do my best to *fake it until I make it*."

"I can get behind that." Shay turned around as we walked into the kitchen, my arms still loose around her waist as I followed behind. Dexter lay curled on his bed, and Stout sat on top of the dog's hind legs. They were talking, although I could only hear Stout's side.

"It's not that high." Stout's arms waved and flailed in the air. Dexter was conveying his side of the discussion through thought or whatever means of communication the two of them used. "No, it's not."

Shay stopped, and I bumped into her. "What are you talking about?" she asked Stout.

The dog barked at the tiny fairy, and Stout flew up in the air. Dexter nipped and just missed taking a chunk out of Stout. "Your dog was telling me—"

Dex barked louder this time, ending with a slow, quivering growl.

"Dexter," Shay scolded him.

"He doesn't want me to tell you." Stout flew up to the top of the bookcase and far from the dog's reach.

"Tell me, what?" Shay asked. She walked closer to her K-9 partner and dropped to one knee in front of him, scratching between his ears. "What's up, buddy?"

I looked up at Stout. "Is he okay?" What could cause a fairy and a dragon-dog to argue? Why would Dexter keep a secret from Shay? And how odd was my life that I was even wondering the answers to these questions?

Stout yelled down at us. "He doesn't want you to know he's afraid."

They must have been discussing the ancestry of the Magick and the Maker. Somehow, the dog must have learned the power of the Gatekeeper demon. Then I realized that thought made little sense as I remembered the dragon-dog's fierce appetite for this class of monster and its pustule embryos.

Shay turned to look at me and then up at Stout. "Afraid of what?" she asked. The silence that followed was a sign that Stout felt a sense of loyalty to our dog.

"If I tell you, he's going to hold a grudge." Stout pushed off the bookcase and hovered beside Shay. I'm sure he felt safe from the dog with my girlfriend between them.

"Against you or us?" I asked.

"Against me!" The fairy buzzed around my ear. "I think it's something he should let me tell you."

Dexter growled again. "Maybe we should take Dexter with us." Shay swiveled around to look at me.

"Maybe. I'd hate to come home to half a fairy," I joked.

Stout landed on the table. "Don't worry, he won't catch me."

I wasn't convinced, but it would be nice to take a walk, just Shay and me. She leaned over Dexter's nose and hugged him. "Behave yourself." I held my hand out to her and helped Shay to her feet.

"You ready for a walk?" she asked.

"I am more than ready to be outside for a little while."

Shay followed me down the stairs, and we paused in front of the table in my workshop. I stared at the scroll and turned to look at the ring burned into the floor. Gatekeeper demons. I wanted nothing to do with them.

Shay bumped my hip to get my attention. "You still bothered about the ancestry scroll?"

"I'm bothered by Gatekeeper demons more than anything."

Shay didn't understand. Well, I thought she didn't understand. How could she? Maybe she'd read through the scroll. Perhaps she already knew how all the Makers died.

"That's understandable, especially after going into the mine." She held my hand and walked us to the door.

"It's more than that." I pulled the handle and got my first glimpse of sunshine after our warm rain.

"You've read through your ancestry?" Shay asked, but I could tell she already knew. At that exact moment, she realized I understood what the Gatekeepers wanted.

"I have."

Shay's fingers snaked through my fisted hand, clenched so tight with fear. "You realize that most of the Makers who came before you were solitary souls?" she asked as she tugged us toward her house.

"I know Jacob chose to be alone, and Sabine didn't. This guy Gorath, there are just a few scribbles about him." Our feet fell together in stride, but there was no rush as we walked.

"And Kai?" Shay already knew the answer. She'd memorized the history of herself and me.

"Kai was the last to hold the Hammer of Brigid," I said. I held up my palm, showing her the sigil.

"Yes, and her death was a brave one."

"It was a brave one?" My voice was louder than I'd meant it. My body trembled at the casual way Shay mentioned death. I wasn't sure how being slaughtered by a Gatekeeper could be brave.

"She protected the few people who were here. The settlers who opened that mine," shay explained.

"The settlers who unearthed the monsters inside," I spat back with frustration in my tone.

Shay squeezed my hand. The more we talked, the more we realized that the town of Bannock existed because of the Maker's sacrifice, but it was more than that. "Kai was alone." Shay stopped to look at me. "She carried the powers of the Maker and the Magick. No one could do that for very long. Remember?"

The memory of the magickal surges Shay had experienced was frightening, as were those first days as we'd come into our power and the transferring of untamed energy back and forth to the earth. Shay couldn't hold our powers alone. I didn't want to think about how much Kai must have suffered.

"How do you think she did it?" I asked.

"It had to be the magick of Brigid and the powers of the hammer." We turned the corner, and I could see the bright orange door of her house. I could also see the "Contract Pending" plaque on top of a "For Sale" sign.

"It's sold?" I stopped, and Shay's arm yanked me forward.

"Not quite sold, but the realtor called me only a few hours after I officially listed it. That's why I was late coming home."

"This is really going to happen?" I grabbed Shay and hugged her tight. My heart was racing, and I couldn't contain my excitement.

She lifted me off the ground and carried us down the sidewalk. "It's just a pile of paperwork at this point."

I kissed her. "And we both know how good you are at that."

"You might say I'm a pro." She lowered me until I was standing on the bottom step.

"Is that why we're dodging puddles? So I can see the sign in your yard?"

"Not exactly," she said. Shay opened the front door, and I could see the stacks of cardboard boxes. There was a tray of markers and a pile of old newspapers.

"This looks like a trick," I said as I figured out her plan. I was helping her box up the house. "Are you putting me to work?"

"I'm putting us to work, yes." Shay closed the door behind me and walked to the room at the back of the house. "I know I've migrated a lot to the apartment already, but I thought we could convert your second bedroom into an altar room like mine." Shay opened the door, and I could see most of her life as a witch packed into what looked like twenty cardboard boxes.

"You've been busy." I poked the corner of a box marked "books."

"I have. The last few days, I've stopped by for lunch, and I've delivered a bunch of stuff to the shelter. When I dropped it off, I made arrangements for them to pick up all the furniture we don't plan to keep."

I walked around the room. The east wall was Shay's designated apothecary. The last time I was here, there'd been hundreds of bottles and jars filled with plants and flowers. Was Shay keeping secrets again? Had she fallen back into old bad habits? I didn't like the idea of her doing all the work alone. "Why didn't you ask me to help you?"

She leaned against the empty bookcase. "I think I needed to be sure. I needed to walk through this house and say goodbye with no other emotions involved."

Was she worried about my emotions? Was I emotional? I just wanted her to be happy, and I was sure we would be happy at the carriage house. "I'd never want you to do something you're not ready for."

"That's just it. I think I knew it the first time we talked about it."

I remembered the moment she was referring to, the two of us standing in her kitchen, me asking her how much she adored her life inside this house. She liked it more than anything, and I realized she was giving up her beautiful backyard and our porch swing.

My hand ran over the block letters spelling "incense" on the side of the cardboard box. "But you love it here," I said.

Shay pushed off the wall and walked closer to me. "I love you, and I love us, and I think we should be together."

"I've thought that since…" I looked into her eyes, and I saw the skinny, frail fifteen-year-old girl who'd stolen my heart, "I've thought about being with you since as far back as I can remember."

"So it's happening." Shay smiled.

I waved my hands around the room. "It looks like we are in the process of making it happen." Her laugh was an elixir, and I planned to hear it for the rest of our lives. I clapped my hands together. "So why am I here?"

"Would you laugh if I said it was for heavy lifting?"

I was already laughing. "Nope, I'm here to lift all the heavy things." I flexed my bicep to show it off even though I was pretty sure Shay could out-lift me. I heard pounding on the front door and a loud hello.

"That's Dani," Shay said.

"More heavy lifting help?" I joked.

"Exactly."

"Shay?" Dani walked through the front door as we came out of the back room.

"Hey, D."

"Hi." I gave a weak wave.

"Hello, Wildwood. Good to see you. I saw the sign in the yard. I guess the sale went pretty fast." Dani shook her thumb at the real estate sign outside.

"I already have an offer, and I need to move out the big stuff."

"That's why I'm here." Dani cracked her knuckles. "What needs a new home?"

"I'm just moving books and bottles today," Shay explained. "Most of the furniture is going to the shelter. I think the only big thing for sure is the apothecary cabinet."

Dani held up her hands, shaking them in surrender. "I'm not moving that thing again. No way! You said it would never move again."

"I remember what I said." Shay threw her arm over Dani's shoulder. "But I didn't know how different life was going to be when we dragged that cabinet in here." Shay led her friend down the hall and into the back room.

"Oh, come on!" Dani saw the boxes stacked and the empty shelves. "You're mean, Pierce. I thought we were moving boxes of books."

"I promise beer and burgers when the job is done."

"Like last time." Dani froze in place. I wasn't here last time, and I didn't know what she meant, but Shay did, and she stopped laughing.

"Not quite like last time." Shay's voice was quiet, solemn.

"Benton made a mean burger," Dani added.

"She sure did, and she would agree that I said this sucker would stay."

Shay ran her hand over the scrolled etching on the cabinet door. The absence of their friend was the piece I didn't understand until this moment. I didn't know what to say, so I waited for the two of them to work through the memory. I started carrying boxes to the living room, and when I returned, Dani was hugging Shay.

"Everything okay?" I asked, afraid to interrupt.

Shay pulled out of Dani's hug and wiped her eyes on the back of her hand. "It's fine. It's just going to take some time."

I looked at Dani and saw the same fight against tears raging in her eyes. Grief is a solitary experience, and I didn't know what to say. I'd only known Benton for a short time, and as lovely as she was, we were barely friends.

"You summoned us here to boss us around." I tried to break the tension. "What's the plan?"

"Really, Pierce? Who moves on the same day they list their house for sale?" Dani joked as she began shimmying the cabinet out of the corner.

"I've been planning this since before the funeral," Shay admitted. "I just didn't tell you."

"Or me!" I pointed to my chest. "I would have made space in the back room upstairs."

"The wall is empty. We can work around the rest."

Shay left the room, and a few seconds later, she returned with a wheeled cart. Between the three of us, we moved the three-piece cabinet from the bedroom to the back of Dani's truck. I packed the boxes of books around the edges, and Shay and I hung out the tailgate, keeping everything locked in place as we drove the few blocks to the carriage house.

When we pulled up, I jumped off the back and ran inside to swing the double-wide service door open. I didn't use the door often, but today, the barn-style entryway would give us a straight shot up the stairs to the second floor.

Shay removed the tie-down straps and hopped off the tailgate. "Let's take out the boxes and get them out of the way." Shay loaded my arms, and we made quick work of stacking them to the side.

My carriage house has 13 stairs. I know because each made a creaking sound as the weight of the cabinet settled on every one of them. When we hit the top step, it was no problem to wheel the cabinet into the new magick room. Then we brought up the side shelves and set them in place.

"The cabinet looks great in here," Shay said, her hands resting on her hips in the sexiest superhero stance.

"Like they made it to fit in the space," Dani agreed.

I wrapped the tie-down straps around the cart. "You want the boxes up now?" I asked.

Dani grabbed the handle and dragged the cart out of the room. "We can just load this up." She said as she walked toward the kitchen. Dani stopped hard, and the steel handle fell from her hands, crashing to the floor. She stood frozen in place, and I didn't know why.

The sound of excited fluttering wings filled the air, and for a second, I thought Dani had never seen a fairy before. Here, it was the exact opposite. It looked as though she'd seen a ghost. "Stout?"

The fairy hovered in front of the tall cop. "Danielle! It's excellent to see you again."

She turned around to look at Shay. "How long?" Shay didn't have time to respond as Dani turned back to talk to Stout. "You're still here? You're still with us?" Dani held out a hand like she'd done it a thousand times. Maybe she had. It was apparent the two of them knew each other. "How long?"

"It's just been a day," he explained.

Dani turned around with a tiny fairy standing in the palm of her hand. "You went back to the mine?"

Shay didn't say a word. She just nodded in confirmation.

Dani looked at me. "You found it, didn't you?"

I didn't know how to react. Should I tell her I found the hammer? Did she already know but didn't believe that we would ever find it? How much was she going to share once we told her that the hammer gave me more power?

"We did," Shay answered for me.

"Can I see it?" Dani asked, and I was in awe of her composure. Her father, Jacob Kota, was meant to carry the Hammer of Brigid. She must have wondered how it looked. I didn't know what to say. Was it cool with the Goddess for her to see it?

"If it's alright with Wildwood, yes."

I didn't know of a single reason why Dani shouldn't see it. "It's in the workshop."

Shay picked up the cart, and they all followed me down the stairs. Stout was hovering in the air around the hammer resting on the table. Dani sat in the chair, staring at the shiny chunk of metal teetering against my modest hickory handle.

"It's beautiful." Dani didn't touch it. She only stared in silence.

I stepped closer to stand beside her and picked up the hammer, giving it a little swing in the air. "It's something. The power of the Goddess is so alive when I hold it."

"That's because it was destined to be yours," Stout shared as he landed on the table.

I set the hammer down so Dani could see the other side. When I opened my hand, she grabbed my wrist. "You've used it?"

My hand was wide open, revealing the sigil scorched into my palm. "I have." I pulled my hand away.

"What did you make?" Dani's reaction to the hammer was intense, and I stepped away.

"We made an axe," Shay answered as she moved closer to stand beside me. "Last night. Why?"

"Can I see it?"

The hammer and its power moved her in a way I hadn't experienced. It was like the tall cop was under a spell. "Sure." Reaching across the table to get the axe, I handed it to Dani.

She touched my Maker's mark stamped on the head. "You marked it. What does it do?" Dani knew a lot about Brigid's Hammer and its power of creation. She also knew that some kind of magic was born into the weapon.

"So far, it never misses," Shay said as she flicked her finger against the steel.

"Even when *I* throw it." I took the axe from her and headed for the target wall. I adjusted my feet to take a focused step and launched it into the splintered center of the red circle. "Not bad, right?" I walked across the room and pried it loose. When I reached the throwing line, I turned and launched it again. It hit the center.

"Can I try it?" Dani asked, and I couldn't find a reason to say no.

"You've thrown an axe before?" It seemed like a silly question to ask, since she and Shay were best friends who shot at paper targets for fun.

"I have." She held out her hand, and I plunked the handle against her palm. I moved closer to Shay, and we watched Dani launch the blade at my throwing wall. She wasn't as accurate as Shay, but it didn't bounce back like my usual failings.

"This has outstanding balance." Dani shook it in front of her and made a few swings in the air.

"It's almost identical to the one she made from the demon metal," Shay explained.

"So, you didn't make this from demon steel?"

"No, I wasn't sure what the hammer would do to it. I just wanted to work with the material I'm familiar with."

"Dani, what aren't you telling us?" Shay asked. She stepped close to her friend.

"I've seen what the Maker can do. I've just never seen this." She held up the axe.

"I don't understand." I was confused by Dani and by her reactions this evening. It made sense that she would know Stout, but the two of them had secrets. I wondered what they were and if they would hurt Shay or me.

Stout bounced off the table, and the fluttering of his wings made me think about his relationship with the Maker before me. "Did Jacob ever forge anything like the axe?" I asked.

"You mean infusing magick into non-magick material?" Stout answered, and I saw the look on Dani's face. Dani launched the axe one more time, and it hit the wall, but missed all the rings of the target.

"That hammer," Dani murmured. "The Goddess and her hammer." She was muttering under her breath, and she almost sounded intoxicated. "Looking for that damn hammer was an obsession for my father. He thought it would fix everything." Dani walked toward the table where Brigid's Hammer lay. She dropped into the chair and stared at the Maker history laid out in front of her. "This damn power destroyed my family." She pounded her fist on the table and pushed to a staggering stand. "Sorry, I gotta go, Shay. This is too much. I just can't."

I watched as Shay chased after her friend, and Stout flew back and forth between the past and the present. It made sense that Dani would know so much about Brigid's call because she'd known Jacob and had witnessed his Maker's demise. Dani saw something more in my hammer, and that detail still haunted her.

When Shay came back into the building, she was talking on her cell phone. "She just left. Yes, she's really upset and…" Shay paused. "I'm sure you know more than I do, but we found what we were looking for in the mine."

I couldn't hear the person on the other side of the conversation, but I was sure it was Amelia. Shay didn't say another word. There was no "goodbye" or "I'll talk to you later" when the call ended.

"That was Amelia. She wanted to watch for Dani, so she hung up the phone."

"What's going on?" I asked.

"I wish I knew the answer to that." Shay strode over to the throwing wall and leveraged the magick axe from it. She twirled it around in her flattened palm as she walked to the workshop table.

I held my hand out to Shay, showing her the sigil in my palm. "Seeing this set her off."

"I noticed that," Shay said. "Maybe you should keep it covered for now."

"Maybe I should." I had a pair of fingerless gloves that I could wear in public. It was a dated look, but who would wonder about a blacksmith and welder who protected their hands? I flexed my hand, feeling the energy of the sigil move up my arm. "Do you know what the symbol means, Shay?"

"Not yet, but there's a book over there that can help us." She jutted her chin at the stack of twenty boxes lined up against the workshop wall.

"We have to unpack them to find it?" I knew the answer, but I asked anyway, hoping that she had a perfect idea which one of the twenty contained the right magick tome.

Shay picked up two boxes and carried them to the stairs. "It's in the one marked *M* books."

I looked at the line of boxes against the wall. "Over half of them say that."

She was laughing as she climbed the stairs. "I guess we should get started, then."

I bent down to pick up the largest box; by its weight, I could tell she'd filled it with books, and only books. My girlfriend had hundreds, and tonight we were on a quest to find just one.

CHAPTER VII

EXODUS

"So many books!" I said as I wiped the dust from the binding.

I was so exhausted. It hadn't taken long to carry all twenty boxes of books up the stairs, but it took hours for us to wipe them off and put them on the shelf. Shay was specific about how she'd packed them, so it wasn't as daunting a task as she'd implied it would be. She paused often to remember the origin of a favorite text or quote a passage that she liked. She had read every single book in her collection.

"This is the one." Shay held up the book so that I could see the cover.

I read the words on the spine and wiped my forehead, thinking our unpacking task was complete. *"The Witch's Sigil."*

She passed the book to me before turning back to the box. "Not a very original title, but the artwork in your palm will be inside."

I sat down on the floor in front of Shay and flipped through the book. "There are hundreds of symbols in here." I felt a wave of defeat as I fanned the pages, each one a reminder that I'd spent too much time on bike frames and welding and zero time on witchcraft, magick or my unity with their power. The sheer volume of knowledge seemed impossible to master. "This book is...I never knew there was so much—that magick had so much."

Shay pushed aside a flattened cardboard box to sit next to me. We had two more to unpack, and it was close to midnight. "Let me see." She scooted closer, and her arm wrapped around my waist. "There are sigils that represent just about everything." Shay rubbed her fingers across my palm to open my hand on top of the book. She traced the symbols burned in my skin. "This is a spiral." Her touch was feather light. "But here." She stopped on the bump in the center. "The dot. It's the point of origin. The representation of energy itself. Every part of the sigil comes from it."

We studied the palm of my hand, seeing, maybe for the first time, the sigil for the complex pattern that it was. "I see the dot, but the arrow cuts it down the middle, and are those feathers?" I asked.

"Slow down, sweetheart." Shay stretched her legs to sit behind me and cupped my hand with her own.

I felt a rush of excitement as I flattened the book across my thighs. "I guess I just didn't look very closely before now."

She placed a kiss on my cheek. "It's okay. We'll go through it." Her voice vibrated against my ear, and I leaned into her as she continued. "This vertical line is the connection between above and below. See here?" Her fingertip tickled my skin, flexing my palm.

"How can you tell that?" I asked.

She tapped her knuckles against the book. "It's all in the book, sweetheart." She compared my markings to the page in front of us.

"Right." I wiggled myself further into the arc of her arm.

Shay drew her finger along another line in my palm. "This shape. It looks like a teardrop, but it's actually a flame, and these little squiggles are roots."

Flames and roots, I thought. I understood these symbols even if I didn't recognize them in this form. "So, it has earth and fire?"

"I'd say those are your elements, wouldn't you? And they come from the point of origin. Your center of power. The sigil makes complete sense when you put all the parts into the whole."

"Is this Brigid's mark?" I asked, unsure what it meant for me and for our future.

"I think it's more like a vow to Brigid. You've bound yourself to the power of creation that comes to you through the hammer." Shay squeezed me a little tighter as I tried to understand what she'd said.

Forging as the Maker of Bannock was an overwhelming responsibility. *How was it possible that I could be a source of power?* I wondered. Would I create my work for the goddess if this was my fate? "What if I didn't want to bind myself to Brigid?"

Shay closed the book and set it on the floor beside us. She rested her chin on my shoulder. "I'm thinking...and this is just my thought..." She took a breath, and the pause made me nervous. "Sweetheart, if you weren't supposed to be the Maker, you would have died in those tunnels."

I twisted to turn away from Shay. There was no smile or arching eyebrow. She was serious. I didn't want to believe that searching for the hammer without being called by the goddess was beyond dangerous. "You're not kidding?"

"No, sweetheart. I'm very serious."

I pushed off the floor to stand. The world we lived in seemed to expand beyond human and demon into a realm of otherness. I didn't know what it meant for me as a simple blacksmith or what it meant for the woman who was staring up at me with a concerned wrinkle on her brow.

"What?" I asked.

"Remember, I said it was okay to be afraid."

"Afraid is *not* the emotion I'm feeling." The assumption seemed obvious factoring in all the experiences we'd had in the last few months, but fear was not my first emotion. I held a hand out to help Shay off the floor.

Her arms snaked around my waist. "What are you feeling?"

"I'm feeling like everything is finally making sense."

Shay's eyebrow pinched, coaxing me for more details. "Really? Explain, please."

I stepped out of her arms and opened another box of books. Shay followed my lead as we worked through the last two boxes. "When I came to Bannock, when I got the grant, it felt like the accomplishment of my life." I wiped a few books and handed them to Shay.

"It was, even though I got involved," Shay added.

"That's just it. You were supposed to. We were supposed to be together." I reached for her hand and wiggled her pointer finger alongside my own. I opened my palm and drew our joined fingers across the fading scar from our childhood. "Do you remember this?"

"Yes, Wil. I remember it like it was yesterday."

"We made a vow, Shay. We promised to try even when life got hard." I thought about holding her hand that first time, about drawing my little knife blade across our palms to make an oath in blood. Her blood and mine combined, binding our futures together, just like the powers of the Magick and the Maker. And now, the sigil of the goddess tied me to that hammer, too. "Our life together, you and I, it's bigger than the two of us."

"It seems like the stuff of folklore and legend," she said.

"It does, doesn't it?" I agreed. "So that vow we made extends to our life here. Not just in Bannock, but inside this building. Inside *our* home."

"I like the sound of that." Shay looked at the wall of books. She ran her fingertips over the representation of a life she'd had before me. "This is our home."

"For better or worse." I stopped her hand. "Can you manage a long life with me?"

"I can handle two long lives with you and maybe a few more." She picked up the empty box, ripped off the tape, and collapsed it flat. We had a pile of empty boxes ready to move the rest of Shay into the apartment.

"Do you think you can handle taking me to bed?" I asked as I rotated the watch on her wrist to check the time. "It's almost one in the morning."

"I can handle you and that bed–and maybe a bit more–before you close those beautiful eyes."

She stepped backward, holding my hands as she tugged me across the hall and into our room. When she pushed me to sit on the end of the bed, I felt the boards move on the frame beneath me. I'd built this bed for function and nothing more. Sure, it was solid, but I'd assembled it from scraps abandoned inside the carriage house. It was better than a mattress on the floor, but as I felt the frame tremble, I remembered Shay had a comfortable queen-sized bed.

"Are you going to keep your bed?" I asked.

"I wasn't planning to, no. I figured this one is fine." She put her hands flat on the mattress and gave it a few squeaky pushes.

"But your frame is much nicer than this one." I pictured the solidly built sleigh-style bed frame. "Plus, we get to break it in." I wiggled my eyebrows at her, which I knew she did not find a single bit sexy.

"We're not doing any kind of anything if you keep doing that." She covered my forehead with her hands, and I seized the opportunity to hold her. "Besides, we've already broken that bed in."

I dragged her down on top of me, and her thighs straddled my hips. "Not in our home, we haven't." I tugged at the hem of her shirt to pull it up. "You should take that off."

"Should I?" She leaned back and arched just enough to throw the shirt over her head. We made a couple of choices in the next few seconds, but none had to do with beds, articles of clothing, or the pile of mysteries about our life.

~~~~~~~~~~~~

Shay and I spent our free time the next few weeks cleaning out her house and moving her life of magick into the two-bedroom apartment above the carriage house workshop. When I'd moved into the building, I'd had more tools than furniture and personal possessions. Shay had ten years of her adult life and all the magick artifacts to go with it in her house.

"What about this one?" I held up a dish. Her kitchen cabinets were the last project, and then the house with the orange door would officially be vacant.

"Go." She pointed to the thrift store collection box.

"These?" I held up two coffee mugs.

"Go."

"How about this?" I carried the bucket of dead plant clippings to the garbage can.

"No! Not garbage." She put her hand under the can to catch it. "These are mistletoe cuttings. Not trash."

"Really?" I'd never seen real mistletoe cuttings before. I knew about the plastic holiday ball people hung in doorways to solicit kisses. I didn't follow that tradition; it always felt nonconsensual to me. I also chose who I kissed and when, so I wondered why she had such a big bucket of the plant. "What's it for?"

"It's part of my protection spell. Where I go, it must go too." Shay was careful to cover the top of the container and tuck it into the packing box. "There's already a bunch under the table in the greenhouse."

"There is?"

"Yep, along with a few other things to boost that barrier around the carriage house."

I whispered under my breath. "Stupid Gatekeepers."

Shay pulled the last few dishes from the cabinet. "Sorry, love; I think they're only going to get worse."

"How many did you have to deal with today?" I asked. In the weeks since releasing Brigid's power from the hammer, we'd experienced a surge in demon activity.
~~~~~~~~~~~~

"Dani and I were out near the park, about two miles from the mine, and we had three." She was shaking her head as she folded the flaps on the last box. "They're getting bolder, appearing closer to town in the middle of the day."

"Do you think it's related to Brigid's Hammer?" I asked just before I heard a knock on the door.

"It might be," she said, standing up and brushing herself off. "Dani and I were talking about visiting the mine on Saturday. Maybe do some shooting and check things out."

Shay walked to the front door. The mail carrier was standing on the porch, and I peeked around to see the tall, lean man, his skin a little darker than mine, with a smile that made you want to stop and talk. He was cute, and I'm pretty sure he thought the same about my girlfriend.

"Hey, Shay. I'm glad you're home. I've got an express package that requires a signature." He held it up for her to see.

"Hey, Gabe. Sure, no problem." Shay poked out the door to sign the card, and he tore it from the oversized envelope.

"Thanks, and the rest of your mail is in the box. I have a confirmed change of address. After today it'll be forwarded to Fifth and Main. That right?"

"That's where I've moved, yes. Thanks, Gabe." Shay tucked the letter under her arm and stepped out to get the rest of the mail.

"Not a problem. Take care." Gabe walked down the steps and continued his mail delivery to the house next door.

"This is interesting." She was reading the return address on the large envelope.

"What is?" I asked.

Shay ran her finger through the flap to open it. "It's from an attorney."

"You recognize the name?" I asked.

Shay pulled the pages from inside and set the stack on the kitchen counter. She tipped the envelope over, and a set of keys fell out. Shay's eyes zipped back and forth across the words on the page. Before I could ask a question, her cellphone was in her hand.

"This can't be," she said as she tapped the call button.

"What can't be?"

She wasn't making sense as she passed the cover letter to me and put the phone to her ear.

"Hey," she said after the person on the other end picked up. "Did you get a package today?" Shay asked and was quiet as the other person answered. "This is crazy. I can't take it. She had a family, and this should go to them."

I read through the letter. It was from the attorney in charge of Benton's estate. According to the document, Shay and Dani were the new owners of the retired cop's bar, Slammed. There was no way either would ever give up law enforcement to run a bar. Why in the world would she leave it to them?

"Yeah, sure. We're just finishing boxing up the house. We'll meet you over at the bar." Shay ended the call. "Can you believe she did that?" She tapped a finger against the letter in my hand.

"It's very generous. Benton loved you both."

Shay was scanning through the stack of papers from the attorney. "I don't want the bar. I don't want to be anything but a cop. Benton knew that. I don't understand why she would pass this business on to Dani and me."

I took the papers from her hand. "There's a reason."

"With Benton, there always seems to be, doesn't there?" She shoved the pages back into the envelope along with the keys. "Dani's going to meet us at the bar." Shay carried out the last boxes and put them in the back of my truck. "Can we drop this at the carriage house first? I want to pick up Dexter and take him with us."

"Stout, too?" I asked.

Shay jumped into the passenger seat. "I'm sure he'll be happy to be inside the bar again."

"Only because there's beer," I joked.

Shay laughed, and it was the first sign that she was reconciling with the reality of Benton's gift. I drove the few blocks to the carriage house, and we unloaded the boxes inside the workshop. I moved the scraps of lumber and cardboard left over from building our new shower. After so many messy demon encounters and the struggle to get Dexter into the oversized bathtub, this two-person stall made sense. I stacked the boxes beside it, planning to carry them upstairs later.

"Dexter!" Shay called the dog, and he came running down the stairs, chased by a fluttering fairy. "Good boy." She patted Dexter's side.

"Are we going somewhere?" Stout asked as he hovered in front of my face.

"Yes, and I think you're gonna like it." I set the box of hardware on the table and looked at Shay. "My car or yours?"

"Let's take mine, just in case."

Shay expected trouble. "Just in case" implied something unexpected might happen, and I wasn't excited to think about what that might be. In the town of Bannock, it was a good idea to feel that way, and since coming to power and invoking the Hammer of Brigid, we'd experienced life beyond "just in case" encounters.

"You need anything else?" I asked.

Shay was holding the legal documents in her hand. "Just you."

"That's easy. You got me."

I pushed her toward the door and locked it behind us. Shay hit the button to open her trunk, and she reached in to check for something. I walked around the car, let Dexter into the back seat, and climbed into the passenger side. Stout flew in the window and landed on top of the dog.

"Everything alright?" I asked as Shay sat behind the steering wheel.

"We're good." She tucked the file between us.

I didn't know what to think about the last half hour. Shay was quiet, which was a clear sign that her mind was a tangle of thoughts. I didn't want to guess. "Will you tell me what you're thinking?"

Shay started the engine but didn't move to drive, and her arms rested on top of the steering wheel as she turned to look at me. "You're pretty good at that."

"Pretty good at what?"

She smiled, and the tiny wrinkles around her eyes made me smile, too. "You're pretty good at reminding me when I get caught up in my head."

"I was alone for a long time, too, and I just want to help you if I can." I didn't want to overstep, but we were also moving in together. We were permanently entangling our good times and our bad.

"Benton left the bar to Dani and me, and I don't understand how or why." Her head dropped to rest against her knuckles. "She had other people." Shay's tears fell against the back of her hand.

"She loved you, Shay." I reached to rub her shoulder.

"I guess she did. More than I ever realized, but—"

I interrupted, hoping to break the negative direction of her thoughts. "Why don't we go talk to Dani and figure this out together?"

"That's just it. Dani is part of the will, too." Shay wiped the tears with her hand. "They had a bond so strong that Benton would choose the daughter over the father?"

"I guess Dani is the only one who can reconcile that."

Shay pushed away from the steering wheel and shifted the car into drive. "Let's go talk to her."

I looked at Shay, hating to see her suffer. The people of Bannock who loved Shay had also kept her in the dark about the power of the Maker and becoming the Magick.

"You're staring." She glanced at me while she waited at the stop sign.

"You're beautiful. It's hard not to stare."

Her smile was everything, and even if my corny admiration only helped for a moment, it was worth it.

"You are sweet and thank you," she said.

"You're welcome, and you're also not alone."

I thought I should remind her we were partners in life, not just in the world of the Magick and the Maker's existence. Her solitary life habits continued to get in the way of our lives mingling together. So far it wasn't seamless, and as long as her instinct kept veering in the direction of solitary resourcefulness, we were going to have this barrier.

She reached across the center console to hold my hand and gave it a quick squeeze. "I don't even want to think about being alone again."

"The two of you are so cute." Stout stood perched against the metal frame dividing the back seat from the front, his eyes dreamy as his head rested on his chin.

My body bounced against the seat at the sound of his voice. "Shh—it! Dammit, Stout! Don't listen to our conversations!" I yelled at him.

"Gosh, calm down, Firestarter. I was just making an observation." He pushed away and flew to land on Dexter's back.

"How is it that Stout is *my* fairy?" I asked. "Why couldn't I have the cool dragon?"

Shay's laugh was enough to say she was glad that she got the dragon in this relationship. I was always going to be jealous of that.

CHAPTER VIII

CONFIDENTIAL

"Good, she's already here." Shay turned into the parking lot behind the bar, where we saw Dani standing beside her truck. The tall, dark-haired, casually dressed cop was holding an oversized envelope very much like Shay's. Dani kicked a foot up behind her against the vehicle's bumper, supporting the entirety of her stance. Her jaw flexed as she smiled, and I could appreciate how much alike my girlfriend she was, a similarity that made *me* smile.

"You took your sweet time, Pierce!" Dani yelled as she kicked away to walk closer.

"You remember I'm moving, right?" Shay yelled back.

"Moving slow, is more like it." Dani grabbed the handle of the car door, opening it for Dexter. The dog jumped out, and without hesitation, he sniffed around the parking lot.

Shay climbed out, grabbing the envelope she'd tucked in the seat. "So, you read through the documents?" Shay asked.

"I did. I also sent a scan to Amelia's attorney friend in Middletown, and it's legit. According to the attorney, there are a few things to sign, but you and I own this building and everything inside."

"Why?" Shay asked.

"You read the letter, didn't you?"

Shay walked to the bar's service door and slid her key into the lock. "She said it belonged to us. We were supposed to have it." Shay opened the door. "That doesn't answer the question of why."

Dani pushed the door open wide so all of us could enter. The bar was dark and had the distinct aroma of cooked beef and stale beer. Dexter sniffed his way around the room, but the space was the same: wild-west style tongue-and-groove floors; rich, straight grained mahogany bar with a brass accented foot rail; and mirrored shelves lined with bottles. I admired the replica police badge hanging in the center of the wall. It wasn't a cop bar, but if tradition continued, it would be a bar owned by cops.

"What do you think about all of this?" Dani asked.

I didn't realize she was talking to me until I turned around to look at Shay.

"Wildwood?" Shay's arm fell around my waist.

"What?"

She leaned in to say, "Dani's wondering what you think of all of this."

"I'm not sure." I didn't know what to think or how to feel. We were standing inside a bar that none of us wanted, but now we had to manage. "I'm a blacksmith and a welder, not a bartender or restaurateur. I never thought about a bar at all."

"I can't say that I have, either." Shay tugged at my hip.

"That makes three of us." Dani wrapped her knuckles against the oversized bar countertop. "So, how are we going to figure this place out?" she asked.

Shay walked away and turned over the chairs resting on a table. She sat down and waved for us to join her. "We can't make big decisions today, but Benton's cousins have been running the place since she went into the hospital. Maybe they'll just keep doing it and help us figure it out?"

"I can talk to Diana tomorrow afternoon when they're here to reopen," Dani offered.

Shay's shoulders relaxed. "That's a great start. I have no plan to retire soon."

Dani slapped Shay on the shoulder as she walked back to the bar. "Me either, but Amelia might want to set up shop."

"Do you think so?" I asked, a little too excited to pass off the responsibility.

"Wil doesn't want to own a bar, either," Shay explained as she threw her arm around my shoulder to pull me close.

"It's definitely not my first choice." I walked over to the bar. The glossy finish on the countertop made me think of old saloons with giant mugs of beer spinning and sliding across the surface. I didn't want to be part of a wild-west ghost town beer fest. "I'll just keep doing the blacksmith thing."

"I like you doing the blacksmith thing." Shay winked at me, and I was content that she would hold firm to the verbal agreement.

"Want to have a look around our new bar?" Dani asked as she tossed the attorney's folder on the counter.

"Who's been taking care of the building since the funeral?" I asked. My fingers swiped over the shelf of whiskey. "It's pretty clean in here."

"The cousins." Dani opened the office door. "It's been business as usual, but the attorneys shut it down two days ago. I guess they wanted us to come in and make some decisions."

"What decisions need to be made?" I asked.

"To keep it or sell it, I guess." Shay picked up three glasses and looked at her friend. "We should celebrate, don't you think?" She slammed a bottle of scotch on the bar, and I turned it around to read the label.

"Top shelf, only the best." My fingers wrapped around the neck of the bottle, and I wiggled the cork loose.

Shay pushed the glasses into a line as I poured. "Only the very best for my partners." She blew me a kiss. "This was Benton's favorite."

"What about me?" Stout asked.

I'd almost forgotten he was there. Shay didn't hesitate as she opened the fridge near her knees and took out a bottle of beer. She flipped the cap off using the wall-mounted bottle opener and poured it into a glass.

Stout was already beside her with his favorite bamboo straw from Benton's stash. "Regina took care of me." He shot the straw like a dart into the glass and took a long sip. "So good."

"Shay, come in here." Dani's head popped out from the office door.

"What's up?" Shay carried a glass in each hand, and I followed her into the tiny office. The space was small, just enough room for a steel desk, a few file cabinets, and a couple of office chairs. The three of us were a cozy fit.

"Does anything look odd to you?" Dani twirled her finger, encouraging us to look around the office.

I remembered the last time we were here. I had paid little attention to the room because Dexter was on the scent of Benton's hidden treasure of demon steel.

"Looks like someone moved the furniture around," Shay observed.

"Do you know why?" Dani asked as if she knew something that we didn't.

Shay handed the glass to Dani before kicking the toe of her shoe across a ripple in the carpeting. "Someone was looking around?"

"Someone or some horrible *thing*?" I said, lingering over the last word, hating the idea that a creature of evil had been lurking inside this building. "Isn't the bar protected?" It seemed like a logical question, considering Benton warned us to always cast a protection spell over our homes.

"That bind is fading." Shay set her drink on the desk and fished her keys out of her pocket. She sorted through them until she found the shiny one Benton gave her. She fitted it into the lock and pulled open the drawer. "Empty, same as we left it."

She closed it and fit the key into the center drawer. When she pulled it out, plastic dividing trays sorted everything. Shay picked up a pen. "It's got the bar logo on it." She dropped it back in place and sorted through the rest of the drawer.

I glimpsed a shiny piece of metal that looked like a gambling chip made from aluminum or silver. "What's that?" I pushed the tray aside to remove the token and held it in my open palm. "It's a medallion of someone's maker's mark."

"What's it doing in here?" Shay asked, tapping it before picking it up.

Dani was leaning against the wall, and I could see that she knew what it was. "That coin is pretty old," she explained. "I played with it when I was a child." I could see the frustrated lines on her forehead, and I wondered what memory was turning around in her head. "The last time I saw that thing, my father had it."

"Do you recognize the mark at all?" Shay asked, and I stood in silence, knowing the origin of its creation. Stout and I had seen it in the ancestry scroll, and I wondered what it meant and why Benton had it locked away inside this desk.

"I recognize the mark. It belonged to Kai," I explained. "She was the last to carry the hammer."

"What's it doing here?" Dani asked. "How did Benton get it? And why all the mystery about a Maker who lived hundreds of years ago?" Dani pushed the drawer closed and leaned against the frame of the door. We watched as Dexter began pawing at the floor near the feet of the desk.

"Dexter," Shay called.

His doggy nose popped up, and he barked at Shay to signal he'd found something. The wonderful thing about Dexter was that he was always working. Even if the mysteries of the past distracted us, his nose kept searching for more.

Shay walked closer as he was digging at the floorboards beneath the desk. "What you got, buddy?"

"You should move this." Stout flew toward the wall, hovering just above the floor. "There's a knot in the wood here." He landed on the one-inch hole, careful not to fall through. "Just hook your finger in, and it'll open."

Shay followed his directions and slid her index finger inside. The floor raised just enough with a gentle pull to allow the desk to swing out of the way. We didn't move, not an inch, as we took in the sight of a hidden staircase.

"Not another basement," I whispered under my breath. We already had experiences with dark basements and magick rituals. I wasn't ready to see otherworldly creatures or to disappear into the river down the street.

The dog, on alert, barked at Shay, and she sent him in first. "*Ante!*" Dexter moved forward, down the stairs. There were secrets down here; I could feel them, locked inside the shadowed corners of this bar. More secrets, always secrets. Shay and I had vowed months ago that we would share the scary parts of Bannock, but the people around us hadn't taken that vow, and here we were, standing on a staircase, walking into Benton's hidden world.

"*Ignis,*" Shay said, as her palm flashed with a blue flame. Before I could make a move or say a word, Dani slapped her hand on Shay's shoulder, and the two of them followed the dog into the unknown.

I don't know what power moved me, but I followed the trio into the cellar. I said the word, "*Ignis,*" and stepped behind them into the basement. My free hand pressed against the wall for security, and I could feel a plastic cover plate against my fingertips. The orange flame was bright in my palm, and I stopped when I saw Shay and Dani standing in front of a solid wall with an arched wood door, preventing us from going a step further.

"Stout, what's the trick?" I asked as the fairy hovered in front of Shay.

"I guess the trick is that you have to be Benton," Stout said. "She's the only one I ever saw come down here, and she's the only one who knew the trick to open the door."

"What about the keys?" It seemed like an obvious question. The package from the attorney's office had a set of them inside. Dani must have received them, too. "The set Benton left for you. You both got them, right?"

Dani reached into her pocket at the same time Shay did. They compared each set.

Dani flipped them over the ring as she counted. "I've got six keys."

Shay mirrored the motion. "I've got eight."

It was exciting and curious at the same time. Why all the mystery and suspense to open an oversized dungeon door hidden in the secret basement of a bar called Slammed? They took turns comparing keys, and it sounded like two kids playing a childhood game.

"There's a deadbolt key, Silver." Shay held it up.

"I got that one." Dani dangled the ring with her key. "The next one has a green tag."

"Yep, there's a weird two-pronged fork thing?" I laughed at the description, and the *ignis* flame flashed. Shay looked at me. "What?"

I held out my hand. "Give me your keys."

Shay handed them to me, and I climbed three steps, returning to that plate in the wall. I fit the mini forked key into a slot and felt the prongs grab hold. As it lifted at the pivot point, the light above us flickered on.

"How did you know that was there?" Dani asked.

"I had a vision." They stared up at me, eyes wide and mouths open. "I'm kidding. It's a maintenance switch. Earl had them at the bike shop to keep kids from playing with the lights." I had learned a lot from Earl and his bike shop. He'd given me a bed when I was homeless, and he'd offered me a future when no one else would. Life would have been so different without that man. "Seems weird to have maintenance switches down here."

Shay shook her head, scolding my humor, and I tossed the keys back to her.

"What are the odd ones here?" Dani asked as they continued to flip the keys around the rings.

"These are the two." There wasn't anything special about the brass keys Shay was holding up. They were so plain that I wouldn't have given them a second glance otherwise. They showed signs of wear, which made me believe Benton had used them often.

"Here goes." Shay fit one into the lock, and the key turned with ease. She twisted the knob, and Dexter pushed his nose through as the door opened. The K-9 advanced in search mode and was the first to enter. A heartbeat later, he was also the first to fly backward and slam against the base of the stairs.

"Holy shit!" Shay dropped to her knee in front of the animal as Dexter rolled onto his belly. "Hey, buddy. You okay?" She rubbed his head and ran her hands over his shoulders and back, checking for an injury.

"He says no," Stout translated for us as the dog jumped to his feet. "He says you should go first." Stout pointed to me.

"Me, why? My name isn't in the will." I felt the rush of panic as my instincts told me to flee—fast. "I hardly knew Benton."

Shay stood in front of the doorway, her right hand feeling the ridges and grain of the wall. I thought she was searching for energy shifts as she moved around the frame, but she stopped fast and turned to grab my forearm. "The token. Kai's medallion marker. Did you keep it?"

"No, I left it on the desk." I sat down on the bottom stair, and Dani rushed by. She returned a few seconds later with the medallion cast with the first Maker's mark.

"What are you thinking, Pierce?" She passed the silver disk to Shay.

"Everything's a mystery until it's not. There's a hole in the doorframe." Shay held my hand and pried the fingers in my fist open. She tugged the glove off, and Brigid's Sigil was plain to see. Kai's silver mark fit across it. "This must be the Maker's space. Benton must have been protecting it."

Shay was right. The medallion fit over my sigil, and the rush of magick energized the nerves from my fingertips to my toes. I felt the vibration of Kai's Maker-energy fill me, and when I'd calmed myself, I could hear the Maker's call. I squeezed Kai's medallion tight as I stood.

"I can do this. I can do this." The whispered chant was calming as I passed Dani and Shay.

Dexter jumped up and was a step behind me. I opened my palm flat against the circle in the wood and pressed the medallion against the hole. The enchanted mechanism released, and I pushed the door open wide. The fixture on the ceiling lit the entrance, but the space beyond fell into the shadows. There was a slatted wooden facade preventing me from seeing anything beyond my first step. Shay grabbed my forearm. Startled, I jumped back.

"What?" My erratic heartbeat pounded against my breastbone, and I could feel my pulse quivering my temples.

"I'm right behind you." A shadow covered her eyes, but the tone of her voice was unmistakable. She and Dani were in superhero mode, even though I was the one going in first.

"Shit, woman. Don't scare me like that." I grabbed her hand and pushed it against my chest. "My heart is about to beat right out of my damn body."

I took a deep breath and blocked out everything around me. My knuckles were white from gripping Kai's medallion, and the toe of my boot hovered before breaking the plane over the threshold. An obvious poof left my lips as I released the breath I was holding.

"I'm not flying backward, so I guess I'm in." I held a hand back toward Shay, and she grabbed hold.

"That's good. I guess the Magick and the Maker pass the test," Shay said as she reversed her hand to hold mine tighter. Dani followed, bracing her shoulder against the doorframe as she entered, prepared to fly backward.

When Dani was safe beside Shay, she asked, "Why all the magick security?"

I stepped around the wall, surprised to see a chamber stocked from floor to ceiling with magick supplies. It made our apothecary room look barren. A heap of daggers and swords sat piled on the table against the wall. With a quick glimpse, I counted two anvils and a hallowed spot where an abandoned, decaying coal forge stood. Boxes and books were stacked against the building's longest wall.

"I can't believe this." Shay walked to the bookshelf and waved her hand beside the floor-to-ceiling display of books. Of course, she would only see the books. There had to be thousands of volumes, and I could only guess that they recorded every bit of lore and legend surrounding the art of magick and the pagan world. While Shay was pining over the library, I was stumbling closer to a timeless arsenal of weapons and blacksmith treasures. It was more than I'd seen in my lifetime, and although many of the weapons had tarnished and rusted with age and neglect, I could see the incredible craftsmanship.

Dani stood at the long table, flipping pieces of paper over as she read through. "This was my father's."

Shay stood beside Dani, reading over her shoulder. "That's Benton's handwriting." Shay peeled off the sticky note. "What are–"

"These are their diaries," Stout interrupted. "And this is where they worked."

"Why didn't you tell us about this room? About all of *this*?" Shay asked Stout as he hovered in front of her.

"I did. Well, I did a little. I said you'd get the answers."

I picked up a dagger from the top of a rusty but solid anvil stand and slid it from the sheath to look for a maker's mark. The absence of a hammered imprint made me curious as I walked closer to the heavy wooden table. The legs were nothing more than rough-cut tree limbs attached to a solid slab of timber. Its primitive construction was interesting, and I studied the stockpile of forged weapons stacked on top.

I pulled a knife from the collection and drew the sheath away—no maker's mark. As I sorted through a few more, I couldn't find a single signature on any of them. "Where did these come from?" I asked.

"Those are the mistakes," Stout explained.

I held the long-handled knife in my hand, flipping it back and forth in front of my body to get a feel for the blade's balance. I'd made hundreds of my own, and never once did I put a sheath on a blade that was less than perfect. The knife in my hand was no mistake.

"What are you talking about?" I ran my finger across the beveled edge of the blade, and the sigil in my palm burst with orange fire. I dropped the knife. "Shit!" I don't know why my first reaction was to wave a magick flaming hand in the air, but I did, and the flash was brighter than anything I'd experienced before.

With a quick step, Shay was beside me, grasping my hand in hers. "What just happened?" She pushed her flame against mine to snuff it.

"She can't handle the unmarked demon steel," Stout explained. "There's a curse on all of those pieces."

"Then why the hell are they here?" Shay yelled, kicking the knife on the floor. "Why would Benton keep weapons that could hurt her?"

"Not her," the fairy corrected. "They can hurt everything but her." Stout flew to the floor and stood beside the metal. "These belong to the Magick now."

"Wait, what?" Shay dropped to one knee to pick up the smoldering blade at her feet.

"Stop!" I yelled and grabbed her hand.

"It's okay." Shay turned her wrist and, without effort, broke my hold. "It's okay." She picked up the blade by the handle and ran her finger across the bare steel. Nothing happened except another level of confusion was added to our seemingly endless supply.

"Why?" I wondered what would cause Benton to assemble a stockpile of weapons that could harm even her paired Maker. "Why would you want a weapon that could hurt me?"

"I wouldn't," Shay said as she buried the blade inside the sheath.

"But Regina would," Stout explained. "After the Maker, Jacob, betrayed her, she didn't trust him."

"Dad went a little mad," Dani added as she walked closer to the table. She pushed at the handles sticking out from the pile. "I never wanted to believe that he would hurt Benton, but this is proof that there was something evil happening, too."

"What else aren't you telling us?" I reached to grab the fairy hovering in front of me.

He dodged out of my way. "I haven't even told you half of what's going on behind the veil of *Ghost Town* status in Bannock."

"The veil?" I started pushing the arsenal on the table, careful not to touch the bare steel. "What veil?"

"Haven't you ever wondered why everyone in this town stays here?" he asked. "Why they don't move out of a place crawling with creatures like the *Huic Ostiarius*?" Stout flew from my hand and crossed the room, landing on Dexter's furry back. "Or how this dragon-dog ended up here?" The dog's butt dropped to the ground.

"I don't know. It's some kind of weird magick, isn't it?" I had wondered about it more than once, but living in continuous magickal mystery didn't always feel real.

"It's good fighting against evil, and every time the demons push forward, we have to push back." Dani interrupted. "I don't know about the enchantments put on these weapons. What I know is that once the bond between Benton and my father severed, my father was never the same."

"And neither was Benton." Stout pushed away from the dog and flew to the shelf of books on the north wall. "This." He tugged at the binding, knocking off clumps of dust as it moved forward. Shay stepped close enough to grab it.

The tattered spine, bound with string, stretched and creaked as Shay opened the cover. Books were everything to the woman in front of me. "It's in Pictish. I can't read this without a reference." Shay closed the book and tossed it on the table.

I grabbed another title and noticed it, too, was not in English. "What language is this?" I handed it to her.

Stout ran across the first few pages, flipping them with his feet. "I know this one."

"It's Theban," Shay explained as she stopped the fairy from turning any more pages. "They call it the Witches Alphabet."

"Do you know it?" Dani asked as she leaned a little closer to look at the pages.

"A little, but I'd need additional references to translate it, too."

"This shelf of books must be hundreds of years old." My fingers traveled across the spines of the ancient texts. Why was this library assembled in a secret basement under a bar? "How is all of this here?"

"Slammed wasn't always a bar," Dani explained as she picked up the book from the table. "It was once a general store, and before that, it was the town apothecary. I remember Benton talking about the jars she found in storage behind the bar, but she said nothing about this cellar."

I could see the betrayal on Dani's face, but she wasn't the only one who'd been left in the dark. Shay stood beside a cabinet that reached from floor to ceiling with three-foot-wide bi-fold double doors. Her fingers moved to the handles, and I grabbed her wrist.

"Are you certain you should open it?" I asked, unsure why since she was part owner of everything inside.

"Open it," Dani encouraged.

Shay held her hand on the knob and twisted it. "It's locked." She tugged it again, harder.

"Try one of your keys." Stout flew in front of us.

Shay walked back to the door and removed the ring of keys from the lock. "I guess I can eliminate this one." She held up the brass key for the chamber door. "And we know this is the only one that you don't have, Dani." Shay separated the rest of the keys and tried the one remaining. It fit, and she rotated it to unlock the door. "Got it."

We were standing side by side by side, the three of us, but no one wanted to open the doors.

"Are you going to open it?" Dani's voice broke the silence.

"I don't know what to expect in there." Shay had each of her hands wrapped around the handles.

"It's an apothecary." Stout flew up to land on Shay's forearm. "Open it. Anything you've ever needed to protect this town–and yourself–is in there. Don't be afraid of who you are."

The words coming out of the six-inch tall creature from the fairy realm packed more power than he could ever understand. *Don't be afraid of who you are.* Until my early twenties, I feared everything good would always be out of my reach. I wondered if Shay ever felt the pull of insecurity left behind by our childhood, too.

"Did you forget ten minutes ago when Dexter flew into the stairs?" I turned to look at the dog who'd made himself comfortable, curled in a ball in the corner. He wasn't even curious about what we were doing, which meant there was minimal risk of danger to anyone in the room.

"Dexter would be right here if he felt a threat." Dani nodded toward the doors, directing her friend just to do it. "Open it."

Shay pulled on the handles, and the tall wooden panels folded in the middle, opening until she tucked them to the side. The wall was beautiful, lined with arched cubbies, some open and some sealed tight with tiny doors. Four metal candle holders rested on the shallow, waist-high countertop. It was fascinating in a way that stole my breath. Shay's mouth hung open, and I could understand why.

"Honey?" I touched her hand. It was apparent that she was overwhelmed when her head turned to look at me. Her soulful green eyes were glassy with tears.

"I wish Benton was here," Shay whispered.

"She kinda is, in a way." Stout flew up to sit in an open cubby filled with delicate blown glass bottles. "She put this together for the next in line."

"Next in line?" Dani asked.

"The next Magick," Stout said.

Shay reached to pick up a container. "I need her to tell me what to do."

"You already know what to do," I said over her shoulder as I reached to take the bottle from her hand. "*Ignis*," I whispered in her ear, and my sigil hand burst with a glowing orange flame. "You've gotten us this far." My forehead rested on her temple. "We're going to be okay."

I set the jar back on the shelf and waited for Shay, wondering what was going through her mind. Was she scared? Was she wondering how this giant wall of plants and mysterious things managed to be in this musty basement?

"What's the plan, Pierce?" Dani opened a tiny door on the wall to reveal three bottles inside. I wondered why they were behind the closed cubby. "What are these?"

"Don't touch them!" Stout flew into the door, using his head to slam it closed.

Dani pulled her fingers away just in time to prevent a solid pinch. "What the hell, Stout?"

"Red is the only one allowed to touch anything behind a closed door." He waved a finger like a scolding teacher. "Remember, everything in the apothecary belongs to the Magick."

"What about the Maker?" I asked, reaching to open a different tiny door.

"Before I met you, I'd say you shouldn't touch anything, but there's something different about the two of you. You're bound by more than the powers of Brigid."

I looked at Shay as she stared at the wall in front of us. At that exact moment, something became clear. I understood our childhood made us different, not just because of how the world neglected us, but also because of our continued displacement. It was the life-saving pact made on a warm afternoon when we were fifteen years old. I thought about that day, and it was like an old-fashioned movie as the memory played in my mind. I could hear Shay's question.

"What are you doing, Wildwood?" Her voice had changed little in thirteen years. I still found it a welcome distraction. I remember explaining how I talked to the earth and the adorable look she'd given me when she thought I was spouting silly talk.

I remember holding that handful of dirt and what it meant to connect to something bigger than who we were at fifteen, and I remember the innocence of youth, closing my eyes to hear what the earth had to say.

The memory of Shay's fear was still vivid as she felt, for the first time, the power move inside her and the sudden rush that left her wanting more. We felt whole together on that warm summer day, and wholeness was a rare experience for two girls in the foster care system.

And then there was the question.

"You do this all the time?" Shay asked, and I nodded as I cradled her body, weak from taking in so much energy. She didn't freak out; in fact, she wanted more. Her stunning green eyes looked up at me as she said, "Whatever just happened, it felt really good."

And she listened as I talked about Gran and light work. About being six and feeling like someone honestly cared. Gran taught me to communicate on a different level, and it was like the Earth was talking to me.

Shay asked what the Earth said, and I explained that it wasn't words, really; it was a vibration, but I understood what it meant.

I remember our tangled hands and her innocent voice longing for a connection when she asked, "What we just did? Have you done that with anyone else before?"

I hadn't, and as I thought about it now, Shay was the only one, and she wanted to learn more right from the start.

"I trust you, Wil. I really do."

"Before we do anything, we have to make an oath," I said.

That cut to our palms was innocent, meant to connect us when the inevitable separation came.

"An oath for what?" she asked.

"We need to promise that no matter where we go, or who we become, that we will remember how all of this felt, and we won't give up on being whoever we want to be."

She didn't hesitate. Not for one second. "Okay, yes." She wriggled tight into my arms, adjusting until her left hand rested in my own, and it was that feeling of her body against mine that had kept me going in the dark days that followed.

"Do it," she consented.

"Take a breath and then let it out. Go really slow."

She followed my direction, and, on her exhale, I drew the tiny blade across what Gran called the Jupiter Mount. She didn't flinch, and I mirrored the slight cut on my palm. Shay turned and looked into my eyes as our palms clamped together.

It was trust that brought us here, to this moment, standing in the confines of a magickal cellar, stocked full with stabbing things, and all I could remember was my tiny knife blade meeting the skin of Shay's hand and the words we had spoken...

"You're a part of me, and I'm a part of you."

My eyes glazed with tears as I stared at my faded scar. What had we done? Could a single innocent act have set this binding in motion?

"It's us, Shay." I reached for her hand and held it to my heart. "You are a part of me." I paused, tears streaming from my eyes, giving her a moment to remember. Her eyes opened wide as she realized what I was saying.

"And I am a part of you," Shay whispered back. It didn't take more than half a breath for Shay to understand.

"It was the blood pact," I said.

"It was the blood pact, but it was more than that. It was an Earth spell that bound us together beyond everything." Her hands caressed my cheeks as she brushed the tears from my eyes with the pad of her thumbs.

"It put the Magick inside the Maker and the Maker inside the Magick." Shay stepped closer and wrapped her arms around me. "We're meant to be here, Shay." Her lips pressed to mine, and I felt a sense of calmness and understanding as I opened my mouth to her kiss.

The sound of a loud cough and the clearing of a throat broke us apart. I was aware of more than Shay's kiss, and I pulled away, staring into the warmest green eyes. "I love you with all that I am, Shay," I whispered over her soft lips as my forehead rested against hers.

"I love you more than I ever thought possible."

"You two should get a room and preferably not one down here in the cellar." Stout flew away from the apothecary wall and landed beside Dexter. Before we could answer him, he yelled, "Hey, honeymooners! Maybe you should come over here and see what your dragon is doing?"

"What is Dexter doing?" Shay turned, but her arm held tight as it looped around my waist.

"He's eating something."

"Dexter, *rigescunt indutae!*" she yelled in a voice that made me jump.

The dog didn't move. If I had to guess, Shay had ordered the dog to freeze. She walked across the room and pulled the debris from Dexter's mouth.

"What is it?" I asked, hesitant to get close enough to see or touch it.

"Maybe it was a piece of a demon." Shay pinched the remnant with her fingertips and held it up. "It might be a spire or some other part."

"What other part?" I hated to ask the question.

"It's the articulated arm bone of a Philous Ouiac," Dani supplied. "I know it's hard to tell with Dexter's teeth marks, but those little barbs." She pointed to the small hooks peppering the boney material. "They walk sideways, but if they brush against you, those little barbs push out and hook onto their victim. What's worse is they're hollow and inject a potent venom. The actual damage happens when they pull away."

From her description, it sounded like Dani admired the weapon this demon was, but I was trying to shake the chill I felt from the words *potent venom*. "If I can make a request, I would like to never see this demon alive." I raised my hand to get their attention.

"This would be a nasty class-one, baby," Shay said.

"I haven't seen a barbed class-one in ages," Dani confirmed. "We suspected that the P.O. is what might have wounded Benton." This seemed to confuse Shay, her eyebrows knitting together as she said, "It was a profile we sent to the hospital, but —" Shay threw the demon remnant on the table. "Why would this bone be down here?"

Stout flew to the farthest corner of the room and hovered in front of the crumbling brick foundation of the forge. "You have to understand that she needed you to come to power, Shay." The fairy maneuvered to create a protective space, and judging by his leading comment, he was planning to share something big. As I watched Shay, I was sure Stout would break my lover's heart. "The venom is quick and infectious."

"Stop!" Shay held up her hand. "Don't tell me she did it to herself?" I stepped closer to Shay but didn't make a move to touch her.

"She couldn't hold the Maker's power anymore." Stout didn't stop talking. "When Wildwood forged those punch daggers...Regina was relieved. She knew she could stop fighting the power that had become a burden."

Shay stumbled back against the apothecary wall and slid down until her butt hit the floor. It was the truth we'd never spoken about but somehow both knew. Benton had poisoned herself with demon venom and staged the attack. She'd sacrificed herself, knowing it would set our transformation in motion.

Dani walked to the stairs and left the cellar. She didn't say another word, and she didn't return. I could only imagine how she felt, losing her father to a demon attack and losing Benton the same way. But I couldn't worry about that any longer because Shay was hurting.

"Hey." My arm was slow, cautious, as it moved around Shay's shoulder. "Talk to me, baby."

"She didn't have Parkinson's. That was just another lie. Her body failed because she was fighting the imbalance of the Magick and Maker's powers."

Shay's face fell forward, buried against her knees, as she fought the coming emotions. When she turned to look at me, I could see the vulnerable girl I'd fallen in love with all of those years ago. Losing the people we call family is never easy, but knowing a loved one had sacrificed herself so that you could live is an impossible burden to bear.

"What can I do?" I asked.

"I don't know," she said with a sniffle.

I pulled Shay into my arms and held her as the tears came. We were going to get through this no matter how many secrets we uncovered.

Dexter heard Shay and pushed his face into her lap. She didn't say a word as she fluffed the fur around his ears. I could never remember comforting Shay when we'd lived with Mama Pierce. She simply hadn't reached out to me, told me she was hurting. The world of foster care was unpredictable, and so few things were ever our own. But our pain was, and Shay had held tight to hers. The day they came for Shay, we didn't get to say goodbye, but I never stopped longing for her. The cellar around us was filled with five lifetimes of Magick and Maker history, and for now, we would try to make it our own. I don't know how much time passed as we sat in silence, but I wondered what our next step would be.

"Sweetheart, what do you want to do?" I asked. "Do you want to go home?"

The muscles in her jaw clenched as she looked at me. "I want to keep going through this room."

I pushed off the ground and held a hand to help Shay to her feet. "Are you sure you want to stay?"

"Yes." She walked toward the office stairs and paused when she noticed a second staircase spiraling up. "Where do you think that goes?" she asked.

My boots clanked against the wrought-iron steps as I climbed to the top. I pushed against the wall to reveal a doorway and peeked out before yelling down at Shay, "It opens into the stockroom at the back of the bar."

"That's handy," she said as she looked around the cellar. "Where are Dani and Stout?"

I knew Dani had walked out, but I didn't know which direction the fairy had flown.

"She left," a voice said from a dark shelf of the apothecary wall. It was Stout, and if I was reading the angles of his body, hands, and head correctly, he was crying, too.

"Come down here," Shay said as he revealed his location on the top shelf.

Stout stepped off as if plunging himself toward death. His wings opened just before hitting the ground, and he walked across the dirt and pebble floor.

"Dani has a long history with the powers you possess." Stout was speaking to the two of us. "Maker energies are almost impossible to balance without the Magick. You've already experienced that with the surges."

It was interesting to hear him speak so casually about the days when Shay would wake up with her scars lit by Magick energies. We'd sat together for hours, chanting and burning herbs just to keep Shay from sinking into a magickal abyss. How did he know?

"Who told you about the surges?" I asked. Shay was silent beside me, which seemed out of character for the curious cop.

"I saw them. You just couldn't see me."

"That's creepy, Stout." I crossed my arms around my body to shake the chill that came every time he referenced his stealthy months in the carriage house. "You're not allowed to be incognito anymore."

"I know. We made a contract, and I won't break it." Stout hovered in front of me. "Can you trust me when I tell you I'm on your side?"

"That's a little hard to do when we're standing in a secret room that you didn't tell us about," Shay shot back. Her hand traveled over the cubbies as she turned the labels on the jars. I couldn't read a single one, but she appeared to understand as she sorted through them. "Why is all of this here?"

"Benton didn't want it destroyed when Jacob died. She spent weeks bringing it into the cellar."

"How?" Shay didn't turn around to talk to him or acknowledge his presence. "How does an arsenal of weapons exist that would kill her partner?"

"Jacob did that. He severed the bond and doomed Regina to a half-life. A half-life of pain and isolation."

"Why did that bastard have to take it out on Dani?" she asked, mostly to herself.

I felt like a voyeur in this exchange because I knew nothing about the history between Dani and Regina beyond their family feud with Jacob. I wondered if her love for Amelia was the cause. Could a gay teenager break the bond between the Magick and the Maker?

Stout continued, "Dani just wanted to be herself. Jacob believed he could force her to be something, someone she's not." Stout landed on the shelf Shay was touching. He walked across the scar on the back of her hand. "Jacob died alone in his misery, and he deserved it. I don't feel sad about that, but he took Regina with him. Jacob Kota was a selfish son of a bitch."

Shay held a finger out, and Stout walked across it. "Benton didn't deserve…she shouldn't have sacrificed herself for us."

"It was a simple choice for her to make." He walked to Shay's palm. "She believed in you. And in Wildwood, too."

Shay looked at me. I was standing still, quiet, waiting for her to need me for whatever came next. We'd have to decide how the four of us would proceed, who we would be for the city of Bannock. Shay let Stout down on the narrow apothecary countertop as she held a hand out for me. I was happy to close the space between us.

"I believe in Wildwood, too," she said, only inches from my face. "I believe the two of us will do whatever it takes to make all of this work." Her arms came around my hips, and her fingers tucked into the back pockets of my jeans. "We'll make this work." Her forehead touched my own, and I believed every word coming out of her mouth.

"I'm right here." Shay closed her eyes as I whispered. "We're going to go through this entire building until we answer every damn question we have."

She took a deep breath. "Okay," she said.

I kissed her. Standing in the middle of this chaotic room, I kissed her as if nothing else mattered.

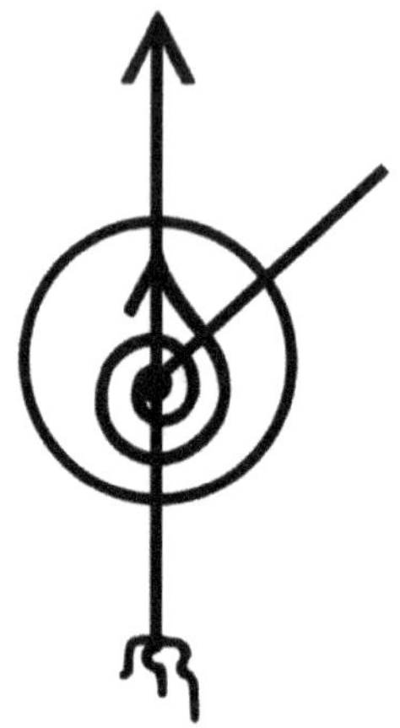

CHAPTER IX

OFFENSIVE

"It's going to take years to get through all of this." I dropped my canister on the table, and it made a clanking sound as it fell against a jar full of unidentifiable plant roots. "Why didn't she just mark the damn bottles?"

We'd spent the last two days going through countless eight-inch cubbies on the wall in the bar's basement. It felt like a task that would never end as I took one jar down just to discover the label needed translation. Benton used some Latin terms, which were easy for Shay. Pictish and Theban were the languages of choice for most of the bottles, which required Shay's research to convert. Trying to decipher the ridiculous quantity of containers was daunting.

"Some of these are hundreds of years old," Stout answered my question. He was spinning the containers around to make it easier to find anything written in English.

"Does…" I held the bottle so I could read the label, but it was in Latin, so my pronunciation was a guess. "…*Herne Cornu* have an expiration date?"

Stout flew to hover in front of me. "Don't touch that with your bare skin unless you want to enact a totemic mating ritual."

I threw the bottle at the fairy, and he caught it mid-air and carried it back to the *H* section of the shelf. "What the hell is that?"

"Don't worry, sweetheart. If you accidentally enact the mating ritual, I've got you covered." Shay stood up from the table where she was working and gave me a reassuring wink. She had more than a dozen books spread out in front of us, and when I had a label that needed translation, she got that job done. "Anyway, Herne's Horn takes more than flesh contact. You also have to chant and be completely naked," Shay added.

"Whew, because it's not like we ever do those things." I pretended to wipe the sweat from my forehead. In fact, we'd done those two things almost every night since Shay and I had come into our powers. Although we felt balanced in the light of day, when we rested at night, somehow, one of us woke with more power than the day before.

"I think we should call it quits for the day," Shay said as she turned the label on Herne's Horn so it was facing forward. "My eyes are seeing these symbols as the same." She walked to the wrought iron staircase, giving us access to the first-floor stock area. Her feet hit the first stair, and I was close behind her. "Come on, Dex," she called to the dog, and the four of us climbed up to the first floor.

I could hear the sound of business as usual at the bar. After our first visit to the cellar, Dani had contacted Benton's cousins, and they agreed to run the bar until we could figure out what to do with the day-to-day operations. I could smell the burgers on the grill.

"Are you hungry, Shay?"

"I'm too tired to be hungry," she answered.

"What if I get some food to go?" I offered.

She wrapped her arm around my waist and leaned against me. "Rare with fries, please," she whispered in my ear.

"That's my girl." I kissed her cheek. "Go home. I'll get the food and be right behind you."

Her head fell to my shoulder. "Are you sure?"

"I'm positive."

She planted a kiss on my cheek. "You're amazing," she whispered in my ear as she stepped away to leave.

"Don't fall asleep before I get home." I waved at Benton's cousin, Diana, and she nodded to tell me she was coming to take my order.

"I'll be awake. Don't worry." She pushed away from the bar and ran her fingers through the tangles in her hair. "Come on, Dexter." She patted his neck, and the dog was at her side. They were more than partners in law enforcement, they were family, and I loved to watch the two of them together.

"What do ya need?" Diana asked. She was a sweet woman, barely five feet tall, with broad shoulders and strong hands from a life behind the bar. She wiped the top of the counter in front of me.

"Can you make me two rare burgers with fries to go?" I asked.

Diana wrote it down on her notepad and looked up. "Want a beer while you wait?"

"Sure, why not?"

She poured a pint for me and set it down. I took a sip as I turned around to look at the customers in the bar, catching a glimpse of a familiar face.

Andrea Peters sat in the corner, swiping her finger across her tablet as she spoke on her phone. I was glad Shay had left the bar because the last thing I wanted was a confrontation with a woman who didn't respect Dani or Shay. When I turned my back to her and saw Bill Bailey from Bailey's farm, I gave him a nod. He waved for me to join him, but I held up my beer in a gesture that would suggest I was good. He walked over.

"Hello, Wildwood. How's business?" he asked as he stretched out a hand.

"Business is good." I set down my beer, wiped the fingerless gloves over my pants, and shook his hand.

"My youngest wants to work at the forge. You doing classes yet?" His question got my attention. I was ready to do classes and wanted students in the workshop.

"Should be soon, yes." I walked behind the bar for a pen and a piece of paper and scribbled my cellphone number on the back of a Slammed business card. "Give this to him and have him call me so we can set up a time."

"That's real good. He'll be happy I ran into you." The farmer tucked the card in his front pocket. "I hear that Shay's part-owner of the bar now?"

I nodded, unsure how much I should share. "Yes, it seems so."

"And Officer Forrest, too?"

I was uncomfortable talking about the bar, even if I liked Bill and had no reason to think he meant us harm. "Yep, they're still working out the details, but don't worry. Slammed isn't going anywhere."

Diana walked up with my order wrapped in a brown paper bag. "Here you go, Wildwood. I put it on your tab, and I threw in a couple of salads just to add some green."

"Thanks, Di. Shay will appreciate it." I left a ten-dollar bill on the bar and turned to leave.

"Take care of yourself, Bill." I patted his shoulder.

"Goodnight, Wildwood. I'll see you later."

I waved as I walked out and was happy to take in a deep breath of the cool night air. The carriage house was a few blocks from Slammed, an added perk to small-town life. I heard the river's rushing waters and detoured down Center Street, where the river crossing was less congested. Bannock was quiet for a weeknight, and as I navigated the intersection, I sensed something behind me. I heard the flapping sound reminiscent of a paper card in bicycle spokes and saw the winged fairy buzzing near my head.

"Something's coming, Wildwood." Stout's voice was loud in my ear, and before I could take a breath to speak, the overwhelming rush of fear drove adrenalin through my body.

"Run!" he yelled as he zipped at full flying speed toward the carriage house.

I did not know what the *something* was, but I tucked the bag of food into the bend of my arm and ran as fast as my feet could go. I looked back over my shoulder to see two huge flaming-orange eyes and four skeletally thin demon legs moving toward me.

I couldn't determine the species because looking back hindered my pace. The weight of my boots felt like bricks, and I wished I could run just a little faster as the sound of claws scraping on the concrete sidewalk grew louder. I swore at myself for the detour down Center, but it didn't matter now. I could see the carriage house as I turned the corner onto Fifth Street.

I hoped Stout was inside getting help from Shay and Dexter, but I didn't see any movement. The demon was closing in, and as fast as I could run, I couldn't maintain the gap. I hoped that the creature would feel the pain once it ran into the protective barrier around the carriage house. Somehow, through all the chaos, I was still clutching the bag of food like I was about to score a touchdown.

The realization hit me. I was going to have to save myself. One block—I had one block left, and then I had ten yards and five yards, and my fingers were on the handle. I ran hard into the solid door, and it did not give way. I turned to see the taut-stretched skin over the skeletal monster just feet from me.

"Shay!" I yelled her name, but she didn't respond.

I pushed against the door once more with the total weight of Maker force, and without hesitation, I fell into the workshop entrance. The demon lunged forward, passing through the street's light, and I saw the full length of his body, twice my five-foot-eight inch height. I waited for the claws on its raptor-like arms to hit me, but just before making contact, it flew back and pounded against the tree across the street.

I was lying on the workshop floor, dizzy from running, struggling to catch my breath. The bag of food fell out of my hands as I crab-walked, scooting myself backward until I was far enough away from the door to get to my feet.

I looked around the workshop for Shay. Where was she? I didn't see Dexter, either. And where was that drunk fairy who was supposed to help protect me?

"Shay!" I yelled again, this time more concerned for her now that I was behind the protective barrier. I tossed the mangled bag of food on the table and ran up the stairs. "Shay!"

I ran into each room, frantic to find her. Where the hell was everyone? Sliding the greenhouse door open and walking through to the rooftop, I looked down to see the demon lurking in the dark and watched him turn toward the motion coming from the river.

It was Shay and Dexter, shifting locations. Wherever they'd been moments before, their full-body forms appeared across the street from the carriage house. It took a few moments to adjust to the shift, a disorienting journey from one place to another, but seconds later, they were running at full speed toward the front door. The demon saw them, and it pushed off on all fours, running foot to hand, foot to hand, headfirst toward my family. I ran back through the apartment and down the stairs, reaching for my axe hanging next to our go-bag. Abandoning the protection of our magick barrier, I threw the carriage house door open.

My heart was racing, but I couldn't think as I watched Shay skid to a halt. The demon advanced on her, and Dexter feathered out in complete dragon form, launching at the monster. I stood in the street, watching as he ripped the head from the demon. Shay ran toward me, and before I could say her name, I heard the ticking flutter of fairy wings.

"I found her." Stout was hovering over Shay's shoulder.

"Are you hurt?" Shay asked.

"Did it hurt you?" I asked.

Her arms came around me. "We need to get inside," Shay said, carry-walking me toward the carriage house.

"What about Dexter?" I asked.

Shay and I watched dragon teeth sink deep into the flesh and bone of the now-unidentifiable monster.

"He'll come when he's..."

We heard the bone-chilling screech before the two fire-eyed demons came into view. Shay took the axe from my hand and ran toward our attackers. After a few springing steps, her feet left the ground for two seconds before the axe head struck, and Shay held tight to the handle as she swung it over and over before removing the head. My body felt disconnected from the experience as I watched. Demon gore slathered Shay's arms and torso.

Dexter tore through the last creature, and before I could blink, the fight was over, and our dragon morphed back into dog form. His shell-like neck and torso billowed into fur, and the beak-like snout crinkled into a shiny wet nose.

It didn't matter how many times I saw Dexter transform; it always left me stumbling over the pathway between reality and fantasy. What an incredible life I had! Shay was walking toward me, my axe in her hand, dripping with the dark black ink-like blood of the headless demon. The same mess coated her t-shirt and cheeks. Wearing all the remains of their fight, she looked incredible.

"Are you okay?" Shay asked as she put her hand on my shoulder.

"Am I okay?" The question came out louder than I'd expected, fueled by the adrenalin of my chase.

Her knuckles were so white from gripping the axe that I had to pry it from her hand. "Dex and I walked down to the river. He was playing in the water, and then Stout came flying in." Shay explained. "And–"

Stout interrupted. "She wasn't in the apartment, so I followed Dexter's scent, and I found them."

"You did great, Stout." Shay held up her hand, and the fairy landed in it. "You did great."

Stout looked at the bottom of his feet as he stepped in the sticky remnants of demon covering Shay's hands.

"Honey, I think we should get inside." My fingers gripped Shay's bicep, tugging her toward the carriage house. She seemed confused as she looked into my eyes. "Honey?"

She turned toward the sound running toward us. "Dexter, come here, buddy." She clapped her hands together, and the K-9 dropped to sit in front of her. Her hand ran over his fur and came back covered in more of the smear left behind from the fight.

Shay walked away, back toward the little bits of the creatures that had attacked us. "Where are you going?" I asked.

"I just need to look."

"Look? Look at what?" I followed her, reluctant to get closer to the scene, still holding the axe in my hand.

Shay kicked through the grass and launched a few bones and bits of demon flesh at the gutter. She pushed the top off the public trash bin and picked up the demon remains to drop them inside. She pulled out the bag and dragged it back to the carriage house.

"What the hell are you doing?" Her actions confused me, but I'd never battled a demon in the middle of town. We always built fires to dispose of their remains, but Shay was collecting every piece she could find.

"I need to check something."

"Wait!" I pushed in front of Shay, holding a palm to her chest to stop her. "Slow down."

She took the axe from my hand and held the bag of demons in the other. Her eyes looked wild as her red hair fell loose, tangled in knots with bits of flesh and blood dripping from the tips.

"You're supposed to be protected." Shay's voice was loud. "These bastards shouldn't even be this far into town." She tugged on the bag and launched it at the carriage house door. "Shit!" she touched the axe to her forehead.

"What are you talking about? What do you mean, they shouldn't be in town?" I grabbed her arm to hold her in place, and her body language felt foreign, stiff, unlike the woman I loved. Something wasn't right.

"They almost got to you." Her voice was small.

I struggled to see the beautiful green eyes of the tender woman I laid beside every night. Her eyes were dark, shadowed now by the battle and some kind of magick.

I held my hands out in front of me, twisting and flipping them so she could see my unmarked skin. "Look, I'm fine. Not even a scratch."

"There were three damn demons right over there!" She reached into her pocket and pushed the release button on her trunk, then dumped the bag of demon parts inside. When she slammed the lid and turned around, I was in her face.

"What the hell are you doing?" My hands gripped her shoulders as I pinned her against the car. "Tell me what the hell you're doing!" My heart was racing, and my blood was pumping as I thought about the last ten minutes of my life. I wasn't inside Shay's head, but putting together everything I'd just witnessed, I knew something wasn't right.

Her hip thrust forward, and when I pushed back, she stopped to look into my eyes. I saw it then. Even though I knew she was trying to hide it, she was being powered by fear. Her hands trembled in terror, mingling with the power to do something about it.

"Shay, honey, please. You're scaring me."

Her chest heaved with every breath, and her eyes went wide as her body fell against the car. She took a slow deep breath and blew it out through puffed cheeks. "We need to go inside." Her arm grabbed my waist, and she lifted me off the ground. As much as it seemed she was in control, I didn't know what she was thinking as she turned me around and pushed us toward the carriage house door.

"Dexter!" she yelled, and he followed us inside. When he settled by Shay under the carriage house lights, I got my first glimpse of the wreckage that was my demon-fighting girlfriend and her dragon-dog partner.

"The two of you are a mess."

She didn't hear a word I was saying. "Are you hurt? Did it touch you or cut you?"

I grabbed both of her shoulders and shook her body harder than I'd planned. "Shay Pierce! Damn it, look at me!"

Her eyes blinked and clamped shut as if she was coming out of a fog.

"Can you even hear me?" I asked, and her fingers gripped the back of my bicep.

She squeezed hard. Her breath hitched as if she'd broken the surface after a deep-water dive. "Wildwood."

"Yes, love. It's me, and I'm not hurt. Not a scratch." I pulled her into a hug and spoke through the tangle of demon smear in her hair. "Your spell protected me. I'm safe. We're safe."

"But we *aren't* safe." Shay held me tighter, and I felt the thump of metal on my back as she spoke against the side of my head. "Dani and I put up protective barriers around the mine. They shouldn't be here."

"When did you—" I stopped asking because it didn't matter when. But if it didn't work, that meant someone had interfered. I pulled away from our embrace. "Never mind. We need to clean up, and you need to get that demon out of your hair and off of me." I held her hand and stretched it out to show her how much sludge was on her body. Her pants had chunks of bloody flesh, likely from the mess that covered her arms.

"The axe you made. This axe." She held it up for me, still clutching tight like an additional appendage. "This axe is a demon killer." Shay turned around to lock the carriage house door. "That creature didn't stand a chance."

It was frightening to see her hold on so tightly to the weapon. I wasn't sure what she was thinking or feeling, but she was still riding the adrenaline rush from the fight. "Can I have the axe, please?" I reached to grab the shoulder of the handle, and Shay released her grip. I laid it down on the table and took hold of each of Shay's hands.

The sound of her breath was quick, like she'd run a marathon, which made sense in the current situation. One careful step at a time, I led her to the shower I'd built in the back of the workshop. It wasn't complete, but there was no chance the three of us were strolling through the apartment covered in tonight's demon drippings. I pulled over a stool from the office and sat Shay down on it.

The showerhead sprayed out a forceful stream when I turned it on, and while I waited for it to get hot, Dexter jumped into the oversized fiberglass enclosure. I guess he was going first.

I heard Shay's head tilt back to settle against the wall. Maybe the adrenalin rush was fading, and the cool-headed cop I loved would reappear.

My hands ran through Dexter's fur, and I washed away the blood and bits with soap, rinsed him clean, and toweled him off. He ran across the workshop to settle in his sacred circle on the floor. When I turned around, Shay was standing beside me with her shirt half over her head. It was then that I saw the gash on her torso.

"Hey, honey, you've got a pretty big cut here."

Her arms tangled in her sleeves as she turned to look at her body. "Shit, I didn't even feel it."

I had a single thought at that moment about the venom of a demon that had infected Benton. "This thing that attacked you. Is it venomous? Poisonous?" I asked her, and when she didn't answer, I pulled her shirt out of the way and threw it on the floor. "Shay?"

She was confused, so I made the decision that the venom was toxic, and we needed to purge the poison from her body. My only thought was a heavy application of demon sift. I helped her sit on the floor and ran to the office to get a container of the sacred dust. When I returned, Shay was half-dressed and standing in the hot spray of the shower's water.

"Goddess women, what are you doing?" I stood in the shower's opening where the curtain should have been.

"My skin is...it burns, and I just needed to get the blood off." She rubbed the bar of soap over her arms, unaware that her pants were still buttoned around her waist.

"Shay, you're supposed to take all of your clothes off."

She looked down at the lower half of her body and shook her head. "I thought I did."

I grabbed her hand and tugged her out from under the spray. "Look at me." I turned off the water.

"I'm try—ing." Her reaction was sluggish and her words slurred.

I grabbed a towel from the shelf and rubbed it over her wound. Less than ten minutes had passed since our demon attack, but here she was, falling under the power of the toxins in her blood. Shay's body jerked away when she felt the sting of the sift's magick.

"Ouch, that's not good." She pushed me aside, but I steadied myself as I poured another handful of anvil dust onto her wound. She wiggled out of my hands. "Shit, stop! That hurts like hell." Shay stumbled back against the reinforced shower wall.

"I know, but that demon did something to you, and I don't know what else to do."

Her hands slapped against the wall as her back arched away from me. I held her as the two of us slid to the floor of the shower. It was torture to watch her writhing in pain as I poured more sift onto the slice in her side. It was slow to start, but when the magick element of the demon anvil dust worked, I could see the bubbling black ooze seep from her wound.

"Oh, goddess. No more, Wil! It hurts."

Tears fell from my eyes, and I felt like a monster, but this was the only thing I could do. "Breathe, Shay. It'll pass. Just let it work, baby."

Shay's eyes went wide just before her head slammed against the shower wall behind her. She gulped air in heavy bursts and puffs like a person about to give birth. It seemed like every time we needed to use the demon sift, it took longer and was more painful. The ooze puckered and hardened until all that remained were dried, flaking bits of sift mixed with the demon toxin.

"Shay?" I shook her shoulder.

"I...wha—?" Her words were still slurred as she struggled to open her eyes.

"Honey, you need to help me. We have to get your wet pants off."

I popped the button on her jeans and unzipped the fly. The only help she could give was to raise her hips and butt so I could pull the wet denim off. It was a soggy tug of war, but a few minutes later, the two of us were standing beneath the hot spray. Most of Shay's weight was resting against the wall, and I could stabilize her enough to wash away the remains of our fight. The longer we stood together, the stronger she became until she could hold up her own weight as I did my best to scrub her skin.

"What just happened?" Her hands came up to rub her face. Shay was asking questions, and that was a promising sign. If Shay was good at anything, it was asking questions.

"One of those demons cut you," I explained. "You had a bad reaction to the poison, and it was all I could do to get you inside to clean the wound."

"What about Dexter?" She stepped into the spray of water, letting it run over her face. She turned to look at me. "Is he hurt? He took on—"

"He's good." I held her cheeks in my hands. "He jumped in here before you did." I ran my hand over her shoulders and down her back. "I'm pretty sure he was in dragon form when he hit the first demon, anyway."

"I should check him." She turned around.

I pushed the center of her chest, forcing her against the shower wall. "Stay…right…here, superhero."

The tiny lines around her eyes crinkled as her cheek pressed up with a bit of a smile. "I keep getting knocked on my ass. That's not a very spectacular superhero maneuver." Her head fell back against the wall.

"You're my superhero, and I'll let you know when I've finished with you. Right now, you need to stay here with me."

"Yes, ma'am."

"Now, let me see your side." I lifted her arm over her head and ran my fingers over where the wound had been. "This looks good. Not even a scratch." I held her face in my hands. "Do you remember what happened?"

Her eyes looked brighter, clearer, and she leaned forward to stand under the spray of the shower. Turning off the water and stepping out to towel dry, she wrapped herself and handed a towel to me. I couldn't tell if she was thinking or avoiding my question.

"Shay?" I rubbed my body dry and knotted the towel in the center of my chest.

"I took Dexter down to the river. I just figured you'd take longer, and I wanted to do a few training exercises in the dark. Keep him sharp." She picked up the dirty clothes and carried them to the washing machine, dropping them in with a detergent packet and pushing the power button. Her hands rested on the edge of the machine, but she didn't turn around. "Stout found us, and he said something was after you, and it was all I could do to get here. Everything after that is a blur."

"I outran it," I told her. "I don't know how, but I got through the door, and that bastard hit the protective barrier and shot into the tree across the street. But you weren't here."

"It was just a training exercise. I wasn't thinking about—"

"You don't have to think about anything because the barrier protected me. You protected me even when you weren't here."

"I should have stayed with you." She picked up her shoes and walked toward the apartment stairs.

"You can't be with me every minute of the day, and besides, I had this killer axe." I picked up the blood-stained demon weapon and carried it with me up the stairs. I wanted to clean it, but I needed to listen to Shay.

She dropped our shoes on the floor and walked to the bedroom. I set the axe in the bathroom sink before following her. Shay's towel was on the back of the door, and I watched as her head popped through the neck of her t-shirt.

"I want to protect you from whatever is coming." She pulled on a pair of shorts.

I dropped my towel and walked across the room to stand in front of Shay. "Look at me." Her eyes focused on my own and I turned my naked body in front of her. "I don't have a single solitary scratch on my body. Not one, anywhere."

Her hand stretched out to touch my cheek. "I lost my mind when Stout flew up to find us, but Dexter knew, and we just had this connection, tunnel vision, to get to you."

I kissed her because she needed to understand that I felt protected and empowered by her love. "I knew I'd be safe when I got here, and I was."

She picked me up, and I wrapped my legs around her waist. "You did great," she said as she carried me to the bed and lowered us to the mattress.

"The barrier protected me. Your barrier protected me," I whispered against her lips, just inches away from my own.

Shay's head fell to my breast, and I could feel her quiet sob against my body. "I don't know what I would do if something got to you."

I ran my fingers through her hair, turning her head so I could see her face. "I'm safe. Right now, we are safe, and tomorrow, we can figure out the rest."

The weight of her body fell to the bed as she rolled off of me, but I held her against my shoulder. "I think I need to lie here with you for a month."

I grabbed the edge of the blanket and wrapped ourselves together. "I think maybe a day and you'd go stir crazy, but I'll take you for as long as I can get you."

"Good." Her leg draped over my hip, and I was content to fall asleep with her in my arms. I heard her stomach rumble, and she laughed against my shoulder.

"Just ignore it. I don't want to get out of this bed for anything." She tucked her hand under my hip.

"You know I have a bag of food downstairs," I said.

"No." The word vibrated in my breast.

"I think I should feed you."

She wrapped tighter around me. "No."

"Okay."

I felt her heartbeat against my bare skin. Her breath was even, and although I couldn't see if she was asleep, I didn't plan to say a word. Shay needed to rest, and I needed to close my eyes and stop thinking about that demon face at my workshop door.

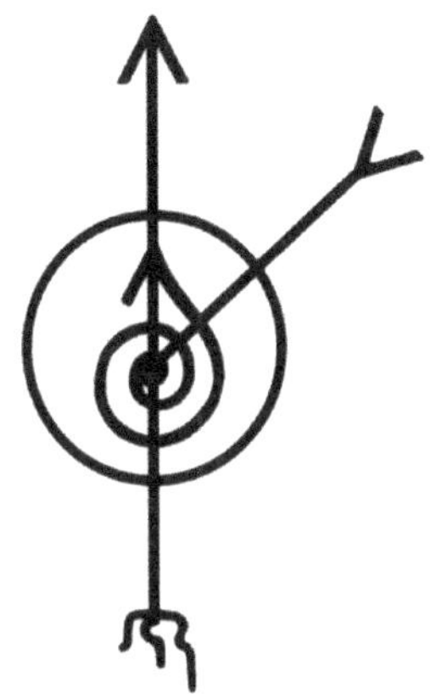

CHAPTER X

HAUNTED

The streets of Bannock were quiet as I walked along the sidewalk. I could hear the rumble of noise coming from the only business still open after midnight, Slammed. The bar music was loud and pulsing as I walked by, and although I held a dog leash in my hand, Dexter was nowhere in sight. I heard the flutter of a paper card in a bicycle tire and looked to my left as a fairy blew by on a miniature tricycle, flying beside my ear.

I tried to catch it as it went by, but the palm of my hand caught fire, and the sigil burst into a giant orange flame. I didn't summon my ignis *fire, and I froze when I heard the words.*

"Something's coming, Wildwood. You better run!"

I looked over my shoulder, and two massive glowing eyes were behind me. The snarl of a salivating demon and the scraping of talons against the concrete sidewalk vibrated in my ears. I was running, but I didn't move, and when I looked down, my shoes resembled mortared red glazed bricks.

The carriage house door was visible, but no matter how many steps my bricked feet shuffled, I just couldn't get to it. I held the bag in my arms, but when I looked closer, it held wriggling pustules of demon embryos, and I didn't know why I was cuddling them in my arms. The Gatekeeper's talon tore into the back of my shirt, missing my skin but ripping half of the fabric away. The demon lunged forward, knocking me against the door...

I jumped up from the bed, sweat pouring down my face as I gasped for air. My heart was racing, my chest heaving, as I moved from my nightmare into consciousness.

"Wil?" Shay was half in my lap and half wrapped around my naked body.

"I'm okay," I said. My breath was ragged, and it was apparent I wasn't okay. "I'm good. It was just a dream." I kept repeating it, but I was having trouble convincing myself that I was awake, so I pinched my arm. "It was just a dream."

Shay sat up and reached over to brush away the sweat-soaked hair sticking to my face. "Hey, look at me." A warm hand caressed my cheek.

I couldn't distinguish her touch from the ravaging grasp of the demon in my dream, and I grabbed her wrist. "Wait. Don't touch me." I crab-walked away from her until I pinned myself against the headboard of our bed. My gasps for air paced with the rate of my heart. "Don't touch me."

She held up her hands in surrender. "Wildwood! It was a dream." She repeated the words I was saying.

I closed my eyes, chanting. "It was a dream. It was a dream." I rested my sigil hand over my heart, feeling the heat when I looked down. "*Ignis*," I said the word, and my palm ignited. For reasons I couldn't explain, this felt normal, and I took a slow, deep, calming breath.

"Wil?"

I looked at Shay, and I could see the hurt in her eyes. "It felt real." I clenched my sigil hand in a fist, and the flame burned away. "It felt real." I closed my eyes and slammed my head back against the headboard. "It felt so real."

Shay kneeled beside me, her hands resting on her thighs. "Tell me what just happened." She kept her distance.

"It was coming after me, but I couldn't get away. It caught my shirt and grabbed it; it almost got me." I huffed the words out through quick breaths. "It almost got me." My hands came up to cover my face, and I forced back the tears.

"I'm going to touch you, Wil." I could feel her body shuffle across the mattress as her weight tipped our bodies together. The touch was warm against my cold skin, and I felt something else.

"Please." I don't know what I was asking for, but when her hands held me, everything felt right.

"I'm here." She pulled me into her arms, and the power of her magick was a lifeline pulling me back to her. "I've got you," she whispered over my head as she held me against her chest. My arms circled her body, and I laced my fingers tight behind her back.

"It almost got me, Shay." I realized I was reliving the terror of last night's attack. As much as it was a dream right now, it had all been quite real a few hours ago.

"I know, baby." She rocked us back and forth. "I'm sorry I wasn't here."

I said nothing because I didn't know how to respond. She hadn't been here, but the truth was she couldn't babysit me every minute of every day. Being the Maker meant that I also needed to fight for myself.

"It's not your fault." I felt something touch my shoulder, and I looked up to see the tears falling from her chin. My fingers brushed her cheek. "Please don't."

"I almost lost you." Her body shook against me as she cried.

"Your spell. The magick surrounding this building saved me tonight. Even when you weren't here, you protected me."

She pulled me into her lap. "We have to do more." She shuddered against me.

"What do you mean?" I asked.

"Our powers. The monsters of Bannock are going wild," Shay explained. "I don't know what happened, but they've been active outside the caverns, and now more species are coming into town. Something is drawing them out, and I think it's because of Brigid and the powers you're carrying."

"This is because of me." It made sense that the ability to transform anything into a demon-killing weapon would attract attention.

"Now that the hammer is yours, they're going to come for it," Shay continued. "We have to double up. We have to be more diligent, and you and I can't take anything for granted until we reinforce the barrier around this building and around you." She squeezed me tighter.

"What about you? You're in danger all the time." I pushed away to look at her face. "You know, I'd stand in front of every demon to protect you." I brushed the hair from her face.

"I feel the same." She kissed me. "I'm so sorry you were alone."

"I'm going to be alone again, so you're right. We need to do more." I felt the chill of the room against my naked body and reached for the blanket.

"Are you cold?" she asked as she pulled me between her open legs. Her hand traveled down my naked back and over my hip.

"Yes, just a little."

"Let me get you some clothes, sweetheart." She tried to pull away, but I held tight to her.

"Not yet, just stay." I tugged the blanket over me and snuggled into her arms, glimpsing the clock on the side table. "It's only midnight?" I blew out a breath from my puffed cheeks.

"Yeah, baby. We just fell asleep."

"We never ate dinner," I said as I heard the rumble of her stomach.

"You heard that?" I felt the shake of her chest as she laughed. "Think those burgers are edible?"

The idea of holding her while her stomach rumbled for food felt selfish, so I pulled out of her arms. "Why don't you go grab the bag from the workshop, and we can heat it back up?"

Shay snugged the blanket around my shoulders. "Keep warm. I'll be right back." She kicked her feet into slippers and walked out of the bedroom.

I fell back on the bed, and a few seconds later, our massive German Shepherd came into the room. His face landed on the mattress beside my head. "Hi, Dex." I stretched my hand out from under the blanket to pat his head. "Did she send you in here to watch over me?" I listened for our fairy, but I didn't hear him, and I was happy he maintained the boundary that kept him out of our bedroom.

Dexter's giant dog eyes were staring at me, and I wished I knew what he was thinking. I closed my eyes, trying to shake the dream. It didn't take long for the smell of hamburger to make its way to the bedroom.

"You ready for some food?" Shay asked, and my head popped up to look at her. She carried a plate in each hand, and I kicked the blanket aside with my feet to make space on the bed.

"I've never had burgers in bed before."

Shay set the plates on the mattress. "I haven't either. Well, not with someone else."

I laughed at her comment and picked up the plate. The food smelled delicious, even if it was a greasy burger and fries. "I didn't realize how hungry I was." I took a big bite.

"I might have already eaten a bit." She held up her burger to show me it was half-eaten.

"A bit?" I grinned.

"If you remember, I was hungry."

"I remember." I took another bite and noticed Dexter was gone. "Where did Dexter go?"

"I filled his dish. He's eating. *Not* burgers."

"Poor guy." I ate a few fries. "At least you didn't give him those salads."

"He could probably use a salad or two after eating that demon." She held up her burger for me to touch like we were clinking glasses together.

"Cheers to that," I said.

We sat together, eating the burgers, and I couldn't help but think about my run through town. "I guess it was good that

Diana packaged the food well." Shay's eyebrow raised with curiosity, and I continued. "I ran three blocks with these tucked under my arm." I picked up another fry and popped it into my mouth. "That bastard chased me almost all the way."

"I've been trying to figure out why they are moving into town."

"The demons?" I asked.

"The Gatekeepers, more specifically." She wiped her mouth with the napkin. "When I was heating our food, I was thinking about Brigid's Cave and that maybe we disturbed more than the hammer's head."

"Honey, Dexter ate about a hundred embryos." The thought of him licking the tunnel walls and popping the spawning demons in his mouth made me put my last bite of hamburger down. "The image makes me not hungry anymore."

"It is kinda gross," she agreed and picked up my plate to stack it on hers. "And I see a lot of gross on the job." She carried the plates into the kitchen. "You want a drink?" she yelled.

"Water would be good."

I heard her walking back, and she returned with a glass of water in her hand. "Nothing for you?" I asked.

She nudged the switch with her elbow, dimming the lights. "I poured Stout a beer. He's pouting because I took a sip."

I laughed as she handed the glass to me. "What's with Stout's beer-drinking, anyway?" I asked, before taking a long sip of my drink.

She lit the salt lamp beside the bed. "He says it helps his magick," Shay explained as she sat beside me.

My head fell back against the headboard. "Beer makes a lot of guys think they're magick."

Shay laughed at my joke as she tucked the blanket around our bodies. "I wouldn't know about that. Never had the experience."

"Not terrible, but whoo, tough crowd sometimes."

Her arm snaked under the blanket, and she pulled me closer. "I don't think I missed anything." Shay pulled me in between her legs. "I think I like you and me just fine."

I turned my head to kiss her neck. "I like us too." She held me in the quiet, and I was content to listen to the beat of her heart.

After a few minutes, her voice broke the silence. "We need to talk about the barrier around the carriage house."

I raised my hand to cover her lips. "Shh, no magick barriers or spells tonight."

"What about—?" She tried to speak, but my hand pressed tighter.

"No. No more talking. I just want you to hold me so I forget about everything that happened tonight. We can worry about the spells tomorrow."

Her arms tightened around my hips and relaxed against the soft skin of my abdomen. "No spells," she conceded.

I closed my eyes, safe in the protection of her embrace.

CHAPTER XI

RUNED

I woke up in almost the same position I'd fallen asleep in. I settled my head against Shay's shoulder with the blanket only half-covering her as she lay tucked around me. It was well past her five-thirty alarm as daylight peeked through the edge of the window. I lifted my head to look at her, and she was still deep in her dreams.

It was rare for Shay to sleep beyond the first alarm, and it didn't occur to me last night to ask if today was her day off. My arms held tighter, willing us to stay connected a few moments longer, but I thought about her injury during the demon attack last night. My fingers ruffled the hem of her shirt, baring her abdomen and the spot where her wound would've been. With gratitude, I pressed my lips against her warm skin. Demon sift was our saving grace.

"Tickles," she whispered in a sleepy, drunken tone.

"Hi, baby." I kissed her again.

Her arms squeezed me. "Hi, yourself."

I pushed away from her hip so that I could see her face. She had a smile, and although her eyes were closed, she was certainly not sleeping.

"Did you get some rest?" she asked.

My legs tucked under me, I looked at Shay. "I feel rested. How about you?"

"I'm not ready to be awake yet."

"It's Thursday, Shay. Do you work today?" I gave her a little shake, and her beautiful eyes opened.

"Not today. Good thing, because I'm not getting up for a while." She slid further down the mattress, turned to her side, and snuggled against her pillow. It was odd for her to retreat into sleep, and I wondered if her wound and our use of demon sift did have the lasting effect Stout had mentioned.

I climbed out of bed to get dressed and go to the bathroom. When I returned, she still hadn't moved. I kissed her cheek and went to the kitchen to make some coffee.

Stout was hovering over the sink, trying to turn the hot water tap. "Can you run this for me?" he asked, making short bursts of flight at the handle, trying to force the rotation.

"Sure." My hand met with a bit of resistance as I cranked the knob.

He flew into the stream of water, and I saw a shadow of blue wash down the drain. When he finished, he shook off, similar to the way Dexter did when he crawled from the river after a frolic.

"What was that?" I asked him as I pointed to the trickle of blue on the chrome of the drain.

"Residual powder," he explained. "It's from the fairy dust I used on the two of you last night. I didn't have water to wash off after."

I opened the top of the coffeemaker and filled the pot before turning to look at him. I shoved the filter into the machine and dumped three scoops of grounds inside. "What do you mean, fairy dust? What did you do?"

"I heard the nightmare, and when Shay came out to make the burgers, I put a bit of fairy dust in your food."

"You spiked our food?"

"To help you sleep, yes."

"NO!" I yelled at him. "No, you can't do that to us without permission."

"I had permission." He landed on the counter with a stomp of his foot. "Shay said she wanted to help you, and I told her fairy dust would work."

"You're kidding me, right?"

"I took an oath. I can't do anything without Shay's say-so."

It made little sense that she would use magick to help us sleep. That's not how we lived our lives. Magick had consequences, an exchange of one thing for the other, and we didn't use it without consent.

"What did you say?" I demanded. "I want to know exactly what you said."

"I don't remember exactly, but it's not a big deal. You got to sleep, didn't you?"

"I did, but Shay doesn't want to wake up."

His legs pushed off the counter to hover in front of me. "What do you mean, she doesn't want to wake up?"

"I mean, she is still sleeping, and it's six a.m."

"Well, that's not like her." He pointed out the obvious as he floated around the kitchen before returning to hover in front of my face. "You used the demon sift, didn't you?" His question felt more like a reprimand.

"Last night, the demon injured Shay during the attack. Yes, I had to use it."

He flew down the stairs, returning a few seconds later carrying a bottle of my anvil dust. "Demon and fairy don't mix." He pushed on the bottle cap, trying to open it. "Demon and fairy don't mix!" he yelled louder.

"What are you talking about?" I grabbed the bottle and twisted the top. "What happens when you mix them?" I asked.

Stout flew to the cabinet where we kept our dishes and returned with a small bowl. "Get some salt, a pinch of thistle, and—" He paused for a few seconds to think. "And two sprigs of willow."

There wasn't time to ask what the combination would do, but I was on board if this would wake Shay. I ran to the back room and threw the apothecary doors open. The canister labeled thistle was easy to find, and I knew we'd tied the willow to the door, so I broke two branches off and waited for the next instructions.

"Grind the thistle and willow," he directed. "Where's the salt?"

I reached for the container on the stove. "Table salt okay?"

"It'll do." He waved a dismissive hand. "Pound all of it with the mortar and pestle."

One by one, I threw the ingredients into the stone grinder to crush them together. Bits of willow tumbled over the edges, but the mess didn't matter as I continued to mix the ingredients. The fairy forced his thick body through the mouth of the bottle of demon sift and exited with a generous handful. He carried it to the mortar and dumped it in. Two seconds later, a loud hacking rumble came from his mouth, and he spat three giant mouthfuls of fairy saliva over the pestle.

"That's gross!" I yelled. "Was that necessary?"

With the weight of his entire body, he grabbed the stone pestle and moved my hand to continue the grind. "Just keep mixing!"

I forced the ingredients together, watching the solids swell into a glob of mush. "Now what?"

"You need to rub the paste under her eyes and nose." He gestured, touching his eyes and upper lip as an example.

"Are you serious?" I leaned in to sniff the concoction, which smelled like rotten tree bark. Shay might wake from the aroma alone.

"She has to take it in." He flew up to the top of the bookcase. "Be careful," he warned, "because she's gonna be kinda pissed."

I processed his last words as I ran to the bedroom with the stone bowl in my hands. *"Pissed?"* I wondered. Why was she going to be pissed? The thought faded as I pressed my thumb into the mixture and rubbed the dark paste under Shay's eyes and nose. As it streaked across her skin, the paste changed from black to dark red.

"It's turning red!" I yelled over my shoulder to him.

"That's great," Stout answered. "It means it's working."

Seconds later, Shay's hand came up to rub at the smear under her nose. The back of her hand looked covered with a streak of blood. Her eyes popped open, and she glared sideways at me as if I'd just banged spoons to all of our pots and pans to wake her.

"What are you doing?" Her voice held a tone of anger. Shay looked at her hand. "What the hell is this?"

"It's a misunderstanding, I think," I tried to explain as I took a few steps away.

Shay did not have a temper. She rarely raised her voice in anger, so the suggestion that she might be pissed was accurate.

Shay pushed off the mattress. "Misun—What? What's going on?" Her legs fell over the side of the bed, and she tried to stand.

"Side effect of an anvil dust and fairy powder combination," I said as fast as I could to make the reality as painless as possible.

Shay rubbed the side of her head. "A fairy powder and what?" she asked, confused, but I wasn't sure I understood it either.

"Stout might have mixed them." I was trying to keep it simple as I watched Shay struggle with the idea of what was happening to her.

Her head fell forward, and I couldn't see her face through the tangle of red hair. "From the fight last night?"

Her fingers combed through to pull her hair, and with a twist and a twirl, she tied it into an unruly knot. When she turned to me for an answer, the look on her face was pure anger.

Stout's words–*Be careful because she's gonna be kinda pissed*–rang in my ears.

"Wait, baby, please." I dropped to my knees in front of her. "I think he misunderstood."

Her hands clenched into fists, and I heard a growl coming from behind me. Dexter's nose pushed under my arm as he threaded his way to Shay. He was protecting me—from her. The dog barked once, and when Shay didn't react, he barked two more times. I stood silent, giving the K-9 space to work.

Her glassy green eyes blinked open, and her hands splayed across her thighs. Dexter's eyes stretched wide, and I wanted to know what silent exchange was taking place between them. He pushed her hand up to force it on his nose, and Shay leaned forward to kiss his snout.

"Thank you, Dex," she said, and he dropped his face in her lap.

I reached to touch her chin, raising her head to look at me. "Shay?"

Her eyebrow flexed as she looked up. "I'm alright." Dexter wandered back into the kitchen.

I dropped to the floor to kneel between her legs. My hands rubbed across her thighs, cautiously at first, to test her receptiveness to my touch. "How do you feel?"

"Not quite right, if that's an actual feeling." Her hands rested over my own. "Will you please explain what happened?" She pinched the bridge of her nose. "What do you mean, it was a mistake?"

I stood up to find Stout because I didn't know how to describe the events of the last ten minutes, and I wanted him to tell Shay what he'd done.

"Wait." She tugged me into the V of her legs and wrapped her arms around my waist. I could feel her heart racing against my abdomen.

"Gosh, love. Your heart. I can feel it pounding."

Her head turned as she took a deep breath. "I'm confused. There's something—I can't figure it out, but I feel so—"

"Pissed?" I interrupted.

"Maybe, but more disconnected." Her hands fell to my hips, and I stepped back so she could stand. "I need to talk to Stout. He needs to tell me what this is."

I followed her to the living room, where our fairy sat perched on the kitchen table.

"Before you get punchy and slappy on me, you said I could." He stood his ground, even if he was occupying less than a square inch of space.

Shay sat down at the table. "I won't get violent."

"You won't?" His tone was doubtful.

He crossed his arms in defense, waiting for whatever was coming. When he flew up to the top of the bookcase, I watched him, curious to know what he was doing. I heard his wings fluttering as he zoomed in front of us holding a thimble. He didn't say a word before blowing across the top of the thimble to release a puff of powder into Shay's face. The gray powder spread across her skin and blazed bright red before disappearing.

"Ugh." Shay coughed, and I fanned my hand to push the smoke away. "What the hell?"

"Are you drugging her again?" I yelled at him.

"It's a test." Stout hovered in front of us. "I'm just making sure my powder is at full strength. I haven't had a lot of beer in the last few months."

Shay put her hands in the air. "Hold up." She pointed at the table in front of her. "Come here and stop flying around. You're making me dizzy." I walked to the sink to wet a washcloth and grab a dry hand towel.

"You can't crush me." He hovered over the table before dropping to the surface.

Shay took the towels from my hand to wipe off her face. "I don't want to crush you. I just want to know what you did last night."

"You wanted to help Wildwood sleep," he reminded her.

Shay shook her head. "I said I hoped the memory wouldn't keep her from sleeping."

"Is there really a difference?" he asked.

"Yes!" I yelled.

Shay looked at the red stains on the cloth and held it up for the fairy to see. "Clearly, there is a difference." She threw the towels in the kitchen sink. "You do *not* get to use fairy magick on us. That's demon shit!"

"I am not a demon!" he yelled back with almost as much weight in his voice as Shay's. "Never put me on the same list as those mindless monsters!" He stomped his foot.

"Then don't come after me where I sleep," Shay spat back. "The carriage house is our home. This apartment is a sacred space. It's where we are safe to live. You don't do magick here."

"I only did what you asked!" Stout shouted back.

"No, you didn't."

Watching my lover fight with an action-figure-sized creature shredded the seams of my reality. He was forceful in his insistence and holding his own against my superhero girlfriend, which I found pretty exciting and inappropriately impressive. But he'd used fairy powers on us, and the use of that magick had put Shay in jeopardy.

"Stout." Shay took a slow, calming breath. "As long as you are in the carriage house with us, we have to make an agreement."

"What kind?"

"Magick happens with full consent. There is no question. There is no crossing that boundary."

I thought about the first time Shay and I had had this conversation. She'd been hiding every part of herself from me– the existence of otherworldly beings, fighting those creatures, and her life as a witch–yet somehow she'd believed keeping me in the dark protected me. It hadn't, and I still had the tiny scar on my cheek as a reminder.

"My fairy magick can help you the same way that your demon sift does," Stout explained. "I thought last night when you cooked the hamburgers that you were asking me to help you."

"I was telling you how difficult it was to see Wildwood suffering," Shay said.

"I guess I read more into it." He was pacing back and forth across the table. "Maybe we need a signal."

"We need a signal? What for?" Shay walked toward the coffee pot and took down a mug. "Coffee?" she asked, waving the pot over a second mug.

"Yes, please," I answered.

The mood in the room changed as I watched Shay's hand pause while replacing the pot in the machine. She carried the cups to the table.

"What about a drink for me?" Stout asked, and Shay gave him a glaring sideways stare.

"I thought you drank beer," she said, opening the refrigerator to get cream for her coffee.

"That's right. Everyone has their morning routine." He flew to the refrigerator door and propped himself inside to prevent Shay from closing it. "Don't judge me."

Shay replaced the creamer and pulled out a bottle of beer. She popped the cap and poured the amber liquid into a glass. He was already waiting with his paper straw. Their entire interaction was only a few seconds long, but it was enough time for everyone to take a moment to think about what had just happened. The fairy sucked down a quarter of his drink before Shay sat beside me at the table.

"How are you feeling?" My hand tapped her fingers, and I waited for her to look at me.

"I'm upset with myself. I should have known better." Her lips puckered to blow across the top of her mug. "There are so many outside forces working against us right now, and I can't be worried about the inside ones." She looked at Stout, who was still sucking down his glass of beer.

He paused. "I'm always on your side." He took another sip.

"You need to ask more questions," I said. My hands wrapped around the mug, and I enjoyed the heat in my palms.

"You need to know that we can't solve everything with magick, Stout," Shay said, her tone leaving little room for question.

"But we can solve a lot of things." Stout stood on the rim of his glass, shuffling the straw across the bottom to get every drop.

"With communication." Shay touched the straw to get Stout's attention. "And consent."

"I swear it." He spit in his hand and rubbed it across his chest. It was an odd gesture, but I'm sure it was a fairy way to seal the deal.

"Good," Shay said as she leaned back in her chair. "So, let's talk about mixing demon sift with fairy powder."

"It's powerful magick." Stout flew to the tabletop and sat in front of Shay.

"I've used it before," I said. "For–"

"For Shay," Stout interrupted. "You needed it for the spell, and I delivered. That's what I thought I was doing last night."

"You're saying we can mix it, but that we can't ingest the combination. At least not while we've used one or the other."

"Exactly. You can use as much demon sift as you want, but it's painful, and it's supposed to knock you out."

I wondered about demon sift, and her body's reaction to it. He'd commented before about how little it affected Shay after the first few times we'd used it, but I wasn't sure if he understood, either. "But the sift didn't knock Shay out. It just burned and bubbled, and a few minutes later, we washed it away. No cut. No scar."

"It's not supposed to happen that way," Stout explained. "The magick in demon sift is supposed to undo physical harm. There's a high cost for that, and it usually draws from your own power."

"But it doesn't," Shay said. "I mean, the sift hurts. But that's it. It seems like every time we use it, the pain gets more intense, but after about a minute, no pain, no wound. It's like I wasn't injured at all."

"Your reaction, its healing abilities…they don't make sense." Stout pulled his straw from the glass and motioned with his hands for a second drink. "Please?"

Shay adjusted her body to stand, but I put my hand on her shoulder to stop her. "I've got it." I opened the refrigerator and removed the last bottle, pointing to it. "We're going to need to pick up some more."

"Regina made drinking beer really easy at the bar." Stout watched as the frothy drink filled his glass.

"Convenient, I guess," I interjected. "We've put together that your beer drinking makes fairy powder, but a few minutes ago you spit into the mortar. So, is your spit the source of your powder?"

I couldn't believe I was asking such a ridiculous question. Using spit from any creature to reverse magick was new for me, but to save Shay, I'd used it with little hesitation. So fairy spit and fairy dust were the same, but what the heck were they for?

"What does your powder do?" Shay asked before I could. "I know a little about your powers to protect life and creatures of kindness. Is your powder part of that work?"

"It's not as good as demon sift. That's practically a cure for death. Fairy powder is more about making calm in the chaos and reversing poor decisions."

"But using it makes people mad?" I asked, confused about Stout's fairy world.

"Yes, mostly because it's twice as potent in liquid form."

Shay sat listening. I wondered how long it would take for her to put together all the components of this morning's episode: the red under her nose, the encounter with Dex, and her unusual level of anger. By the look on her face, she was just about there.

"The liquid form?" Shay asked, staring at the towel on the kitchen counter. "You smeared fairy spit on my face?" She stared at me, and the look was enough to invoke panic as I thought about the entire situation.

"I didn't have a choi–"

"She really didn't, Red," Stout cut in just as I was assembling my defense. "You were pretty out of it, and we needed to act fast."

Shay got up from the table and left the room without saying a word. Although it was her habit to walk and wander when we were in research mode, we weren't researching anything at the moment. She returned a few seconds later with a bottle from the bathroom and set it on the table.

"Is this you?" she asked.

The liquid sloshed against the side of the glass container. It was the test sample from the day we'd received the mysterious delivery.

Stout put his hand against the glass. "Yes, it is."

"Benton told you to leave the envelope at my house?" Shay sat at the table.

Stout's head dropped with a solemn nod, confirming that Benton had made sure we could complete the transfer of power that would balance Shay as the Magick. We sat in silence for the longest time. I thought about Shay and her relationship with Benton, but I couldn't forget that Stout had had a life with Benton, too. I didn't know what to say or do. Benton had been the human force that brought Shay and me together in Bannock. It was clear now that our power would transfer, and Benton's death was an unfortunate and unavoidable consequence. All of those factors were out of our control. We needed to stop chasing answers and start taking action.

"What are we going to do now?" I couldn't stand the silence, and it felt like the right question to ask.

"They're going to keep coming." Shay stumbled over the words. Was she talking to me or to Stout? I couldn't decide as the statement rested between us. "Now that the hammer is free from Brigid's cave, they'll come."

"Yes, they will," Stout agreed. The two of them focused on the piles of notes and books covering the table, and it felt like they weren't listening to me.

"So, what do we do?" I asked again, a little louder to get their attention.

Shay's hand slid to grasp mine. "We pump up the protection on the building and make you something like my armor."

Stout flew up to the top of the bookshelf, and I watched as he tugged on the string hanging off of Benton's funeral flag. A few seconds later, he was hovering over us with a tiny black bag clamped in his toes.

"Start with this." He dropped the bag in front of Shay. "This is cemetery soil from the Magick's grave. It's powerful; it'll be like conjuring with two sources at once."

"Yes," Shay said, picking up the little black bag, "but there's only enough for one spell. We need to make sure everything is right."

"Regina had a powerful bind on the cellar at Slammed. I know where her spell book is, along with other things that will help," Stout promised. "We can go to the bar, and you can read the spells."

Shay looked at her watch. "If we go now, we can get in and out before Diana comes in for the one o'clock crowd." Shay turned to look at me. "Do you think you can fire up that old forge in the cellar?"

"Not without proper ventilation and more tools than I care to haul over there." I thought about the rusted hood vent and what bugs and other forms of wildlife might have a nest inside. "It would take a week at least."

"We don't have time for that. We'll bring everything back to the carriage house and work."

"What are you thinking?" I asked.

Shay held my hand and tugged it into her lap. "I want you to make a gauntlet, and we're going to charge it with Magick and Maker powers so that it will protect you when you're outside of the carriage house barrier."

"I'll get to work on that right away."

We had the demon material from Benton sitting on the worktable in my office. I had multiple pieces of class four demon to experiment with, but I wondered if my new friend could suggest the right piece.

"Once you're physically protected, we can work on boosting the carriage house barrier," Shay suggested.

"That's a good plan, but maybe Stout should help me with all the materials Benton left?"

The fairy flew closer to me. "That's easy. Use block number seven. It's from the same thing that you used to make Shay's cuff."

"How do you know that?" I asked.

"I was with Regina when she marked it all. She was very thorough."

"So, we're set." Shay laid her hands on the table. "Let's get out of here and grab what we need from the bar." She called her dog. "Dexter!"

It was my first time outside the building since the attack, and although I considered myself brave, the fingers tangled around my hand were comforting. Shay gave me a little tug toward the patrol car. Knowing that magick wares filled the trunk would make the trip easier. She dropped Benton's charmed backpack on my lap and looked behind her to check that Stout and Dexter were in the back seat. Driving the few blocks seemed like a waste of resources, but we weren't taking chances until the protections were in place.

Shay slid the key into the service door at the back of the building, and a few minutes later, we were following Dex down the staircase hidden in the back room.

"What does Regina's spell book look like?" I turned to Stout for the answer.

"It's at the base of the Apothecary." He flew toward the cabinet wall, and I was a half-step behind him as he pointed. "Shay, you'll need to open the—"

I was already tugging on the hinged pull knob when I felt power surge through my fingers. I pulled my hand away. "Whoo, that's a little intense."

Stout was already across the room. "Touch it again," he said.

"Why?" I asked as my hand hovered near the knob.

"Are you messing with her?" Shay asked as she held a hand up to stop me.

"The power of the Maker is messing everything up," Stout explained. "There are some things that the Maker shouldn't do, especially now that she carries the power of Brigid."

"I think we already came to the consensus that our powers are symbiotic," Shay reminded him as she opened the cabinet door. "What we do, we do together."

"Not since Jacob," Stout said. "Jacob turned on Regina, and after that happened, no one entered without permission."

Shay dangled the ring of keys in front of the fairy. "This basement chamber belongs to Dani and me. There's a reason that Reggie made that decision, and Wildwood and I are together, bound by more than Maker and Magick powers. So, she has permission to be everywhere."

"It's not supposed to work that way." Stout hovered in between Shay and me.

"That doesn't matter anymore. This is how it is now." Her voice was louder as she set the boundary.

"You should just be careful," Stout warned. "Wildwood's still the Maker, and that mark on her hand is still there, even with that glove covering it."

I tugged at the wristband of the fingerless glove covering Brigid's mark. "Once we finish inventorying this cellar, will we still need to be careful?"

"Probably not," Shay answered before Stout could.

"Hold on, Red. You've got a lot of magick to undo before your girlfriend is safe down here from Regina's barriers."

"One thing at a time." Shay dropped to a knee to inspect the contents of the cabinet and pulled out a small cardboard container. She seemed familiar with the box as she tipped the flap over to remove a shotgun shell. "Why are these in here?"

Stout's smile was close to a laugh. "The last resort, Benton called them."

"What does that mean?" I asked, frustrated by his ability to answer without getting to the facts.

"Those are killer shells. The big guns, if you will."

The words echoed in my ears. Big guns. I disliked guns of any kind, but living with a police officer whose best friend was also a police officer meant that I was surrounded by firearms most of the time. I wasn't afraid as much as I understood the damage a gun could do, and I chose axes, knives, and hammers instead.

"Big guns for…?" Shay asked.

"Anything demonic that crawls from that mine," Stout explained.

Shay tilted the container, and two shotgun shells rolled from the box into her hand. Three seemed like an odd number if you were fighting for your life. I understood Shay had excellent aim, but three shells were limiting when demons were involved. She dropped the rounds back into the box and set them on the counter. "I'll put these in the armory." She winked, and I thought about the rugged, dented box of ammunition she kept in the bedroom closet. She returned to the cabinet and passed me a four-inch-thick book. I needed two hands to hold it as Shay stood up beside me.

"This is pretty amazing." Shay ran her hand over the cover. It looked like animal skin. "Do you know the history here?" she asked Stout.

"You know what a grimoire is?"

"A book of spells, yes." Shay was quick to answer, and I was relieved I hadn't had to guess, although I thought I knew. "I was asking if you knew about this book in particular?"

"It's the history of your power, Red."

"Are you saying this is older than Benton?" I asked as I handed it to Shay. I didn't feel like it was my place to be the first of us to open it, as she had twice my experience in her practice as a witch.

"This has magick that goes back to Kai." Stout flew closer. "She stretched the cover from the skin of the same deer that holds the ancestry scroll."

Shay ran her finger over the primitive design on the cover. The only decoration was the hand-tooled full moon circle, touched by two delicate half-moons. The title letters were Pictish, like the writing on my hammer.

"This belongs to both of us." Shay looked up at me. "This is the history we always wanted to be part of." Shay turned to Stout. "Can you translate the cover for me?"

He landed on top and walked across the words as he translated. "Magick balances the Maker, and the Maker balances the Magick."

"This is—"

"Unbelievable," I interrupted. We stood in awe. The book should have been in a museum, not in the hands of a blacksmith and her witch lover.

Shay opened the cover. The first page was stiff like cardboard; it resembled a piece of translucent stretched hide, I thought. I was familiar with the tanning process, but the picture that adorned it was new. It was an eight-sectioned circle filled with symbols and signs. "Do you recognize this, Shay?"

"En colligo maleficarum." Shay read it out loud and then translated it. "The gathering of witches."

"What does that mean?" I asked as I trailed my finger across the circle.

"This is the calendar of the year," Shay explained. "I've never seen it quite like this, but there are eight celebrations. The four great festivals–Yule, Ostara, Mabon, and Litha–celebrate the solstices and equinoxes, and the four lesser festivals celebrate the cross-quarter days. Our goddess has her celebration in the cross-quarter," Shay added.

"Really?" I tried to follow Shay's explanation around the page. "What is her celebration called?" I asked.

"Imbolc. It's the festival of Brigid, and we celebrate in February."

I thought it was odd that a festival for a fire goddess would fall in the cold of winter. "Why is it in February?"

"It's a celebration of the days becoming longer." Stout landed on the open page. "It's a perfect time for the gathering of witches into a coven."

"We don't have a coven," Shay pointed out. "I've always been a solitary practitioner, and I'm certain that would be the same for every Magick that came before me."

Stout nodded his head. "For obvious reasons." He flew off the book and hovered in front of us.

"Why do you think it's on the first page?" I asked.

"The calendar, the moon phases, and the seasons are all powerful on their own, but when you align your magick with the power of the moon or the seasons, it can infuse incredible forces."

"Like the spell in the old courthouse?" I asked.

"Exactly like that." Shay turned the page and found a continuation of the Pictish script. "Stout, you're going to have to help translate this."

He walked across the page. "It's a spell for power balance," Stout explained. "Kai would have used this a lot."

It was difficult to forget the memory of Shay and the surges she'd endured when my powers came. I hated to think of the suffering Kai would have faced as she carried the abilities of both the Magick and the Maker for so long. "Balancing all the power must have been an incredible burden." I didn't mean to say it out loud.

Shay turned to look at me. "Yes, it must have been."

"Don't be so quick to feel sorry for Kai," Stout gently chided. "She was incredibly powerful and a fierce fighter. All magick has a price no matter who carries it or who uses it."

"That's very true." Shay teetered the book while trying to turn the page. "Can you help me find the spell we need, Stout?"

The fairy hovered above the unturned edge and flew closer to stick his arm deep in the pages. "It should be here."

I ran my finger until it touched Stout's place-holding arm, then flipped to the yellowed parchment insert. "It's in Latin." I was excited when I recognized the language.

"Very good, love." Shay planted an enthusiastic peck on my cheek. "This should be pretty simple." She laid the book on the table and walked to the apothecary shelves. She plucked small bottles from the cubbies, broke a twig from the wall, and paced back and forth, referencing the book and picking items from the shelves. The last tool was a dust-covered, drip-smeared candle, and I wondered why we didn't use one we already had.

Shay put the collection into Benton's backpack, and I felt a sense of relief, knowing that the enchantment of that bag would mask the contents. Only the three of us would know what we were taking from the cellar. "What do you need from the forge?" Shay asked as she slipped the backpack on her shoulder.

I walked away, moving closer to the blacksmithing tools that had changed little in half a millennium. "Honestly, I don't think I want to take anything from here."

"Why not?" Shay asked as she stood beside me.

I picked up a pair of tongs and pulled them apart at the pivot. They were rust-covered and a challenge to move. "These tools haven't touched hot steel for a long time." I tapped against the hammer rack. "These feel a little haunted," I explained as I walked around. "If Jacob was the Maker before me, these should go to Dani. That's if she even wants them."

"Do you know why this forge set-up would be down here?" Shay asked Stout as he zipped between the dog resting in the middle of the room and the two of us.

"Regina brought it here."

"Obviously, but it doesn't make sense." Shay picked up a hammer, spinning the handle to rotate the head. "Did she ever use it?"

"I…don't know." His answer sounded evasive.

It was curious for a forge to be in the basement of an old building, so I climbed on the stone and mortar base to look closer at the venting hood. I reached up inside, and my knuckles hit a solid surface.

"This is some kind of panel." I turned toward Shay. "Did you bring a flashlight?"

A smile broke wide across her face, wrinkling the tiny lines around her eyes. "Yes, but I think you have one, too." She waved her hand, wiggling her fingers.

"Oh, ha. I guess I forget sometimes." I removed the gloves and stuffed them in my pocket. "*Ignis*," I whispered, and my left hand sparked with an orange flame. I pushed my light up as close to the obstruction as possible, surprised to see a framed steel door. "It's some kind of exhaust door."

I felt a hand on my leg and looked down to see Shay leaning in to inspect the hood. "What was Regina up to?" she asked.

"I wonder where this goes?" I said, thinking about how toxic the fumes from a coal forge setup could be. "This little door had to lead somewhere. Maybe she used it to camouflage the exhaust smoke."

"But she wasn't a blacksmith," Shay said and looked at Stout for confirmation. "Was she?"

"She was definitely not a blacksmith," he said.

"I don't get it," she said.

I clenched my palm to extinguish the flame and grabbed Shay's hand as I jumped down. "To answer your question about using this, I wouldn't light this forge, not as it sits, but maybe someone could have." I wasn't ready to answer questions about what and how. There was a reason Regina had gone through the work to assemble a forge in this cellar, which meant that she'd had a plan. Maybe after we inventoried the cellar diaries, we'd understand.

Shay was circling the anvil, dragging her fingers across the face. She seemed deep in thought, and I didn't want to break her focus. I dusted my hands on the thigh of my pants and pulled my gloves back on.

"Why would the Magick of Bannock assemble an operational forge in her workspace?" Shay was thinking out loud.

I didn't have a guess, and I didn't know if our fairy had one either. "Stout?"

He flew to the top of the vent hood. "Benton thought she could use Kai's spell to find balance. She wanted to summon the Maker's powers, so she built this. It never happened." Stout climbed up into the same cone-shaped pipe where I found the metal door. I could hear the squeak of the rusty pieces of metal sliding against each other.

The sigil in the palm of my hand felt warm. I removed my glove, and the glow flashed the *ignis* flame without me summoning it. "What the hell?" I yelled as I clamped my hand into a fist.

Shay looked at me and stepped closer to help. "What happened?"

"I'm not sure. Stout climbed up and opened that trapdoor, and my sigil heated."

"Stout, what are you doing up there?" Shay leaned over to yell at our fairy as small lumps of cloth dropped one by one. Shay picked up the first bundle, covered in a tangle of spider webs and dust.

"What are they?" I asked as Shay rotated it to see the marking tag.

Another bundle dropped, and I counted six in total. I heard the squeaking of the metal door closing again and watched our soot-covered fairy exit the hood. He landed on the bundle in Shay's hand.

"You're holding history right there," Stout explained.

"History?" I asked.

Stout pushed the marking tag over to reveal a name written in charcoal block letters. "This is from Gorath."

I considered the history of the name. Gorath Strinegart was the Maker in the late 1600s, and this was him, but what part of him were we holding in our hands? I stepped back at the thought of Shay possessing a four-hundred-year-old Maker in her hand.

Shay didn't falter as she picked up another bundle from the forged top. "What do you mean by history?" she asked.

Stout hovered over the bundles. "Grave soil."

It was unclear to me what the power of grave soil meant, but I thought I understood what it was. Someone had taken the time and effort to collect the soil from the graves of every Magick and Maker who'd lived before us. Magick took many forms and used all the elements. The earth element carried an incredible pull for me, and the energies of past Makers and Magicks must have set off my sigil flame.

"Can I ask a question?" I touched Shay's hand.

"Go ahead."

"Is grave soil what I think it is?" I was hesitant to touch any of the six bundles in front of me.

"If you think it's dirt from the graves of the people in our ancestry scroll, then yes, it is."

I had more than a few questions about the little dirt-stuffed packets in front of us, but the most urgent was, "Why?"

"Why would someone take soil from a grave?" Shay asked, mirroring my question.

"Well, yes. Why would anyone take *anything* from a grave?"

I remembered the bag of soil that Shay had tucked in the flag resting on our shelf. She understood the power locked inside the soil. Magick was something she nurtured, and I respected that Shay was always a step ahead with her magick.

"As Stout said earlier, it's a powerful vessel for earth energy. I guess I thought you'd understand that."

"I've never thought about the dirt from a grave."

"We are all energy, love." Shay turned each of the bundles over and lined them up. She sorted the Maker packets from the Magick ones, took off the backpack, and tucked all of them into the inside pocket.

"What will you do with them?"

"I'm going to use the grave soil from the previous Magick and Maker to put up a serious barrier around the carriage house." Shay tugged the backpack closed and put it on her shoulder. "If you don't need anything else. Let's head back to the carriage house."

"I mean, we have the dirt from the graves of our ancestors. What more could we need?"

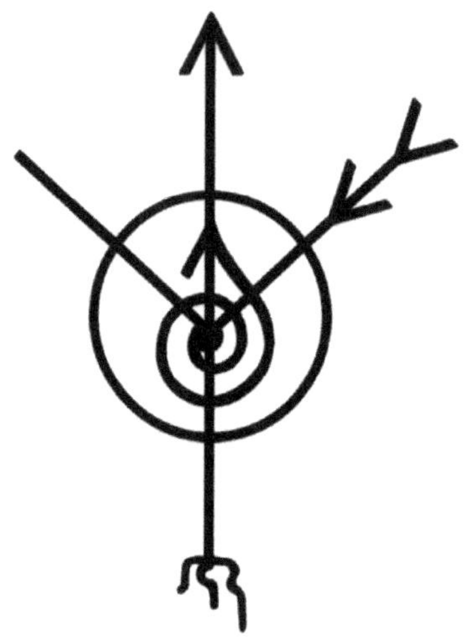

CHAPTER XII

SANCTIFIED

"Is it weird that I'm excited?" I asked.

"Maybe a little, for you," Shay said.

She squeezed my gloved hand before pulling it into her lap. I was feeling less anxious after finding the grimoire and the grave soil. I trusted Shay to craft a powerful spell with these new components. We were about to put a barrier around the carriage house, and this solid plan moved us closer to safety.

When the four of us arrived at the door, I turned the key in the lock, thinking about the history behind the oxidized piece of metal. This key must have opened this door thousands of times before it became mine. My hand rubbed across the peeling white paint of the rustic solid-core door, and I appreciated its strength because last night it had saved my life.

"Do you want to help me with the prep work?" Shay was standing behind me as she asked.

"Sure, but can I do something really quick? It'll only take me about a half-hour."

I couldn't stop thinking about this door and my new life with Shay. We were going to make memories inside this carriage house and be happy once we rid this town of its monsters.

"There's plenty for me to do. Stout and I will go through the grimoire and organize the spell."

"That's perfect." I kissed her square on the lips, and the enthusiastic response reminded me that her magick was wildly erotic.

"I'll be up when I finish." I pushed her toward the stairs. "Can Dexter stay down here with me?"

"Sure." Shay waved a hand to steer the dog to the ring on the floor.

"Perfect," I whispered to Dex as Shay climbed the stairs. "Can you guard the door for me?" I asked, not expecting a verbal answer, but he moved to lie by the open frame.

I started popping the pins from the hinges and laying the solid slab of wood across my sawhorses, careful to cover my mouth with a respirator as I ran sandpaper across the surface. I wiped the dust down and washed the door with a thin solvent solution. With the prep work complete, the exterior side of our door was ready for a fresh layer of paint. It took less than ten minutes to roll a fresh coat of color across the surface, and I used a heat gun and fan to speed up the drying process. The finished result was perfect, and I raised the door on its end to lean it against the frame to dry.

My thirty-minute guess was more like forty-five, but when I climbed the stairs, Shay was twisting her wrist, mashing leaves and stems with the grinding stone.

"How's it going up here?" I asked as I hugged around Shay's hips to kiss her cheek.

"I've got almost everything set for the spell. I just need you and your hands." She pointed to the gloves I was wearing.

I smiled, thinking about how she might like me to use my hands. "I love doing magick with you."

She tugged off my gloves one finger at a time.

I stepped around her to look at the jars and bowls she had assembled. "Are we going to be upstairs or down?"

The last time she'd performed a spell of protection, we'd used the workshop. I wasn't sure if we could repeat it in the same space.

"I'm thinking we should enact the ritual inside the sacred circle and work from the ground up."

I ran my finger across the page of the grimoire open on the table. "What can I do?"

Shay stopped grinding the herbs and poured them into an empty glass jar. "You can take this down along with the backpack, and I'll bring the rest." She looked around the room. "Where's Dex?"

"He's downstairs. He's still helping me with my project."

Shay stopped working to inspect my appearance, and I realized my body was chalky with dust. "What have the two of you been up to?" she asked.

"It's a surprise. You'll just have to wait and see."

I took advantage of the time I had to carry the supplies down and checked the surface of the fresh paint. It was a little tacky across the center, but it felt dry enough to hang, and it would be okay if I didn't close it all the way. Dexter was standing guard.

"Good job, Dex." I patted his shoulder just before sliding the hinges in place. I dropped the pin through the top and closed the door just enough so that Shay could enjoy the dramatic unveiling.

I heard footsteps before I saw her. "Are we ready?" Shay wore her deep purple cloak, and I could smell the censer coal smoldering in the clay bowl in the center of the tray she carried. Spell-casting was one of the most exciting parts of loving a witch. The smell of oils and incense would linger on her skin long after her work was done. At some point today, I could hold her in my arms and bask in the sweet aromatics of her magick.

"I'm ready." I stopped in front of her. Shay's hands were full, with papers and books tucked under her arms. I held my palms up for her to fill them. "What can I do?"

"Take this." She tilted her shoulder so I could grab the thick grimoire, and I carried it to the center of the room.

"You should do protective magick in that ring," Stout suggested as he hovered near my ear.

"I was planning to do all our magick inside. It's where the three of us are most powerful," Shay explained.

"Good." He hovered behind us before flying back up to the apartment.

"The magick won't let the Gatekeeper out?" I asked, mainly as a joke.

"No, it won't." Shay was quick to answer as she set the dust-covered candle in the middle of the room. "New magick in a sacred space."

"So why the dirty old candle?" I asked as she used her *ignis* flame to light the wick.

"Pick it up," she said.

I dropped to one knee and held the three-inch diameter candle in my hand, rotating the surface until I saw the deep zig-zag grooves carved into the side. "What does the symbol mean?" The wax dripped on the floor.

Shay stood behind me, resting her chin on my shoulder. "It's a sigil." Her finger traced over the marks. "It represents an intention. See this hole?" The glow from the flame backlit the lines and swirls carved into the wax, but there was a clear round divot in the wax.

"Yes." I touched the circle poked into the candle.

"This is the origin–or the first letter." Her fingertip swooped across the line. "Imagine all the letters in the alphabet are on the sigil wheel. The wheel has two rings surrounding a circle. Each ring is cut into segments: thirteen around the outer ring, holding letters A through M; eight parts to the second ring, holding letters N through U; and the center cut into five pieces holding V through Z. The entire alphabet is part of the wheel. I can show you what the chart looks like later, but when I create a sigil, there's a supernatural purpose behind it. For example, if I want to mark an object to increase its magickal powers, I'll etch the word 'power,' or if I wanted more passion, I'd draw a sigil for 'love' or 'heart.'" She kissed my cheek. "But to create the sigil, the first letter of the represented intention begins at the origin hole." She touched the round divot in the wax.

I tapped each of the four points on the candle in my hand, trying to determine what the design might spell. I looked at Shay for some help. "So, what does this say?"

"The origin letter is a 'B.'" She dragged my fingertip along the gouged groove. Her motion was smooth, sensual, as she whispered against my cheek. "Second letter is 'R.'" I closed my eyes, anticipating the next sound. "Then 'I.'" The tiny hairs on the back of my neck tingled from her warm breath against my skin. The last stroke was slow and long. "And 'D.'"

My heart was racing, but I had enough sense to put the letters together to spell "brid." "Wait, what?" I twisted my neck to look at Shay's face. "'Brid?' What's 'brid?'"

"Not a what, my love, but a who." She tipped the candle upright and held it so I could see the carving. "Brid is your goddess. She is the hearth keeper. Your Brigid."

"But why?" I asked as I watched her set the candle back on the floor.

"Big spells require powerful magick, and who better to protect the Maker than the goddess who is the source of it all?"

"Wow," I said as I watched the flame dance on top of the pillar of wax.

"'Wow' is right," she said as her hands fell away.

I heard a creak from the door behind us and felt a gust move through the room. Shay turned fast, and in one fluid motion, pushed me out of the doorway. Her body was rigid, on high alert, as she walked over to inspect the door that I'd left unfastened.

"Did you leave this open?" she asked.

I nodded, a little spooked by the abrupt change in emotion. "I was fixing it."

Shay pushed against the solid wood, and the draft from the motion extinguished our candle flame. I hoped that wasn't a sign, but she didn't even notice as she said, "We should be hyper-vigilant about open windows and doors right now, babe." Her voice had a scolding tone.

"I know. That's why I had Dexter keeping watch."

Her head tipped as her eyebrow raised with a silent but curious nod. "What were the two of you up to?"

"It's nothing big. You'll understand later."

She walked across the workshop to the candle and whispered against the wick. It burst into flame, and she set it down on the floor.

I smiled as I remembered the first time I'd seen her light a candle without a match. The spell to bless our athame had been breathtaking and sensual, but watching her, at this moment, whisper across the wick of our blessing candle made me believe in everything Shay could do. I hadn't understood her magick at first, but in our months together, I'd learned so very much.

"Have you always had candle magick?" I asked.

Candle magick was the ability to manipulate the fire element. The power that came with the Bannock Magick and Maker transformation was elemental, but Shay had carried it long before I loved her or even understood what it was.

Shay's cheek raised with a delighted half-grin. "Yes, I have." She looked at me as she explained, "I read about it once. It was just a vague mention of the concept. It fascinated me, so I did a little research, and once I tried, I found I could create heat. That was the beginning, and after a few weeks, I could spark a flame." She set up the space for our spell, and as she placed each item, I couldn't help but enjoy the elegance of her body in motion. "It's intuitive." She winked at me and the action warmed my soul.

"Goddess, save me. You are an incredible woman." The words came out of my mouth before I could censor them, and her smile was almost as bright as the candle lighting her face.

"I think you're pretty wonderful yourself." She held up a gallon-sized glass vessel and a dish of herbs. "Would you like to come and adore me over here, please?" she asked.

That's a dumb damn question, I thought as I took a few steps closer. "Yes, I think I would." Shay sidestepped, and I noticed her naked feet. "Are we grounding for this spell?" I asked.

"Good catch." She winked at me. "Kick off your shoes and socks. This incantation needs all the elemental strength we can draw."

I followed her instructions and placed my shoes and socks next to Shay's by the door. Since discovering the importance of demon sift, I'd kept the workshop floors swept clean. Under most circumstances, I would never walk barefoot in the shop. This spell was something different, and as Shay moved to trace a thick chalk line on the floor, I waited for her next instructions.

"That amber vessel. Can you pull the stopper and cover my line with the mixture inside?"

"Sure." I removed the spongy, tapered cork and tucked the jar into the bend of my arm. "What is it?" I poured a small amount into the palm of my hand. It was granular, dark, and dusty and didn't look like the bright white salt I expected. I sifted it back into the jar.

"It's black salt."

"Oh, well, that explains it," I said with a hint of sarcasm.

She reached behind to pat my hip. "If you'll give me a second, I will explain."

My hand passed from one corner to the other of my lips, making a zipper-shutting motion.

"That," she continued, pointing to the jar tucked in my arm like a football, "is a combination of pink sea salt, black pepper, and the ash of magick."

"Ash of magick?"

"After every spell, after every act of prayerfulness and intention, I collect the ash left behind from burning. I mix it all and sift it into a fine powder. That is the ash of magick."

"Wow, I didn't know that was a thing," I said as I stared into the open container, thinking about how many sticks of incense and pods of charcoal were mixed inside.

"Mmm hmm, there are many parts that make up my life."

"I see that."

"Black salt is an important part of what we're about to do. So follow my mark and make a thick line all the way around us."

"I guess the ash explains why it's black," I said, cupping my hand to create a pouring spout and tracing the outside edge of the ring on the floor.

"I charge black salt with the power of my magick and use it for protection. Today, with intention, we will make a powerful barrier."

"But if the ring is on the floor inside the carriage house, how does it protect the outside?"

Shay picked up four candles from the tray. "We're going to start here." She pointed at the center of the ring. "The workshop is where you spend almost all of your days. The forge is where you craft with Brigid's hammer. Everything, good and evil, will come to the carriage house."

"That makes sense."

She set one candle at the east point of the ring, careful not to break the line of black salt. "Once we cast the spell inside the circle, we'll move outside and plant these on the ground." Shay walked back to the tray and held up six tiny pouches with obsidian chips tied on the drawstrings.

"What's inside them?" I asked.

She set the bundles down and continued placing the candles around the ring. "I blended the grave soil from the ancestors. Their magick is our magick, and once we set it on the earth, no demon with evil intentions will ever enter."

"What about humans?" It seemed like a harmless question, but Shay took a moment to ponder it.

"I guess it might make someone feel anxious or uncomfortable, but it won't repel humans the way it will drive demons away."

"You said you used some of the soil. What did you do with the rest?"

"We're going to take it back to the bar and reactivate the barrier there. You and I will probably spend a lot of time in the apothecary in the future."

"Makes sense."

The future. I smiled at the thought of our future together. Shay and I were building a life that seemed more significant than our humanity. She carried the incense censer to the center of the ring and set it on the floor. Her mash of herbs rested beside the smoldering dish, and it felt like it was time to invoke our incredible magick. She waved me inside the circle.

"You ready?" she asked as she held a hand to me. I stood beside her and listened. "There are three places to be. One is yesterday, one is today, and the other is tomorrow." Shay unhooked the cloak from her neck and dropped it to the floor. "Yesterday, they were among us."

Shay picked up the tiny pillows of grave soil. One by one, she placed them around the ring of black salt. "Regina, the Magick, share your power, so it is known." She placed the soil pouch on the floor beside the east candle and blew across the wick to light the flame. "Jacob, the Maker, share your power, make it known." She placed his pouch on the outside of the ring by the east candle. She stepped to the next candle, moving with the hands of time. "Graison, the Magick, share your power, so it is known." Shay continued around the ring, placing the grave soil of each Magick on the inside of our salt ring and the soil of each Maker on the outside. She blew each candle wick into flame.

When she circled to the north point, she stopped. "Wil, I want you to do the final one." She handed me the pouch filled with Kai's grave soil.

"Should I say what you said?" I asked, anxious about making a mistake.

"Yes, baby. You've got this."

I held up the pouch, noticing that it was two smaller parts tied together. "Kai, the Magick and the Maker share your power, so it is known." I dropped to a knee, placing one segment of the bag on the inside of the ring and the other on the outside. It felt like the right choice, and Shay shared an approving smile as I stood.

Shay bent to blow her breath across the top of the last candle, and the wick flickered with a flame. Her voice was breathy as she said, "We are the ancestry and the power of this circle." Her voice stole my heart, and I froze as I took in a breath. Shay's hand reached forward to steady me. "You still with me?"

"I'm good."

She continued. "Mother goddess, keeper of the hearth, today you are the custodian of our flame." Shay opened her palm. "*Ignis.*" The blue flame burned, and she pointed to me. "Light yours, please."

I raised my hand. "*Ignis.*" The orange glow from my palm was bright, shining through the sigil. I wasn't sure if I'd ever tire of the magick that Brigid entrusted to us.

"Sit down across from me." Shay winked as I looked into her shining green eyes. She picked up the delicate silver spoon, scooped a generous amount of the ground herbs, and poured them on the censer coal. The smoke was thick and lingered between us. She cupped her hand, drawing the smoke toward her heart.

She snaked her purple robe so that it was touching both of us. "I want you to do everything that I do. Okay?"

"Yep." I pulled the smoke toward my heart. Her flame hand rested on her knee, and I mirrored the position.

"Goodness and love are the sources of us." She held up her other hand and clapped them together. The mashing of her palms burst with light, and as they separated, the energy grew into a dense orb of blue flame.

I clapped my hands, saying, "Goddess and love are the sources of us." It was almost like a dream as I felt the vibration surge from my heart, travel through my chest, and down my arms, until the rise of energy transformed my flame into an orange orb. My fingers tremored, and I sat in awe, commanding more power than I'd ever held before.

Shay stretched her hands toward me, and as I mirrored the motion, her fire tangled with my own, a mass of green flame hovering between us. It felt impossible to reconcile what was happening in front of me, so I trusted Shay. As much as I wanted to scream with excitement, I sat in awe of her, the Magick of Bannock, as the bonding of our power created this magnificent exchange.

"There is only one authority to protect us, and that is virtue. I draw upon the goddess and our ancestors to build a barrier against the evil we do not see to protect all who are present." Her hands dropped to her knees, and as I moved mine, the flame remained, hovering in the space between us.

Shay poured another spoonful of herbs on the censer coal, and the cloud from the smoke cradled the orb.

"Fire, water, earth, air," I repeated the words after her. "Be in this ring, be in this life, be in us."

Her hands pressed to the ground alongside her thighs. As I moved mine, I saw a flash of images in the flame in front of my eyes. The depictions played through like an old movie. I saw Regina standing with Jacob, fighting side by side as if it was yesterday. I watched the Magick and Maker pairings of Sabine and Graison, Hebra and Gorath, and then I saw Kai. My heart raced at the sight of someone who looked so much like my own reflection. For the first time, I felt connected, known in a way that hurt my heart. The feeling was so overwhelming, I closed my eyes to stifle the visions.

"Stay with me, Wil." Shay's voice was a caress, a gentle hand leading me back.

"I'm here."

"These walls are called home, shelter. Build it up to keep us safe." Shay raised the grimoire. "I'm going to say all the next parts. You just need to focus on the magick in front of us."

"Okay," I said, doing my best to concentrate with all the energy moving between our bodies.

She opened a stubby hexagon-shaped bottle of red oil and set it in front of her. "It is as it has been," Shay began. "We are born from the water of a womb, and with our first breath, the fires of life ground us to the earth. My spirit is all elements in one." She extended her middle finger and dipped it in the oil. Her hand moved across the floor in front of her as she traced a five-pointed star. "Water." She said the word and dabbed a spot of oil on one of the star's points. "Air." She dabbed the next tip. "Fire." Dab. "Earth." Dab. Her finger stopped on the fifth and final point as she said, "Spirit."

The swirling flame in front of us moved higher until it almost touched the exposed rafter in the workshop. Shay opened a one-inch square drawstring bag and removed a piece of white cloth streaked with a rusty-colored stain. "By the blood of the Magick, I ask the goddess to protect all who balance the energies of life. For today and all of our tomorrows." She dropped the cloth on the floor and spooned another pile of herbs onto the censer coal.

My mouth was open, I knew it, but I couldn't stop myself from feeling awe for the woman in front of me. Her eyes were closed, and I wondered if she was still performing part of the ritual, but I didn't dare break the silence. Before I could take another breath, her glistening green eyes were staring at me, and she smiled.

"So mote it be," she whispered, and I repeated the same.

"So mote it be."

Shay transferred the saucers and containers from the circle back to the tray she'd carried them on. I sat still, watching her move around the workshop. When she returned to the circle, her knees came close to mine until they touched. She held her palms to me, and I pressed mine against hers.

"*Ignis.*"

Bright blue flames burst against my palm, and without saying a word, my orange flame mingled with hers. Magick between us was almost as satisfying as having Shay inside me. The erratic pounding of my heart matched the heaving of my chest as we sat together in silence. The smoke of the incense hovered in the air. I wanted to close my eyes and meditate on the words of the spell, but the glow from our hands and the hovering orb lit Shay, and she became a perfect manifestation of the Goddess of Fire.

She opened her eyes and smiled as she noticed my stare. We sat, palm to palm, until the candles were half to the floor. "You ready to go outside?" she asked, her voice a breathy whisper. I nodded and took hold of her outstretched hand.

We were careful as we stepped over the ring. Shay picked up the small jar of oil and slipped the sigil etched candle into a protective glass cylinder to carry it outside.

"Bring the black salt, please."

I picked up the container and took a quick double step to get in front of her and open our door.

Shay's sharp gasp was the exact response I was hoping for when she saw the fresh paint on the door. "You did this?" She held the candle flame up in front of the bright orange surface.

"It makes it easy to find." I winked at her. "I also wanted you to remember to be happy in our new home."

"I'm the happiest I've ever been in my entire life." One arm came round my shoulder as she kissed me. "This is so thoughtful."

"We're going to be happy here. I promise."

"I like the sound of that," she said before leaning inside to call the dog. "Dex!" The animal was at her side. "*Vigilant ad me.*" She whispered the watch command, and the dog's ears perked as he stayed close to her hip.

"For protection?" I asked as I patted his shoulder.

"Yep, he's going with us until we've completed the barriers."

I nodded. "So, what's next?"

"Windows and doors," she said as she set the candle under the threshold. She opened the jar of oil. "Dragon's blood oil." She held it up for me to see. "Powerful protection. I'm going to draw a pentacle in oil on every pane of glass on the ground floor."

I looked up at the second story. "What about those?" I asked.

"We'll do those on the inside of the glass." She dipped her middle finger into the oil and traced the lines, saying one word with each stroke. "Water, earth, fire, air, spirit. Deities of love and goodness protect us." Shay turned to me. "After I bless each window and door, I want you to make a line of black salt under it."

I thought about this step in our protection spell and wondered aloud, "Did you do this part when you buried the Gatekeeper?"

Shay turned to look at me. "No, I didn't know that we would attract this kind of evil when I did that spell."

We walked around the first floor of the building, marking each pane of glass and leaving lines across every opening of the carriage house. Dexter was on high alert, staying close to Shay's hip. Once we circled the building, I had only a handful of black salt remaining.

"There's not much left." I held the container up to show her.

Shay covered the jar of oil and stood in front of the bright orange door. She pressed her hand against it and closed her eyes. "It means so much that you did this." She bent down to pick up the candle.

"I have to confess. When you told me you sold the house, I wanted to take the door with us on that last day."

"You never said." She opened the door and waved Dexter inside.

"That door and what it meant for you…I just want you to feel that way when you're with me."

She pressed her hand on the center of my chest, pinning me to the frame of the door. Her lips crushed against mine, and my heart raced as I opened my mouth to deepen our kiss. My arms dropped to my thighs, and the container slapped my knee. I could smell the incense on her skin and decided I'd paint every door in our house if she'd kiss me like this for the rest of her life.

She pulled away, and I stood, eyelids heavy, with a ridiculous smile on my face.

"Thank you," she whispered against my lips.

"You're…welcome." I drew the words out to emphasize precisely how much she melted my heart.

"Come on, sweetheart. We've got more work to do." She hooked the collar of my shirt and dragged me inside. "Dexter, upstairs."

The dog jumped the risers to the second floor.

"What about the circle?" I pointed to the ring on the floor where the four candles were still burning.

"We'll come back down when we finish upstairs." Shay held the tray, and I carried my almost empty jar of black salt and the old candle. "I'm going to draw the pentagrams, and you can make the lines."

I stood at the top of the stairs. "What about securing the greenhouse?" I pointed to the oversized door suspended by antique metal wheels. "There's a lot of glass."

"I'm going to mark all the panes." Shay moved through the apartment, drawing pentagrams on the windows. "Check the apothecary cabinet in the magick room. There's another container of black salt on the countertop."

We went from room to room, marking the rest of the apartment with stars and lines of black salt, until we ended up on the rooftop in front of the greenhouse.

"Now what?" I asked.

"Now we lay a thick line of salt around the glass, and the carriage house protection is complete."

"That's it?"

We walked through the greenhouse, and Shay stopped to wash her hands in the mud sink.

"You need to fire up the forge and make a gauntlet." She held up her wrist to show me hers. "And I want to talk to Dani about protecting the bar. She should probably be there when we do it."

"Does she have protection around her home?" It hadn't occurred to me before this moment, but Dani and her wife were part of the magick, too.

"I've never asked about details, but knowing that she and Benton were patrolling the tunnels in the mine, I'm sure Benton protected them."

I thought for a moment about what Shay had just said. If Benton was the Magick, she could have protected the people she called family. What did it mean now that Benton was gone? "Does a spell end when the person who cast it dies?"

Shay was drying her hands on a towel and stopped in front of me. "Unfortunately, yes. Magick is not everlasting."

"I guess we need to go to the bar and talk to Dani and Amelia?"

Shay nodded. "We do, but first, you and I have one more thing to take care of." She tossed the towel on the table beside me.

"Oh, what's that?"

Her hand reached the slide on the greenhouse door. I heard the squeaking whistle of the old wheel rolling across the metal track. Shay's hand rested on my hip, and with a quick motion, her thumb flicked the button on the waist of my jeans.

Her voice was breathy against my throat. "Maybe just a little more magick?" I heard the slow tick—tick—tick of zipper teeth as her hand slipped inside my jeans.

"Oh, yeah. I like the way you think."

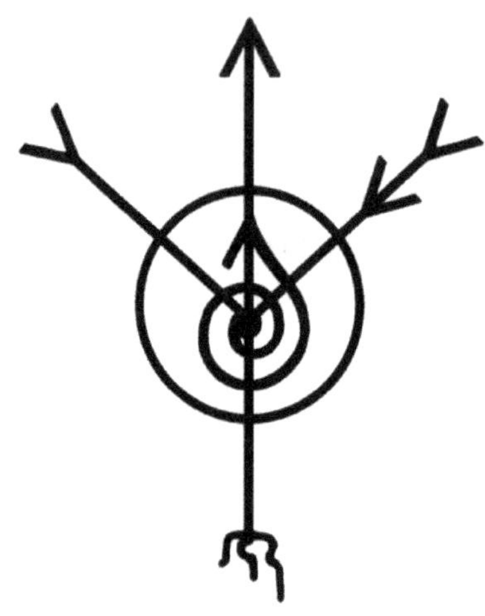

CHAPTER XIII

FLY

"Goddess, Shay. How do you do that to me?"

It wasn't a sincere question so much as a statement to the lover she was. I've never had sex on the floor of a greenhouse. Or on the table in a greenhouse. I've never wanted to do either of those before, but as Shay pulled on her shirt over her head, I wanted to do all of it again.

"I was a single witch for a long time, and I bottled up enough sexual energy to eclipse this whole town." She crawled over my outstretched legs. "I think it's you turning me inside out just as much."

"Baby, you've got me anytime you want me."

Her lips touched mine. "I like the sound of that." She fell back on her heels as she looked for something.

"Are you making me go back to work?" My hands flopped to my lap as Shay stopped to smile at me.

"We need to talk to Dani and take care of the cellar at the bar. There's too much history down there. It's important to keep it protected."

I knew she was right, but I also just wanted to stay naked with her for a few minutes longer. "Right now?" I did my best wide-eyed puppy dog pout. It had no effect on her.

She bounced to her feet. "Yes, right now."

I dangled her underwear from my finger, and she didn't flinch as she grabbed her jeans tucked behind the plant stand and pulled them over her legs. It was a cruel punishment to think about her like that for the rest of the day.

"So mean."

She held her hand out to me. "You're going to live."

"After all of that spell casting, I better." Our hands palmed together, and she tugged me to my feet and into her arms.

"I love you," she whispered against my lips.

"Your love is kinda hard to miss." The kiss was soft, lingering, and a promise that there would be more. "Oh, and I love you right back."

She stepped out of my arms and pulled the greenhouse door open. "Let's go." She patted my leg, and I realized I was still completely naked.

"Maybe I should put some clothes on?"

"That would be nice for all of us," I heard Stout yell from the kitchen, and suddenly, the last hour replayed in my mind.

"You can't be serious?" I grumbled. "Please tell me you weren't listening?" I punched my hands through the sleeves of my shirt and pulled it over my chest, grabbing the bundle of clothes that were my pants and socks.

"Dexter and I were downstairs watching the spell flames. Neither of us is interested in the overly abundant carnal exchanges that happen around here."

I shook my head. No part of me wanted to think about dragons or fairies when I was intimate with Shay. They were part of the household, and that would take some adjusting. I let the conversation end.

Shay was standing at the table in the kitchen. "What's the plan?" I asked as I kicked my foot through the leg of my pants.

She turned around and leaned against the table. "Your shirt is not only inside out," she said, tugging the tag with a playful half-grin, "but it's also on backward."

My pants were half dangling on one thigh. "Superhero, you are too much." I whipped the shirt off over my head, flipped it around and put it back on, hopped the other leg into my jeans, and zipped them. "Now that I'm properly dressed, what's next?"

"I'll call Dani." She hooked the sleeve of my shirt as she walked to the bathroom. "Have her meet us at the bar." Her fingers feathered across my chest, spinning me around to follow her.

It was difficult to concentrate. "What should I do? How can I help?"

"Two things," she said as she washed her hands. "We need to make more black salt, and we need to refill the container of dragon's blood oil."

I shrugged my shoulders, having no clue how to accomplish either task. "I'm not sure how helpful I'll be, but I'm in." My hip bumped against hers as I lathered the soap and ran my hands through the stream of water.

"It's not complicated, and everything is in the magick room." She dropped the towel over my shoulder. "Come with me."

I splashed two handfuls of water over my face, wiped them off with the towel, and followed her into the magick room.

Shay was half in the closet carrying out a metal pail. It didn't look heavy as she set it on the floor beside the table. "Incense and ritual ash."

"Is there a bucket of salt in there too?" I asked, mostly as a joke.

She was inside the closet again. "It's not in a bucket." She carried two gallon-sized glass jars of salt.

"How did I not see this?" I took one jar from her hand.

"You should sleep less." The wink, followed by a quirked half-grin, was a show of attitude that made me pause.

"Sneaky woman. I'll be on alert from now on."

I set the jar on the table, and she bumped my hip as she went to the apothecary wall for a few additional ingredients. This magick room was impressive, even to me. Shay's collection was almost as involved as the stash Benton had in the cellar at the bar. Jars and metal tins, bowls and blackened basins were tucked in between carefully tagged twigs and herbal sprigs. There were moments when the combination of aromas could overwhelm, but somehow, there was careful balance.

"It's probably a good idea to be on alert for many reasons."

I shook my head and watched as she pulled out the bottom draw on the cabinet. If anyone asked me to describe the black pot she took out, I would call it a cauldron. "Playing to stereotypes?" I flicked the metal tub with my fingertip. The cauldron was misshapen and had many dents from years of use.

"I am not. There are no bubbling brews in this." She set the pot on the table. "But this pot is big enough for what we are going to do."

"Explain, please."

I stood across from her and watched as she removed the covers on all the containers. Her hands, peppered with knife wound scars, were beautiful even without the power of magick moving through them. Her fingers flexed, muscular and slim, and I closed my eyes, thinking about them trailing across my soft belly. The contrast between her strength and tenderness wasn't lost. I enjoyed them both.

"Wildwood?" Her voice was loud, and she might have called my name more than once.

"Mmhmm?" I opened my eyes.

"You with me?"

I wasn't, and she knew it. "Sorry, just thinking."

"Yeah, I could see that. Focus, please."

"Right, focus. I can do that." I leaned closer. "Where were we?"

Her smile was reassuring "Pink sea salt." She passed the jar to me. "You're going to scoop this into the pot while I do the ash mix. We'll go slow. I do four handfuls, and you do one. Keep the salt over the pot and no spilling. We don't want to introduce chaos to the mix." She looked at me, and I tipped my head with an affirming nod.

"No spilling. Should I use a scoop instead?"

"No, just work over the pot," she said. "It's important to set the intention for protection while we work. Earth energy, okay?"

"Got it."

Shay set her ash bucket on the table and counted. We measured back and forth, four to one, until it satisfied Shay that we'd made enough of the mixture.

"That should be good." She opened another container, holding it up for me to see. "Black pepper and crushed coal." She answered my question before I could ask it, as she poured half of the container in her palm and sprinkled it across the top. "Now we mix." Her hands plunged deep, and she tipped her head, inviting me to help.

"Should we say something?"

Shay shook her head. "No, just think about the power of the earth and how it protects us. How it's always given us strength." Her hand brushed against mine as we continued to pull the salt from the bottom through the ash and pepper mix on the top. After a few minutes, Shay stopped.

"What now?" I asked.

"We just need to put the black salt into a storage container."

The jar was beside me, and I held it over the pot as Shay used both hands to transfer it. "What about the dragon's blood oil?" I asked. "Is the oil like the resin we used to bless the tools?"

She smiled at me. "Yes, the oils come from a palm tree, and I get it mailed from an adorable practitioner who owns an apothecary in the Middle East."

It surprised me to hear that she ordered her witchy goods. "Really?"

"The world is full of witches." She tipped the pot and emptied it.

"I know that," I said, with a hint of displeasure in my voice. "I just meant, I guess I didn't realize that you'd use things from outside the country."

"Some magicks are more powerful than others, and I have to reach out beyond our borders to get them. That's probably how Herne's Horn ended up at the bar." She carried the pot to the drawer, and I followed her with the bucket of ash. There was still plenty if we needed to make another batch of black salt. "I would imagine Herne's Horn comes from somewhere in England. I'm not sure."

I shook my head. "Do you think it'll take me ten years to know half of what you do?"

Shay let out a tiny laugh. "I'm still learning myself. There's no destination when it comes to understanding the power of magick."

It was impossible to feel less than adored when standing beside her. "You've got a solution for everything."

"Not everything, but self-deprecation doesn't serve either of us." She pulled out a five-inch square drawer and removed a jar. "You'll get there. Be patient with yourself."

"I'll try."

She held out her hand to me. "Put this and the salt in the backpack. I'll grab the grave soil and call Dani."

I thought about the time and that there would be people in the bar for lunch. "What about all the customers that are at Slammed this time of day?"

"We can use the back stairs."

She walked out of the room, and I followed her with the massive bottle of salt in one hand and a jar of oil in the other. Shay went to the closet in the bedroom and opened the trunk she'd made, filled with a temporary altar and magick supplies. She removed all the contents until she could pull out a soft piece of animal skin.

"What are you doing there?" I tucked the jar of black salt into the bend of my arm.

"The grimoire needs to be bound." She refilled the trunk and pushed it back into the closet.

"I'm not sure what that means," I said as she passed by me on her way to the kitchen table. I grabbed the backpack from the chair and set the salt and oil inside.

"This book of magick. It's powerful just sitting right here." I raised an eyebrow, questioning her explanation. "If this fell into the wrong hands, it could be dangerous, so I want to safeguard it when it's unprotected outside of the carriage house."

"Won't the backpack do that?" I asked, thinking Benton enchanted it to keep everything hidden.

"Benton's magick is fading. The charm over this bag won't last much longer." She began tracing a symbol over the swatch of leather. "I figure we have a few days, and then everything that Reg blessed will lose her magick."

"Do you know how she enchanted the backpack?" I asked.

Shay folded the edges of the leather until she covered the grimoire. She wrapped a thick stranded braid of cord around the bundle, cinched it tight, and waved the book in front of me. "I'm guessing the answers are in here. We can use the ancestry magick to keep us safe."

I felt my shoulders relax as Shay's confidence trickled over to me. "That's a relief."

"Yes," she said as she dropped the bundle inside the bag. "I'm just going to call Dani, and then we can go over to the bar." She pulled her cell phone from her pocket and walked toward the bedroom.

The apartment was quiet, and I took a moment to check on Dexter and Stout. The bottom of the backpack touched each stair as I stepped down, and I could hear one side of a curious conversation.

"You're not too big, and you'll learn how to do all of it," Stout said as he hovered near Dexter's nose. "You just need to get a good start, trust your magick, and science will do the rest." The fairy dropped in front of the dog and padded across the workshop floor without leaving the ground. His wings were curled down around his body, making them almost invisible. Dexter's ears perked up as he heard me enter the room.

"What's going on?" I asked and watched as Dex crossed his paws and dropped his head on top. Stout leaned against the dog, and it was obvious the two of them were downplaying their conversation.

"Nothing, really. We were just talking about—" Dexter snorted at the fairy and puffed him into a mid-air tumble. "Hey, fire-face. Knock it off!"

"Talking about what?" I asked, curious to know their big secret.

Stout flew closer to me, and Dexter chased after him, nipping in the air. "He's afraid." Dexter stretched his body, crouching into a feral stance as he growled at Stout. Shay walked in and caught the last seconds of the heated exchange.

"Dexter!" she yelled. The K-9's butt dropped to the floor, and he froze in place. "What the hell is going on?"

"Dexter is mad at Stout about something, and Dexter doesn't want me, or us, to know what it is." I rambled the explanation quickly to assuage the tone of Shay's voice.

"What the hell is the big secret?" She stared at the fairy hovering above us.

"He—" Stout began, then cut himself off.

Dexter didn't move as he transformed into his complete dragon shape. His jowls disappeared behind the shell-like beak, and his soft black and brown coat of fur rippled into impenetrable scales. His mouth opened to release a soul-splitting screech so loud I had to cover my ears.

"Dexter!" Shay yelled at him to stop, but the animal snapped at Stout.

The fairy flew up to the ceiling rafters to escape the raging animal. Shay stood between me and her dragon until he met her stare. She was fearless, and I wasn't sure how she put her entire flesh and bone body in front of the transformed beast. I couldn't see the beautiful German Shepherd any longer.

"Stout! Come down here and tell me what's going on." She tugged Dexter's neck, guiding his face down to hers. Her hand caressed the space between his eyes. "You, behave!" She booped the dragon on his nose. I stayed behind Shay, watching the mystery of the secret conversation unfold.

"He says he'll eat me if I tell you." Stout didn't come down from the ceiling.

Shay yelled at Dexter. "Transform, right now!" He shook his body as if he was whipping water from his fur, and I watched as the gentle-eyed dog returned. "Now, tell me!" Shay yelled up at the fairy. "And come down here. I'm tired of this ridiculous volley between the two of you."

Stout drifted down and landed on my forearm. "You won't let him eat me?" The squeak in the fairy's voice was the first sign of genuine fear I'd heard from him. He honestly believed our boy would eat him.

"I won't let him eat you," I said.

Shay dropped to a knee in front of Dexter and hugged him around the neck. "It's okay, buddy. Let Stout tell me." There was a pitiful whimper, and the furry animal flopped to the floor in surrender.

"What's the big secret?" Shay asked, this time with a tone that didn't disguise her irritation.

"He can't fly, and he doesn't know how to control his shifting." Stout blurted and flew up to the ceiling. Dexter didn't raise his head, but a smoky puff of defeat snorted from his nose.

Shay turned to look at me, and I shrugged. "What do you mean, he can't fly? And he's done pretty good shifting us when he needs to," she said.

"He's—" The growling made the fairy pause.

"Dex!" Shay's fingers tangled in the thick hair around his collar.

"He's afraid."

Shay fell over the top of her dog, snuggling him. She whispered into his ear, something I couldn't hear. I didn't want to ask, but I needed to know. "I guess I understand that shifting us might be hard; it *is* a little disorienting. But how can he be afraid to fly?"

Stout flew down to the floor in front of us. "He just is. I've tried to explain it to him, but he won't even try."

"It's okay, buddy." Shay sat up and pulled the massive animal across her lap. "I don't care if you never fly. And we can practice shifting until it feels right."

The beings in front of me stretched the boundaries of reality. My fearless girlfriend was holding tight to a dragon-dog, the same dog who couldn't control his power to shift and was afraid to fly, while a tiny fairy creature effortlessly zipped and hovered in front of her. I gave myself a slight pinch as a reality check and had mixed feelings when I felt the sting on my arm.

"I get we know little about dragon aviation," I said, "but once he can control shifting us wherever he wants, does he really need to fly?"

Stout landed on the floor beside Shay. "She's got a good point, fire-face." He hesitated to get closer to Dexter.

"Yes, she does." Shay lifted the dog's head to look into his eyes. "You hear that? We don't care if you can't fly." She smashed her face against the side of his snout. "We don't care, Dex." The cell phone buzzed in Shay's pocket, and she twisted to retrieve it. "Pierce," she answered. I couldn't hear the conversation on the other end, so I waited. Shay pushed off the floor. "Yep, we're on our way. We just had to take care of something." More muffled sounds and then Shay laughed. "Our pants are on. Jeez, give me a break, D. We'll be right there."

"Dani?" I asked as she ended the call.

"Yes, she's at the bar. Said it's pretty quiet." She pointed to the backpack. "You ready to get some magick on?"

I threw the bag over my shoulder. "Yes, I think I am."

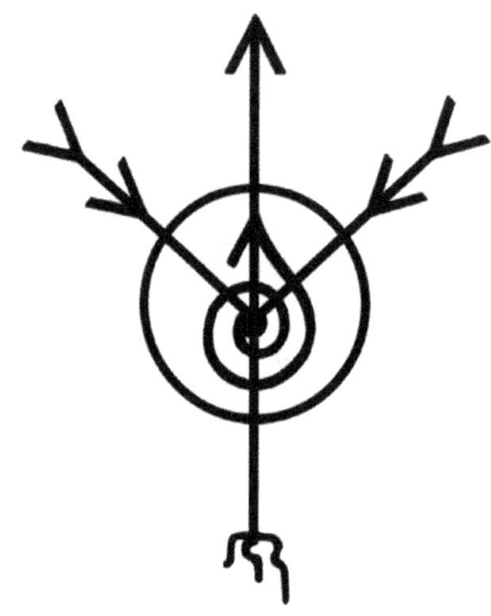

CHAPTER XIV

AUTHENTICITY

We drove again, taking the patrol car the few short blocks to the bar. Dani was waiting outside, much like she'd been the day before.

"Sorry, you had to wait," Shay said, pulling the car up beside her. Shay hit the trunk release, and I walked around to grab the backpack, letting Dexter loose from the back seat.

"It's not a big deal," Dani assured her. "I could have gone in, but I thought it would be better if we all went together. Keep a low profile and all." Dani unlocked the back door, and we all followed her inside. The steel shelves sat packed with cases of liquor.

"Restocked the shelves?" Shay asked.

"Amelia and Diana have been taking care of business. Amelia will be here later. She might be a little too excited about the bar."

"Really?" She and Dani wedged their hands in the wall to pull the hidden door open.

"Yep, I'm pretty sure she and Diana are going to split the workload to keep this place on track."

I let out a sigh of relief, a little louder than I'd intended. "That's fantastic to hear," I said.

"Yes, I couldn't agree more." Dani laughed as she walked through the doorway and down the stairs. Dexter and Stout followed her, and I helped Shay pull the door behind us.

"I didn't mean to imply—"

Shay tapped her fingers against my mouth. "It's fine, love. None of us are ready to retire and pour beer all day."

I kissed her fingertips. "I'm really glad." We descended the stairs together, hand in hand.

"So, what's the plan?" Dani asked as she turned a chair over to sit.

"Wildwood and I just put a barrier of protection around the carriage house."

"I thought you already had one?" Dani asked.

"Something came after her last night," Shay explained as she unpacked the bag. "Somehow, they know about the hammer, and they're coming for it."

"Yes, I suppose they would. According to dad's journals, the powers of evil have been trying to possess that damn thing for hundreds of years." Dani leaned her forearms against the table in front of her. She knew more about Brigid's hammer than she was willing to share, and I wondered why she was holding back from us and, more specifically, from Shay.

I hesitated for a second, wondering if I had the right to interrogate our friend, but last night was terrifying, and secrets kept meant trouble for all of us. "What do you know about the hammer?" I blurted the question.

Dani took a quick breath, and I wondered if her reaction was frustration or disappointment. "I know my father was obsessed over the damn thing." She picked at the splintered wood of the tabletop. "His desire to find it possessed him like a drug."

I didn't understand why Jacob had never found it. I'd only had the Maker's power for a short time before hearing Brigid's call, but I understood the uncontrollable thirst to find it. That compulsion forced me to the mine, drawing me toward the unknown dangers buried in the dark.

"Why did you and Benton patrol the tunnels?" I asked, deciding that I needed answers.

"There's a lot of nasty stuff down there." Dani's definition of stuff was intentionally vague, and I wasn't sure if I appreciated the ambiguity.

"Stuff?" I raised a questioning brow.

"You've crossed the salt lines in the switchbacks. The Gatekeepers aren't the only things breeding in the tunnels."

"Why don't you just blow up the mine and kill all of those bastards?" It seemed like an obvious solution. Without an easy entry, there wouldn't be a clear exit.

"Explosives won't stop them from coming." The look in Dani's eyes was an obvious message, a solemn statement that was also chilling.

I pulled the hammer from the backpack I was carrying. "It's all about this, isn't it?" I set Brigid's Hammer on the table.

Dani stepped closer, her finger hovering over the head of the hammer. "This damned thing has damaged a lot of lives." She pulled her hand away and shoved it in her front pants pocket.

Shay unpacked the elements of the spell. "Do you want to talk about what happened?"

"To me?" Dani asked as she returned to her chair. "I lost my mother because of that thing, and then I lost my father because Mom was gone."

"But you were a baby when your mother died." I thought about the few things I knew about Dani's past. Was her life without a mother similar to mine? Living with the loss because of murder was a separate pain. "As I said before," Dani explained, "Dad was obsessed with finding Brigid's hammer. He was a blacksmith, kinda average when I see what you can do, Wildwood." I held up a hand to protest, but Dani kept talking.

"Don't worry. It's not an insult to Dad. He just never trusted the power of the goddess."

"Didn't Benton help? The Magick and the Maker are supposed to balance each other," Shay insisted.

"The struggles between Regina and my father were always a barrier."

I reached to take Shay's hand, grounding myself in the power she carried, unable to imagine fighting the magick between us. Our connection to the Goddess was more than a mystical duty; it was a covenant beyond the physical and greater than the spiritual.

"Dad couldn't stop researching Brigid. You've seen the notebooks. But I never understood why commanding the force of nature in that hammer overpowered everything. And don't forget my mother. I'm pretty sure she interfered, and that's what got her killed."

"Did anyone ever get close to finding the hammer?" I asked.

Dani stood up and flipped her chair around. She straddled the seat and rested her forearms against the curved back. "No one could find a trace of it." She flicked her thumb to point at me. "Until you."

My breath hitched in response to Dani's words. The search for the Hammer of the Goddess had taken me less than a day. The call had possessed me, summoning me in a way that was impossible to fight, the pull almost crippling. I can't imagine searching for a lifetime and never touching it. I felt guilty for finding it in such a short time. "What makes me so special?"

"I don't know." Dani's voice broke, and I saw the glaze of tears in her eyes.

"And your mother?" Shay asked. "She died in the old courthouse. Why was she there?"

"You've seen the report." Dani ran her fingers through her hair. "There was only one reason for her to be there, and no cop in Bannock would ever write it down."

"Was she trying to invoke the power of Brigid's wall in the basement?" Shay asked.

I felt like the odd person in the room, eavesdropping on a private conversation, and I could tell that Dani had a guess about her mother's decisions and the fate of her misguided visit to the old courthouse. Why would she want to interfere with the power of the Maker?

"I'm not sure anybody knew what my mother was doing except for the person who killed her." She brushed a tear from her cheek with the heel of her hand. "We may never have answers because of the way the crime scene was investigated."

"Hey, I'm sorry." Shay rubbed Dani's back and hugged her from behind. "I didn't mean to stir up so many old memories."

"I don't talk about my family much, you know. I haven't thought about my dad in a long time, and I like to believe everything would have been different if mom had been around."

"Why do you say that?" I asked.

"I guess, maybe I just hoped that her love would have come with fewer conditions than his did, and maybe she would have supported me. I like to tell myself that, anyway."

I didn't know how to relate to the concept of a mother's unconditional love. I had substitute people who had acted as mentors, but I never knew what it was like to be held by a woman with biological ties. My heart missed that connection, and on occasions like this, my head did, too. That ache to be known was an emotion I understood.

"You're talking about coming out?" Shay pulled up a chair and sat beside Dani, admitting, "I don't have a coming out story."

"I don't have one either," I added. "I never had an adult who cared enough."

"I have a story." Dani's eyes glazed as she remembered. She leaned forward to rest her cheek on the backside of her hands. After a slow, deep breath, she began. "I always had this disconnect." She stared into the space of the room, eyes unfocused as she shared. "There were all of these parts of myself that felt jammed inside the wrong space. I didn't know how to explain it when I was five or six. I just felt it." She pushed off the back of the chair and walked toward the table of weapons.

"When I was sixteen, I met Amelia. She came to Bannock looking for a wild adventure. She'd read some crazy story about walking across the country and decided she was going to do that before adulthood grabbed ahold of her." Dani's eyes twinkled with happiness at the mention of her wife. "You've met her. Adulthood hasn't gotten her yet."

Shay smiled. "I like that about your wife."

"So do I," Dani added with a smile. "Melia walked into this town, and the day we met…the attraction was instant. Well, at least, it was for me. The first few months she was here, she moved into our family cabin. Without Dad's permission, of course. I went out there one afternoon and found her asleep in the loft. I almost had a heart attack, but she was so apologetic and adorable. We sat together the entire day just talking." Dani pulled out a short sword and picked at the pummel of the handle. "I fell in love with her. It was immediate. It was impossible not to."

"She's a wonderful person," Shay said as she walked to stand beside me and hold my hand. "I've always envied your marriage."

"Thanks, I guess." Dani twirled the handle of the sword, sweeping it from hip to hip. "Amelia was my best friend first, and then she was my only friend."

"Because you're gay?" I asked.

"That wasn't a problem in the beginning." She dragged the sheathed sword tip through the dirt on the floor. "Here's what you don't know." She stabbed the sword into the pile and pulled out a dagger. Dani paused for a long moment. "When I turned nineteen, I told Amelia a secret I'd never shared with anyone. I don't think I'd actually said the words out loud before that day, but I knew when the words were out there, it would either end us or connect us for the rest of our lives."

Countless ideas raced through my mind as Dani paced the room. Was she sick or abused by a hurtful father? Was she somehow involved in a terrible crime? She needed to pick up the pace in her storytelling.

"It was the late nineties. The world was very different and —"

"D, if it's too hard, she doesn't need to know," Shay interrupted.

"Nah, it's about time I shared this, Pierce." She straddled across the chair. "When I met Amelia, I could finally be myself."

Dani walked to the apothecary wall and removed two containers from the shelf. I couldn't see what she was doing, but she set the cans on the table a moment later. "You see these canisters?" she asked, directing the question at me. I nodded. "Read the labels."

I was glad that Shay had already translated these two. "This one is garlic." I held it up. "And this is lavender." I raised it for Shay to see.

"Open the first one," Dani instructed, and I twisted the cover off. The second it opened, I knew the contents did not match the title scribed on the side. It was delicate and aromatic, soothing, and reminiscent of love–nothing like the pungent scent I was expecting.

"This has the wrong label," I said as I reached for the second container. "The outside doesn't match the inside." My explanation seemed simple.

Dani didn't say another word as she waited for me to take in what I'd just said. *The outside doesn't match the inside.* I repeated it in my head until I realized what she was saying. Danielle Forrest explained that her nineteen-year-old outside hadn't matched her nineteen-year-old inside. My friend is transgender. I smiled at her, and she knew I understood.

Dani continued. "I didn't have anyone until I had Amelia, and when I told her I'm a woman, she didn't even flinch. She didn't question, and she never faltered, not for a single second. She just held me, and honestly, she's never let me go."

I wasn't sure what Dani expected, but for me, nothing had changed. "Thanks for trusting me with your truth," I said.

"Hey." Shay wrapped her arms around her friend. "I love you, D. I love you just exactly as you are."

Dani stepped back. "I'm thankful for that. It's just the people in this town. They come and go. At one time, the population was less than sixty-five, with only a few of the founding families left, so the story didn't need to be shared any longer, and I was safe to be just myself."

The thought of a young Dani suffering without her dad made me angry, and knowing that he would break the bond with Benton because he couldn't love his daughter made me vengeful. "But your father?" I asked.

"My father was—complicated, and his love had so many conditions that they almost killed me. He rarely acknowledged me after Amelia and I married. He sent me away every time I went to talk with him." Dani's words were so quiet I would have thought I imagined them.

"And Reggie became your family," Shay said. "She stood beside you."

Dani's forehead fell against the back of her hands, and her shoulders shook from the tears that came. Shay pulled her into her arms, and I couldn't help but hope that love could comfort our friend.

Dani looked up at Shay. "Reggie helped us when Dad kicked me out."

"When you said she chose you over the Magick and Maker bond, you meant it literally," I said as Shay leaned back against the table.

"My father forbade any communication, and I asked Reg to be there with us when we told him. I had hoped that the bond of their friendship would make it easier for him to understand."

"But that wasn't the case, was it?" I asked, keeping my distance so that Dani felt safe with Shay.

"I think it made it worse. My father felt betrayed by all three of us, like it had anything to do with him. He said some pretty vile things and threw Amelia and me out." My heart was breaking for our friend. Watching her tell the story of ultimate rejection was just another hidden scar on her soul. "Reggie tried to change his mind every time she saw him, and then one day, he just stopped coming into town. He lived in that damn cabin and hunted those caves."

"Do you think he knew what breaking the bond would do?" Shay asked.

"He didn't care. After that conversation, he became a monster ten times worse than any demon that ever crawled from the mine."

"But you stayed in Bannock? Why?" I asked, curious to understand how a wanderer like Amelia would settle in a demon-infested town.

"We stayed because of Mom, because I wanted to know why she died."

Shay grabbed hold of Dani's shoulders and pulled their bodies closer. "Maybe we can help you with that. Maybe the Maker and Magick powers can help us find the person who killed her, and we can bring you the closure you've been looking for."

"Maybe." She didn't sound very hopeful. "There are no witnesses. They didn't collect any biological evidence. Her body was cremated, and after so much time has passed, I'm not sure where to look."

"How about we tackle one thing at a time?" Shay asked, walking back to the table. "When we finish here, we should look through those boxes. Perhaps Benton knew more than she could share. Hiding the truth of her Magick powers would have had to come first, but obviously, there was more."

"You think she was protecting me?" Dani asked as she studied the jars on the table.

"It wouldn't be the first time, would it?" Shay wrapped an arm around Dani's shoulder, giving her a tight side hug.

"I guess not." Dani stood in front of the table, picking up the massive jar of black salt. She pushed the bundle of leather. "What ya got here?" Her hand pulled away fast, as if she'd touched an electrified fence.

"It's Benton's grimoire," Shay answered.

"You protected it?" Dani blew on her hand as she shook it. "That's very good."

I found it interesting that we'd protected the bundled tome even from Dani. We trusted her as family, but the spell had prevented her from touching it. Why?

"What did you feel just then?" I asked.

"She felt the safeguard of the Magick and the Maker. We're going to call Amelia when we are ready to perform the spell. All four of us should be here when we invoke the powers so that the cellar is accessible to all of us in the future. I brought these, too."

Shay removed four stones from the side pocket of the bag. They were shiny, black, and glass-like, with flecks of silvery-white inside that shimmered as they caught the overhead light.

Dani smiled when she saw the stones, and I was excited about enjoying the expertise of her rock hunting experience. "Black tourmaline. We're going hardcore."

Shay smiled. "We don't have time to play anymore, and since Wildwood's magicks are young, we need all the power we can get."

"What's black tourmaline?" I asked.

Stout flew down from the apothecary. "It's a rock."

The sound of his voice mingled with the flipping and flapping of his wings made me jump, and I yelled. "No, shit!" I shook my head. "I meant, why are we using black tourmaline?"

"Why didn't you just ask that?" Stout hovered over the stones.

"Why don't you let me explain, Stout?" Dani interrupted just before I could slap the fairy across the room.

"Would you, please?" Shay encouraged as she moved the backpack to the floor. She snapped the altar cloth in the air, guiding the fabric as it floated to the tabletop.

"Does it really matter?" Stout said. "It's a rock from under the ground, and it's formed like every other rock. Lots of pressure and crystallization." He hovered in front of Dani. "How'd I do?"

"You didn't do well at all," Dani said as she picked up the stones. "What you need to know, Wildwood, is that the stones will protect us, and they'll repel many levels of evil. Amelia wears a piece pinned in her bra, and I've got a piece on right now." She tugged at the collar of her t-shirt to show me the little black gemstone around her neck.

"D, when is Amelia coming?" Shay asked, as she opened the jar of salt.

Dani looked at her watch. "She'll be here soon. I'll call her and tell her to use the back entrance."

"Don't bother." We turned to see Amelia coming down the spiraling stairs. "I'm here, and you've got me for half an hour."

Dani walked to the stairs to meet her wife. Just before hitting the bottom step, they were eye to eye. Amelia rested her hand on Dani's cheek. "Oh, my love, you've been crying?"

Dani's head fell against her wife's palm, and they whispered words between them. I didn't turn away, captivated by the intimate exchange and wondering how long it would take for Shay to just look at me and know what I was feeling. Love–deep, pure, soulful, connecting love–is a wonderful thing.

Dani put her arms around her wife and turned the two of them until they faced the center of the room. "Hello, everyone. I understand we've got some magick to do?" Amelia's voice was delicate and carried a sense of calm so delightful that I was happy she was here.

"Hi, Amelia." Shay hugged her tight. "I'm almost set up. What would you like to do?"

Amelia surveyed all the elements on the table, her fingertips hovering but not touching, as if she was running through a mental checklist. "Where's your spell?" she asked.

Shay waved her hand over the grimoire laid open on the table. "Stout and I put this together." She thumbed to the page and wedged a stone in the book's gutter. The loose page lay to the left of the spell book.

"This is very good," Amelia said. "Did you already protect the carriage house?" Shay nodded. "Great, let's roll with this." She didn't waste one moment as she bossed us around. "Danielle, why don't you do the candles? And Wildwood? You'll do the salt lines." She held up the jar to me. "You know what to do?"

I nodded. "All the doorways and windows."

Amelia's smile was almost as big as Shay's. "Very good."

She sidestepped, giving Shay the space in front of the book on the table. Shay picked up the sigil candle and blew a flame across the wick. I was still in awe of her candle magick, but it didn't seem to faze our friends. She lit the incense censer and spooned her herb blend over the top until smoke hovered above the table.

"Goodness is the source of us." Shay held up her hands and clapped them together; the *ignis* flame burst in her palms.

I tugged off my gloves and stepped close enough to mirror the action. We repeated every step from the carriage house spell, floating the green orb, creating a ring, setting candles, and marking every access point in the entire cellar. Shay placed all the grave soil pouches behind the secret metal door above the forge, adding Benton's soil to the mix. When she returned to the table, the only thing left for us was to bless our black tourmaline amulets.

Dani removed the necklace she wore, and Amelia unclipped hers. They laid them on the table, and Shay motioned for them to place each in their own small silver bowls. She poured water on the stones and pinched a sprinkle of salt over the top.

"There is only one power to protect us, and that is goodness. I draw upon the goddess and her ancestors to build a barrier against the evil we do not understand." Shay's voice was calm, asking in a way that left no question that a magickal exchange was happening. "Fire, water, earth, air. Be in this stone, be in this life, be in us." She passed each silver bowl through the flaming orb, and I watched as the water boiled but had no effect on Shay's hands.

"It is as it has been," Shay began. "We are born from the water of the womb, and with our first breath, the fire of life grounds us to the earth. My spirit is all elements in one." She extended her middle finger and dipped it in the oil. Her hand moved to touch each stone. "Water. Air. Fire. Earth. Spirit." Her finger stayed on each stone as she repeated the chant four times.

Shay tore four pieces of a white cloth streaked with a rust-colored stain. "By the blood of the Magick, I call on the goddess to protect all who balance the energies of life." She dropped one piece of cloth over the top of each bowl and held them in the orb until the flame burned them away.

"So mote it be," she said, and the rest of us repeated the same. Shay stepped back from the spell book, and the orb fell like ash over the table.

Amelia was the first to take her bowl. "That was beautiful, sweetie."

"Thank you." Shay picked up a silver bowl and removed the stone inside. I waited for someone to give me instructions.

Shay smiled. "That one is yours, Wil. We won't touch it because its protection is pure, and once you hold the stone in your hand, it's merged with you."

"How should I wear it?" I asked, feeling the warmth that lingered from Shay's magick.

"That's really up to you," Amelia said as she tucked hers back inside her brassiere.

I smiled at her action. Wearing anything that restricted movement felt uncomfortable, so I almost never wore a bra. I didn't wear jewelry like Dani, but I might just have a solution. "Since half the time I'm not wearing one of those…" I motioned at Amelia's shoulder strap. "I'll mount it on my wrist cuff after I forge it."

"That sounds like a great idea. Maybe you can add it to mine." Shay raised her wrist. "Help me mark the windows," she said to her friends, and we each took one of the four panes of glass.

Amelia leveraged herself on the small ladder beside the table of weapons. As she climbed down, she grabbed hold of a carved piece of wood. "This is beautiful." Gripping it in her left hand, she turned it over to reveal a scorched circle.

"What is it?" I asked as I stepped closer to the contoured piece of wood.

"It's an archery riser." She passed it to me.

"That doesn't really answer my question." My palm fit into the curves as my thumb wrapped around the grip, and I noticed threaded bolts attached to each end. "A riser for…?"

Amelia's smile was brilliant as it crinkled the corners of her eyes and sent an excited glow to her cheeks. "It's the grip for a takedown bow."

"A bow? Like a bow and arrow, bow?" It made little sense that a bow, or part of one, would be in the cellar with an apothecary and a forge. "Why would this be in here?" I handed it back to Amelia.

"A few parts are missing; most important would be the upper and lower limbs and a string to draw it together. My best guess is that someone was going to make them in that forge." She pointed the handle toward the abandoned blacksmith setup.

"I don't shoot a bow. You shoot?" I asked Shay. She shook her head no, and I glanced at Amelia and her wife. "Either of you?"

Dani pointed toward Amelia. "She does, and she's an excellent shot."

"I can hit a target." The ridiculous modesty was endearing, and if her skills were comparable to Dani's with a gun, I was sure she was beyond capable.

"I'll research a takedown bow and rebuild this if you're willing to test it?" I said.

Amelia smiled. And that was the answer I needed. "It looks like you've just added more work to your to-do list," Amelia said as she turned to her wife. "Are you coming up to help me?"

"To be your bar bitch?" Dani joked as she kissed her.

"You're hired." Amelia turned to leave. "Come up and have a beer when you're done down here."

Stout flew close to her shoulder. "I'm going up now." He raced to the top of the staircase, and I could hear the buzzing of his wings until Dani and Amelia made it to the top. A few seconds later, Shay and I were standing together in front of the burning candles.

I wrapped my arms around Shay's waist. "You smell so good."

"Do I?" She was teasing me, and I liked it more than I wanted to admit.

"Every time I watch you do magick, I just want to hold you, be close to you, and never let you go."

"I think I like how that sounds." Shay touched her lips to mine.

I pulled away. "Yeah?"

"Oh, yeah."

I had a lot of feelings about what had happened between all of us. Magick had a way of opening the mind and making the unattainable seem possible. Amelia and Dani's love felt like the ideal, a relationship goal I dreamed of having with Shay. From the outside, I saw the now, the playful joy of their lifetime together, but it hadn't always been so, and I wondered how Shay felt about the information Dani had just shared. She tugged at the loop on my pants before stepping away.

"Did you know about Dani?" I asked as Shay began packing the altar supplies.

Her hands stopped moving, and she looked up at me. "I did."

"Did it bother you when she came out?" I'd only known Dani for a few short months. Shay had been her friend for close to ten years.

"Bother me?" Her eyebrow raised. "Why would it bother me?" She picked up the bottles and put them into the bag.

"I don't think it should, but that's just me. I'm a 'you be you, love is love' kind of human." I folded the altar cloth she handed to me.

"D and I spend a lot of time together. We've talked about almost everything." Shay's hands hovered over the drawstring of the backpack. "She knows about Andi, about the attack."

I ran my finger across the longest scar on the back of Shay's hand. "But not about the scars on your chest?"

"After the attack in the tunnels, she knows everything now."

"How did she react?" I asked.

"Dani didn't, really. She knew some details because of my hands, and she put two and two together. She asked me what happened, and I explained the story."

"You never told me that you talked about it."

"It wasn't a big deal. We talk about a lot of things at work."

"Do you talk about me?"

Shay smiled. "Probably more than I should."

Giving a wink, she grabbed my hand and pulled me up the stairs.

CHAPTER XV

METAMORPHASIS

We sat in the bar long enough for Amelia to stuff our bellies and for Stout to drink his fill. I was anxious about going out onto the streets of Bannock, and when it was time to leave, I was glad we didn't have to walk in the dark. I wondered how long my anxiety might last. The attack had brought up plenty of thoughts —what I should wear when I was alone was one; tying my boots and carrying some kind of weapon was another. I looked in the back seat, staring at the dog and his fairy friend. They were there for me last night, mostly.

"You're awfully quiet," Shay mused as she reached to hold my hand.

"I was just thinking about last night and that damn demon." I rolled my hand over so she could hold it.

"The nightmares are going to take some time to fade." Shay pulled into the parking lot of the carriage house. "Be patient with yourself and remember: you fought back and won."

"It isn't even that. I just don't understand why Dexter didn't sense them. Why didn't he shift you to get to me sooner?"

"He's afraid of those powers, so maybe that's the hesitation," Shay said as she put the car into park. "Or maybe the connection between the two of you isn't as strong as it is with me?"

"I wish we could just talk to him without our fairy interpreter."

"He said that the demons were hidden." Stout gripped the metal partition dividing the squad car's front seats from the back.

"They were what?" Shay's head whipped around to look at Dexter and Stout.

"He said that he couldn't sense them. That someone cast a shadow over the demons so we couldn't sense their attack."

"Is that even a thing?" I asked. "Can someone put up a barrier to get through? To get to me?"

"Not after what we just did." Shay was confident in her reply. "Nothing is foolproof, but I don't know anyone around here with that kind of magick."

"You said any*one*. What about any*thing*?" The word lingered on my lips. Everyone in the car knew that Bannock had many non-human beings flying and crawling around.

"Like I said, nothing is foolproof." Shay hit the button to release the trunk, and I walked around the car to grab the backpack as Shay let the passengers out of the vehicle.

I shoved my hand in my pocket and felt for the black tourmaline gem inside. If this stone added strength to my protective barrier, it might be time to make sure it fit somewhere on my body. "I think I want to work on the gauntlet tonight."

Shay rolled her wrist over to check her watch. "It's getting kinda late."

"It won't be the first time I've worked on a project through the night," I said as I pushed the orange door open, waiting as Dexter and Stout went inside.

Shay stood for a moment, staring at the bright orange door of our home. "It means so much that you would do this. It makes me feel seen and loved."

I leaned against the exterior rock wall of the carriage house. "I'm glad that you see it that way, because I want you to feel happy when you're here and when we're together."

"I do." She wiped her eye with the back of her sleeve.

"Are you crying?"

"I think I'm just processing all my emotions from the last few days." Shay's palm pressed against the surface of the door. "Sometimes, it feels like your love is more than I deserve. Like it's impossible that—"

I wrapped my arms around her. "My heart was waiting for you. It's just that simple."

"Simple." Shay laughed. "You make it seem that way."

"Good. That's all that matters." I kept a close hold on her as we stepped together into the building, and I pressed a kiss to the back of her neck. "Will you sit with me while I work?"

"Of course, I will." She turned in my arms. "I love watching you at the forge."

I couldn't hide the smile on my face, and I didn't want to. "It makes me very happy to hear that." The backpack dropped from my shoulder to the table. "I'll fire up the forge, and we can get to work." I opened the bag and removed my hammer, unsure why I'd brought it to the bar because we'd had no plans to use it. Some part of me hadn't wanted to leave it at the carriage house. It wasn't a human entity, but something about it felt alive.

"I'll run this up to the magick room and be right back," Shay said as she threw the strap of the backpack over her shoulder.

While she was gone, I walked through the open space of the workshop. Even with the complications of demon hunting, I loved my life as a blacksmith. My hand brushed the face of the anvil, something I'd done hundreds of times before, but now, it was different. I felt Brigid's energy in and around me. The earth song I'd heard in my head as a child played louder now in my heart, and the workshop walls held a life force calling me to the forge. I slid my office door open, ready to sort through the stack of Benton's metal. I wanted the material, just like the class-four demon steel I used for Shay's wrist cuff.

The valve on the propane tank opened with a simple spin of my fingers—a well-practiced maneuver–and I sparked the ignitor at the mouth of the forge, listening to the sweet song of fire coming to life. "Safety first," I said to no one as I fastened the apron around my neck, but I paused before putting on my protective glasses because I felt her presence. Shay stood, stopped at the bottom of the stairs, her arms stretched over her head as she flexed her shoulders with a fingertip hold of the doorway. She knew exactly what she was doing, and I made the short walk to grab her around the waist.

"You ready to watch me work?" I asked, turning the two of us around. She slid down the length of my torso until we were face to face.

Gripping the back of my neck, she kissed me with her warm lips. I was so lost in her touch, my eyes remained closed for several seconds after she pulled away.

"I am so ready," she said with a whiskey-soaked, honey-sweet tone, and I squeezed her tight before letting go.

My fingers traced along the back of her bicep and danced down toward her hand. "I picked a piece of class-four that I hope will behave like yours." I tapped her wrist cuff and noticed she had a gallon sized jar in her hand. "What's that?"

"I had a thought..." Shay began as she held it between us. The contents wiggled like gelatin.

"You usually have excellent thoughts." I winked at her.

She grinned, and tapped my nose. "Damn, you're cute. Stop distracting me, though."

"Please, continue." I made a zipper motion across my lips, showing that I would keep my mouth shut.

"This is a sample of embryos I've been collecting from the tunnels. You want to try an experiment?" She waved the bottle in front of us with a tick-tock pendulum motion.

Experimentation was a major part of blacksmithing, especially demon blacksmithing. "You want to see if it turns into forgeable material?" I asked.

She nodded, and the electrified reflection in her eyes was the only answer I needed. I opened the cabinet in the workshop's corner and pulled out a small graphite casting crucible.

"What's that?" Shay asked.

"It's a basin made from graphite. It can handle the high heats used to turn solid metals into liquid. That's what we're going to do. Give me the jar." She passed it to me, and I twisted the cover off. Even though it was an arm's length away, the smell was overwhelming, and I fought my reflex to gag. "This smells like death." I popped the cover over the top.

"I should have warned you." Shay took the jar from my hand.

I nodded. "Uh, yeah, that would have been nice." I walked to the cabinet to put on my respirator and gave Shay a less sophisticated face mask. With our faces covered, the smell was undetectable when I uncapped the container again. I dumped all the embryo material into the crucible and set it in the forge to heat.

"What now?" Shay asked, her voice muffled by the mask.

"We wait, and we watch." I spoke loud so she could hear me, crossing my arms as I rested against the anvil while Shay stood looking over my shoulder.

She took a deep breath, lifted her mask, and whispered in my ear. "What are we watching for?" The warmth of her breath tickled my skin.

"One of two things," I explained. "The samples are either going to get very hard or really soft."

Shay's eyebrow raised in a question. "What do you mean?"

"The embryos are fleshy, and part of me thinks we're going to get a molten reaction."

"Like lava?"

"A little bit, but not so destructive, I hope."

"If it doesn't become molten, it'll be solid like the other demon steel?" Shay paid attention to the details of the forge. Since the first time I'd accidentally transformed demon horn to a forgeable material, she'd been interested in the blacksmithing part of my life.

"I put it in the crucible because I'm pretty sure we're going to get liquified demon embryo." The material was already breaking down, puckering and bubbling like liquid lava. I tilted the long handle so Shay could see the transformation. "Yep, there we go."

"What can we do with liquified demon embryos?" Shay asked.

"We cast it."

Her question was smart, inquisitive, if you'd never smelted metal before. I removed my mask, hesitant to take the first breath, but delighted to discover that the smell was gone. The idea of casting metal made me think about Kai's token from the cellar at the bar. I pulled the crucible from the flame and set it on the ground in front of us. The open end of the container puckered and burst with flame, and Shay took a huge step back.

"Give me one second," I said as I bounced up the stairs two at a time.

I sifted through the piles of paper on the table until I found Kai's medallion and wondered if Kai had poured this from embryo material hundreds of years ago. There was no way to test my theory without destroying it, and I wasn't ready to do that now. When I returned to the forge, I handed Kai's token to Shay. "This. I think Kai cast this from the same material in there." I pointed to the white-hot crucible containing the molten embryo.

"Can you make one?" Shay turned it over in her hand.

"A medallion of my mark?" I asked.

"Yeah, is it complicated?"

I walked to the cabinet where I kept the crucible and carried out a bucket of sand and a set of metal frames. "It's not complicated at all." I laid the materials on the table and set the metal frames side by side. "The tough part is choosing what we should make. This is casting sand." I scooped a handful and squeezed it into a lump. "It's kinda cool because I can pack it until it's very hard, but it'll stay soft enough to make an impression."

I poured the sand into each half of the frame and packed it tight. "This marking tool is for finishing leather. I use it as a brand." I pressed the round Maker's mark into the packed sand, leaving behind my hammer symbol slashed with the spokes of a wheel that looked like a pentagram. It was an unplanned mark, designed to memorialize my new life as the blacksmith of Bannock. The marking tool made a perfect impression in the sand.

"That's almost the same size as Kai's," Shay said.

I nodded. "What I think I'll do is attach my mark to the new gauntlet," I said, taking the black tourmaline from my pocket, "and set this stone in the middle of the hammer."

"That's a lot of protection."

"Let's hope so." With my fingertip, I drew a line in the sand, creating a trough for the liquified embryos to flow through. I put the two halves of the sand-filled frame together and bolted them tight. "This makes a good seal." I put the crucible back into the forge.

"This is exciting." Shay rubbed her hands together. "Have you poured metal like this a lot?"

"Yes. You never met my friend, Mick." My hand smoothed the surface of the sand. "When I moved into the carriage house, he helped me with a lot of the heavy work upstairs in the apartment. We experimented with casting."

Shay looked up at me. "Just with casting?" she asked.

I didn't miss the subtle quest for information in her expression. I'm bisexual, and I had dated a few men, but Mick was never one of them. "Yes, just casting."

Her eyebrow raised with a question, and I thought about him for the first time in months. Mick was an enormous wall of a man who loved the gym. He was gentle but definitely rough around the edges and awkward in most social situations. But he was loyal, and for reasons we never discussed, he loved taking care of me.

"I never dated Mick," I said as I poked the center of the liquifying embryo with a steel rod.

"Never?"

"Oh, hell no, the guy was too much for me. He was so in love with his freedom that there wasn't room for anyone in the relationship he had with himself."

The answer made Shay laugh and satisfied her curiosity. "What did you cast?"

"We messed around with art pieces and natural materials. He made a few knife handle enhancements for me."

"You're not a fan of casting metal?"

"You can tell?" I tipped the crucible to check the viscosity of my embryos.

"It's obvious."

"The fail rate is pretty high, and I hate wasting time just to make a hot mess." I slipped my piece of the class-two demon into the forge behind the crucible, placed the metal frame filled with casting sand on the floor, and wedged it between two concrete blocks. "You should take a few steps back just in case this pops when it hits the sand."

"It seems dangerous."

"Everything in this room can be dangerous." I winked at her before pulling on my heavy-duty leather gloves, my hands wrapping around the crucible handle as I stepped closer to the spout of the metal frame. Once the liquid was poured, I had a few seconds before the cool air hit, and the transformation to solid began. There was just enough smelted embryo to fill the impression, and I carried the hot assembly away from the workspace so it could cool on its own.

"Did it work?" Shay squatted down for a closer look.

"We won't know for a while." I checked the seams of the metal frame for leaks, and it looked like the material stayed in the sand for a good pour.

"How long is a while?" She let out a frustrated sigh as she pushed off from her knees to stand.

I dropped the smelting gloves on the table and replaced them with a forging pair. "About as long as it'll take to forge the wrist cuff." I gripped Brigid's Hammer in one hand and pinched the demon billet with a pair of tongs. A second later, I struck my first blow to shape the material to match the gauntlet Shay wore on her left wrist. My new hammer was beyond magickal. One strike moved metal faster, wider, and I could see the cuff appear with each swing. I turned the billet over and placed it in the forge.

"Are you going to do this edge?" Shay asked as she held out her arm.

My fingertip ran along the thin hammered grove in the polished metal. "I am. It's going to be a little bigger here." I pinched the width of her wrist with my fingers. "So, I can solder my maker's mark in the center. If our casting experiment works out."

"It'll work out. I can tell." Shay pulled up a chair, turned it around, and straddled the seat with her forearms resting on the arched back.

"We'll see soon enough." I gripped the gauntlet and continued shaping it on the anvil. After ten minutes of twisting, tapping, and striking a solid groove all the way around, it was time to roll the cuff and fit it for my wrist. I pushed the project into the flame and snaked my finger to summon my girlfriend a little closer. "Come over here."

"I'd love to." Shay stood in front of the anvil. "What can I do?"

"Hold out your wrist."

She held out her naked wrist with a playful grin.

"Cute," I snorted, "but how about the other one?"

She leaned forward to kiss my cheek and put her hand in mine. I gripped the cuff and turned it just enough to remove it from her arm. Then I laid it on the anvil and traced the shape of the curve with a piece of soapstone.

"You're going to make them the same?" she asked.

"This is the general shape. I'll make mine a little wider to fit my arm." I tried to slide her cuff over my wrist, but it was too narrow. "Not quite the same." Shay took a step back as I turned to pull the project from the forge. I rolled the cuff over and tapped light strikes around the anvil's horn. I finished shaping the curves and turned off the propane feeding the forge.

"Are you finished?" Shay leaned forward in her chair.

"With the hot parts, yes. I need to polish it, and if our pour went well, I'll solder the medallion to the face." I pointed to the wrist cuff, careful not to touch the hot metal.

"Can we look at the casting?" Shay asked. Her cheeks lifted with a smile, creating cute wrinkles in the corners of her eyes.

"You excited?" I asked as I held a hand to lead her over to the project on the floor.

I removed my glove to check the temperature of the frame with the most sensitive part of the back of my fingers. It wasn't hot, but I picked it up with tongs just to be safe. I pounded the casting against the steel storage container that held the sand. The blocks of packed sand fractured and crumbled away from the solid misshapen medallion. The hardened embryo resembled a not-too-tasty-looking metal lollipop.

"Why is there a stem?" Shay asked, stepping in for a closer look.

My tongs pinched the metal, and I walked to the quench bucket to give it a cold water dunk. I removed it and turned it over on the face of the anvil. "This looks so good." I used my apron to wipe the water away. "The stem is just the neck of the mold. I'll grind that off." I traced the outline of my Maker's mark with my pinky finger to scrape the clinging pieces of sand from the etching. "How do you think demon castings will behave?" I asked as I held it up for Shay.

"I would be guessing." She rubbed the face of the medallion.

"You're usually a very good guesser." I bumped her hip.

"I've never collected embryo material. If they're connected to Gatekeepers, they will behave a lot like the punch daggers— hard to break and flames when you use it. It's impossible to know what it will do if a different demon slathered its spawn on the walls of those tunnels."

"We know two things," I said.

"What's that?"

"It melts, and it gets hard."

She laughed as I tapped the medallion against the face of the anvil. "That's not very helpful." she said.

I tugged Shay's hand and pulled her with me to the grinder. I pinched the medallion in the vice to anchor it and sliced the metal stem material from the edge. With a few quick strokes of the hacksaw, I had a nearly perfect one-and-a-half inch circle.

I held it to the light. "Time for a little shine-up."

I applied compound to the felted surface of the buffing wheel and flipped the power on. The Maker's mark medallion drifted back and forth across the wheel, buffing and polishing the front and sides until the surface was smooth.

"What do you think?" I handed it to Shay and turned off the machine.

"It's even better than Kai's."

"She didn't have the equipment I have." My knuckles rapped against the machine as I walked to the anvil to check the temperature of the cuff. It was cool enough to touch, and I handed it to Shay. "This is going to look pretty good." The Maker's mark medallion fit the face of the wrist cuff. "I'll have to solder it on."

Shay squeezed the clasp on my apron, releasing it from my waist. "Not tonight. Finish it tomorrow, and maybe we can take it out to Dani's and test its powers," she said as she raised the worn leather over my head.

I hooked my apron on the hanger and followed Shay upstairs. The day felt like it had been both long and short, but the experience of blacksmithing with Shay had invigorated me. The heat from the sigil in my palm radiated through my hands, and I realized that Brigid's gift of the Maker power had a similar effect to Shay's magick.

"Can we burn off a little of this energy?" I held up my sigil hand and the *ignis* flame burst from it.

"That's pretty hot."

"Exactly my point." The cuff and medallion dropped from my hand to the tabletop. "Bed?" I asked with a wiggle of my eyebrows.

Shay's hands covered my forehead with a gentle press. "Oh gosh, you can't do that." She giggled as I wrapped my arms around her. "Not if you want to get any more action."

"I'm all in for action," I whispered against her mouth, lifting her off the floor and taking cautious steps down the hallway leading to our bedroom.

"That's very good." Her lips pressed to mine, and we fell against the frame of our bed.

~~~~~~~~~~

Shay's alarm buzzed at six o'clock, and I wasn't happy to feel her move away from my backside. *Why did she have to work at all?* I thought as I rolled over to wrap around her waist.

"Good morning." I peppered the curve of her hip with kisses.

"Good morning, yourself." The delicate hairs on her back came to life with pimpling bumps.

"I slept like a baby," I said, and it surprised me that the nightmare hadn't come.

She turned around, and her cheeks flushed as she smiled. "Did you?"

"Someone rocked me right to sleep."

Shay climbed across my hips, straddling me as she moved in for a kiss. "I think there was mutual rocking. I'm glad you slept."

"Blacksmithing helped, I think." My hands rested on Shay's hips. "When I use the power of my hammer, I feel balanced."

"The relationship is symbiotic." Shay's body moved away as she climbed off the bed. "Maybe you and that hammer should keep working."

I stretched to grab her wrist, but she moved faster than I could. "Maybe that's a good idea, but come back to bed." The sound of my voice was desperate and whiny as my arm flopped over my face. I heard the shower turn on and followed Shay into the bathroom. "You want company?"

"You don't have to ask."

The curtain separated, and her arm reached forward to grab mine. I stepped over the high tub and was met with warm hands and a heart-stopping smile. Water ran over her cheeks as she kissed me. My thumbs hooked the ridge of her hip, and I pulled our bodies closer.
~~~~~~~~~~

Shay's fingers curled around my wrist, and her quick move to break my hold crushed my hope of pleasuring her under the hot spray of water. "We have time for a shower only."

I pouted, and she tapped my lower lip with her finger. She lathered her body, and I ran my hands over her shoulders, down her back, and her hand grabbed mine before it could travel into forbidden territory. She turned around, still gripping my fingers, criss-crossing my arms in front of me. Her breath hitched as her forehead touched my own.

"Shower, only."

She leaned back, and the rain of water bounced off her head and sprayed my face. She sidestepped my stunned form, and a few seconds later, she pushed me under the water's flow. Shay left me standing alone, and by the time I'd washed and rinsed, she was hanging her towel on the hook by the door.

"That's so rude, Officer Pierce!" I yelled as I turned the water off, and a hand came through the doorway to toss a towel at me. "So rude." The words were a whisper as I wiped my body dry. I hooked the towel by the door and was upset to see Shay jumping into her uniform pants. "You're in a big hurry this morning."

She looked up at me as she opened the collar of her undershirt and pulled it over her head. She punched her hands through the sleeves, and the letters BPD stretched across her breasts as she pulled the shirt to tuck it into her pants. "I want to talk to Dani this morning."

"About going to the range?" I asked.

"That." The velcro ripped away from the vest she wore. "And I want to make sure she can come out there with us."

"Always be prepared," I said as I pulled on a t-shirt and pair of jeans. "Right?"

Her fingers slipped the buttons of her uniform shirt closed, and she tucked it into the waist of her pants. "That's the way we roll, sweetheart."

My shoulder thumped against the doorway as I leaned to watch her finish dressing. She locked her duty belt around her waist and checked the magazine on her service weapon. "I think I'm going to finish the wrist cuff and set my stone."

Shay looked up from the safety check she was doing on her taser. "Are you sure you want to set the stone before the test?" The wire lead cartridge was in her hand as she triggered the electrodes, and the spark lit the handle green. She reassembled the taser before placing it in the alternate hip holster.

"Yep, we should test the full power of our magick." I stared at her standing in front of me in full uniform.

"I agree, but I wasn't sure how you'd feel if the entire experiment shattered."

Her hands rested on my hips, and she kissed me. My eyes were closed long after her lips left mine, waiting for more. I didn't hide my smile, and my brain was working hard to put together a response to her statement.

"Shatter?" I opened my eyes, and she was gone. When I walked into the kitchen, she was making herself something to eat. "Why do you think it will shatter?"

"I don't think it will, but I've never shot at black tourmaline before." The timer on the coffee pot buzzed to alert it had finished brewing. Shay was whisking two eggs in a bowl.

"With the protection spell and my hammer's powers, I hope it'll stop bullets like your breastplate." I took down two mugs from the shelf and poured coffee for us.

"If Dani is up for it, I guess we'll find out." Shay threw a tortilla on the open flame of the stovetop to crisp the edges. A few seconds later, she dumped the eggs into the shell.

"Will you come home for lunch today?"

"If I can." She took a bite of her food and checked the time. "Gosh, babe. I need to go." She wrapped her breakfast in a napkin and kissed my cheek. "I'll call you and let you know the plan."

She made a few quick steps, throwing her duffle over one shoulder and calling Dex. It was curious that he hadn't come when the velcro sound of her vest had played a few minutes ago, but the German Shepherd was at her side now, and she handed her food to me before dropping to one knee to wrap the vest around the K-9.

"I love you," I said as she stood up.

"I love you right back." Her kiss was quick, and she snatched the food from my hand. There I stood at the top of the stairs, watching my whole world walk out the door.

~~~~~~~~~~

Imagine my disappointment when Shay called at noon to explain that she and Dani had an appointment to visit Amelia's attorney in Middletown. Since they both had the day off tomorrow, the timing was perfect, but I had to reconcile spending two nights alone.

"Keep the carriage house locked tight," she said, and I could hear Dani making kissing noises in the background.

"I will." The forge fire pulsed behind me as I set my project inside.

"I love you."

"I love you, too." The words were just above a whisper. Shay didn't need to know that I was afraid or that I didn't want to spend a single night without her, let alone two. Then she was gone.

~~~~~~~~~~

"It worked out perfectly," Shay said through the static-filled cellular connection. "We signed and certified the documents, and none of the family members contested the will."

"So, you own a bar?" It wasn't news so much as a confirmation of Benton's wishes.

"We co-own a bar." She laughed, and I heard Dani yell in celebration.

"You're hooked now, Wildwood!"

Hooked was right, because I wasn't a simple blacksmith any longer. I was the Maker of Bannock, wielder of Brigid's Hammer, and pourer of beers. It sounded silly in my head, but if I looked to the future, owning a bar in our retirement might not be such a terrible burden.

Shay giggled as she said. "Goodbye, I love you."

"I love you, too. See you tomorrow."

The call ended. I tossed my cellphone on the workshop table and returned to the fire in the forge. The two-foot lengths of steel soaked up the heat, turning bright orange in color. I sandwiched the pieces together and clamped them into the bending jig I'd made. My forehead beaded with sweat, and I used my upper body to shape the steel into a perfect, long S-hooked curve. I anchored the material with vise grips. Benton's bow riser rested on the table, and I turned it over to size up the threaded screws.

Measure twice, cut once, I thought as I sat in the chair by the table. Amelia was going to love her surprise.

~~~~~~~~~~~~~

Twenty minutes past three o'clock on the following day, the carriage house door opened, and Dexter ran through the workshop to lie in the sacred circle. I was standing at the forge, moving a piece of metal from the anvil into the flame. When I turned around, my red-haired superhero was standing in front of the table with her uniform shirt unbuttoned just enough to reveal her vest. Her ponytail was already down, and delicate waves of red hair framed her face. I was staring, and she was waiting.

Two days. It had only been two days, and it felt like I was seeing her after a hundred years.

"How was your day?" she asked, her voice breaking into my musings.

The question rolled around in my head. *How was my day? It had been two days without you, but who was counting?*

"I've been very busy," I said finally.

"That's so good."

Her eyes moved over the length of my body, stopping on my face. She licked her lips, and I was done. I tossed my tools on the anvil and stepped close enough to caress her cheek before leaning in for a kiss. We stood together, tight in each other's arms, until I was content that an intimate reunion could wait. The forge was not a place for sex, especially after two days apart.
~~~~~~~~~~~~~

"The trip went well?" I asked as I stepped out of her arms, knowing if the two of us didn't separate, we would be half-naked up the stairs before taking another breath.

"It did," she said as she waved her knuckles over the twisted metal on the table, checking the temperature. "What's this?"

I smiled as I pulled off my gloves. "I had my first one-on-one workshop with Riker Bailey this morning."

"Really?"

"I got a call from Bill. I ran into him at the bar the other night, and he asked if I was doing workshops yet, and since you were gone, I arranged for him to bring Riker over."

"That's exciting," Shay said as she pulled up a chair and sat beside the workshop table.

"Bill paid me, overpaid me honestly, and I'm pretty sure Riker wants to come back."

Shay reached her hand across the anvil and grabbed my arm to squeeze it. "I know that's something you want to do. Congratulations."

My fingers touched her hand. "It's the start of what I've always wanted to do. Teaching and sharing blacksmithing with the people in this town."

"Bill's a good guy. He'll tell everyone, and so will Riker." Shay stood up. "I'm going to run up and get out of this uniform. Can you be ready in a few? We're going to meet Dani at the range."

She looked at her watch and didn't wait for an answer as she carried her duffle up the stairs. I shut down the forge, leaving the project inside to cool. Workshop clothes would be fine, and I needed little else as I hung up my apron and waited for Shay to return. She came down the stairs with a shotgun in her hand, a dark green canvas bag over her shoulder, and a top-handled steel box—the same box we'd taken to the range last time. I knew if she opened the cover, a variety of ammunition would be inside.

"Loading the armory?" I teased as she set the box on the table. She and Dani called the trunk of Shay's patrol car the armory, and for years, they'd practiced out at Dani's homestead. The joke was long-running.

Her smile was the best answer. "We're going to give the gauntlet a test. I told Dani to bring ear protection for more than just the noise of our guns."

"Are you thinking the freeze factor will be part of this?" I held up my gauntlet for her. It was the first time that Shay had seen the almost complete project, and I knew she'd share my excitement about the final results.

"You waited this long to show me?" She dropped the canvas bag by the ammunition case and laid the shotgun beside it. I removed the cuff, and Shay took hold to study the finished product. "This is beautiful." She turned it over, looking for the stone set in the center. "The black tourmaline didn't fit?" The faint lip pout expressed her disappointment about the absence of my gem.

"My stone stuck out too high, and I thought it would break the protective magick if I altered the size." I took the rock out of my pocket.

"Your intuition was right. Changes should happen in a sacred space. We can break a piece off later, but maybe forging with Brigid's Hammer will be enough." She held my hand as she slipped the cuff onto my wrist. "You ready to load the armory?" She winked before putting the ammunition case in my hand.

"I am." I made a quick check of the workshop before cinching fabric around the surprise I'd finished only hours before.

CHAPTER XVI

PRIMED

This was the first time I'd returned to the firing range and homestead area around the mine since answering Brigid's call to the hammer, but it didn't feel dangerous today. Perhaps it was the support of the magickal people and beings around me. Dexter lay in the back seat of Shay's patrol car, and Stout sat in the rear window ledge the entire drive, never making a sound. The trip up the gravel road was the same winding route, and the wood-framed shooting targets stood like ravaged monsters in the open field. Dani was standing in front of the solitary table that marked the firing range's safety zone.

The smile on Dani's face was toothy-wide, and I knew they were planning more than a few quick shots at my wrist cuff. They were going to blow off some emotionally charged steam. I looked toward the one-room cabin sitting on the hill behind us where the little flag stood upright to show that Amelia was also on the property. Shay honked the horn two times, and a few seconds later, the flag dropped, and the dark-haired, copper-skinned woman stepped out onto the small porch. She waved as she made her way along the winding, pebbled path. I noticed she had her cane today. Maybe this would be the day I learned more about her life.

"Hey, you two." Dani waved across the yard as we exited the car.

The trunk lid popped open, and Shay reached inside to remove the shotgun, canvas bag, and canister of ammunition. Shay opened the back door of the patrol car, and Dexter dangled his paws out the open door. Stout's feet kicked out across Dexter's hind legs, and the two seemed content to watch from afar. Since Stout came from a magick-filled world, I wondered how he felt about guns and shooting at the range.

"Hey, D. You started without me." Shay stopped next to her friend, dropped the canister beside her, and laid the shotgun across the table.

"I was just about to hang up a few targets." Dani removed the rubber band from the paper silhouettes and unrolled them in front of her.

"Put 'em up." Shay slapped her friend on the back and waved me closer. "Come on, sweetheart. Let's give that wrist cuff a thorough testing."

I reached around to grab the cuff and turn it off my wrist. Amelia was two steps behind me and gave Shay a half-hug.

"Hello, Shay. How are you?" Amelia asked as she reached to touch my arm. "Hello, Wildwood." Amelia's voice was soothing, and if anyone ever felt like a safe person to be near, it was the woman holding my arm.

"Hi, Amelia," Shay and I said almost in unison.

"Did you come out to see our test?" I asked, and I squeezed her hand before it fell away.

"Danielle has been talking for days about coming out here. She had to remind me during every phone call that she and Shay needed to blow off steam. I guess it's time, and I'm glad Diana can manage the bar without me."

"Business is good?" I asked, knowing that it was great and that the arrangement with the Benton family was, so far, a success.

"The bar practically runs itself," Amelia said. "And Diana knows how to manage inventory. She's impressive, and we're lucky to have her."

"Lucky is right," Dani agreed. "Makes it possible for us to do this." She opened the canister of ammunition and pulled out a box of shotgun shells.

"I'm glad we're all here together," Shay said as she took the cuff from my hand. "Wildwood's been working on a new project, and we're excited to test it." She handed the cuff to Amelia.

"This is beautiful, Wildwood." Amelia turned the bracelet in her hands, getting a closer look at the details hammered on the surface. "The mark on the medallion is unique," she said. "How did you make this?"

"Experimenting with the material we found in the tunnels," Shay answered for me, and I was grateful because I wasn't sure if they should know that we were smelting demon embryos.

"What material did you use?" Dani asked as her hand hovered over that cuff, hesitant to touch it.

"Embryos," Shay answered.

Well, I guess we can *tell them*, I thought, then explained, "I melted them down and cast the medallion from the molten material."

Dani took the cuff from Amelia. "You combined demon elements again?" It was difficult to read her expression as she examined the wrist cuff, holding it up to the sunlight. "What's it do?"

"That's what we're here to find out," Shay said as she slapped her friend on the shoulder. "You and I are about to take a few shots at it."

"What about the mine?" Amelia asked. "The last time we 'took shots' at demon steel, we had some angry, unplanned visitors."

"That's why I wanted Dani here." Shay took a few steps toward the ten-yard target. "If we have visitors again, we'll need more hands to take care of them." She hooked the wrist cuff over a groove in the slatted wall built to hold paper targets.

"What are we using?" Dani yelled as she pendulum-waved the shotgun shell in her hand.

"How about we start smaller with a few service rounds and go from there?" Shay stood behind the table, looking downrange at my wrist cuff. Dani was loading her handgun, and Shay mirrored the action. "Everyone gets ear protection." Shay held up her wrist. "Remember that my cuff has an interesting ability to freeze you where you stand. We can only guess how this new one will behave, so cover up."

"Really?" Amelia asked, and I explained.

"The first time my wild girlfriend smashed her cuff with a hammer, I couldn't move for almost five minutes."

"Why would you wear something that could knock out your girlfriend?" Dani asked.

"It doesn't anymore, not since she put in her Maker's mark and came into her powers as the Maker," Shay answered. "Everything is different since—" She hesitated and looked at Dani. "Since we went into the tunnels and found Brigid's Hammer."

"I guess you have to listen to the magick." Dani shrugged.

"I'm not going in those tunnels," Amelia said as she backed away from the table.

"We aren't going anywhere but right here." Dani slapped the tabletop with both hands. "Are you going to stay and watch the test?" she asked her wife.

"Yes, as long as we stay right here; you've got me curious, and I want to see what happens."

Shay passed the ear protection to each of us and called to the dog. "Dexter!"

The K-9 jumped from the backseat and ran across the gravel to stand by Shay.

"We ready?" She yelled so we could hear her over our ear protection, and we each responded with a thumbs up.

The two women transformed, switching from girlfriend and wife right into police officer mode. Hand gestures replaced verbal cues, one studying the other before pointing their guns downrange. Smiles stretched their cheeks as they aimed at the wrist cuff. It was adorable right before it became terrifying.

"You go, Pierce." Dani spoke loud enough for all of us to hear through our muffled ears.

"Firing!" Shay yelled, and her finger squeezed the trigger, releasing the first shot. The bullet struck the cuff with a solid hit. Once the cuff flopped back against the slatted wall, Shay shot again. The cuff moved but didn't fall, so Dani took aim.

"Firing!" she yelled, and a second later, the cuff flew up in the air and landed in the dirt. They laid their guns on the table and took off the ear coverings.

"Damn, that was outstanding," Dani said.

I'd anticipated their enthusiasm, but as I watched Dexter, I noticed his calm posture. He didn't react to any of the bullet strikes fired at the transformed remains of multiple demon embryos. I hadn't expected chaos from him, but I thought he'd at least make a howl or a whimper.

Shay looked at me. "What?"

"Dex didn't react. The shots didn't set him off."

"I had a feeling that would happen," Shay explained. "Since the tunnels and finding the hammer, you and I have balance, and I wondered if the Magick and Maker powers would include Dexter."

I dropped to one knee in front of our dog. "Who's a furry dragon?" I fluffed the fur around his face and scratched his ears.

Dani walked out to pick up the wrist cuff and carried it back for all of us to see. Shay and Dani had both hit it, we were sure. But it didn't surprise me when they couldn't find a scratch on the surface.

"Shotgun?" Shay looked at her friend with an excited grin.

"Hell yes!" Dani carried the cuff downrange.

Now *this* I wanted to see. I knew little about guns and ammunition, but even I was aware of how big a blast a shotgun could make.

The distance was five yards farther, and she set it on a box on the ground. I was sure my wrist cuff was about to perform more aerial stunts. We covered our ears, and they let loose two shots, each hitting their mark and popping the cuff into the air and out of sight in the field. I wasn't sure we would find it in the tall grass, but Shay called to Dexter, and the dog darted out into the range and returned with the cuff in his mouth.

"Nothing." Shay held it up for me to see. "Not a ding, not a scratch. The cuff is bulletproof."

"Just like yours." I tapped the cuff on Shay's arm.

"What does this mean?" Amelia asked.

"It means that we can finally go into the tunnels and kill all of those bastard things." Dani looked at her wife. "Wildwood can make weapons for all of us."

"I'm not going back in there, Danielle." Amelia turned to walk away, but her wife grabbed her hand.

"I'm not asking you to go inside. I'm telling you, we can stop the evil that's growing down there. Do what my dad couldn't."

Amelia's dark eyes widened. "What your dad wouldn't do, you mean. Even after this." She pointed to her prosthetic leg, but stopped herself from saying anything else with me standing there. But I didn't have to guess anymore. It was clear now that she'd lost her leg in something unrelated to caving. Maybe she wasn't going to share anything with me today, after all.

"You don't have to remind me." Dani stepped close enough to pick up her wife and carry-walk her a few steps away.

I put my hand on Shay's shoulder, and we walked to the patrol car to give them space to talk. "How much do you know about all of that?" I asked.

"Only what I've already said. Some kind of accident while they were spelunking." She looked over my shoulder, and I turned to see Amelia glancing away from me.

Amelia had heard my question to Shay, and I felt the flush of embarrassment warm my cheeks. The last thing I wanted to do was offend the woman who had only ever been kind to me.

"We were nosing around in those damn tunnels," Amelia said, her voice raised. "We were exactly where we should not have been, and Jacob was no help. That asshole made it worse."

"I wasn't trying to be nosy," I said as I struggled to explain. "I just wondered if you'd survived a demon attack."

"I survived. No thanks to the Maker of Bannock." She put her hand on my shoulder. "Not you, Wildwood. Danielle's father, Jacob." She said his name in a way that sounded like a foul word.

"It's okay. You don't have to share your story if it's going to bring up such horrible memories." Shay stepped closer to me and wrapped her arm around my waist.

"We seem to be tied together by these terrible memories, Wildwood." Amelia's voice was almost a whisper.

"Melia…" Dani's own voice was a warning.

"What, Danielle?" She slammed the base of her cane against the gravel. "We were stupid kids, looking for answers to grown-up questions in a place we didn't belong."

Dani turned to look at me. "I wanted to know how my mother had died. I needed to understand why my dad spent more time searching for Brigid and whatever gift she had for him than he did for whatever killed my mother."

"So, you went looking in the tunnels?" Shay asked.

"I followed Benton. She patrolled those tunnels alone for years, and I thought I could go in there on my own." Dani looked at her wife. "I was wrong, and Amelia paid the price for my stupidity."

"I was a willing participant." Amelia rested her hand against her wife's cheek before turning to address Shay and me. "We went into those tunnels looking for something, but we didn't know what it was until *you* found it almost twenty years later, Wildwood."

Dani wrapped her arms around Amelia. "The switchback in the embryo tunnels. We didn't make it ten yards before the demon attacked. I was trying to protect Amelia, and she was trying to protect me. She did the better job."

"Danielle, that's not true. There was nothing I could do. The creature dug its claws deep into my calf and tore half of my leg away before I could scream." Amelia's body trembled, and Dani held her tighter. "We had basically nothing for weapons. Regina patrolled the mines with nothing, or so we thought. So, we went in thinking we'd be safe. Regina had the powers of the Magick. We had our bare hands and a flashlight."

"How did you get away?" I asked.

"I cut off its arm or leg–whatever was tearing into her. I used the only thing I could find, a damn shovel, and I beat it until it stopped coming." Dani shook her head. "There was so much blood, and I carried Melia out to the grass. I used my belt to slow down the bleeding and drove her to the hospital. You have to understand that the demons weren't as wild as they are today. I'd never seen one face to face until that day in the mine."

"The official report was a cave-in accident," Amelia said. "Everyone knew Danielle was obsessed with the mine, and we had a solid story. At least we *thought* it was until two people questioned it." She smirked.

"Benton and Jacob?" Shay guessed.

"Exactly," Dani answered. "Once Benton knew, well, that set my destiny as a law enforcement officer in Bannock. Benton took me into the tunnels to establish patrol boundaries, and she explained the magick barriers and how she moved through the mine."

"Barriers that are fading because she's gone," Shay said.

It made sense now. If Benton had used magick to trap the demons inside, that magick would be fading with every passing day now that she was dead.

"Have you been going into the tunnels by yourself since she died?" Shay asked.

Dani nodded solemnly. "Since she went into the hospital, yes. I felt pretty safe while she was alive, but not since her funeral, since that day we all went in. It brought up a lot of memories, and I haven't been able to go alone."

"You and I will go together. I'll find the spell." Shay put her hands on Dani and Amelia's. "My magick is as strong as Benton's. We can do this now. Maybe I can't undo the past, but we can do something about the future."

"It sounds so simple," Amelia said.

"We know it won't be." Dani held her wife a little tighter before letting her go. "You want to hit a few more targets, Pierce?" she asked over the top of Amelia's head.

"Set 'em up."

I stood beside Shay in awkward silence and felt the tug on my hand before the cuff slipped onto my wrist.

"You going to stay out here or go inside?" Shay asked.

"I think I'll let Amelia kick my ass in cribbage for a while."

Shay laughed, and Dani smiled. "No one will play with her."

"If 'no one' means 'my wife,' then that would be accurate." Amelia patted Dani's cheek after kissing it. "Have fun." She turned to walk to the cabin. "Come on, Wildwood, I'll teach you a new game."

"Better than cribbage?" I asked, knowing that just about any game would increase my odds of winning.

"Ever heard of Rummy?" She didn't bother to look back as she sidestepped the uneven rocks on the path.

I shook my head. "Never played." I opened the trunk of the squad car and removed the wrapped surprise.

"What you got there?" Amelia asked.

"It's something special I hope you'll like, but first, you can teach me a new game."

"That sounds like a plan."

~~~~~~~~~~

Counting by five was easier than fifteen, but after twenty minutes of playing, it was clear that Amelia had a head for cards.

"Maybe I should take up target practice?" I joked.

"We could put up an axe wall, and you and I could try something less explosive?"

I had a feeling this woman was setting me up. "Are you aware that I forged an axe that never misses?"

She laid her cards down on the table. "Really?"

"I'm surprised Dani didn't tell you. It was the first thing I made with Brigid's Hammer."

"Oh... no. Danielle never said."
~~~~~~~~~~

I thought for a minute about Dani's reaction to the axe and the power the hammer infused. "She was—I guess she was upset."

"The history of that damn hammer. I'm not sure my wife will ever come to terms with the loss surrounding it. We've always believed that her mother died trying to find it."

What could I say? I'd never had a mother to lose, but I'd dreamed about having one who cared. Someone who would make snacks after school, check my homework, and listen to my dreams. But that person never came. I'd never had to explain why blacksmithing made me happy or face rejection for coming out as bisexual. There was little time at a foster home to create lasting relationships, and before I aged out of the system, I could count three people who cared about me: Mama Pierce, the woman I called Gran, and Shay.

"I wish I could make it better," I said.

"Thank you."

"Dani told me about herself, that she's transgender." I waited for her to say something.

Amelia looked up at me with an abundance of kindness in her eyes. "Yes, she said as much. She also said that you were supportive."

"She's a wonderful friend to the person I love the most in this world. Nothing is different for me."

"She told you how we met, then?" Amelia stacked the cards on the table and shuffled the layers one over the other.

"That you were out here living in this cabin?"

Amelia laughed. "I had such a wild idea I was going to walk across this country. I barely made it three hundred miles before that stunning woman stole my heart."

"Love at first sight?" I asked, unsure if my guess was correct.

"Hardly, but she was an incredible storyteller, and we sat for hours talking about nothing and everything." Amelia's eyes lit with pure joy, and I could see the memories were happy ones.

"She wooed you." I couldn't hide my giggly grin.

"Stole my heart right out of my chest." She slapped the deck of cards in front of me, and I cut the deck. Amelia made the smoothest left-handed deal of seven cards to each of us before flipping over the top card on the deck. "The day she came out to me, I'd just asked her to go on the road and leave this town behind."

"That never happened, I guess?" I picked up my cards and sorted the two aces from the pair of twos and an off-suited jack, queen, and king. This was going to be my winning hand. I took a card from the deck, the four of hearts, and dropped it on the discarded pile.

She shook her head. "No, we never had that grand adventure. Jacob got involved. Jacob Kota and his bigotry happened, and then my thoughts were about loving Danielle and building a life together, even if it was in this demon-infested town." Amelia picked up my discard and laid down three fours, discarding a seven.

I thought for a moment about Bannock. Being lured here by Benton and the powers of the fire goddess. "But you stayed?" I drew a six of hearts. Not needing it, I discarded it.

"That's all Danielle." She picked up my six and laid down two more. I was about to get caught with a handful of points. "Well, Regina was a large part of it, too. She took care of us when we were just kids. We didn't know up from down after Jacob cut Danielle from his life."

"And after Jacob passed away?" I picked up a two of diamonds and discarded one of my aces instead. Amelia had only one card left, and I decided it was time to get rid of some points.

"He left everything to Regina. Which made little sense because they hardly spoke. I think he wanted to punish Danielle, but Regina let us buy the homestead for fifty dollars as a screw you to that old bastard."

"I wish I'd had the chance to know Benton. She seemed like a genuine friend."

"None of us would be here, literally, if it wasn't for her." Amelia picked up a card and laid down a fourth six, ending the hand. I could hear guns firing at the range and playful laughter.

I shook my head at the handful of cards I was holding and laid them on the table. "Maybe we need different entertainment."

Amelia laughed. "You'll get better." She placed her hand over mine, serious for a moment. "You're very good for Shay, you know."

Her smile was sweet and her eyes so kind, but her words caught me off guard, and the only thing I could think to say was, "Oh, thank you."

"We should thank *you*." Amelia tossed the cards on the table as she stood. "Shay has always been self-sufficient and ridiculously independent, but so solitary that it was almost painful."

I knew why Shay was alone, and until recently, the physical consequence of her teenage inexperience was the barrier between all of us. Shay had been brave the day I'd seen all of her scars, and that courage had made me love her even more. But Amelia was right. Shay had hidden herself away, living half a life.

"She tells me she was content," I said, trying to protect her privacy.

Amelia let out a sad laugh. "We can convince ourselves we're many things to survive."

It was the first time anyone had spoken about Shay in a way that hurt my heart, and it was because I knew she'd suffered alone. "I love her more than I thought I could."

"I'm delighted to hear that." She patted my cheek.

I heard more laughter outside and got up to peek at the women standing behind the table at the firing range. Shay looked happy as she watched Dani count the holes in the paper targets. I walked back to the table.

"They sound like they're having fun."

"The two of them are good at that." Amelia smiled.

"So, you want different entertainment? What did you have in mind?"

"How are you with a recurve bow?" I asked, ready to share my surprise.

She paused from sorting the cards back into the box. "I might be very good with just about any kind of bow." She walked behind her chair and stretched to reach for a long canvas bag hanging over the window. She untied the nylon cord and slipped an unstrung recurve bow from inside. "Danielle had this made for me a few years ago." She guided the loop of the string to the knock on one end and stepped on the stringer to draw the bow and lock the bowstring in place. She passed it to me.

"Hickory?" I asked, and she confirmed with a nod. I drew the bow, careful not to breach the integrity with a dry fire. It felt balanced as I passed it to her and said, "It's beautiful. What's the draw weight?"

"It has a fifty-pound draw. Great for hunting, if you know what I mean." Her wink was a delight as it flushed her cheeks. She pulled a quiver from the curtain-covered cabinet and removed a bundle of steel tipped arrows with neon-orange fletching. "I made each of these."

She rolled them out on the tabletop and I picked through, noticing that Amelia was a talented fletcher. "They're beautiful." I pointed the arrow toward the floor and stared down the shaft. "Perfectly straight."

"That, my friend, would be the only straight thing around this homestead." I laughed, enjoying her sweet voice and casual use of the title "friend." "Since we're showing and telling, what's in that wrap you've got over there? It wouldn't be a bow?"

When I picked up the bundle, the cloth flopped away from my new creation as I handed it to her. "It's a takedown." She said as she laid the three parts on the table. Her hand moved over the polished edge of the upper limb and stopped when she hit my maker's mark. "You made this?"

"Just the limbs. The riser came from Benton's arsenal."

Amelia's fingers pinched the lock screws, and she wasted no time attaching the metal limbs to assemble the bow. The smile on her face was the exact reaction I was hoping for as I built the jig to create the perfect bends in the limbs. Once assembled, she laid her forearm parallel to the length and tilted it back and forth. I didn't know what she was doing until she said, "My guess is sixty inches."

"Exactly," I said, watching as she opened a box stored inside the curtained closet.

"I think I've got one in here." She pulled out a handful of bowstrings, dangling them from her fingertip by the loops.

"These are pretty close." She plucked one from the bundle. "Let's try this." Her hands moved over the bow, repeating the same steps as before until the string stretched the limbs tight. Amelia's left hand gripped the riser as she drew the line to her right cheek. "It's perfect," she said as she held tight, careful not to release the string.

"I'm glad you approve," I said.

Her cheeks flushed red as she smiled. "It draws like a child's bow. Have you tested the draw weight?"

"Not yet. I don't have the setup. You're actually holding the first bow I've ever made."

"You've done a stunning job." Amelia moved to the opposite wall of the cabin and mounted the bow across an anchored timber. "We can check it here." She hooked a compact fishing scale over the bowstring and drew it down until it hit a slash-mark carved in the wall. She guided the string up and pulled it down and up a few more times. "That's not possible."

"What's not possible?" I asked as she raised the scale and pulled it down one more time.

"The scale." She tilted her head for me to come closer to read the scale. "What's that say?"

"It's resting on the twenty."

She raised the string and pulled it to the line again. I watched the red indicator spin once all the way past one hundred to land on the twenty. "One hundred and twenty. There is no way that I could draw a one-hundred-and-twenty pound bow. No way."

"According to that scale, you already have. More than once." It was impossible to hide my pride, and I knew my cheeks were puffed from my massive smile. "Want to shoot it?"

"Hell yes, I want to shoot it." She opened the curtain again and removed a bundle of arrows. "If that's got a one-hundred-and-twenty pound draw, we're going to need better arrows." She cinched the quiver around her hip and fed the arrows inside. "Let's drop the flag and see how our girls are doing first."

"From the sound of it, I'd say they're having fun."

I pushed my hands against the edge of the knotty pine table, and Amelia dropped the safety flag to alert Shay and Dani of our exit. They stood in front of the table, fighting over the red circles drawn around the bullet holes and who had the most kill shots. It was frightening and adorable at the same time.

Amelia locked her stance on the top of the porch landing. She gripped the riser of the bow, nocked the arrow toward the sky, and drew until the string touched her cheek. She held the position for a few seconds and yelled, "Come to the porch!" She held the arrow without effort, pointing it at the clouds.

The women in the yard turned and ran full speed from the firing range. They stopped at the foot of the landing, and before I could take another breath, Amelia yelled, "Firing!" and lowered the bow. The arrow flew true across the yard and into the tattered, blood-red center of the target farthest from the cabin.

"What—the—hell, woman?" Dani yelled as she turned up to look at us.

Amelia stood, locked in firing position, nocking a second arrow against the bowstring. "You should stand still." She pulled the string against her cheek. "Firing!" The arrow landed a hairline away from the first.

"Don't fire again," Shay called from her position beside me.

Amelia stared at the bow in her hand, glancing over her shoulder at me. "This bow is like nothing I've ever used before." The riser rolled over her fingers, and she tried to give it to me.

"Don't. It's yours. I built it for you."

Before she could protest, Dani and Shay were stepping onto the porch. "What are the two of you thinking?" I felt the scolding sting in her voice as Shay glared at the two of us.

"Shoot this, Danielle. It's stunning."

Amelia tipped the bow's upper limb toward her wife, and Dani took hold. She hooked her fingers around the bowstring and tugged it to her cheek.

"The draw is so smooth," Dani said.

"Guess the draw weight?" Amelia said with a giddy tone in her voice.

Dani drew the bow again. "It feels like the ebony recurve. About fifty-five pounds?"

Amelia looked at me, and I looked at her, but she clarified that she wanted me to share the number. "We tested it at one hundred and twenty pounds."

"That's not possible." Dani drew the bow one more time, holding the string against her cheek as she said, "It can't be over sixty." She returned the bow to her wife.

"We checked it. A lot," Amelia insisted as she passed the bow to Shay.

My girlfriend walked to the firing range without saying a word, and the three of us followed. She crossed the field, pulled both arrows from the target wall, and didn't comment as she turned behind the firing line and launched both arrows one after the other. She laid the bow on the table.

"I'm not surprised you hit the target," I said, and Dani laughed. "What?"

"Your girlfriend is the worst with a bow." Dani covered her mouth, masking the laugh.

"Truly terrible," Amelia agreed.

"Really?"

Shay nodded, cringing. "It's so embarrassing to admit, but I'm a horrible shot, or at least I was until this." She took a moment to appreciate the bow's limbs and stopped when she noticed my Maker's mark. "Demon steel?"

"Demon steel meets the Hammer of Brigid." I smiled, and the reflected joy in Shay's eyes was the only reaction I needed. "I thought maybe Amelia might like it."

"I can't take this. It wouldn't be right." Amelia held up her hands in protest.

But I wasn't changing my mind. "It's already done. It's yours." I turned the bow around and thrust it toward her.

"Don't fight it. If Wildwood made it for you, it is yours." Shay threw her arm around Amelia's shoulder. "We should celebrate, don't you think?"

"Hell yes."

My intention to create a powerful weapon had exceeded my expectations, and it was a moment to cherish. Amelia passed the bow to her wife, and Dani kicked one limb against her foot and tangled the bow against her thigh to unstring it. She turned the limb bolts to break the bow down into three pieces.

"Who's buying beers?" Amelia asked.

"Baby, we own the bar. You're buying the beer from now on," Dani reminded her, wrapping an arm around Amelia's waist.

"So, there are no losers here." Shay slapped her friend on the shoulder, and it was refreshing to watch the two of them playful and relaxed.

"Nothing came out of the mine?" I asked, surprised that Dexter wasn't crunching on some otherworldly creature.

"We're clear," Dani said as she fist-bumped Shay. "Just like old times."

Shay pumped the action on the shotgun to unload it and boxed the ammunition. "Why don't we get some food?"

"And beer," Dani said as she discharged the magazine from her handgun. Shay and Dani reloaded their magazines and placed them in the canvas bags they carried.

"You lock up the cabin?" Dani asked Amelia.

"I was a little excited. It's tidy enough, but we should lock it."

There was a definite system to their shooting trips, but although I was new to the process, I didn't feel like an outsider. Dani dropped her duffle over Amelia's shoulder and sprinted up to the cabin to lock the door. Shay carried her equipment to the patrol car and popped the trunk open. Dexter and Stout were in the back of Dani's pickup.

"How was the card game?" Shay asked as she dropped the bag in the trunk.

"Amelia and I decided we're going to build an axe wall out here so I can win at something." My laugh didn't sell the idea.

"She kicked your ass, didn't she?" Dani said as she took the bag off her wife's shoulder.

"She's learning," Amelia defended herself.

"You hate to lose. Admit it." Dani picked Amelia up and carried her to the passenger side of their truck.

"It's been a long time since I've lost, so I don't know." She wrapped her arms around Dani's neck and kissed her hard.

"Ouch," Shay said as her fingers traveled down my forearm to hold my hand. "Did you have fun?" Her voice had a tone of concern.

I wanted to say that getting my ass kicked in card games was the thrill of my life, but part of me enjoyed getting to know Shay's family. "Amelia is great company."

"That's a very diplomatic answer." Shay smiled at me, and I wondered if she was worried that I didn't like the shooting range. It wasn't a secret that I didn't like guns, but I loved Shay, and I also loved seeing her happy.

"We're going to build an axe wall," I said.

Shay's head bobbed "yes," and she yelled at Dani. "We're going to build an axe wall. Right over there!" She pointed to the space in front of her patrol car. "Wildwood's decided."

I tugged our joined hands. "Maybe I should have asked?"

Dani and Shay were always so serious and intense that it threw me when they teased each other. It was going to take a while for me to feel comfortable with the playful side of their relationship.

"It's okay. These are my people, and now they're your people too." Shay leaned against the trunk of the patrol car and pulled me in between her legs.

"I like your people," I said.

She smiled, and her eyes drifted to my lips. Her hand came round the back of my neck, and she pulled me in for a kiss. Shay's lips were soft, and as she leaned back, she said. "That's very good because my people like you, too."

I rested my forehead against hers and took a deep breath. The truck horn blasted, and I jumped, knocking Shay off balance.

Dani yelled out her window, "I've got your dog and your fairy! We'll meet you at the bar." She honked the horn one more time. "Keep your pants on, Pierce!"

I couldn't hide my smile. "Yeah, they sure do like me."

CHAPTER XVII

CONVERGENCE

"What are you thinking about?" I wedged my back against my seat in the patrol car. Shay's eyes were focused on the road. Almost too focused.

She hesitated, took a quick breath, and said, "I was thinking about you and me, and Dani and Amelia." She turned her head to smile before looking back at the road.

"That's a lot to think about," I said. "Care to be a little more specific?"

Her eyes glanced up at the rearview mirror before she spoke. "I was just thinking, wondering mostly, how I'll feel about you in twenty years."

My palms started to sweat, so I rubbed them on the denim fabric covering my thighs. "Twenty years, huh? That's a long time."

Shay looked at me again, doing a quick double-take, noticing my nervous posture. "You don't think that far ahead, do you?" She reduced the speed of her patrol car.

My head fell against the back of the seat as I turned to her. "I've never thought further than setting up the carriage house."

Shay maneuvered the car to the side of the road and shifted it into park. "Do I fit into the setup?" Her hands remained on the steering wheel, and it occurred to me that my flippant answer might have been a little insensitive.

"We live together," I said, thinking it was apparent our commitment went beyond the next few months.

"Yes, but we've never talked about what comes next."

What comes next? I heard the words, but it took time for my mind to sort through what she was saying. What comes next after living together? Being happy? Having my best life as a blacksmith and welder? What comes next in a happy relationship?

Amelia and Dani have a happy life. A life that Shay admires and wants for herself. It hit me like a punch to the face.

"Marriage?" The word burst from my mouth without a thought to how she might respond.

Shay's eyes went wide with surprise, and I was curious about her reaction. "I wasn't thinking about getting married," she explained. "I was thinking more about being in love with you for the rest of my life."

She wasn't thinking about marriage? Why wasn't she thinking about it? I guess I wasn't thinking about it either. "So, you don't want to get married?" I asked.

"Well, yes. I mean…no." She was flustered. "But that's not what I was—"

"Shay, stop." I reached across the car to touch her hand and pulled her closer to me. "I'm not proposing to you. What I am saying is that if I wanted to marry anyone, it would be you."

She turned her head to look at me. "I don't know if I want to be married, but I know I want to be with you. Just you."

It didn't seem complicated, this understanding. I was cool with the idea of marriage, and Shay was not. Our relationship was young, and my love for her felt bigger with each passing day. We could figure out the rest. What was the rest? Family? Did she want…?

"Do you want children? Have you ever?"

"No." The green of her eyes darkened, and I saw sadness as she looked at me. "I don't think I have it in me to be a parent."

I tried to hide my surprise as I thought about the woman sitting beside me. Shay was kind, tender, and passionate. She made me feel loved in a way I never thought possible, and she would be an incredible mother. But part of me was relieved because I didn't want to be a parent either.

"Do *you* want children?" Her question came out as a whisper, as if she was afraid to know the answer.

"No, it's never fit into my plan, which is to have no plan until I need a plan."

She smiled and said, "You realize that having no plan is actually a plan?"

"Fair enough." I let out a short laugh, more from emotional relief than actually finding humor in her words. I felt okay that we could be happy together, just the two of us. Well, maybe three, with Dexter–four, with Stout. But it was safe to leave either or both of them unsupervised. "We have a dragon and a fairy to contend with."

She shifted the car into drive. "Which we should rescue from Dani and Amelia because Stout is probably on his second beer, and who knows what Amelia is feeding Dexter." Shay checked the mirrors, looked over her shoulder, and pulled out onto the road.

"Are we going to be okay?" I asked as I settled into the seat. Shay said nothing, and the silence made me nervous. "Shay?"

"Young children are a trigger for me." Her eyes were looking forward, focused on the road ahead. "Maybe it was growing up in the system. Watching people come and go. I never want to put a person on this planet who might end up like we did."

"In foster care?" I asked, even though I knew what she meant.

She nodded, and I could see her eyes glisten, but tears didn't come. "There's no one. If something happened to you and me, there's no one to take care of any kids, and I just could never do that."

"It doesn't always end badly," I said. I wasn't trying to convince Shay to change her mind, just give her hope for a different future.

"Sometimes it does." She wiped her cheek with the back of her hand and stretched to put on her sunglasses. "People leave."

"Shay." Her words were a strike to my heart. It shouldn't have been a surprise that having a family would frighten her, but this was more than fear of failure.

"Maybe it's just not for me, you know?" she added. "Since Mama died, going through that alone…and now Benton." She turned into the parking lot of the bar.

"I will never leave you."

Shay put the car into park. "Someday you will."

My thumb pressed the button to unclip my seat belt, and I reached across the front seat to grab her arm. "Not by choice. It'll never be by choice."

"I know." She pulled off her sunglasses, clipped them to the visor, and turned to look at me. "You make me believe in things I never thought I could."

"Oh, love. I want to spend a million days with you just so you can believe in everything." I touched the tear on her cheek.

Her eyes closed, and I wasn't sure if I'd said too much when she squeezed her eyelids tight, and tears fell freely. "I want that, too."

"That's good." My hand snaked behind her head, and I pulled her in for a kiss.

Her lips were warm as she leaned away. "Just you and me."

My forehead touched hers. "You're all I'll ever need."

Two huge paws slapped against Shay's window, and a giant Dexter tongue lolled from his mouth as he looked for his partner.

Shay took a slow cleansing breath, rolled the window down, and turned to look at her dog. "Hi, Dex." Her hands ruffled the fur around his face. "I think having him is enough."

"Yes, I think you might be right."

"Down, Dex." His paws fell off the door, and Shay opened it. His nose was in the crack, and he was in her lap a second later. "Hey, buddy."

Dani was standing at the service door of the bar. Shay pushed the animal off her legs and got out of the car. "Sorry, it took so long. We made a stop."

I opened my door and walked around the vehicle.

"It's fine. Amelia and Stout are looking at something, so I took your boy for a walk. He was getting nervous, pacing around the bar, and I thought he might just shift himself to go search for the two of you."

"What's up, buddy?"

The dog didn't make a sound, but his head turned, and a few seconds later, he maneuvered himself in front of Shay. His body was stiff, at attention, and in protection mode, and Shay's smile disappeared when a woman came around the corner.

"What do we have here?" Her voice was thick with a drawl of superiority.

The woman's dark hair was sharp around her face. The tan skirt just touching her knees was neatly pressed, as if she hadn't sat all day. She tucked her handbag into the bend of her arm, and I noticed the color matched the dangerously pointed shoes on her feet. If she wasn't constantly antagonizing Shay, I might want to know what secrets she was keeping.

"*Assistant* Mayor Peters." Dani's head tipped with as minimal a greeting as anyone could give.

"Hello, Officer Forrest. How are we all today?" She stepped around the side of the building as if she intended to enter through the back door.

"We *all* are just fine." Dani crossed her arms over her chest and sidestepped to lean and block the entrance.

"What can we do for you, Andrea?" Shay's voice sounded tired and Dexter didn't move as he kept himself pinned against his partner. Shay's arm raised, and she pushed my shoulder until I was safely standing behind her.

"I understand you inherited a bar." It wasn't a question, and I found it interesting that she ignored Dani and directed the conversation at Shay.

"We did," Shay answered as her hand patted Dexter to calm him down.

Andrea stopped moving toward the door and leaned against the patrol car. "I'm curious about the building, not the business. Do you have intentions to sell it?"

"I don't think either of us is interested." Shay looked at Dani. "You agree?"

"One hundred percent, and I probably wouldn't sell it to you even if I was desperate," Dani added as she stepped closer to the Assistant Mayor.

"Well, that's disappointing." She opened her purse to retrieve a business card. "Why don't you call me, Shay? Maybe we can discuss it privately, and I can convince you it would be beneficial for everyone involved."

Shay took the card but didn't put it in her pocket. Dexter's upper lip curled away from his front teeth, and although he didn't growl, his rigid body position made it clear he didn't like Andrea Peters. He didn't want her standing as close as she was to Shay. The dog barked twice, and the sound startled the Assistant Mayor enough for her to step away.

"You have my number."

Shay held the card up, flicking it between her fingers and thumb to make a snapping sound. "I do, but don't expect a call."

Andrea turned to walk away. "That would be a terrible shame." She waved a hand, and the three of us watched her walk around the building.

"What the hell was that about?" Dani asked as she snatched the business card from Shay's hand. "She is a terrible person. Why would you humor her?"

"She's harmless," Shay said dismissively. Dexter stepped away from her and dropped his butt in front of the door, waiting for us to open it.

"She is so into you," I said, with a hint of teasing jealousy in my tone.

Dani didn't hesitate to agree. "Wildwood's right; she's absolutely into you."

"That's too bad." Shay held her hand out to me, and I was delighted to hold it. "I'm happily and indefinitely taken."

"Anyone who knows you could see that." Dani smiled and turned to open the door. "You two hungry? Diana is making burgers, and I've got a table in the back."

"Amelia and Stout?" I asked.

"They're looking through some things." Dani pointed to the hidden panel, discreet about saying out loud that they were in the cellar.

"What kinds of things?" I asked, curious to know what the two of them might discover in the boxes downstairs.

"Stout had this idea, and he needed someone to help him with the heavy lifting." Dani sidestepped a case of whiskey on the floor.

"And he took Amelia instead of you?" I said with a laugh. Shay tugged my hand and squeezed it.

"You've seen my wife. She can take you in a fistfight." Dani held up her balled hands, rolling them in front of her like a boxer.

I let go of Shay's hand and held mine up in surrender. "I wouldn't even think about taking her on."

As we walked into the bar, I was happy to see more than a dozen people inside. Business was good, and that was great for the women in front of me.

"Beer?" Dani asked, pointing at Shay and me.

"Yes, please," I said, and Shay nodded her agreement. She pulled out a chair, and Dexter scooted under the table. I sat down beside her and wiggled close enough to whisper in Shay's ear. "I hope I didn't piss her off."

"You're fine. You fit right in." She kissed my cheek. "Dani's a real smartass, and I think she's finally comfortable enough to be that way with you."

"As long as you're sure."

Shay kissed me. "I'm positive."

"Positive about what?" Dani asked. She had a beer in each hand, and a third one gripped in the triangle of her fingertips. She set them down on the table.

Shay didn't say a word; instead, she stood up and reached into her pocket to answer her cell phone. "Pierce," she said as she stepped away from the table.

"What was the positive?" Dani pulled out a chair, and Dexter snuck through the opening to follow Shay. I watched as she put down a hand and the dog threaded in against her thigh.

"I asked Shay if I'd offended you."

"What would offend me?" Dani asked.

I looked down at my beer. "Joking about Amelia. I—"

Dani held up a hand. "Everyone already knows she's the tough one in this marriage. I'd be an idiot to think otherwise."

If she was being kind to make me feel better, it worked, but I sensed the sincerity in her tone. "She is pretty wonderful."

"The absolute love of my life." Dani's voice broke as she said the words.

I thought about it, realizing I was in a place where I could relate to having a lover who was also the love of your life. "It feels good to have someone who loves you, wants to be in love with you."

"It does." Dani took a sip of her drink. "Amelia likes you, if you couldn't tell. She thinks you're very good for Shay, and I told her I agree."

I felt the heat flush my cheeks, and I took a sip of my drink to change the awkwardness of the conversation. "Thanks, and I think she's very good for me, too."

Shay walked up behind me and held my shoulders. "What did I miss?"

"Mutual admiration society." I winked at her.

"What, are you ordering hats?" Shay joked.

Dani looked at the two of us. "Must be an inside thing?"

"Something like that," Shay said as she pulled out a chair and waited for Dex to find a place to lie down.

"Everything okay?" I asked, curious about the phone call.

"The station. I have a K-9 meeting in the morning." She pointed at the glass in front of her to confirm it was her own and took a sip.

"Review time?" Dani asked.

I knew nothing about police procedures and what was involved in being a K-9 handler. Shay made it seem easy, and I never considered what she had to do to keep Dexter. "What does that mean?" I asked.

"The department just wants to run through the paperwork. It's all crossing T's and dotting I's," Shay said, which explained nothing.

"Anything to worry about?" I asked.

Shay's hand touched mine. "Everything is wonderful. Dexter is performing exactly as they'd hoped, and I'm sure they just want to see us in action so they can justify the funding."

"I thought Benton arranged for Dexter?" Dani interrupted.

"She did," Shay said.

Why had Benton arranged for the K-9 acquisition? I wondered. She was a civilian, and even though she'd had a long life in the department, I didn't understand why she would be involved. Unless she was the one who found him?

I asked Shay if that was the case.

"What do you mean?" Shay took another sip of her beer. "She was at the town meeting when they voted. In fact, she was the most outspoken, and she advocated for me to get the training."

My brow furrowed as I thought about Dexter in our lives. Benton was involved in so much of our magick that it made me wonder if she'd known about our dog, about what he might become. "Where did Dexter come from?"

"He was a rescue. Lots of service dogs are," Shay explained. "I think it was a puppy mill seizure from a few towns over. Do you remember, D?"

Dani looked away for a second, thinking. "Pretty sure that was in Grant's Pass. A nasty place in that town. I've always felt there was an otherworldly presence in the foothills. It's about twenty miles south as the crow flies."

My eyebrow raised, and I looked at Shay for an explanation. I'd never heard the term before. "As a what now?" I asked.

"As the crow flies. It means if you could travel straight south from here to there, it would be about twenty miles, but since you have to navigate old mountain roads, it's more like a sixty-mile one-way ride."

"Ahh, so isolated and empty, kinda like Bannock."

Dani nodded. "A lot like Bannock. And I think they were breeding German Shepherds as safety animals. If I remember correctly, their department seized over fifty dogs that day."

"I wasn't at the raid," Shay added. "But that sounds about right."

"You're saying that Dexter came from a small town like ours? Do they fight demons there?" I asked, trying to put together how we ended up with a dragon-dog.

"I imagine they do. I don't know many towns around here that don't have their fair share of activity."

"That doesn't strike you as odd?" How was it possible that this part of the country was so casual about sharing their lives with demons?

"They've always been here," Dani said.

And that was the simple truth. We lived in a world peppered with the supernatural.

"And for you?" I asked Shay.

"You've just never been as awake as you are now. Demons and magick are everywhere."

If I hadn't been sitting, I probably would have fallen over, but it made sense. My life now had enormous demon activity, and perhaps if I'd been looking for them my entire life, I might have found them. Demon encounters and otherworldly beings were standard for the women sitting at the table, and I realized now that this was my normal these days, too.

I leaned forward in my chair to ask my next question in a whisper. "Do you think someone knew Dex would transform?"

Shay set her glass on the table. "You mean did they breed him to be a dragon?"

"Is that even a thing you can do?" Dani leaned back in her chair.

I bent down to look under the table at the massive dog curled up on the floor near my feet. "I'd say a solid yes." My head popped up. "It's definitely a thing someone did."

"Let me get this straight." Dani held up her hands, waving them in the air. "You think Benton knew about Dexter's ability to transform and set things up so he would become Shay's partner?"

"Do either of you believe in coincidences?" I asked and turned to look at Shay. "What are the odds?"

Shay snapped her fingers, and Dexter came out from under the table. "The only way to know for certain is to ask the only thing that's been alive as long as Benton."

"Stout." I said, and I started to get up from my chair.

"When they come up, I'll ask." Shay put her hand on my knee. "Let them finish downstairs, and then we'll talk."

Before I could say another word, a tray of hamburgers landed on the table beside me. "Who has the bloody burger?" Diana asked as she set a plate in front of Dani.

Shay held up a hand. "That would be mine." She rubbed her hands together, excited for the food. "This looks so good."

"They're burgers, honey." I picked up a fry and popped it into my mouth.

"I know, but I'm so hungry." She took a generous bite and made a satisfied sound that made me shuffle in my seat.

Amelia and Stout stepped up to the table. "You started without us?" Amelia said, as she took a small bite of her wife's burger.

"Hey!" Dani turned away from her wife and cradled her burger. "You said you didn't want any."

"No, that's not what I said. I said I didn't want my own." She wiped her lips on a napkin and dried her fingers. "I just wanted a bite." She reached into her pocket and slapped a deck of cards on the table.

Shay leaned in for a closer look. "What did you find?"

"There is no way that I'm playing cards with you. I don't care what they are." I pushed the pile away with the back of my hands. "Not a chance. My ego can't take it."

"These are special cards." Stout walked over the deck, creating a fan across the open tabletop.

I set down my burger and wiped my hands before touching the top card. The backside was plain, with two sketched leaves I guessed were oak. The paper was thick cardstock, but with no slick coating like a modern deck of playing cards. I turned it over on the table.

"What the hell is it?" I asked as my finger traced over an image I'd never seen before.

The charcoal-style sketch was an unbelievable monster. The head looked like a bear, but was skeletal where it should have been fur and flesh. There were no hands or paws, just three claws at the end of the arms and legs. There was a number on the card and a brief description that I read aloud in a whisper. *"Buscreas, class-one, potent venom injected from claws, night vision. Vulnerable to spells of evisceration and class-one steel."* I looked at the sketch and laid the card on the table in front of me.

Shay picked it up. "Where did these come from?" She studied the front and back before pushing the cards into a pile and picking up the deck.

"They were in—" Amelia stopped herself before revealing out loud where she'd been. "They were in Benton's things."

Shay pulled one card after another, looking at the pictures and scanning through the descriptions. "Do you know if they were hers?" Shay asked.

Stout stayed close to Shay. "They belong to the Magick and the Maker and are part of their tool reserve." Stout landed on Shay's hand. "These didn't come from Regina. They were passed on to her, just like most everything down there." He whispered these last words.

"They're like trading cards," Dani joked as she picked one from Shay's hand. She studied it for a second and placed it back on the deck. "I think the only person ever to trade them was the keeper of your magick because all I see are blank pieces of heavy cardstock."

Amelia smiled and tapped the deck. "Stout said he could read them, so I figured they were enchanted or something like that."

"Written in *sanquis* blood?" I looked at Shay.

"They must be if you, Stout, and I can see them." She shuffled through a few more cards before setting the deck on the table.

I drew the top one, looked, and threw it down on the table, face up. "I know that one intimately."

"Huic Ostiarius," Stout said.

It didn't matter if the name was in Latin or English; it brought a chill to my spine regardless. The Gatekeeper demon's flesh-ripping hands had been close to my body too many times.

"These are hundreds of years old," Stout continued.

"How do you know that?" Shay asked.

"We pulled out a box," Amelia explained. "Under the table of weapons, there was a trunk. Stout wanted me to open it."

"So you did?" Dani asked, pulling her wife into her lap. "Anything could have been inside."

"It belonged to Hebra," Stout said. "She was the Magick after Kai and made those cards. Probably to learn their powers, and maybe she didn't have access to writing journals."

"I guess things were very different back then." I stacked the cards and handed them to Shay. "Maybe you should put them away for now."

Shay stood and stuffed the deck into her front pocket. "We can go through them at home." She picked up our plates and carried them to the bar, returning a few seconds later. "Any more drinks?"

"I'm good," I said.

Dani and Amelia looked at each other, asking the same question. "We're good, too. I think we're going to head out."

Amelia stood, and she and Dani came around for hugs. "Good shooting out there today," Dani whispered in Shay's ear.

"You, too."

Amelia kissed Shay's cheek. "Goodnight, both of you." Her hand touched my shoulder. She turned away, and the two of them left the bar.

"You ready to go home?" I looked at Shay, who was sliding her chair away from the table.

"I am so ready to go home." She reached her hand out to me, and I held tight.

Home sounded perfect right now.

~~~~~~~~~~

Shay had little to say on the drive home. When we arrived back at the carriage house, she turned off the car and released the trunk lid. "Why don't you grab Dex, and I'll get the rest."

"I'd love to."

I opened my door and turned around to release Dexter from the back seat. It was dark in the parking lot, and the energy made me pause. Every shadow seemed haunted, and I had a feeling something was lurking in every one.

"See anything, Dex?" I asked the dog, and he moved without concern to the carriage house door.

Shay's arm came around my waist. "What's up?" she asked as the duffel bag bounced on her hip.

"Something feels off," I said as I held tight to her and took the ammunition case from her hand.

"Spooked from the attack?"

I shook my head. "I don't think so. Maybe."

"Let's just get inside, and we can clean up and do some meditation."

"Meditation?" I winked at her, and even in the dim light, I could see the mischievous smile on her face.

"We should also do a cleansing ritual for this." She tapped the cuff around my wrist.

"We could do both." I grabbed her arm to look at the time on her watch. "Although, it's getting kinda late."

"Do you want me to tell them that?" She pointed up at a nearby window.

Although Stout was upstairs, I could hear him yelling, and I could only guess he was talking to the dog. "You're going to get yourself fired!" Stout's voice was loud enough to hear from the workshop.

"Hey!" Shay yelled up the stairs as she climbed to the second floor.
~~~~~~~~~~

"Yes?" Stout hovered in front of her face.

"What are the two of you yelling about?" Shay watched the dog flop onto his bed as she sat down at the table.

"I want you to understand that I don't know where Dex came from. All I know is that Benton got him for you." Stout was anxious, rubbing his hands as he paced back and forth over the tabletop.

"Did she know he was a dragon?" Shay asked. I was sitting beside her at the table, watching the two of them discuss the dog balled up in the corner of our living room.

"She knew he would be a protector." Stout dropped into a cross-legged position.

"My protector?" Shay ran her fingers through her hair.

She didn't do it often, but when she did, I knew she was trying to calm her thoughts. Until today, I'd never questioned where Dexter came from, and maybe I should have, but who wouldn't be happy to have a dragon?

The fairy held up his hand in front of Shay. "Don't take it out on Dexter. He knew nothing. He's an innocent."

She looked at me. "Why would you think I'm mad at Dexter? I would never hold him responsible. I just don't understand why all the secrets keep coming out around the Magick and Maker's powers."

"Benton did what she had to do to survive." I touched her cheek so she would look at me when I said it. "We've all done things we aren't proud of to get to where we are."

"Forget it." Shay stood up and walked away. Her anger seemed misplaced, and a few seconds later, she returned to ask, "Why would Dexter get fired?" She sat down.

"He's a dragon," Stout explained. "He's been alive for over two hundred years and only took the form of a dog because Regina asked him to."

"She set it up so I would get him, and we could work together." Her voice was low, almost a whisper. "And I would have a protector."

Shay pushed away from the table and walked out of the room, but I stayed put, staring at the dog, whose eyes followed

Shay until she was out of sight. I heard the greenhouse door slide open, and I went to talk to Shay.

She was cutting herbs and placing them in a glass bowl. "Can I help you with this?" I asked, unsure what she was doing.

"No, I just need to think." She snipped a second leaf from the bay plant.

"Tell me what's going on in your head."

She moved between being frustrated or quiet most of the evening, but sometimes that was Shay. She'd been on her own for most of her life, and the habits of solitude would take time to change, but she needed to remember that she wasn't alone.

Her hands stopped moving, and she turned to look at me. "I'm tired of all the damn secrets." I didn't say a word, just nodded, and waited for more to come. "It feels like Benton was two different people, and that I never knew either of them."

"Well, she *was* two people, but she let you know what she could. Those damn secrets kept her safe, and they kept you safe, too."

Shay's eyebrow raised, and she squinted with a questioning glare.

"The cellar at Slammed has so many tools that give us an advantage," I continued. "Benton left a massive arsenal, a collection of diaries and files. But the most important thing she did for you was to leave behind something she never had."

"Dexter?" Shay tossed the clippers on the bench.

I nodded. "She made sure that when we came to power, we had the ultimate companion." I stepped in front of Shay and rested my hands on her hips.

"I need to stop being surprised that there were so many damn secrets and lies, don't I?"

I drew a finger across Shay's cheek, brushing her hair away from her eyes. "Listen, I'm not saying it's right or wrong, but what's done is done." I kissed her.

Shay pulled back. "I'm so tired, Wil. Can we just do the blessing and go to bed?"

I held the cutting bowl and walked with her as she clipped the rest of the plants. "Are you sure your magick is in the right place for a cleansing?"

Shay reached over the table to slice a piece of bark from a log. "It will be, yes. You need to be able to go out with that cuff knowing that you're protected."

"I'll be safe."

Her hands hovered over the herbs in the bowl. "Yes, my love. You will be." I followed Shay into the magick room and prepared to stand beside her. "Here." She passed the bowl of plants and a pair of scissors to me. "Cut these into little pieces and mix them together."

Magick and spells and the combining of components always made me apprehensive. I didn't want to make a mistake, not when they could hurt her or me, so I stared at the saucer filled with the plants she'd collected. "You want little pieces?" I asked.

She smiled. "Don't overthink it. This part is always intuitive."

Magick, loving Shay, being in this relationship—every part of my life was intuitive, and if she trusted me, perhaps I could trust it, too. I snipped each leaf and stem until they were a crumbled combination of textures and hues that smelled like a kitchen in the middle of a forest.

Shay moved around the room, assembling the altar and lighting the candles. The sound and scent of the censer charcoal was an indicator that the ritual was about to begin. I turned the cuff sideways to slide it off my wrist and laid it in the center of the table in front of me. I moved to step away, but Shay's hands fell on my shoulders, and she wrapped around me from behind.

"This one should be on you."

I felt the weight of a robe fall over my shoulders and looked down, expecting to see her deep purple cloak wrap around me. Her thumb pushed the bone-colored toggle through the leather loop, and the forest green robe weighed on my shoulders. The fabric was soft against my skin, and I raised my arms, gripping the braided trim with my fingers.

"Shay," I squeaked out her name through the clutch of emotion. We were coupling our magick, bonding her powers and mine in a way that felt like a covenant.

She whispered in my ear, "We're going to do a lot of magick in this room. You should be a part of it." Her lips touched my cheek, and a few seconds later, a soft velvet hood covered my head.

I turned to look at her. "This is..." I didn't have a single word that expressed my emotions.

"It's perfect. *You're* perfect," she said as her hands slipped inside my robe to rest on my hips. Her kiss was tender against my lips. Moments later, she stepped back, and I took a deep breath, blowing it through my lips, fighting the happy tears.

"Thank you." I struggled to form the words, lost in the gesture's thoughtfulness.

Shay's hand rested on my cheek, and she wiped my tears with the pad of her thumb. "I love you, and you're welcome." She adjusted the shoulders of the cloak and stepped back. "You ready?"

My cheek rose with a half-grin. "As I'll ever be." I turned to the altar in front of us.

"The circle is cast," Shay said as she stepped around the ring of salt on the floor. She whispered across the wick of a thick black candle, and the flame flickered to life as she set it on the floor. "You want to start?"

I shook my head. No, I wasn't ready to pour protection over my creation. Shay stepped around the table to stand beside me. Her hands moved over every object, first touching the tiny silver spoon to scoop incense over the smoldering coal. It was impossible to identify any single scent as the haze of smoke spiraled around us.

"Goddess divine." Shay's voice broke the silence. "Be in our circle, we ask of you. Cleanse this cuff with purposeful intention; purify the energies of the amulet to protect and vibrate the skills of Bast, goddess of protection." Shay held my cuff in her hands, sprinkling water and salt over it. "Spirit of earth and air, bring strength and truth. Release the hindering forces housed within and protect the Maker as she wears it." She reached for my hands and turned them over, placing the cuff in my palms. "Forged from fire and called to be and do our will, we cast away evil and draw a barrier around the wearer." With Shay's guidance, we passed the wrist cuff through the candle flame. "Our obeisance to truth and the boundaries of love and nature, for good to call out evil." She poured a cup of moon water over my hands, reciting, "Blessed by the goddess to be true, in love and honor, dispelling evil. In peace and trust and in all that is our faith." She looked at me as she said the last words, nodding encouragement for me to repeat them. "So mote it be."

"So mote it be," I whispered before taking a deep, calming breath.

As so many times before, the first few minutes after an incantation left me invigorated. The smell of incense and sacred oils was intoxicating, but the most dramatic experience was the surge of energy the earth sent in response to her words. Today, I felt it through every cell of my body, warm and radiant. Shay threaded the cuff around my wrist and drew my hand to her heart.

"Protect her," she whispered. Her forehead rested against my own. "Please."

I felt a rush of pure love move from her hands into my body. She placed an elemental barrier inside of me, and I did not know what it meant or how it would take hold, but I trusted the connection.

"You're incredible." My voice broke as I said the words.

CHAPTER XVIII

TRANSLATION

I didn't feel Shay leave the bed the following morning, but I woke when I heard the velcro separate before she threw her bulletproof vest over her head. Dexter was at her feet, and something was comforting about the early routine.

"Good morning, beautiful." I watched her arms slide into the sleeves of her shirt.

"Hey." She stopped to lean over the bed and kiss me. "Good morning." She hovered long enough for a second kiss and returned to her routine of getting dressed. "What's on your schedule for today?" she asked as her fingers worked over the buttons.

"I've got a few calls to make. Maybe another workshop." I sat up in bed and combed my hair away from my face. "I've got an errand to run, too." My head fell against the headboard as I watched her cinch her duty belt around her waist. "What about you?"

"I'm not sure. I have that meeting with the chief about Dex. It's probably just a routine run." She drew her service weapon and checked the magazine. "Should be done at three, unless I'm not." She looked up at me and smiled.

"I'll be here. Unless I'm not." I winked at her, and she climbed across the bed and straddled my legs.

"You are so bad." Her palms pressed beside my head, trapping me for one more long, crushing kiss.

My eyes were closed when she leaned back.

"Only for you." I curled against my pillow and watched her go. I wasn't ready to leave the warmth of our bed, but a few minutes later, my cell phone rang.

"Hello?"

"Ms. Blackstone." I didn't recognize the caller's voice.

"Yes…?" I drew out my answer.

"Assistant Mayor Peters here. I was wondering if I might interest you in a meeting this afternoon?" The way she'd said my name, it seemed Andrea Peters was looking for something, and after our conversation at the bar, I had an idea what it might be.

"I have a few appointments." It was a lie, but I needed time to figure out what she was planning, and I wanted to talk to Shay. "Perhaps we can meet in a few days when my schedule is open."

The silence on the other end of the call lasted long enough for me to think she'd hung up. I was about to hit the end call button when I heard her say, "Two days. I'll meet with you on Thursday afternoon."

"I'll be here at the workshop." I wanted to ask more questions to determine if she was using me to get to Shay, but before I could, the phone beeped twice, and the call ended.

"Unbelievable," I said out loud as I tossed the phone on the side table.

That woman had a way of making me uncomfortable and knocking me a little off balance. What could the Assistant Mayor want from me? I didn't own the bar, and I had limited experience with magick. I thought about our previous encounters here and at the bar and remembered the files she'd given to Shay just after Benton's death. Perhaps the documents had secrets to reveal, much like Benton and Stout.

I jumped out of bed and threw on a t-shirt and sweatpants. I wanted to find the folder from Andrea. Shay's move from the house into my apartment was mostly unboxed. Her books filled the shelves, but a few unpacked boxes remained. These held notebooks and folders Benton had left before going into the hospital. I opened the first and dug through each clipped and bound stack. Nothing looked like the file I remembered. I sorted through another and another until I'd exhausted every box in the living room. I couldn't find the document, so I moved into the magick room and opened the drawers of the apothecary wall.

"Why are you tearing the carriage house apart?" Stout flew down in front of me.

"I'm looking for–" I stopped talking to concentrate on the stack of folders tucked into the wall's corner. My fingers fanned the pages until I'd scanned the pile. Nothing.

"Looking for what?" He landed on top of the file stack.

"Andrea Peters' file." I waved the stack just enough to flip my little fairy into the air. "Right after Benton died, she gave us a file. I want to know what's in it."

"There's evil in her, Wildwood. You should be very careful."

"Evil? What do you mean by evil?" I stopped searching. The tone in his voice made me shiver. If our tiny fairy knew something I didn't, perhaps I should listen. "She's got it strong for Shay, alright, but I wouldn't call that evil."

"There's more than lust for a woman in that bitch's stare. I know it." Stout hovered beside my ear as I wedged the file back on the shelf.

"If you think there's more, why don't you help me find the damn file?" I pushed off the wall to stand and scanned the cubbies and shelves for loose papers.

"Maybe Shay has it with her. Did you think of that? Maybe she's having it decontaminated." He flew to the top shelf and paced.

My cheek puffed with a frown. "What are you, a child? It's not like Andrea has cooties."

"Cooties?" He flopped to sit on the edge of the cabinet, kicking his legs back and forth. "Cooties are child's play. That bitch is hiding something, and none of it is for the greater good."

"Then stop talking and start looking. Now that I have full Maker powers, I think I'll be able to read those pages."

I opened all the drawers and searched each closet in the apartment, exhausting every place the file could be. I dialed Shay's cell phone, but her recorded voice answered. "You've reached Officer Pierce. I can't take your call. Please leave a message." The long beep followed.

"Hey, love," I said, hesitant to give details about what I was looking for, "can you call me? I'm trying to find answers to a question, and I'm hoping you can help." I ended the call and tossed my phone on the table. "I guess we're on our own." I looked at my fairy friend.

"Maybe she took it to the bar?" His knees bent to launch himself in the air. "Maybe we should go look in the cellar?"

"Why? Are you thirsty?" I asked, only half-joking. He was probably ready for his first beer of the day.

"I wouldn't say no if you offered me a cold drink, but I was only thinking about helping you." He crossed his arms over his chest with a pout as he hovered in front of my face.

"I guess I'll have to take your word for it." I grabbed my boots and laced them. "Let's go look at the bar."

My fingers squeezed the cuff on my wrist. We were about to test the power of Shay's magick and the efficacy of its protection. I stood at the door of the carriage house, remembering the attack, and wondered if it would look ridiculous for me to carry my new axe down the sidewalk of Bannock. I picked it up.

"You should take it," Stout suggested.

I clenched the unwrapped handle. "Yeah?"

He didn't say another word as he landed on the back of my hand, patting my knuckles, reassurance that this weapon should accompany us. I turned the honed edge toward the floor and tucked the handle into the belt around my waist.

It was a change to see out-of-state license plates in front of the general store and the recently reopened antique shop. Tourism was picking up in Bannock just as demon activity was on the rise.

As we walked by the police station, I considered stopping to talk to Shay, but I hated police stations. I had an aversion to the system behind the solid brick walls. Shay hadn't returned my call, and her patrol car was not in front of the station, so it was easier to just keep going. We walked the last block to the bar and went in through the service door close to the hidden stairs. It was hours before Diana and Amelia would come to open the bar for lunch, so Stout and I felt safe to make our way to the cellar.

"Where should we start?" he asked as he launched from my shoulder.

Shay's organization of the apothecary wall made the answer easy. "Files are all over there." I pointed to the long table with boxes stacked on top. "I guess we start at the top." I patted the highest one marked *archive*.

"You flip the top, and I'll dig through." He skipped across the lid of the box, running in place.

It seemed like an impossible scenario to watch a tiny creature imitating the Running Man dance move. I followed his direction, and together we searched the endless compilation of documents. When his feet touched a gray flap of tattered animal skin, Stout launched in the air.

"Use your Maker hands to turn this one over. It's knotted together," he said, hovering close to my ear.

I reached into the box, removing the unbound papers, but didn't understand the characters burned into the leather. I hesitated to untie the cord holding the parchment inside and asked Stout, "Can you translate?"

He waved his hands in surrender. "I can, but I won't."

Stout flew to the corner of the cellar, as far from me and the ancient tome as he could get. My fingers traced the deep grooves of the letters. "I think maybe this is Pictish. I know you can translate it. Just tell me what it says."

"That's soul-splitting magick, and I'm not fooling around."

"What do you mean, soul-splitting?" I turned the book over, and there were no external markings aside from the letters on the front. "What's in it? Damn it, Stout! Just tell me."

"I want a beer first." He flew to the base of the stairs.

"Translation first, beer second." I waved the book in the air. "What's it say?"

"Rasavatam!" The word came out of his mouth like a curse on his tongue, and he slapped both of his hands over his mouth. I waited for thunder to crash or sparks of lightning to fly in the room, but they didn't. Nothing happened.

"Raz-a—What?" I didn't know how to repeat the word.

"It says Rasavatam. And it's not Pictish. It's Sanskrit," he called from the staircase. "Don't open it, don't look at it, and *do not* read it without the Magick standing right beside you."

In the last few months, I'd experienced magick in impossible situations—demon attacks in my carriage house, spells to lock monsters in concrete, demon sift to heal bleeding wounds, the magickal presence of fairies and dragons. I set the book on the table and took a giant step back before sending Shay a quick text message that included an image of the cover. Might as well ask her what she thinks.

"Can we get that beer now?" Stout asked as he hovered over the railing of the spiraling iron staircase.

"We didn't find the file, Stout. I want to know what Andrea is hiding." I filled the box with the stacks we'd removed and opened the next. We went through two more until we got to the final one.

"Maybe you should ask Shay if she has it?" Stout stood on the cover, preventing me from lifting the lid with the reverse energy of his loud wings.

Before I could respond, my phone vibrated on the table, and I read the message out loud. "'Just finished my review, and it was amazing. I'm coming to check out that book. See you in a few.'" I smiled at the text. With Shay, "a few" could mean hours or minutes. I was hoping for the latter.

"Good. She can answer all the questions." Stout leaped off the box and up the stairs. "We have time for a beer." It wasn't a question or a suggestion, but since he'd spent the entire afternoon going through the Maker and Magick archives, I decided he deserved a cold beer.

"Okay, let's go. But as soon as she gets here, we're coming back down to look some more." I climbed the staircase and listened for movement in the back room. After a moment, I slid the panel, and the two of us wandered to the service door to wait for Shay.

A few minutes later, a shiny new patrol car pulled up in front of me. Shay sat in the driver's seat, and I noticed her name scrolled above the handle on the door. My eyes skimmed over the two-toned side of the SUV and stopped when I saw the title, "K-9 Dexter," painted on the panel above the rear door handle.

Shay opened her door and stepped out. "What do you think of my new ride?" Her arm came around my hip as she tugged me close.

"This is—wow, this is amazing," I said.

I had thought little about the meeting today, believing it was a routine evaluation of the K-9 unit's value to the community. The vehicle confirmed Dexter was here to stay.

Shay beamed. "It's amazing. I'm still pinching myself to make sure it's real."

I heard Dexter's bark, and Shay pressed a button on her vest to release him from his new cargo area. When the door opened, I got my first glimpse of the dog's transport system. They had replaced the back seat with rubber-lined reinforced steel floors, a stationary water dish, and metal grate dividers. Dexter liked it so much, he was content to stay in his space.

"Made himself right at home, huh?" I asked as Shay headed to the back of the car.

"He loves it." She opened the divided doors. "And so do I. All of my gear fits in the cases back here." She patted the metal cubbies. "I just pull this, and the magick happens." She tugged the hinged handle, and I could see her demon-hunting gear fit into the foam-lined drawers.

"I guess this means that they're happy with your performance?" My hip bumped against hers.

"The chief went on and on about Dexter, about his conduct as a K-9 unit." She pushed the drawer into the locked position and closed the rear doors. "An anonymous donor funded the vehicle. The board said, in the long run, we could be a public relations asset, and that's all the Mayor needed to hear."

She stopped moving, giving me enough time to wrap myself around her for a hug. "I'm so damn proud of you." I kissed the side of her face.

"Dex sealed the deal." She pointed to the passenger side. "Hop in front. Let me show you."

Her excitement was enchanting, and I let go of her waist to run around the side and get in. The front seat technology upgrades with their numerous electronic controls were overwhelming.

"This box here." Shay tapped her knuckles against the four dip-switch panels. "This protects Dexter from heat." Her half-laugh was adorable. "I guess for a typical K-9 officer, heat exhaustion might be an issue. I'm not sure how it would affect my dragon, though."

"You're saying if he got locked in here, this control would protect him?" I turned around to look at the dog behind us. Dexter slurped from the foam-padded water container welded to the vehicle floor.

"Yep, and this button here." She hooked the loop on her shirt. "This opens the side door to release Dex in an emergency."

The word "emergency" swirled around in my head. I'd never thought about opening the door during a traffic stop or when she was chasing a human threat. Shay had a way of making me forget people could be just as dangerous as the monsters crawling out of the tunnels at the mine.

"This is the protection I never knew you needed." I reached across her new computer console to hold Shay's hand.

"It's more than I thought Bannock PD would ever do." Shay turned her shoulder to show me the sliding door behind us. "One more thing." She flipped a lever, and the panel grate slid to open the divider; Dexter's head and body popped through. "Hey, buddy."

Dexter pushed his face toward me. "Hi, Dex. I guess you like your new ride?" He propped his paws on the armrest.

"What are your plans for the rest of the day?" Shay asked.

"It's funny that you bring that up. I was hoping you could help me find something."

Dexter pushed off and returned to lie on the floor.

"Sure, what are you looking for?"

My back pivoted to rest against the door. "I got a call from Andrea Peters today, and she wants to meet with me on Thursday."

"Does she?" Shay's right eyebrow pitched with curiosity. "About what?"

"She wouldn't say, but I plan to find out."

"Maybe I should be there." Shay squeezed my hand and let it go.

I nodded. "I will not say no."

Shay pressed the button on her vest, releasing the door behind me. "Dexter, *ante!*" she yelled, and the dog leaped out of the vehicle.

"So cool!" I said as I opened my door and followed them to the front of the car.

Shay ordered Dexter back into the car, latching the door closed and saying, "It's impressive for sure."

Stout landed on the back of her shoulder. "Can I get my beer now? I know we didn't find the folder, but Wildwood promised."

"First, get back in," Shay said. "We're taking a quick ride."

I ran around the side, pausing when Shay pressed a button on the dashboard that brought the vehicle to life. The display of switches lit up with different colors, and her roof lights rolled back and forth from red to blue. I slid into the seat next to her.

"Buckle up." She yanked the strap and locked her seatbelt in place.

"Where are we going?" I fastened my belt.

"I want to show you something." She put the car into reverse and backed into the street. A few seconds later, we were headed out of town. I recognized the route toward Dani's place and the firing range.

"Are you shooting with Dani?" I leaned away from her and closer to the car door. "We're going to her property, right?"

A delighted grin pushed at her cheeks. "To the property, yes, but we aren't shooting."

Shay's excitement was charming as she stared forward to focus on driving. I noticed she'd tied her red hair back in a tight ponytail, but her hat lay on the dashboard. Today's uniform looked perfect, pressed and starched, as if she'd taken it from the dry cleaner's hanger. I realized it was odd. Why would she look so fresh after a day of performing for the mayor?

"Are you wearing a fresh shirt?" I asked.

She looked down at herself. "Yes."

"Why?"

"I could tell you, but I think it'll be more fun to show you instead." Shay was on a mission, and it involved her new vehicle and something at the mine.

"You're not going to tell me what we're doing, are you?" My hand gave her shoulder a push, and she turned off the highway onto the gravel road.

"Nope."

The wait for answers ended when I saw the tall person standing beside the firing line table. I couldn't tell who it was at the moment, but I had a sneaking suspicion. I was also curious about the pile of padded material on the ground in front of whoever it was.

"Dani, is the surprise? That *is* Dani, right?"

Shay shifted the car into park and jumped out. "She's part of the surprise." She unbuttoned her shirt and reached behind her seat for another. This one had a tear across the front, and the top three buttons were missing.

"This morning's shirt?" I pointed at her from my seat in the car.

"Yep." She put the ripped shirt on. "Hop out and stand in front of the car. You're about to get a show."

I opened my door and turned to see that the pile in front of Dani was protective gear. My law enforcement family was apparently about to perform a K-9 demonstration. I waited against the hood of the patrol car as Shay walked across the field, yelling at Dani, who stood covered from head to toe in protective padding, her face hidden behind a wire-mesh mask. It was clear that our dragon-dog was about to attack Dani, and I had to admit I was a little excited to see them in action.

Shay shouted, "Police officer! Get down on the ground!" and advanced on Dani, drawing her taser. I turned as I heard Dexter growl and bark. Dani held her arms over her head, pretending like she wanted to hit Shay.

"*Custodire!*" Shay yelled as the kennel door of the patrol car opened and Dexter leaped out. He was fast, and before I could turn my head to follow his path, he was on Dani, tearing at the padding around her throat. His actions were ferocious, and seconds later, Shay called him to return to her. "*Reditus!*" Dexter's head lifted. He turned and ran, stopping at Shay's side.

"You good, D?" Shay asked, and I saw a padded arm lift from the prone body and imagined a thumbs up somewhere inside the gloved hand.

"I'm good. That was excellent execution." Dani rolled to her side and shook her shoulder until the arm pad released. "Good job."

Shay patted Dexter on his side, and the thump was loud as he fell against her leg. "Very good boy, Dex." She gave the dog one more pat before sending him back into the patrol car. "Dexter, *in.*" The K-9 returned to his kennel, and Shay closed him inside.

The entire experience happened in less than a minute, and my heart was chasing the excitement. Shay looked at me, her eyebrow raised as she asked, "Pretty great, isn't it?"

I reached for her hand and tugged her close to press her palm against the heart thumping wildly in my chest. Her smile said everything.

"That was insane."

Dani dropped the last leg pad on the ground. "His reaction was even faster than before."

"I'm pretty sure the dragon part of him wants to come out and fight," Shay said as she walked over to help Dani with the padded armor.

Dexter was half-dragon. Or was he all dragon *and* all dog? It was confusing to work out how he transformed, and the reality was that he was always a dog and always a dragon. I wondered how he controlled himself in the craziness of an attack.

"Good job, Dex." Dani shuffled her fingertips through the grated window to scratch the fur between the dog's ears.

"The three of you were impressive, but, Dani, aren't you a little scared to have a dragon attack your throat?"

"You saw her uniform." Dani pointed at the tattered shirt Shay wore. "She spent a lot of time with him earlier today."

I looked at the shirt again and stared at my girlfriend. The rips in her uniform were not from a human attack but from the claws of a particular K-9 dragon. I hooked my finger through the tear over Shay's left breast. "Dex did this?" I tugged it before letting go.

Shay pulled the shirt off and tossed it through the window. "The first time I called him out, he charged full steam and transformed mid-air. Dex didn't touch Dani because I stepped in his path. His claw grabbed the material of my shirt, and as soon as Dexter realized what he'd done, he transformed into his K-9 self and sniffed my entire upper body, checking for an injury. I could see the fear in his eyes, and he sat on the ground waiting for me to assure him I was alright."

"And?" Why had she stopped? I waved my hands, encouraging her to continue.

"I just hugged him, said I was okay. Then we tried the drill again, but this time I told him only to transform if he sensed a demon attack."

"And that worked?"

She smiled. "It did. We've been drilling for the last few hours." Shay pushed the release button, and Dexter jumped out of the vehicle and wandered in front of us. "He did a great job. Didn't you, Dex?" The dog barked twice and laid down in the dirt.

"So now what?" I asked as Dani threw the pads into the back of Shay's patrol car.

"I vote for a beer." Stout flew up to my face. "I think I earned a beer, don't you?"

"Earned a beer?" Dani questioned. "What did you do? You just sat and watched."

"I helped Wildwood. We looked through the cellar for hours."

Shay looked at Dani, and the two of them turned to look at me. "What?" I asked, feeling the full effect of their law enforcement stare. "I was trying to find Andrea's file."

"Why?" Shay led Dexter into the kennel of the patrol car, leaving the door open.

"Andrea wants to meet with me, and Stout thinks she's evil, and he freaked me out."

"She's evil all right," Dani said, laughing sarcastically. "Peters is a classic scorned lover."

Shay pushed into Dani's shoulder. "One date hardly made us lovers."

"It was two," I was quick to point out. "And *I* knew I loved you the first time I held your hand."

"Okay, two dates. Peters and I never held hands or kissed. I could barely sit with her in the restaurant. All that arrogance in one person." Shay waved off the experience.

"She's not looking for love, not anymore." Stout's declaration was a warning. "She's looking for power, and I'll bet it has everything to do with the Magick, the Maker, and your capacity for creation."

"Brigid's Hammer?" I asked.

Stout flew close to my ear and whispered so that no one else could hear. "She's lusting after you. Not for passion, just for power. Be careful." His wings buzzed as he flew back to the patrol car.

"How do you know?" He didn't respond to my question, and I stuck my head around the door. "Why would you say something like that and just fly away?"

"What did he say?" Shay asked as she closed the door, locking the K-9 and the fairy inside.

"That the Assistant Mayor is lusting after me for my powers."

"He's probably right," Dani said, walking toward her car. "Thanks for the fun, Pierce." She thumped the hood of the vehicle with her fist.

"No problem," Shay said over her shoulder as she opened my door. "You going to the bar or home?"

Dani rotated her wrist to check the time. "Amelia's already at Slammed. I'm going home to change, and I'll probably meet her over there."

"She likes the bar, I guess?"

Dani smiled. "More than I thought she would."

"That's very good."

"Happy wife, happy life!" Dani yelled from her window just before starting the car. "I'll see you later."

"Later."

Shay held out a hand to slap against Dani's as the car pulled away. When Shay turned back to me, she had a serious expression on her face. I sat in my seat and waited for her to come around to the driver's side. Before I could ask a question, her head turned toward the fairy in the back.

"What the hell do you know about Andrea Peters?" Her voice was loud, commanding; it caused my chest to tighten.

"She's coming for you. I don't know why or how, but I can feel it."

"Just like that?" Shay asked as she turned to look at me. My hands clenched to hide the sweatiness inspired by the intensity of my girlfriend's voice.

"Just like that."

He didn't say another word, and neither did Shay. The silence that fell between us was unnerving, and it was evident that Shay had similar ideas about the Assistant Mayor but was hesitant to express them. Was she worried about me? Was it possible that Andrea had powers of magick as well? I needed to know what was going on inside Shay's head.

"Can we talk about the file that Andrea gave you?"

Shay was quiet. Her eyes glanced up at the rearview mirror before looking at me. "What do you want to know?"

"I'd like to know where it is," I said a little louder than I'd meant, but this was not the time to revert to keeping secrets.

Shay's hands gripped the steering wheel, and she drove in silence until we parked in front of the carriage house. I noticed the bright orange door leading to our home and remembered the promise of happiness and love. I didn't move to get out of the car, instead turning to look at Shay.

"Where is the file, honey?"

Her forehead dropped against the steering wheel, and she rotated her head to look at me. "I have it. It's locked in the back."

"In this truck?"

She pushed away from the dashboard and grabbed the handle for the door. "I didn't want it in the carriage house."

"When?" How long had she driven around Bannock with the file in her car? Was it dangerous? How was it possible that everyone but me knew Andrea was a threat?

Shay's eyebrow raised, questioning. "When did I take it out?"

"Yes."

She took a deep breath and released it through puffed cheeks. "I took it this morning. After she approached us about the bar, something didn't feel right, and I just wanted it gone."

Shay was always going to put herself last in our relationship and throw herself in front of every potential danger coming for us.

"But you put it in here." I patted the metal divider behind my head. "You've been driving around with it all day."

"Andrea can't come after me. Not while I'm wearing this uniform and not while that guy is with me." She hitched her thumb, pointing at the dog behind us.

"What's in the file? Do you know?"

Shay shook her head as she dropped her foot to the ground to exit the car. I pulled the door handle and ran to meet her, holding my hand to her chest until her back pushed against the tailgate of her SUV. I wasn't dancing around the subject of Andrea Peters and her mysterious file. Shay was going to give me a solid answer.

"What's in the file?"

Shay didn't resist or try to push me away. Her hand came up, and her fingers wrapped around my wrist. I stared at the scars on her hand and thought about all the secrets she'd kept those first weeks after our reunion. Was this another secret, or was she trying to protect me? She closed her eyes.

"Shay, please tell me." Her shoulders relaxed, and I let go as her body slid down until her ass rested on the truck's bumper.

"Once I tell you, you can't un-know. I'm not just protecting you, Wil." Her head fell against the back window, and she stared up at the clouds in the sky.

What could be so significant as to cripple my girlfriend? We knew about Benton and the Magick of Bannock. We'd learned about Jacob and the Makers before him. The hammer was mine and bound to me by the goddess. What could be so terrible?

"Is it that bad?"

"It's more information than I wanted, and it's proof that Stout is right about Andrea." She stood up fast, knocking me off balance. Shay grabbed my bicep, pulling me into her arms. "People I love will never forgive me...or Benton." She tugged me into a tight embrace, and I felt her tremble as I held her close.

"You? Why you?" I whispered in her ear.

Shay released her hold and turned to open the back of the SUV. She removed the keyring from her duty belt and unlocked the base drawer in the new vehicle. As Shay pulled it open, I could see a locked box resting upright inside. She slid a different key in that case after removing it from the truck. When it opened, I could see the file and handwritten notes on top. She'd translated the documents from Andrea.

"What does it say, Shay?" I hesitated to touch the contents, waiting for her to explain what she knew.

"Secrets. Shit! So many damn secrets."

She closed the box and turned to release Dexter from the truck. I followed her inside the carriage house and up the stairs to the apartment. Stout flew by, chasing Dexter to his bed on the floor. Shay dropped the box on the table and walked to the bedroom to change out of her uniform, so I opened the box and removed the handwritten pages along with the file that I'd searched for all day.

The folder looked the same, worn around the edges and discolored from age. We weren't the first people to possess these pages. Shay returned wearing jeans and a t-shirt, and her hair was loose around her face as she sat down beside me.

"It's not redacted," I said as I laid Andrea's pages side by side on the table.

"No." Shay picked up the document with the Roman numeral I in the corner. "It surprised me when I opened it." She passed the page to me.

"What language is it?" I rotated the page, noticing that it was similar to the book we'd found in the cellar this afternoon. "It looks like something from a fantasy quest movie."

"It's Sanskrit, sweetheart."

I turned to look at Stout, who was sitting on the floor in front of Dexter. He jumped a little when he realized what Shay had said. The fairy sprung from the floor and hovered over the page. Shay turned it over so the fairy couldn't see it.

But he must have seen something because his eyes grew wide. He was speechless for a moment, his eyes darting from the page to Shay and back again several times. Finally, he swallowed hard and took a deep breath.

"Execution?" he asked, trying to put together what he'd seen.

"Wh–?" My voice caught in my throat. It was my turn to be speechless, it seemed. "*What?*"

Stout's voice was grave as he said, "That note in the corner? It said 'execution.'"

CHAPTER XIX

FRACTURED

"Execution?"

Saying the word made me tremble because I'd felt the pain of otherwise-innocuous words more than I could count throughout my life. Words like, *you're moving,* broke my heart just about every eight months until I turned eighteen and aged out of the system. *Misplaced* became an identity long after my caseworker used it to explain where my only pair of shoes had gone. The word *dead* was just another way to describe how I felt inside every time social services arrived at my foster home. But the words, *I'm sorry,* were said so often that they became as meaningless as the word *family.*

"Execution" was a word I *never* expected to hear. My pulse pounded in my temples, and it was all I could do to keep from falling out of my chair. Andrea had given us a file, and the first descriptive word we could read was someone's or something's execution.

I tapped the folder with my finger. "What do you mean, execution?"

"Goddess of Fire!" Shay yelled, and I turned toward the sound of her voice. Her forehead rested on the table, and the file pages were crumpled in fists squeezed so tightly that her knuckles were white. "Damn her!"

The woman I adore, usually calm and reserved, was raging in front of me. The power of this file's secret was beyond what I'd expected, and Shay didn't plan to share it, ever.

"Sweetheart." My fingers hovered close to her clenched fists, but I was hesitant to touch her.

Shay's arms fell away, and the pages dropped to the floor. Stout perched to fly down and read them, but she stopped him.

"Don't look, Stout. Please." She sounded more plaintive than I'd ever heard her before. "Trust me, you don't want to carry the burden of this. You knew about Benton, about the decisions she made about Wildwood and me. This is bigger and—just let me carry it."

Stout hovered over the file, and I couldn't tell if he was angry or sad at the mention of Benton's secrets.

"Is it that bad?" I asked as I grasped her hand and led her to sit.

"Yes, I'm afraid it is."

I bent down to pick up the pages and collect them into a pile. I stuffed them back into the folder along with a thin piece of leather-like material. Stout saw me pick it up and flew over to look at it.

"You know what that is?" He pointed to the material and looked at me and then at Shay.

I shook my head as Shay answered, "I think it's animal hide or something like that."

The fairy pressed his face against the stiff postcard-sized page. His nose wrinkled in disgust as he dropped it on the table. "That didn't come from a forest creature. That's the flesh of an immortal being, saturated with the most dangerous kind of evil." He flew to his perch on top of the bookcase. "That shouldn't be in here."

Shay picked up the card of flesh and placed it in the file folder. "What do you mean, it shouldn't be in here?" She put all the pages in the box and locked it tight.

"You cast a protective barrier, and that barrier should have stopped you from bringing that inside the carriage house." He waved at the box on the table. "It shouldn't be in here. There's something wrong with your barrier."

The rush of fear hit me like cold water against my skin. My breath hitched, and I lost myself in the flash of memories: Shay and I laying in a field, learning how to communicate with the soul of the earth; Mama Pierce sitting across from us as we ate a simple meal; Shay's eyes that first time I touched the scars on her chest and we made love; Dexter's snout resting on my leg right before his dragon nose spouted smoke; and Stout, our fairy friend, drinking the last drip of foam in the bottom of his glass. My family. The people my heart held dear. And in the time it took for me to draw a single breath, they could disappear from my world.

"What are we going to do?" I asked as I tapped the top of the lockbox.

"I'm going to talk with Dani." Shay went to the magick room, returning a few seconds later with a vial and her demon test kit. She pulled on a pair of gloves and unlocked the box, then removed the card, tore a small piece from the corner, and placed it in the vial. "She'll know who I should take it to."

"Why don't you just test it yourself?" I asked, watching her push a cork into the vial and tuck it into the elastic band of the test kit.

"Something Stout said." Shay locked the card in the box, tugged the vinyl gloves from her hands, and threw them in the trash. She tapped the box with the back of her hand. "If it is evil, then we need to treat it that way and take precautions."

"What about the barrier?" I asked.

Shay took a deep breath before saying, "I don't know."

"What do you mean, you don't know?" It was more aggressive than I'd meant, but I relied on Shay's experience and expertise to get us through. If she didn't know, who would?

"Until that confrontation with her about the bar, I thought Andrea was a pest, not a threat." Shay picked up the kit and the lockbox and placed them in her work duffle. "Dani and I can put our heads together and get the sample tested." She hooked the bag to the wall.

"She's at the bar. Maybe we should just go talk to her now?"

I heard the buzz of Stout's wings as he fluttered to the table. "I could sure use a beer."

"What a surprise," I said as I pushed my chair under the table. "What do you think?" I looked at Shay.

"We can go to the bar. I'll talk to Dani, and Stout can get his beer." She kicked into her shoes. "Come on, Dex."

It had become our routine to drive, even though we could walk from one end of Bannock to the other without breaking a sweat. As day turned to night, safety replaced the casual strolls we'd grown accustomed to. Shay was silent as we got to the car, and I wondered about the weight of this secret.

"Tell me what you're thinking?" I leaned against the corner of the patrol car door. The seats of the new vehicle were comfortable.

Shay's expression was unreadable. "I haven't been this scared in a very long time, Wil."

"You're scared?"

Shay's silence was confirmation enough for me.

"But you fight the most terrifying things I've ever seen." The revelation of her fear put me on edge.

Shay turned the key to start the car. "This is bigger. I can feel it. Something's stirring up those terrifying things, and now I'm almost certain that Andrea has a role in it."

I thought about the Assistant Mayor and how she moved through our life. She was sophisticated. That wasn't hard to miss. She had a way of making me feel uncomfortable, even in the space I called home. The more I played through our limited interactions, the more I could see that she was working an angle.

And maybe Shay was right. But Shay confronted chaos all the time.

"What part is the most frightening?"

Shay leaned against the steering wheel and turned to look at me. "I've always had Reg. My first thought was to run this by her, get her thoughts, and then I remember that she's gone, and it brings up a thousand questions and one thought." Her head fell against the steering wheel, and her green eyes darkened as she confessed. "Peters had a hand in taking Reg. Reg was a powerful practitioner, and she's gone." Shay cleared her throat as her voice broke over her last words. "Reg is gone, and I have to figure all of this out *and* keep you safe."

My hand reached across the car to touch Shay's shoulder. "You aren't alone in this. You have me and Dani and Amelia."

"Yes." Shay sat back as she shifted the car into drive and pulled out from the parking space. "I have all of you, I know. It feels like too much when I think about it."

"Too much?" I asked.

"Before, it was just me. It was my wound to heal if I got hurt, and I've had a long time to figure that out. But now it isn't only me." She glanced at me, then back at the road.

"You're doing a great job, love, but we don't expect you to take care of all of us."

Her hands shuffled across the steering wheel as she turned into the parking lot at the bar. "I love you for saying that, but something inside of me knows that isn't true. The powers of the Maker put your lives in my hands."

I waited for Shay to shift the squad car into park. I opened my door and walked around to her side. Her eyes followed me, and I could see the fear she tried to hide. She pulled the door release and kicked her feet out onto the running board. Before she could get out, I gripped the top of the frame and wedged myself between her legs.

"You are the love of my life."

"Wil . . ."

"No." I touched her lips with my fingers. "Please, let me say this. I know I've said it before, but I want you to hear me this time, damn it!" Her eyes closed in anticipation. "You and me?

We are here. We're together. And you don't have to face any of this alone. I won't leave you."

Shay kissed the tips of my fingers before pulling them against her chest. "I know you would never *choose* to leave me, but…"

"Don't!" I said with more emotion than I'd intended, and her shoulders flexed. "Don't give any of your power to the things that are coming."

"You make it sound so easy," Shay said, "but it's not."

"We're going to figure this out, baby. I trust you and your powers as the Magick."

"And you as the Maker?" She looked up at me with questioning eyes.

"I'll forge a thousand weapons, whatever you need, and we will get through this together." I tugged her into my arms and held her tight.

Shay's hands tucked around me, and she relaxed in my embrace. Her sigh was a whisper, and I felt her breath penetrate the fabric of my cotton shirt.

"A thousand?" Shay tilted her head to look up at me. "That's a lot of weapons."

"Baby, that's nothing." I kissed her forehead. "We're going to be okay."

Her arms fell away, and she grabbed the frame of the patrol car to stand. Before I could take a breath, we were face to face, heart to heart, and she kissed me, soft lips against my own. Her hands cupped my cheeks, and I steadied myself against the patrol car door. She pulled away, and all I could do was feel the energy of her love fill me.

"Wow!" I said as the smile stretched my cheeks. I opened my eyes. "What was that about?"

"That was for reminding me." She kissed me again. "And that is for loving me through all the unbelievable." Her fingers slipped through the hair around my cheek, and her forehead touched my own.

"You're so strong," I whispered against her lips. "But we're stronger together. Don't forget that."

"I'll do my best to remember."

"Good." I kissed her once more before dragging her out of the car. "Let's go figure out what the Assistant Mayor is up to."

Shay hit the release button on the dashboard, and Dexter jumped from the back of the SUV. I heard the flapping hum of Stout's wings before he landed on the roof of the car.

"The two of you are so sweet." He picked at his mouth. "I think I need a dentist for this cavity."

"Ugh!" I let out a frustrated sigh as I swatted at the fairy. "Stop listening to our conversations."

Shay caught my hand just before it hit Stout. "We did kinda lock him in."

"Bullshit!" I wriggled my fingers into the webbed steel to show how big the holes were. "He could get out if he wanted to."

"Maybe I could." He threaded himself through and kicked at my fingertip. "But this is way more entertaining."

I pulled my hand from the grate and turned toward the bar. "Asshole," I whispered under my breath as I walked away.

"I heard that," Stout seethed as he flew beside me.

"Hearing is one of your talents, isn't it?"

His fairy wings were loud, and he shot in front of my face, stopping me fast. "I might be an asshole, but you're kinda mean and maybe a little rude. I'm just trying to help." His arms crossed over his chest, and he hovered before me, so close to my face that if he weren't three inches tall, it would feel almost menacing.

"Help us? That's fine! But private conversations are private!" My voice raised enough that Dexter turned, taking a protective stance. I wasn't sure if he intended to protect me or the fairy floating inches from my nose.

"Dexter!" Shay called the dog.

Stout turned to the animal, and I could see his hesitation before he said, "Fire-face says we're both being assholes."

Shay laughed.

"Hey!" I protested.

"You are kinda acting like assholes," she said as she opened the service door of the bar. Dexter squeezed between us to run inside, perhaps to avoid the confrontation or maybe because he could hear Amelia in the back room. I was about to protest when I heard the groans coming from the K-9.

"Hello, you handsome guy." Amelia was scratching the tummy of a wriggling, prone German Shepherd. She looked up as we walked through the door. "Hey, all." Dexter's paw hooked around her leg, keeping her locked in place to continue the belly rub.

"Hi, Amelia."

Shay reached over the pile of dog to give our friend a side hug. I offered a half-wave and followed Stout to the bar. The fairy didn't waste time as he flew to the tap and waited for me to pour him a drink. I thought we could both use one before heading down to the cellar.

"Danielle is downstairs," Amelia whispered as she reached for the glass jar of bamboo straws. Stout was quick to claim one and spear it into the froth-topped pint.

"Already?" Shay asked as she kicked her boot against the polished brass pipe surrounding the bar's base.

"She said something about a notebook. I was too busy talking to Diana to ask questions."

"It's no big deal." Shay pushed back and turned toward the storeroom. "Are you coming?" She directed the question at me, but the tiny fairy sucking down his entire beer without taking a breath captivated me. "Wil?"

My eyes drifted toward Shay. "Sorry, what?"

"I'm going downstairs. Are you planning to come, or are you going to watch the fairy drink?"

Looking left toward Stout and then right toward my girlfriend, I grinned. "I'm definitely going with you." I was a few steps behind Shay as she approached the hidden door. My hands snaked around her waist, and I held her, whispering in her ear, "I'm always with you."

"That's good to know."

I kissed the back of her neck, and before we could make a move toward the door, it slid away, and Dani was standing in front of us. "Jeez, you two. You need to get a room."

"Uh-huh," Shay said with a throaty laugh. "We will, eventually." Her fingers tightened around mine with a reassuring squeeze and then fell away. "Whatcha got there?" Shay's chin jutted at the papers in Dani's arms.

"One of my father's journals. Well, not so much a journal, but some notes." She tipped the loose pages so we could see them.

"How do you know they're Jacob's?" I asked.

"His chicken scratch handwriting." She rotated the page so I could see the horrible cursive-style scribbles on it.

"Does he say anything important?" Shay picked a page and scanned the text. She had an unbelievable ability to read through a document and pluck out the critical information. Her expression didn't change as she placed it on top of the pile. "That's quite the conspiracy theory, don't you think?"

"As I've always said," Dani said, "Dad was a little crazy toward the end, and here's the proof."

"What did he say?" It was curious how Dani and Shay could communicate without giving away the specifics. It was also frustrating to feel left in the dark.

"That page, well, he made a lot of assumptions about Reg and Andrea, of all people."

"You're being kind, I think." Dani stepped through the door and walked down into the cellar. We followed close behind her as she continued. "I'd call them accusations, and they're pretty harsh. He considered the two of them a threat, and he needed a spell to counteract the Magick's weapon stockpile." She dropped the documents on the table and pointed to the swords, knives, and other weapons stacked against the wall. "All of this was to fight Benton. I can't wrap my head around that."

"We know from experience who Benton cared about, but Andrea is another story altogether." Shay looked at me. "Where's that tome you found today?"

I moved a box, and I nudged the book across the table to her with as little touching as possible. "This is the one."

Shay picked it up and tilted the cover towards the incandescent bulb dangling over our heads. "Rasavatam." She whispered the word, and Stout was hovering beside her ear a few seconds later.

"Be careful, or you'll summon things you might not want." The fairy spoke loud enough for all of us to hear. Shay opened the cover, but I could tell by her hesitation that she was thinking about what he'd said.

"Rasavatam." She repeated it. "Sanskrit for sure." Shay's eyes drifted back and forth across the page. She closed her eyes.

"Shay?"

"We will manipulate the nectar of life. Alter what has come through the way of hydrargyrum." She turned to look at Stout. "Help me with the last word?"

"The water of silver," he said, flying away as if he'd lit the fuse on a stick of dynamite.

Shay looked at us. "Anyone know it?"

I shook my head. "Never heard of it."

Dani stepped closer to Shay. "I'm almost certain that the water of silver is Mercury. Not the planet, but the element."

I knew little about the elements in the periodic table, but I was sure there were stories written about the use of mercury in mining, and that it was the solution that made the Hatter mad.

"Mercury? Doesn't that make people go a little bat shit?" I looked at the pile of notes written by Dani's father.

"It can be toxic under many circumstances, but I'm not sure how that fits with this." Dani tapped the book Shay was holding.

"Science of the ancients," Stout explained as he attempted to close the cover of the book. "Reciting Rasavatam would invite a heinous level of immortality."

"Heinous seems extreme." I waved my hand to swat him away from the book.

"That's because you don't understand." Stout's wings whipped faster to counter the whoosh of my hand.

"If this is some kind of ancient magick, and Reg had this book in here, do you think she understood the weight of its power?" Dani moved to the pile of archive boxes Stout and I had looked through earlier in the day. "Reg left all of this for us. It has to mean something."

Shay turned the first page of the book, and although the text was impossible for me to read, my girlfriend was concentrating on transcribing some of it. Dani stopped digging in her box, and I stepped closer to look over Shay's shoulder at the pages.

"What does it say?" I whispered in her ear, the tickle causing her to lift her shoulder.

"It's magick." She laid the book on the table and clenched her hands into fists. When she opened them, I could see the power of those written words flow from the pages to her palms. "It's fierce, almost to the point of overpowering."

"Don't mess with this." The tiny fairy flew down to the table, and with all of his strength, he slammed the cover of the book tight. "We've stretched the forces of nature thin for the Maker and the Magick. Don't tempt fate." Stout planted his feet in the grooved letters written on the book's cover.

"Does the text of the Rasavatam scare you?" Shay asked.

"You bet your ass it does." He sat down. "This magick changes human life, and I'm not just talking about physically. It alters the heart and the soul, and once you do that, it can't be undone."

"How do you know that?" Dani asked.

"Look at her hands." He pointed at Shay. "Look at the power pouring from her fingers. And she only read the first page–translated half, at most. But she has to fight to contain it."

I was looking at Shay and hadn't stopped since she'd set the book down. I could feel the energy of the words she'd read, and I was frightened. In the past, our experience with spells and the unknown consequences had left me babbling and seeing sights of the magick realm I hadn't known existed beyond tales and lore. Magick was also strenuous on our physical forms, and right now, I wasn't certain Shay could balance her powers.

My hand hovered over hers. "Baby?" She didn't answer. "Shay?" I touched her hand, and when the warmth of my skin met the ice of her flesh, I felt more magick than I'd ever felt before. My fingers clenched tight, and her head turned to look into my eyes. The realization was instant, and I closed my eyes to watch the images play.

"Can you feel it?" Shay whispered, or maybe I heard her in my head. It was hard to distinguish between them. I felt it: not just the evolution of energy, but the force of humanity pounding like a heartbeat between us.

"I feel it."

Shay held both of my hands, and we stretched our joined arms to form a circle. It was difficult to know if this was her magick, my magick, or our magick, but at the moment, it didn't matter.

"Brigid," she whispered. Or maybe it was me. The presence was sacrosanct, and I was content to stand with my palms pressed to Shay's.

There have been so few moments in my life where I've felt overwhelmed to the edge of sanity, but this magick passing between us would break me if I had to carry it alone. The sigil in my palm felt warm, and I looked to see it glowing.

"Uh, Shay?" I tugged to let go of her hand.

Her eyes opened as she was reaching to keep hold of me. "It's okay. The magick is balancing. Just give it another second."

"The sigil." I opened my palm to her, and she sandwiched my hands between her own.

"I can feel it. It's okay, Wil. We can balance it together."

Her forehead touched mine, and I relaxed as the power fell away and moved down toward the earth. She took a deep breath and pulled me in tight. Her arms were comforting, but I could not enjoy her due to the question filling my head.

"What the hell kind of magick was that?" I whispered in her ear.

"That was Rasavatam," she said, and the warmth of her breath against my cheek sent delightful tingles over my body, making me forget for a moment what had just happened.

"Maybe you should listen to Stout and not read that again." I gripped my hands behind her back, hugging her and letting go.

"Did it scare you?"

"Hell yes, it scared me. It didn't scare you?"

"No, not at all. The magick felt big, like it was all around me. And somehow, I understood it was mine."

For the first time since the magick of the book had come alive, I noticed we were alone in the cellar. I turned to where Dani had been standing a few seconds earlier.

"Where did everyone go?" I asked, pulling out of Shay's arms.

She walked around the room, but neither Dani nor Stout were present. Dexter lay curled in a ball under the table. Why had he been absent from our magick?

"That's weird. They were just standing here a second ago," Shay said as she stopped in front of the table.

I noticed the piles of research stacked neatly. The only thing left was the Rasavatam, or what I was going to call the Tome of Trouble.

"Upstairs?" I asked, moving toward the staircase.

"They have to be. I hope."

"You hope?" I asked.

What did she mean? Where else would they be? Shay left the book on the table and followed me up the spiral staircase. I heard laughter and delighted in seeing Stout sipping beer from his bamboo straw and Dani laughing at something Amelia had said. They seemed fine from a distance. As we stepped closer, everyone in the bar was content, and Shay and I were the outsiders.

"Shay?"

She turned in front of me; her pale skin was nearly ghost white. "I don't know."

"Stout." She called his name, and it seemed as if the fairy hesitated before returning to his drink. Shay was confused and so was I. She waved a hand in front of Dani's face, and the taller cop didn't notice us in front of her.

I realized what was going on far too late. My mouth dropped open, a gasp escaping me.

"Oh my god," I said, turning to Shay. "They can't see us."

CHAPTER XX

ELUCIDATION

"What the hell do you mean, they can't see us?"

I held my hand out to Shay. I needed to touch her to confirm that the experience was real. Her fingers squeezed between my own, and for a moment, I felt the comfort of her magick. The surrounding room was solid, but we weren't in it, at least not in physical form.

"Are we here?" I asked and regretted the words coming out of my mouth. Of course, we were here. I could feel her, but no one else in the room could see us. "We're standing somewhere, but I'm not sure if it's now or later."

"What do you mean?"

She turned her wrist so I could see the hands of her watch. The illuminated face read seven o'clock. "Look at the time on the wall." Shay's head tipped up toward the bar. The wood-framed clock's pendulum was swinging; the big hand rested on the twelve, and the little hand was on the eight.

"Are we in the future?" I asked, trying to wrap my head around the magick that had taken us from a simple translated text to a hop forward in time.

"Maybe." She shrugged her shoulders.

"Why can't we have just one day without turning our lives upside down?"

She tugged me toward the cellar door and down the stairs to the dusty old book. "I need to look at this again."

"That tome is trouble, and are you sure we should do anything with it?"

Shay waved a hand, directing me to sit in the chair beside her. "I did something, and now I have to undo it."

"What do you think you did?" I asked as Shay opened to the first page of the text. I covered her eyes with my hand before she could read it. "Wait! Before you read a single word, tell me what you translated earlier."

She took my hand from her face and closed the book. "It wasn't much, and I'm pretty sure I didn't translate a word right."

She'd translated something, right or wrong; the magick was happening to us. "Just *a* word?" I asked, thinking that it was possible that every word was wrong and the next thing she read would make the two of us disappear forever.

"Yes, just a word. Stout said the Rasavatam was life and death. I think the spell book is supposed to extend the life of someone with the Magick and Maker powers." Shay stood up and grabbed the folder from the top of the box behind us. "The file from Andrea."

"The file you won't let me read?" The tone of my voice was seeped with accusation and disappointment, but I wanted to know the secret, to understand what Shay was hiding.

"Yes, baby. The file I don't want anyone to read is about Dani and Jacob." She tossed the folder beside the stack on the table. "This." She laid her palm on the book.

The book, that compilation of mysterious incantations, had proven thus far to be nothing but dangerous to us. "The Tome of Trouble?" I hadn't intended for the words to slip out, and Shay's reaction was almost as precious as it'd been the day I'd named the Dagger of Doom.

She hooked her finger inside the collar of my shirt. "You do like to give things interesting titles, don't you?" She leaned in for a kiss.

I was a little breathless when she pulled away, a stunning smile stretching her lips. She could almost make me forget. Almost.

"We've had that tome for less than a day, and it's already displaced us into another time."

"Hardly another time." Shay and I walked across the room to where her K-9 lay sleeping.

She whispered his name. "Dexter, wake up, buddy."

The massive German Shepherd lifted his head and snorted at her.

"Hey, bud. You have a good nap?"

It was comforting to know that the K-9 could see the two of us, but as he woke, he jumped to his feet and pressed his head and torso against Shay's hip, knocking her off balance. My hand caught her shoulder before she landed on the floor.

"What's up, bud?"

She clenched the fur around his neck, and he pushed closer to me, bringing the three of us together. I touched Shay's hand where it rested on Dexter, and I felt the transfer of magick flow between us. It was like the connection we'd made in the sacred circle on the workshop floor. Power mingled with heart and energy and…something more.

Shay closed her eyes and whispered. "I am the light; she is the light; he is the light; we are the light."

After two more times, I repeated the words, and we chanted together. Shay was holding tight to Dexter, and I was holding tight to Shay. My eyes peeked open, glimpsing a thick shadow snaking across the floor, rising stair by stair out of the cellar.

"What the hell was that?" Dani asked as she slapped her hand on the table, catching the pages before they blew to the dust-covered floor.

I looked at Shay as she stared down at the dog and turned toward Dani. "What was what?"

"That draft." Dani transferred the papers from the table back into a box. "It felt like a gust of wind, but that's impossible because we're in the cellar."

"Impossible," I whispered against Shay's shoulder. "Baby, what did we just do?"

"The Rasavatam reversed," Shay explained.

"How did it do that?"

The book resting on the table in front of us seemed to take on a life that was impossible to control. How could we translate the text if it was powerful enough to invoke its magick with a mere whisper?

"Dexter, maybe?" Shay's fingers tangled in the K-9's fur.

"What's going on?" Dani asked as she carried the box to the table at the back of the room.

I flicked the cover of the book with my finger. "This tome is trouble."

"How so?" Dani sat on the edge of the table where the book rested. She didn't move to touch the Rasavatam as she crossed her arms over her chest.

Shay looked at her watch. "In about forty-seven minutes, you're going to be upstairs laughing and drinking with your wife and our fairy."

Stout fluttered in front of her. "I have to wait that long?"

I shook my head. "Is that all you think about?"

"You'll be happy it *is* all I think about the next time you need my fairy dust, Wildwood!" He raised his voice as he said my name.

Fairy dust was definitely a part of our lives, and he was right: we would be wise to create a stockpile of his powerful magick.

"Just go up to the bar." Shay held out her hand, and Stout landed on it. "Amelia will pour one for you."

"Just one?" He held up a tiny finger.

"For now."

His knees bent, and before I could take another breath, Stout pushed off and flew up the stairs.

"Want to explain what you meant?" Dani hadn't moved from her position.

"I read the–"

"Tome of Trouble!" I interrupted. "Don't even say the real name anymore." The two cops stared at me.

"Her title, not mine," Shay explained.

"Damn straight!" I exclaimed. "That thing shifted us an hour ahead of time and out of whack with reality. Stout was right to tell you to read with caution."

Shay tugged a loop on the waist of my jeans. "Take a deep breath, baby." Her voice was a whisper against my ear, and the tickle got my attention.

She turned me, and I closed my eyes to focus on the air going in my nose and out of my mouth. The comfort of her hush shouldn't have been a surprise as I felt the calming spirit of the cycle breathing technique. I opened my eyes, and the two women were waiting, watching.

"Feel better?" Dani asked.

"*No!* But I feel calm." I turned into Shay's arms, and they tightened around me. "How do the two of you do this?" I twisted to look at my girlfriend.

"Years of practice with unbelievable shit," Dani quipped. "The Tome? Tell me."

"I'm not one hundred percent sure how, but the first spell shifted us through time. It was just an hour, but Wildwood and I moved through the room, and no one knew we were there."

"That could be useful." Dani pushed away from the table. "Can you go back in time?"

Shay shook her head. "I'm not sure."

"Hell no! We aren't messing with the magick in this thing." I picked up the book, eager to stuff every page back inside the box we'd found it in.

Shay grabbed my arm. "We have to know, Wil. This tome could be the answer to so many questions."

"It could also be the one thing that could destroy us all," I said.

"You're overreacting, don't you think?" Dani looked at me pointedly.

"Maybe I am, but I don't know how to fix time displacement with Shay's hands, and somehow Dexter needs to be present, too."

"You're a family," Dani said. "It makes sense that the three of you would summon unstoppable forces."

"What happens when we meet an unmovable object?" I knew the answer would be something silly, but truth be told, I felt like a cat, ticking its nine lives away on risky endeavors.

"Don't worry. It'll get out of your way." Dani swiped her hand over the table, kicking up a cloud of dust. Her palms clapped together, leaving shimmering flakes of timeless dirt lingering in the air.

"I wish I had as much confidence as you."

Dani sat in the chair beside Shay. "By the time we get through the archives down here, you'll be as confident as I am."

I shook my head. Magick and archives, books and research–these would never relax me. They only caused more anxiety. Putting a hammer to hot metal brought calm. I needed some time in front of the forge and a project to clear my head. It would be doubly good to escape from my Maker responsibilities for a few hours.

Shay opened the case on the table to remove the sample she'd collected from Andrea's file. "Since we're talking weird and odd…"

"Were we?" Dani asked, leaning forward to see what Shay was holding.

"We are now." The smiles that passed between the two cops spoke of years together as a demon-fighting team. Shay gave the sample to her friend.

"What is it?" Dani held it to the light, rolling the glass tube so she could see both sides of the sample.

"Something evil, according to Stout," I answered for Shay.

"Explain, please?" Dani directed her question at Shay.

"I was translating Andrea's file."

"Okay." Dani set the vial on the table. I wasn't sure if the mention of our Assistant Mayor was the reason, but it got Dani's attention.

"This was in the file." Shay pointed to the sample.

"That little piece of, what? Paper?"

"Flesh," I said, taking a step away from the table.

"Flesh from what?"

Shay removed the folder from the box and flipped through until she found the card of dehydrated skin. "That's the evil Stout was talking about. We don't know the origin. We just know it was in here with the documents Andrea gave me after Benton died."

"You know what's written on those pages, don't you?" Dani didn't move, waiting for an answer.

A silent nod was Shay's reply

"It's bad, huh?"

"Very."

"It's about my father, isn't it?"

"Yes." Shay tossed the folder in the box and closed the cover.

"You're never going to tell me, are you?"

"D, you don't want to know. I promise you don't want to know."

Keeping secrets was not something Shay wanted to do. Watching her struggle with the truth, it was easy to see that keeping Dani in the dark about her personal history would cause problems. Trust didn't come easy, and I worried Shay's need to protect her best friend might just cause irreparable damage.

Dani stood up from the table, knocking the sample vial over. "What gives you the right to keep the truth from me? From m*e*!" She stabbed herself in the chest with the tip of her thumb.

"I'm asking you to trust me, D. Please."

Dani turned her back to Shay and walked toward the forge in the cellar's corner. Her hand trailed over the rusty coal basin, flipping the dangling tongs and spinning the handle on the cast iron blower. It was painful to witness the emotions in the room, but it was obvious that Shay would never give up the secret that Dani wanted to know.

Dani picked up a lump of cobweb-covered coal. She spoke in a whisper as she turned the lump over in her hand; an emotional battle raged inside her, and it was painful to watch. "Trust you?"

"Yes."

She tossed the coal at the forge. "The thing is, I do trust you. I always have." Dani picked up the sample from the table.

Shay nodded. "I promise if there's ever a reason you need to know, I'll tell you."

"I'll hold you to that." Dani held up the vial to the light, tapping her finger against it. "You remember that doctor I told you to call?"

"Yes. Why?"

"Take this sample to her. She'll tell you exactly what kind of evil produced it." She tossed the vial toward my girlfriend, and Shay plucked it from the air.

"I guess our circle of trust just expanded by one," Shay said.

"She's good. It'll take a day or two, so get it to her as soon as you can."

"Roger that." Shay tapped her fingers against her brow and saluted her friend. She opened the box and dropped the sample vial inside. "Are we finished down here?"

"For tonight, I think so." Dani rested her hand on the Tome of Trouble. "Maybe you should keep this thing with you."

"I was planning to."

Shay stacked the box on top of the tome and tucked them both under her arm. It felt reckless for her to carry that book around without protecting it. Was it silly to suggest putting a protection spell on a book filled with spells that probably included ones about protection?

"You're just going to carry the box and that book out the back door?"

Shay raised her elbow to point at her dog. "We have Dexter, and we aren't going any farther than the patrol car."

"Maybe we should just leave it here," I suggested. But her hesitation was an answer.

"I'd like to continue the translations, and I don't want to sleep in this dusty cellar when I get tired later."

"It feels dangerous to take it from Benton's room. She kept it safe all this time, hidden in that box."

"Trust me." Shay slipped her free arm around my waist. "It'll be safe in the carriage house. I'll make sure."

"But will we be safe?" I asked.

"Yes, together we'll definitely be safe."

I followed her up the stairs. Before we pushed the door closed, she grabbed both of my hands and dropped the book and box across my forearms. "Wait one second while I get Stout." She looked at her K-9. "*Custodire!*"

Shay commanded the dog to protect me, and I felt his head tuck tight to my hip. We walked through the stockroom and out the back door. Yes, Dex would defend me with every part of his dog body and with every bit of his dragon self. Before I adjusted the weight in my arms, the passenger door opened, and my butt hit the seat. Shay loaded Dex and ran around to the driver's seat. I felt the intensity of our Magick and Maker responsibilities as we rode in silence to the carriage house. The tome was heavy in my lap, but I felt protected in the presence of my magickal family.

Shay put the truck into park. "Wait while I open the door, then you and Dex can walk in together."

"So you're nervous?" There was a playfulness in the tone of my voice, and Shay turned to look at me. Her smile was ridiculous with confidence.

"Cautious. Not nervous, just cautious."

She stepped down from the truck and crossed in front of the vehicle. Her shoulders were pressed back, and her stride was confident. She wasn't afraid, and I loved that about her. The unknown didn't seem to faze her. A few seconds later, the back latch released, and Dexter waited for me to open my door. I felt the power of their magicks, and for a moment, I wished my mini fairy had the firepower of the dragon-dog pressing against my thigh.

"It's getting late," I said as Shay closed the door and locked the carriage house. "What's your plan for this?" I tapped the cover of the Rasavatam.

"I'm off tomorrow," she explained, "so I think I'll work on translations and figuring out how to manipulate the nectar of life."

"Should I help?"

Her boots were light on the treads as I followed her up the stairs and into the magick room.

"You could keep me company. After the time displacement we experienced earlier tonight, I think all three of us should stick close together."

She laid the book in the center of her table, shrugging out of her flannel shirt and replacing it with the long robe that smelled of incense and essential oils. I couldn't resist the urge to hold her, and her arms wrapped around me in response.

"What was that for?" Her voice hitched as she arched her back to look into my eyes.

"Just because."

"Oh?" Her lips formed a tiny circle.

"Oh, yes."

I kissed her gently until her mouth opened to mine. Her arms, her body, pressed tight to my own, and I surrendered to the energy of our love.

She trembled as her forehead rested against mine, and I felt her breathy voice against my lips. "You're very good at distracting me."

"Distraction wasn't my goal. I just wanted to remind myself why." I felt the velvet of her robe against my arms as she held me tight before pulling away.

"Why, what?" she asked with a curious pitch of her eyebrow.

"Why I can't ever be without you."

"I'm not planning to go anywhere," she said as she walked to the cabinet in the room's corner.

"That book might have different ideas." I sat on the chair, waiting for whatever Shay had planned.

She sparked a flame with her palm to ignite a tall white pillar candle, and the fire flickered as she placed it on the table.

"The Tome of Trouble?" She winked, and although my sigh wasn't a protest, she smiled at my response. "Nothing will change in this room. The power of magick as old as the Rasavatam has been translated for hundreds of years." Shay walked to the wall of books in the magick room. Her fingertips traveled across dozens of texts until she found the one she needed.

I leaned over her shoulder to read the spine of the book. "*Magica, Veneficium et Maleficum,*" I said, sure I was butchering the pronunciation.

"*Magick, Sorcery and Witchcraft,*" she translated as she fanned the first few pages.

No matter how hard I tried, I wouldn't be able to read a single page. Shay's shelves held many books I could never read first, because they were written in obscure languages, and second, because I didn't think I would ever be interested in the ancient perspectives of witchcraft.

"It's a reference text," she said. "Originally written in Sanskrit but translated to Latin."

"What's it for?" I asked. I was curious how this text related to the Tome of Trouble, and it made me wonder if this was the security blanket our book needed.

"This text in Latin is hundreds of years old. And the Sanskrit is *much* older." She opened the reference, fanning the pages until she found the spell she wanted. "This entry is the witchcraft part of this book, and it describes precautions to take when reading curses and blasphemous texts."

"Blasphemous?" The word made me laugh, and I gave myself a pinch to clarify that I was still operating in this reality.

She closed her finger on the page and tapped the cover of the book. "Yes, baby. In 1422, you and I would have been burned alive just for holding this tome."

I dropped into the chair, and my head fell back against the wall. "Shay?"

"Mm-hmm." She didn't look up from the page.

"Why is it you spend all of this time making me feel comfortable with your magick just to scare the crap out of me with phrases like 'burned alive'?"

Her eyebrow raised as she looked at me. "Never doubt that you're safe with me."

"That's not what I was saying," I tried to explain, but maybe I was questioning her skills based on the life I'd experienced in the last year.

My life had changed for more reasons than the Magick and my Maker powers. I had this woman standing in front of me, not only the physical part of Shay but the spiritual, magickal woman who loved me more than I had ever thought possible.

"What are you saying?" She laid a weighted pad across the book to prop it open so her hands were free. She walked through the room, plucking herbs and containers from the shelves.

"I'm just saying that when it comes to all of this, I don't understand how I fit into your life." I fanned my arms in the air, pointing to the components used to keep us protected.

Shay stopped and dropped her supplies on the table between us. She stepped around until she was standing in front of me. Her palms raised as she flexed her fingers, summoning me to her. It was impossible to resist as she held out her hands.

"You, my love, are the most important part when it comes to all of this."

"That's just because—"

Her fingers moved to my lips. "Shh, please. Let me finish." My eyes closed to her touch and the whispered words that followed. "I'm not the woman that you found all those months ago. I've changed; I'm different. And that has nothing to do with the Maker and Magick powers we share. It has everything to do with how you love me. The strength that I have because I come home to you every day. We—" She held her hand over my heart. "We are so much more than the physical, and that is how I know we will be safe."

"Just like that?"

She kissed the tip of my nose. "Just exactly like that."

She was very convincing, especially when she held my hand through my insecurities, and I wanted to believe her. But a part of me knew that one day I'd have to face my fears about the powers of Brigid and my Maker strengths. I could at least be sure that wasn't going to happen today in this room with my girl, so I took a deep breath, releasing it slowly.

"Okay, what can I do to help?" I reached for the robe dangling beside Shay's empty hook.

"You can grind these together and light the rest of the candles." Shay left the room and returned a few moments later with fresh-cut stems from the greenhouse and a peppy Dexter behind her. She broke the leaves into pieces and dropped them into the mixture with one instruction: "Keep going. You're almost there."

Shay placed our athame in the center of the altar cloth and whispered, "Brigid, flame keeper and light, be here with us."

My hand opened, and I whispered, *"Ignis."* The flame flashed in my palm, and I used it to light the four candles placed on the compass point pedestals I'd created for the magick room. Shay closed the door and turned off the lights, and the two of us stood illuminated by the five flames.

"What now?" I asked as Shay stood beside me.

"Now, you and that handsome dog need to sit right there and relax for a while."

"That's it?" I swooped my cloak to pocket a space for me to sit.

"For your part. I'll do the rest of the work."

Her fingertips traced over the words on the second page of our Tome of Trouble, and I was content to comb through the fur around Dexter's face as I watched her, enjoying how fearless she was with magick. She sprinkled a spoonful of herbs over the censor coal and continued her transcription, turning page after page until her notebook was full of scribbles I couldn't read from my chair.

"Will it distract you if I ask a question?" As soon as I asked, I realized how silly it was to phrase it that way.

"You can ask me anything you'd like." She didn't look up or pause as she flipped to the back of *Magick, Sorcery, and Witchcraft.*

"If I fall asleep, will the three of us stay in balance?"

Her hands paused, and she looked up with an adorable smile. "It's not very exciting for you, I know."

"Don't get me wrong, I love watching you. Especially when that robe is over your shoulders, and you smell so good. But isn't there something else I could do to help?"

Her hands pressed on the page, and she flipped the second book over to cover the texts. "Here's what I have so far. The first eight pages are concise rituals performed during the pagan festivals just about every other moon cycle."

I thought about the Wheel of the Year and tried to recall all eight celebrations, remembering that many corresponded with secular celebrations: Yule and Christmas, Samhain and Halloween. But my final thought was Brigid and her festival of fire: Imbolc.

"What are they for?"

"Preparation for receiving the power of the Goddess." She flipped through a few pages of her notebook.

"Brigid?" I asked. I didn't have a long list of goddesses in mind.

Her slight nod was confirmation that this was a guide to the keeper of the flame. If the Tome of Trouble was a guide for our goddess, how had we successfully navigated ourselves to her flame?

"Um, Shay?"

She held the notes to her chest as she looked at me. "Yes?"

"If I'm the Maker and you're the Magick, how is it we skipped the first eight spells of the Tome of Trouble?"

"I think Stout is the answer to that question." She tapped her finger on the paper. "The ritual in the basement of the old courthouse is here." She turned the page on the Tome. "This incantation was on the wall." Shay held up the spell so I could see it. She pulled the notebook back and flipped a few pages and held them out to me. "This is the spell from the Mill."

The Tome of Trouble belonged to Shay. There was no doubt. "You're saying that we were meant to find this text before transferring power so that we'd be ready for it?"

"No, that wouldn't work."

"What do you mean?"

Shay closed her notebook and stacked the reference books in a pile. "The Rasavatam is the book of books. What you and I are…the Magick. Me." She pressed her palm to her chest. "And the Maker." She pointed to me. "We are this book. Our life together. The Rasavatam is supposed to guide us past the evil that's coming and arm us to fight the demons that are already here."

"Wait, what?"

Shay covered the smoldering incense bowl and put her altar tools away in the apothecary cabinet. "We were already under the powers of the Rasavatam. The Magick and the Maker are ageless, not immortal; and to keep us alive, we have to surrender to the magick in this book. The tricky part is that we didn't understand. But somehow it worked despite that."

"We kinda went looking for answers." I shrugged my shoulders, considering the events that we'd endured the last few months.

"That's where Benton and Stout come in. And I have to wonder if this is how the ancestry scroll happened." Shay stood in front of me, holding her hands out to help me to my feet. She unclasped my robe and carried it to the wall, then hung mine and placed hers on the empty hook beside it.

I stared at the books on the table, thinking about the men and women who'd held the powers before us. There was nothing simple about becoming the Maker, and it was doubly challenging to carry the balancing power of the Magick. Kai was the first of us.

She'd taken all of it on her own, and I couldn't help but wonder how.

"Do you think Kai wrote the Tome of Trouble?" I asked.

Shay snuffed out the candles. "I don't know, maybe. It would make sense since this book is written in Sanskrit. Her trial-and-error spell drafting would guide the rest of us to more success than failure."

"What do you think happened to her?"

Shay held my hand as we walked from the magick room into the kitchen. "I think the burden of balance was too much for her to carry alone."

"Do you think it killed her?"

Shay shrugged. "Magick can be dangerous. We know that."

"I'm glad I have you." I tugged her into my arms. "I don't want to go through any of this without you."

She kissed me, and I was content to be in her arms. "You still tired?" she whispered.

"Maybe a little." The tip of my tongue touched the corner of my mouth as I bit my top lip. "What did you have in mind?"

"I think you already know." Her hand slid to the loop of my faded jeans, and she hooked her finger to tug me toward our bedroom.

"I've got a good guess."

Without another word, my hand slapped the light switch on the kitchen wall.

CHAPTER XXI

MYTH

The morning light coming through our bedroom window felt warm on my face. When I'd closed my eyes the night before, I'd seen demons and enchanted tomes, so the daylight felt like an answer to the troubles behind my closed eyes. My mind was more awake than the rest of my body.

I felt Shay's palm press against the bare skin of my abdomen, her body tight against my back. She was warm like the sun, and I felt safe. Her breathing was steady, and it was a minor miracle that she continued to sleep, so I took advantage of the moment and wrapped the blanket tighter around us to keep the two of us in our cocoon.

A part of me craved the centering power of blacksmithing–sparking the forge, hammering out the confusion until the world fell into balance. Today would be an exercise in the balance of Magick from the Rasavatam and the new pages Shay had compiled. She had the sample of strange flesh that I was sure would turn out to be full-blown evil. Nightmares sometimes come to life, and those demons were preventing me from getting some much-needed rest. Shay had ten years of experience falling asleep with hundreds of unanswered questions. I had just started to deal with the darker side of life.

I stared at the cracks in the wall above the window.

"Your worrying is very loud," Shay whispered.

Her words warmed the back of my ear as her arm snaked under the pillow beneath my neck.

"How do you know I was worrying? And there's nothing loud about it."

"Wil, the muscles in your back are so tight, I might need Brigid's Hammer to relax them." She pulled me closer.

I didn't make a sound, but my body shook from my silent laughter. "The sound of your voice is almost the best way to relax me." I rolled toward her, and the smile I received in return was warm and welcome.

"Do I need to guess what the *best* way is?" she asked. Her kiss was tender, teasing, and it was clear that she knew exactly how to calm my nerves.

"You're distracting me."

She kissed me again. "I'm using my lips," she said as I wiggled myself into the firmness of her breast and shoulder. Her hand slid from my cheek down my arm to rest on my hip. "What's your plan for this day off?"

"I'm not off," I tell her. "I've got a workshop, and I have to fill out a little paperwork to justify our existence in this show-stopping carriage house."

"Ooh, paperwork. Very hot."

My palm pushed her shoulder away. "Hot? Really?"

Shay slid up against the headboard, and I was content to circle myself around her abdomen. "You're hot all the time. You should know that by now."

"I'll take your word for it," I said.

Shay's fingers combed through the length of my hair, and I closed my eyes. I thought about Shay, her tenderness last night as she'd caressed me into the late hours. She had beautiful hands. The scars that criss-crossed them were a testament to her strength, and I was humbled every time she touched me. My hand snaked over her ribs and rested on the scar. My fingertip drew back and forth against it.

"That tickles." She swished my fingers.

"I know." My thumb returned to the spot. "That's why I'm . . ."

She gripped my hand and lifted it away from her body. "We don't have time for what comes after your wandering hand."

I twisted my wrist to examine the watch I wasn't wearing. "Looks to me like we've got plenty of time."

Shay pushed me away and rolled her feet over the side of the bed. "You're so dangerous."

"Maybe, but you like it." I kicked my legs around her hips and pulled our bodies together. Her head fell back against my shoulder, and I kissed her cheek.

"I like you." Her words tickled my ear.

"Just 'like'?"

She shook her head. "More than like. But right now, I have to get out of this bed because what I want to do with you will take more time than I have." Her kiss was a brief peck as she broke free from my embrace.

"I can make it quick."

"Uh, uh." She waved her finger, took a big step away from the bed, turned to the dresser to grab a shirt and underwear, and ran to the bathroom.

There was no way she was showering without me, but as much as I tried, she was quick to deflect my roaming fingers after I got in. I stood behind her in the oversized tub, watching the water drive down her back muscles and stagger over the knife wound scars.

"You going to get under the water?" she asked over her shoulder.

"Just enjoying the view." I stepped closer, holding her hips as I turned her around to switch positions under the hot spray.

Her hands came up to comb through my hair. "The view of my backside?"

I tilted my head back, soaking up the shower water as she seized the opportunity to kiss along my exposed neck. It was clear that this was not going to be the quick shower she'd expected. My hands came up to hold her breasts, and her quiet moan was all the encouragement I needed.

"No, baby," I said, swirling my fingers against her skin in languid circles. "Not just your backside."

~~~~~~~~~~

"You want a mop?"

Sex in a footed tub isn't complicated, but it can make a terrible puddle on the bathroom floor. Shay passed me another towel, and I held tight to the old porcelain as I stretched to clean up the last of our spilled shower. Shay's hand fell in front of my face to help me stand.

"No mop, we're good here," I said. Her smile answered the question I hadn't asked. "Pretty pleased with yourself, aren't you?"

"I'm pretty sure you started all of this." Shay waved her hand toward the wet towels draped over the tub and curtain rod.

"Finished it, too." I planted a kiss on her lips before leaving.

Shay followed me into the bedroom and pulled on a dark blue BPD t-shirt as she walked. My feet stopped in front of the dresser as I waited for a response. She moved around me as she dressed and sat in the chair to put on her boots. Still naked, I walked right up to her, planted my feet between her legs, and pushed her against the back of the chair. Our eyes met, and that brilliant smile was the answer I needed.

"I love you," I whispered.

Her hands rested on my hips, and she pulled me close. Her chin pressed against my chest as she looked up at me. "I love you more than anything."

Intimacy with Shay was an experience beyond words. Her life before me had been an exercise in keeping up the tough exterior to protect the fragile, fractured interior. Being inside her,
~~~~~~~~~~

entirely inside her, was a gift, and I never wanted a day to pass without showing her how much she meant to me. Shay squeezed me tight for a few seconds longer and relaxed against me. That was my cue to give her a little space.

"You never told me what your plans for the day are," I said, pulling a well-worn long sleeve t-shirt out of the dresser. The tiny singes around the cuff and lower sleeve marked all the places I didn't get burned. It was funny that everything in my life was some form of hot.

"I'm taking that sample to the clinic," she said. "And then I'll be back here to work on translating more of the text. You'll probably finish in the workshop by noon, right?"

I pushed my feet through the bottom of my pant legs and tugged the zipper in place. "Should be. Riker Bailey is bringing a buddy, I guess. I got a text from him."

"That's perfect. I can help you with some of your paperwork, and then we can dissect the Rasavatam." Shay pulled the socks from my hand and kissed me.

I felt the soft fabric fall back into my palm. "Okay." It was the only word my mouth could produce, and when I opened my eyes, Shay was gone. I grabbed my boots and chased her out to the kitchen.

"You're just going to leave me like that?" The boots clopped to the floor, and I dropped to a knee to pull socks over my feet.

"Nope, but if I stand next to you for a minute longer, you'll miss your workshop, and I'll never get an answer to this." She held up the vial, squeezed between her thumb and index finger.

I kicked my feet into my boots, noticing the wear across the plates of the steel toes. More protection that prevented injury in the hot and heavy parts of my life. Shay was hovering over me with a slice of toast in one hand. She'd already taken a bite, and she reached down to help me stand.

"I guess I'll see you in a few hours?" I asked before kissing her.

Her tongue peeked out to collect a few crumbs from the corner of her mouth. "You will. Come on, Dex!"

Before I could say another word, she and the dog were going down the stairs and out the door. The house was quiet for a few seconds until my favorite fairy fluttered to the kitchen table. He was using his bamboo straw as a pointer.

"How about a cold one?"

Stout was a curious creature, but I understood his need to supercharge his fairy dust. Yesterday's beer glass was still in the drying rack, and I poured an ice-cold beer and set it on the table beside him.

"Shay is gone for the morning, and I've got a workshop in a few minutes. You want to watch us, or are you planning to stay up here?"

Stout was a master at concealing his presence. It was clear now that we knew he'd been in the carriage house all of the months I'd lived in it.

He took a long slurp of the drink. "Can I watch?"

My shoulders lifted with a shrug of indifference. "I don't see why not. Do you think you can just sit and be a silent observer?"

"I'll give it my best shot."

I dropped the empty beer bottle in the recycle bin. "That's great. I've got to go down and set up the workshop." I opened the refrigerator, popped the cap off a second beer, and set it on the counter. "Finish that and come down when you're ready."

The only response was the happy sound of slurping as I walked down the stairs. I checked my phone for any messages, then set it on the workshop table. It was almost nine o'clock, and I had just enough time to cut a few pieces of steel for the demonstration and light the forge. The office door was open, and I caught a glimpse of Brigid's Hammer on the table inside. My hand clenched, reacting to the hammer's call, and as the sigil illuminated, I remembered to cover up with a pair of gloves. I didn't want to explain that to my student and his friend.

A few minutes later, there was a knock, and my first thought was how prompt this fourteen-year-old kid was. I flipped the lock and opened the door.

"Good morn...ing." My greeting faltered a bit when I realized I was staring down at a silk blouse stretched across a bosomed chest. This was not Riker Bailey.

"Good morning, yourself, Ms. Blackstone." The woman on my doorstep cleared her throat, and it was apparent that my misdirected stare did not go unnoticed.

"Uh, hello." My foot kicked the door wider as I peeked around the woman in front of me, searching for two fourteen-year-old boys.

Andrea Peters pushed past me to enter the workshop. Her hand brushed my forearm and rested for a brief moment on my bicep. Her energy felt different, heavy, intrusive, and I shook my head to clear my thoughts and the energy.

Andrea wandered closer to the forge, pausing to survey my tools and the workshop table. Her fingertips swept the face of the anvil, and I watched her inspect every pair of tongs hanging from the rack. Her presence made me uncomfortable, and it was clear that she was here to ask more than a few questions.

"Can I help you with something?" I asked as I kicked a wedge under the door to prop it open. The air in the room went cold. I felt more than knew that I didn't want to be locked inside the carriage house alone with her.

"Actually, I think that you can help me with a lot of things."

Her hands clapped together as she knocked the dust from her palms. She whispered words in a language I didn't understand, and before I could question her intentions, I felt the rush of heat as flames burst out the open ends of my forge. Andrea's eyes opened wide and turned jet black.

"You can help me with this." Her fisted hand opened to reveal a clutch of honed nails. She fanned her fingers and drew one across my left cheek.

Her fingers clenched near my throat, but it wasn't fear that held me frozen against the wall; it was the realization that she was using magick inside our protected carriage house. Andrea Peters was breaking through the one place Shay believed I was safe.

"How are you doing this?" The words squeaked from my mouth as I felt the crush of energy constrict my arms tight to my thighs.

"Your girlfriend's tricks aren't going to work today."

Andrea drew her finger away from my face. I felt the sting of her cut and saw the stain of blood–my blood.

"Ow! What the hell?"

The wound burned and blood streaked down my face. She held the dripping finger under her nose, inhaled deeply, and drew her finger across her tongue. The delighted grin that followed made my stomach turn.

"I knew it was you." She circled around my body, leaning in close as she asked, "Where is she?"

"Where is who?" I tried to turn my head to follow her as she wandered around my workshop.

Andrea turned over the hammers on my table, one by one, inspecting each. "Where is Brigid?"

Andrea's question was confusing. I understood that the goddess existed, but I'd never actually experienced her physical presence.

"I don't know," I said, adding "Honestly!" when Andrea gave me a skeptical look. If the goddess was here, she'd never shown her face.

Andrea grabbed my hand, forcing it to move from the ethereal bindings. I tried to fight, but the force of her energy was more powerful as she peeled my clenched fingers to open my sigil hand. She ripped off my glove.

"You know exactly where she is." Andrea opened her hand, and before I could scream from the pain, her palm lit a brilliant green, illuminating sigil symbols similar to my own.

"Who are you?"

"You'll understand soon enough." Andrea waved her hand, and my body went stiff. "Where is she?"

Her hand clenched, and when she flicked her wrist toward the office door, my body slammed against the wall. The air was knocked out of my chest as I hit the floor. Her hand waved again, and my body flew toward the bottom stair. I was paralyzed by her magick, but I could feel the pain as my back and shoulder impacted the riser. With a fluttering of wings, Stout appeared in front of me.

"What happened?" he asked just before a hand snatched him out of the air.

"Filthy fairy." She squeezed his miniature body. "You belong in a specimen jar."

"Stop!" His voice was a squeal of agony, and I struggled against the magical bindings, trying to save him.

"Why are you doing this?" I screamed as she opened her palm to reveal the limp body of my fairy friend.

"Where—is—she?" she demanded.

Andrea grabbed the tip of Stout's wing, and the fairy jerked awake. His screech of pain was torture to my ears as she pulled the wing from the welted point where it was rooted in his shoulder. I tried to think, to figure out how to find the goddess hiding inside the carriage house.

"Stop! I don't know what you're talking about!" I yelled.

Her hand paused just before tearing his wing from his body. "You do know. You're wearing Brigid's mark."

She tossed Stout's limp body onto the table, stabbed his wings to the surface with two unfinished blades, and crossed the room to where I lay. She knelt in front of me, raising my sigil hand so the two of us could see it.

"Where did you hide her?"

Andrea's palm slapped against my own, and I felt the searing heat of her energy burning through my sigil hand. Her magick was painful, corrupt, and evil.

"I don't know what you're talking about!" I screamed. The pain was making it hard to think.

She dragged her hand across my bloodied cheek and licked her palm. "You've held her. Played with her. I can taste it in your blood."

I felt the rush of earth energy break through the soles of my feet. Seconds later, power moved up my legs, through my hips and torso, until my heartbeat pounded like a hammer through my bones. My head ached from the surge. The goddess, in her infinite power, was pushing back against whatever owned the woman in front of me.

It was clear what Andrea had come here to find.

My eyes glanced toward the office, and she was quick to react, darting over to the table in the other room. Her laugh was wicked, evil; it seeped into my heart like poison.

"By the goddess." She spoke with reverence as she reached to pick up my hammer.

The flash of fire and energy was so bright that I almost missed the woman flying through the air before hitting the carriage house wall. The bond of magick broke, and I scrambled toward the table to find Stout. His tiny body was limp, nailed to the table, but I could see a faint rise and fall of his chest. He was alive!

I stumbled toward the office, trying to reach my hammer, hoping that the bond of Brigid's magick would protect me. My fingers wrapped around the handle, and as I held it aloft, I heard Andrea laugh.

"In virtute manus meae tu es."

I couldn't understand what she was saying, but my best guess was that she was calling something in the room to be hers. My hand gripped the hammer, but I couldn't feel it against my skin.

"Oriri!" she hissed, and my feet left the ground.

My toes dangled a few seconds before I was standing upright beside the table. I wasn't in control. I fought the movement as the hammer raised above my head, poised to strike Stout's limp form crumpled unconscious on the table.

"No!" I screamed, struggling with every force of my will not to drop the hammer down on him.

"Vow to come with me," Andrea commanded, flicking her wrist back and forth to control my arm. The head of the hammer hovered over Stout. "Vow!"

"I'll do it! Please don't hurt him. I'll do it!" Tears fell as I crushed my eyes shut. If the hammer dropped on top of my fairy friend, I didn't want to watch him die.

"So weak. Love makes you so weak." That laugh, her laugh, was like hot steel scalding the presence of humanity.

My body fell against the wall, and the hammer dropped to my thigh. My knuckles were white from the tension of my involuntary grip.

"Screw you!" I struggled to escape with every bit of magick I could draw.

Andrea waved her finger. "Tsk—tsk—little blacksmith." Her wrist flicked toward the door, and my body flew across the room and slammed against the wooden frame. "We're going to take a little ride."

There was nothing I could do to stop the pull of her magick. My feet hovered inches from the floor as her clenching grip carried me out the door and into the back of her SUV. The hammer was tight in my trembling fist. I thought about Stout's unconscious form pinned to the tabletop, and just before something slammed against the back of my head, I thought about the wreckage in the workshop and what would happen when Shay discovered it.

I opened my eyes moments later when my body rolled against the wheel-well of the stripped-out SUV. I could feel the grip of magick pinning my arms tight against my torso. Brigid's Hammer was gripped in my hand, and as the fog of the head injury lifted, I started thinking about how I was going to save myself.

"Don't try to fight."

"What the hell do you want from me?" I yelled at the voice coming from the front of the vehicle.

"I want my powers back, and I've waited a very long time to get them."

The vehicle made a sharp turn, and I slid across the floor. My body bounced as the tires hit obstacles in the road. The best I could guess was that we'd turned onto a gravel driveway or service road. I had no idea how long I'd been unconscious or in what direction we were traveling.

"Where are you taking me?"

She slammed on the brakes, and the force of it threw my back against the anchor bracket of the front seat. I could hear the crunch of rocks beneath her feet as Andrea moved around the car. The back doors opened, and my body floated into the daylight. The bright sunlight was blinding, and I blinked a few times before focusing on exactly where I was.

Andrea gave me a grim smile. "I'm taking you back to the beginning, little blacksmith."

CHAPTER XXII

REWIND

"Back to the beginning?" I repeated.

As my body floated from the vehicle, I could see the mouth of the mine. It was the last place I wanted to go with this woman.

"You've got some lessons to learn, Wildwood Blackstone." Her hand rotated, and my body followed, spinning until I was upright, drifting with my feet just inches from the ground. Brigid's Hammer felt weightless in my hand, where it fit tight to my thigh.

"Just let me go. I have nothing that belongs to you, Andrea." The rush of adrenaline felt like fists to my sides, punching to break through the binds of her magick.

"You have everything that belongs to me."

Her hand jerked toward the tunnel floor, and I felt the weight of gravity as my body slammed to the ground. I couldn't break the fall with my hands, and the gravel of the tunnel crushed against my cheek.

"What the hell is wrong with you?" I spat without thinking, and before I could take another breath, my body slammed against the rock ceiling above me.

"We have a lot of work to do, Wildwood. If you keep yelling at me, you're going to make this more painful than it has to be." The nails on her fingertips sparked as she scraped them across the jagged rock wall. She stepped close enough to hold her pointer finger like a knife to my throat. "Do—you— understand?" Her breath was hot against my face, and I wanted to turn away.

"Mm-hmm." The noise was more like a whimper, and it was all I dared to make as I felt her nail pierce my skin.

"I'm glad we're both on the same page."

She waved her hand, and my body lifted off the ground until I was standing on my feet. I felt my weight transfer, and I struggled to catch my balance as she released her magick hold. I tried to raise my hammer to strike against her, but my arm didn't move.

"Tsk tsk," she scolded, waving her finger in my face. "You're not very smart, are you, little Maker?"

Her fingertip pierced my shoulder again. She twisted her fist, burrowing her finger until her knuckles hit my shoulder bone. My scream echoed through the vacant tunnel, and she pushed harder, deeper, her finger drilling back and forth into my flesh until I couldn't hold the tears back anymore.

"Stop! Please, stop!" I begged.

The words tumbled from my lips as reality faded. She yanked her finger out, and I felt my muscle tear away with the puncture.

"Behave now, little blacksmith." She licked my blood from her hand. "Yes, you are just perfect."

I whimpered in surrender as she gestured toward the darkness ahead.

"We're going to take a walk now," she said.

The sound of her footsteps against the rock floor echoed off the tunnel walls. My feet moved without my consent, and I wondered what it would take to break free from her. I wondered if Stout was still alive and where Shay might be. Had she returned to the carriage house? If Andrea had killed Stout, how would Shay know I was trapped in this mine?

"What do you want from me?" I asked as we moved through the tunnels.

Andrea carried a flashlight and when she turned to answer, the light burned bright in my eyes. "I want her." She pointed at the hammer in my hand. "She belongs to me."

I looked at the image of the goddess etched on the hammer's head. My blood ran down my sleeve, dripping off to hide the Pictish inscriptions. Brigid had power, and as long as my hand held tight to the handle, I had power, too. What I couldn't understand was how Andrea could control both of us.

My body dropped, and my feet touched the ground. Before I knew what was happening, I was walking down the tunnel, three steps ahead of my captor. She controlled every bit of the journey, and the longer we walked, the more I understood exactly where we were going. The dizzying switchbacks were up ahead, and I could see the gouges in the pustule remnants where Dexter had devoured the demon embryos.

"That half-breed monster killed my guardians." Andrea patted the tattered mucus with reverence.

"Guardians?" I asked. I wrinkled my nose in disgust, since it was one of the few parts of my body I could control. "What are they protecting?"

She waved the flashlight around the open space. "All—of—this." I could see her arms spread sideways in celebration. Andrea was a keeper of the darkest, creepiest, and most possessed part of the mine.

As we ventured deeper, I could feel the energy calling me. Brigid's cave was up ahead, and Andrea knew the path. But only the solitary Maker could enter, and that understanding gave me hope. I remembered how my wrist had felt warm, tethered to Shay by the lace of my pants. If I could get inside, the goddess would keep me safe. With each step forward, I felt the Maker's power surge inside me. My empty hand felt free to move, but I hesitated, hoping Andrea wouldn't know and that when I entered the cave, with Brigid's power, I could fight back.

"What do you want with me and the hammer?" I asked, feeling for the first time the magnitude of the wound on my shoulder. I doubted I could raise the hammer high enough to strike a solid blow, but when I got the chance, I would try.

We stood in front of the feathery flames marking the entrance. This would be my chance.

I didn't expect the fist to my back as she pushed me through the opening in the wall. Brigid was there, tickling my skin as I passed through her fire. Andrea was there, too, gripping tight to my shoulder. I thought for a moment the flames would stop her, but the crack in the wall flexed just like before, allowing us to pass through. The fire in the fractured wall still burned, but the light of the crystals had dimmed. The energy was beautiful, even with the evil clinging to my shoulder. I stumbled over the rocks on the ground, but I felt the presence.

She was here. The Goddess of my hammer was inside.

"You're not very smart, are you?" Andrea laughed.

"I'm smart enough to guess that you'll never hold this." I felt my fingers tighten around the handle as my knuckles turned whiter. My sigil's energy burned through, scorching away the stains from my blood to illuminate the head of my hammer.

Andrea leaned back, drawing a deep breath, absorbing the energy like a drug. Her eyes shot wide, her nostrils flared, and when she looked at me, I saw something inhuman inside her.

"What the hell are you?"

"You mean you don't have a guess?" Her fingers flexed and curled as she cracked her knuckles joint by joint. The nails on her index fingers hooked around, and she dug them into a hole in the wall.

"If I had to guess, I'd say you're some kind of monster."

Her laugh was shrill, and she stepped close enough that I could see the hate in her eyes. "I guess if I'm a monster, then you're a monster, too."

Andrea Peters and I had only one thing in common, and that was Shay Pierce. Andrea was baiting me, but why? Was she insinuating that I was like her because of my relationship with Shay? But the two of them had only dated once. Twice, if you counted Benton's interference, and we didn't want to count that at all.

"I'm nothing like you." My body tipped until our faces were inches apart.

"Oh, but you are so very much like me, little Maker." She held her palm to mine, and for the first time, I got a look at the lines shining through her skin. I saw the slashes illuminating like my own.

"How?" I closed my eyes, wishing away what I'd just seen.

"Bind the earth to water," she said with a laugh. "Hold water to the sky." Her flaming palms lifted. "Carry fire to the winds, and the mother's child is mine."

Her hands clapped like the crush of glass, and a sphere of green flame hovered between us. The manifestation was like before, a scrolling of memories that were not my own. I saw the flash of a dark-haired woman standing in front of a forge. The fire danced and puckered as a giant hand billow pumped air into the bright orange coals. It was my Maker ancestor, Kai, and I felt a surge of pride as she struck a mark into the head of a hammer. No, not *a* hammer. Brigid's Hammer. The hammer in my hand.

"Why are you showing this to me?" I asked, captivated by the holographic likeness of someone I wished I'd met.

"You want to know how alike we are?"

She reached for the hammer in my hand, and for the first time since taking me from the workshop, Andrea lost control. Her power over me faded, and I felt the release. My arm whipped up, pushing Andrea against the cavern rock.

The surrounding walls spun, and I felt the weight of gravity pull me to the ground. I was free. As the numbness of her magick faded, the sharp pain of my wounded shoulder flared. My blood dripped, thick and dark, and I tried with all of my strength to roll to my hands and knees to stand. Andrea was doing the same as I picked up Brigid's Hammer and realized I had nowhere to run. She knew it, too, and her laughter was piercing.

"You hold all that power, little Maker, but I have some magick of my own."

She punched her fist against the ground, and a zippering crack opened in the floor. There was no escaping the spider-like creatures that crawled out, scurrying toward me. The dirt under my feet shuffled into the air, creating an ominous filter in front of their telescoping eyes. These creatures came from a place of evil, and somehow Andrea controlled every single one.

The jagged rock of the cavern wall dug into my back, tearing at my shirt. There was nowhere to go, but I raised my hammer in defense. One by one, I smashed each monster, scattering limbs and bodies with every strike. Their blood stained my skin, but I didn't stop.

"Clever, girl." Andrea's open-palmed hand fanned in front of her face, and more creatures crawled from the earth.

"Screw you." My next hammer strike splattered a giant spider demon, spraying the front of my pants with a sticky, green ooze. "I know you didn't bring me here to smash your demon spawn. What do you want?"

The hammer soared through the air as I continued to destroy everything coming at me. I struck out at them over and over for what felt like forever, wondering if it would ever end.

Then, I noticed two things. The spider demons stopped coming, and the etched image of Brigid on my hammer's head was disappearing behind the stain of dark ooze.

Andrea stepped over the remnants of the demons and into my personal space. I heard a plop of goop hit the floor beside me as she reached for the hammer in my hand. It was clear what I'd done—what she'd *wanted* me to do.

"Always the hero." She flicked her wrist. "The Maker always wants to save the day." Her claw-covered finger gripped around my throat. "I was the hero once." Her free hand gripped the handle, and she ripped it from my grasp.

"No." The sound rasped from my lips, and the last gasp of air squeezed from my lungs as her hold tightened.

Andrea blinked hard, and when she opened her eyes, I saw tiny flames reflected against the black of her irises.

I'm not going to survive. The realization chilled me.

I thought of Shay, the love of my life, and what she would do when she found my body. She would never forgive me for leaving her. I felt the darkness coming, clouding my mind. I had to fight, but the grip around my neck was tight as I struggled to keep my eyes from closing.

And then I couldn't fight anymore.

~~~~~~~~~~~

I don't know how long I laid unconscious, but the first sensation was the pain of the wound in my shoulder, and the second was the burning skin of my sigil hand, which was illuminated by the brightest orange glow. I flattened my palm to the earth, seeking strength from the ground. The energy of my Maker powers pulsed from my palm, up through my arm, and into the rest of my body. I felt like a dance club strobe light, and for a moment, I let the energy revive me. I moved with caution, and I tucked my hand under my shirt to hide the earth-energy exchange happening inside me.

"How can this be?" Andrea shouted.

I stayed in the safety of my fetal position, with my back toward her. We were no longer inside Brigid's cavern, and I could feel Brigid's guidance fading. Andrea must have known the goddess would strengthen me.

"How can you betray me?" she called out.

The sound of crashing rock was behind me, but I needed to know who Andrea was talking to, so I rolled my shoulder, stretching my neck enough to glimpse her hand brushing the head of Brigid's hammer. I slowed my breathing, trying to calm the earth energy pulsing through my body. Her hammer arm waved through the air, striking against nothing.

"Mother, please. I want to come back."

Her anguished cries broke the stronghold Andrea had over me, and I was ready to take advantage. I rolled onto my hands and knees, careful to move in silence, but she was aware of what I was doing, and I felt the suffocating squeeze of her hand around my throat. My eyes closed as I surrendered again. The power of the Maker was nothing against whatever Andrea was.
~~~~~~~~~~~

"You bitch!" I felt her energy before I heard the voice or saw her face, but I knew it was Shay.

Andrea chuckled menacingly. "You are clever, Shay, but you're too late."

The shuffle of their feet kicked dust in front of my face. My cough caught Shay's attention, and our eyes met before Andrea's clawed fingers punctured Shay from behind. The attack threw Shay forward and Andrea back.

"Damn you to hell!" Shay yelled as she turned to face her attacker. Andrea's hold over me lifted, and I crawled to my knees, attempting to stand.

The wound on my shoulder continued to bleed. I cupped it with my sigil hand, whispering, "*Ignis.*" believing with all of my Maker magicks I could singe the wound. And I did. The pain was beyond anything I'd ever experienced, but the blood stopped dripping down my arm. I stumbled to my feet, catching my balance against the tunnel wall. The goddess was with me, and I felt the pull of her hammer's power.

Shay's hand grasped mine, and I pulled hard on it to climb to my feet. She shielded me with her entire body, and I got my first look at the wound in her back. It was bad, but there was no time to ease her pain as Andrea moved in on us, my hammer clutched tight in her hand.

The sigil in my palm burned, and Shay's fingers tightened as I felt the Magick and Maker powers fill me. I didn't know if my girlfriend could feel it, too, but I understood in that instant we could escape Andrea's magick together.

"You think that your ridiculous love will make a difference?" Andrea jeered.

Shay took one step backward, and we were shoulder to shoulder, hands clamped tight, the power of the Magick rejuvenating my weak frame. Shay let out a stiff laugh, and a knowing smile crossed her face.

There had been a great evil in Bannock all this time, and she was standing right in front of us.

I heard the growl at the same time I saw two giant paws lunge out of the darkness. "*Custodire!*" Shay yelled, and the fur on his body began transforming into scales.

Andrea laughed. *"Apakaroti,"* she hissed, trapping Dexter between the two states of his dragon-dog self, not fully K-9 and not yet the dragon whose protective ferocity we were counting on for this fight.

Shay grabbed the animal's neck and tugged him behind us. His whimpering was a distraction, but Shay stood firm in her protective stance.

"What the hell did you do to him?"

"It's what you didn't do." She stepped closer. "He loves to eat my guardians, and so my guardians will love to eat him back."

The embryo pustules clinging to the cavern walls weren't the harmless snack we'd believed, and now Dexter was paying the price for our ignorance. Shay's grip tightened on my hand as she dropped to one knee beside her squealing K-9 partner.

"By the mother creator," Shay chanted. "By the powers done, you are whole by my hands."

I felt the magick burst from the earth, rise through the soles of my feet, and move through my body. Shay commanded the element for all three of us, and instead of an *ignis* flame against Dexter's neck, it was a glowing orb.

"Goddess is the source of us," she whispered, and I understood.

"Goddess is the source of us." My voice was just above a whisper as the power of our energies moved into Dexter, returning him to his K-9 self. His nose puffed a burst of smoke before his head fell against the cavern floor.

"Your gifts have grown, Shay." Andrea's hand lifted toward the vulnerable animal.

"Don't—you—dare!" The fluctuation of power in the cavern was palpable, and my hand fell as Shay flexed both palms at Andrea.

"Do you understand who I am?" Andrea mirrored Shay's hand motion, and Shay shielded Dexter and me with her body. "I have been bigger than you for longer than you've been alive!" Andrea's palm lit with a sigil diagram. "She's my mother, too!"

I could hear Shay's sharp intake of breath. "What have you done?"

Andrea reached for the hammer. Her rage focused toward Shay, and my world moved in slow motion. Brigid, the goddess of my flame, was the linking force between the Magick and the Maker. My hammer would not harm my lover, ever. I held my sigil hand toward Andrea with Shay anchoring me to the earth.

The hammer flew from the ground, landing on the floor beside Dexter. His massive paw covered the hammer's head. Shay pulled back the sleeve of her shirt and smashed her wrist cuff against the wall. The force of the cuff's magick knocked Andrea to her knees. Shay barreled toward the woman, kicking her in the chest and knocking her against the tunnel wall. Dexter jumped to his feet and transformed into his dragon self. It was the three of us now, and for the moment, we were safe.

Shay turned to look at me. *"Ignis,"* she whispered, her blue flame illuminating the space between us. "Where are you hurt? I see blood on—" A faint gasp escaped her lips as fingers traveled over my wounded shoulder. "Your shirt."

My eyes fixed on the crumpled woman on the ground. It wouldn't be long before she woke. "That hateful monster!" I said. "She ran her nasty finger through me. I'm fine. It's fine for now. We can fix it later with the demon sift."

Her hand traveled across my shoulder until her palm cupped my cheek. "What did she do to you?" I saw the conflicted emotions in Shay's eyes.

"I'm not exactly sure," I explained. "I have no idea how long I was unconscious, but she said things. I think she's got control of my Maker abilities."

"She does, and I think she's more than a power-hungry monster." Shay's kiss to my cheek was sloppy and quick as she turned toward Dexter, never letting go of my hand. "We need to get out of here. She's got the advantage inside these tunnels, and the cuff's magick will wear off soon."

I didn't say a word. Shay was right. As long as Andrea had us trapped in these tunnels, she could send her demon children after us. It occurred to me that Shay was standing inside the mine, and that reality made me think. "How did you find me?"

"I didn't." She tilted her chin to point at the dragon in front of us. "He found you."

"You shifted here?" I asked, knowing the answer.

"We did, and now he's going to shift you right out."

She pushed my body against the animal, and before I could argue, Shay faded from view, and the dizzying journey from the crystal cavern to the mouth of the mine left me crumpled on the ground. Before I could stop him, Dexter was gone.

A hand grabbed my shoulder. I wanted to push my way to safety, but the shifting travel left me disoriented.

"Let me help you." Dani's voice was gentle, and I grabbed her hand for support.

"We should move away from the mouth of the cave," Amelia said, and I got my first glimpse of her warrior stance.

It was impossible not to pause and take in the beautiful woman. An orange and blue linen wrap draped her torso, twisting to her waist, connected to a flowing tapered skirt. The weight of her arrow quiver creased across her breasts. My eyes traveled to the recurve bow, and the string drawn tight against her copper-toned cheek. She was protecting Dani and me, and for a moment, I wondered if Dexter was protecting his partner.

"Where are Shay and Dex?" Dani asked as we backed away from the entrance to the mine.

Where is Brigid's Hammer? I thought, realizing both of my hands were empty.

"They're coming." I stared at Amelia, who stood perched on the rock beside us, ready to fire her arrow.

"You good, honey?" Dani asked her wife, and Amelia gave a smile in return.

We heard feet crushing the stones of the cavern tunnels, and a dragon burst from the mine with Shay a few steps behind.

"We're about to have some company!" Shay yelled as she slid across the gravel.

"I've got you covered!" Amelia's arms were steady as they held the bow, ready to fire.

Dani and Shay stood shoulder to shoulder beside our dragon, and I felt safe behind them. "Shay?"

"Yes, love." She didn't turn to look at me, but I understood why.

"My hammer—"

Before I could finish, Dexter turned around and jumped toward me. His mouth opened wide, and Brigid's Hammer fell from his teeth. There was no chance for me to pick it up as three raging Gatekeeper demons leapt out of the tunnel.

I heard the rush of the arrow fired from Amelia's bow and saw it penetrate the skeletal flesh of an unsuspecting monster. It fell to the ground, lifeless. Dexter launched at the demon, grabbing the throat and ripping the head from its body. Seconds later, Andrea stepped into the sunlight. I heard the creak of leather and the flex of my demon-forged bow limbs as Amelia nocked the next arrow.

Life moved in slow motion as Shay advanced with Dexter, and Amelia loosed her arrow. I heard the hiss from the spiraling fletching as it soared past. Dani hesitated as Andrea sidestepped the projectile, catching it in her hand. She rotated the shaft, flipped her wrist, and the arrow flew toward Amelia.

"No!" Dani screamed as the impact of the arrow knocked her wife to the ground. Dani scrambled to help Amelia.

Andrea laughed, and her demons advanced toward me. I gripped the hammer in my hand, hoping to channel the fire goddess.

"What the hell are you?" Shay yelled, holding her position in the dirt.

Dani's hands traveled over her wife's body, stopping at where the arrow had struck and yanking it from the socket of Amelia's prosthetic leg.

Andrea was playing with us, but we were ready for her. Dexter launched at the demon flanking Andrea's side, and the clash of gnashing teeth and feral screeches echoed off the hillside as they disappeared into the darkness of the mine.

"Dexter!" Shay yelled, but there was no time to chase down the dragon-dog.

"I'm alright, sweetheart." I heard Amelia say as she pushed off the ground, bow in hand. As expected, this woman was a fierce fighter. She settled on her perch, waiting to shoot again.

"Goddess is the source of us." Shay looked over her shoulder at me, nodding.

"Goddess is the source of us," I repeated, and we began our chant together.

The earth trembled beneath our feet, and for a moment, I thought it was from Shay and me acting in unison. It was not, and the force of Andrea's fist knocked us to the ground, slamming into the side of the mine shaft. Brigid's Hammer flew to the ground, landing in the rocky path between us.

Dani whipped the strap across her shoulder, revealing her gun. She racked the shotgun and raised it to her shoulder. "You better not move, Peters. Not one inch."

"Officer Danielle Forrest—" She paused. "Or should I call you baby Kota? How fitting for you to stand in front of me pointing that ridiculous weapon."

"What's the game?" Dani asked, adjusting the butt of her gun tight against her shoulder and sidestepping to stand beside Shay.

"The game?" Andrea laughed as she said the words. "The game is so repetitive it's almost ridiculous. Kota family members certainly enjoy making the same mistakes."

"What the hell are you talking about?" Dani yelled. I heard the shuffle of rocks behind me as Amelia, still holding the bow with a nocked arrow drawn tight against her cheek, inched her way down from her perch.

"Danielle..." Amelia's voice was a whisper.

"I'm fine." Dani stepped closer to the Assistant Mayor.

"The Kota family has a sad history in this town. Have you heard the story, Wildwood? I'm sure Shay's read you my report." Andrea didn't wait for a response, just plowed on with her story. "Mary Kota was an interesting lady."

Dani's body rocked forward, thrown off balance by the sound of her mother's name. "How could you know anything about my mother?" Her gun fell away from her shoulder as she inched closer to the Assistant Mayor. "You should—"

"Mary and I met," Andrea interrupted. "It was just that one time. She was a curious woman–a little too curious for her own good." She raised her hands and snapped them down, mimicking the motion of breaking a twig.

Andrea was luring Dani in, and what better way than to talk about a mother she didn't remember.

"Don't—take—another—step," Amelia warned, aiming her arrow at Andrea.

The Assistant Mayor positioned herself so that Dani was between her and the rest of our group. "You wouldn't want to hurt your beloved Danielle, would you?" Andrea took another step, and with inhuman speed, she snatched the gun from Dani and tossed it on the ground. Her taloned fingers gripped Dani's throat, and I watched in horror as Dani struggled for air.

"Let her go." Shay's voice was even, her body posture calm as I'd ever witnessed. It was captivating to watch her transformation to cop mode with her hair loose around her face, but after ten years of demon hunting police work, Shay knew what she was doing.

"Let her go? Well, that wouldn't make sense now, would it?"

Sneering, Andrea dragged Dani toward the mine, obviously hoping to take her inside. We couldn't let her gain the advantage.

Andrea's choke hold tightened as she pulled Dani against her chest. "Mary Kota was a problem for me, and so was her husband, Jacob. He had a little more fight in him, though, even without the power of the Maker. You've seen the photographs. I know how to eliminate problems. Much like the problem you are right now. Maybe…" Dani struggled to break free, but Andrea was more creature than human. "Maybe I should snap your neck, just like I snapped your mother's."

I watched the color drain from Dani's face, but Shay didn't move. Almost as if she wasn't surprised. Then it hit me. *This* was the secret she'd been keeping. Shay's hand clenched around the grip, keeping the taser aimed at the women in front of us.

"You killed her?" Amelia asked, flexing her arms. She moved away from Shay, trying to get a clear shot at the Assistant Mayor.

"If I take out this one," she said, squeezing Dani–who looked exhausted, slumped over Andrea's arm–tighter, "there's no one left. I'll have eliminated the whole family, and the Kota bloodline will be one—less—obstacle." Andrea's words were punctuated by her tugging Dani back into the mine, their feet shuffling through the dirt.

"Obstacle for what?" Amelia asked, angling her body for a clear shot at Andrea.

"My freedom."

Andrea's arm constricted, and her back arched. I watched in horror as Dani's feet lifted off the ground, and her arms fell limp to her sides. It was impossible to tell if the move injured her or crushed her windpipe. Dani's body fell into the dirt.

"That's one down." Andrea stretched her arms in front of her, celebrating the ease with which she'd eliminated our friend. "Which one of you is next?"

She raised a finger toward me, but before she could do anything, Andrea flew back against the crumbling frame of the mine's entrance, pinned to the wood by an arrow. I turned to see Amelia nocked another arrow against the bowstring, and launch it into Andrea's shoulder, striking millimeters from the first.

"By the power of my father!" Andrea yelled, and fire burst from her palm, burning through the arrow's shaft and releasing her from its hold.

Her magick was powerful, but Shay didn't hesitate to fire her taser, hitting Andrea in the center of her chest. The pulsing charge sent Andrea backward as she jerked and contorted until she fell to the ground.

Amelia dropped her bow and scrambled to her wife's side. She tugged at Dani's collar, searching for a pulse. "Oh, blessed be. She's alive."

I stood frozen in place, trying to process the events of the last few minutes. I wasn't a trained professional, and I certainly wasn't a bundle of calm in dangerous situations.

"Wildwood!" Shay yelled my name. It was loud, and perhaps it wasn't the first time she'd called it.

"Uh, yeah." It was all I could say, and it was clear to my girlfriend that the entire situation had put me in a state of shock.

"Wil, can you do this?" Shay shoved the taser handle into my palm. "If she so much as twitches, you pull that trigger."

I gave a nervous nod as my eyes traveled down the spiraling lead wires to the spot where they were embedded in the Assistant Mayor's chest. I glanced toward Dani's limp body and watched as Amelia and Shay carried the unconscious woman away from the mine. Could I pull the trigger on the taser? I didn't know. I wasn't sure if it was in me to cause another person harm. It didn't matter, as seconds later, the metal wires flipped with wicked accuracy at my head, catching me very close to the scar on my cheek from my first taser wire experience.

"Ow! Damn." The taser fell from my hand as I touched the stinging slice on my face.

Andrea was on her feet again, her eyes wild with rage as she plucked the taser probes from her chest. "Brigid, mother goddess, release them from the Ancient's hold and restore the power to me." She raised her palm toward the hammer lying on the ground, and the heavy metal dragged toward her, leaving a snaking gouge across the crumbled ground.

"No!" I yelled and dove toward the hammer.

Shay's hand grabbed my shoulder, and she stepped in front of me. "Together," she said, and we raced to prevent Andrea from regaining control.

Shay reached Brigid's Hammer first, and as her palm wrapped around the handle, her *ignis* flame glowed bright white before flashing a solid blinding blue. Like a hurricane wind whipping a sapling tree, the wave of magick energy pushed Andrea back. We took advantage of her loss of control and staggered together into a group. I stared at Amelia, who sat, mouth agape, holding her unconscious wife. I couldn't tell what she was looking at until I felt the heat and witnessed the unbelievable sight of Shay beside me.

In the months that Shay and I had been together, she'd surprised me with her magick more times than I could count, but the power coming from her hand now was something beyond the deities of the heavens. My pause felt like a freeze-frame moment, and it took a few seconds to realize that my mouth was hanging open.

Shay stood before us, shoulders back, chest out, in the most power-filled stance I'd ever seen; her arms were pulled back, gripping tight to the Hammer of the Goddess. The Pictish-adorned hammer became a glowing hilt with Shay's two-handed grip clutching tight to the handle. We had hundreds of forged swords in the bar's cellar, but none compared to the weapon in Shay's hands. The *ignis* flame she carried generated the solid blue blade. Brigid's Hammer, my hammer, was Shay's exquisite sword.

It was a thing of dreams and fairy tales to watch Shay swing the flickering blade toward Andrea. The Assistant Mayor stumbled to her knees, attempting to avoid the blade. Andrea raised her hands, and a Gatekeeper demon jumped from the mine. Shay sliced the blade left and right, felling the demon before any of us could react. Andrea sent demon after demon, and Shay batted her sword back and forth, advancing with each kill until she hovered over Andrea.

Shay raised the sword over her head and swiped down with the full force of her shoulders, but the blade didn't slash through our attacker.

Andrea held her palm out to Shay. "It remembers me," she said, struggling to her feet.

Everything made sense in the whisper of her words.

It remembers me: the search for answers.

It remembers me: the attempts to get closer to Shay and me.

It remembers me: the revelation of Benton's history with Andrea and Jacob.

It remembers me: the disdain for Dani, and most of all, the quest to possess Shay.

There was a ghost in Bannock. It was standing before us, somehow back from the grave, searching for her place in our magick-filled world.

"Kai," I whispered the name.

When I turned toward Andrea, my eyes locked on a pair of dilating irises, and the Maker part of my history was reflected back at me.

"But, how?"

CHAPTER XXIII

RAVELING

"It isn't possible," Shay said as she swiped the sword at the first Magick once more. But once more, the flaming blade passed through Kai's body.

Kai's head swept backward, bobbed forward, and we watched in horror as the skin of the Assistant Mayor's synthetic face peeled away to reveal the decaying flesh of an unidentifiable life force. Her palm flashed, similar to our *ignis* flames, and I saw the mark burst over the skin on her wrist. The primitive red "K" appeared, one slashed line at a time, and a red ring sizzled around to touch the edges, bringing the original Maker's mark into existence.

"*No!*" Shay screamed, and with the full force of her magick, she lunged forward. "You cannot be her!"

"But I am." Kai's hands caught the flaming sword as it dropped toward her neck. "You can't kill me with a weapon that these hands forged."

The impact of the sword collided with the power of their magick. The explosion sucked the air from the space between us. Shay flew to the ground, and the transforming Kai fell in the opposite direction. Her cries of pain tore through the sound of flying gravel, and she kicked pellets of rock and sand at all of us. I tucked my shoulders to my ears, trying to cover them from the sound as I scrambled over the ground, frantic to get to my girlfriend.

"Shay!" My hands traveled over her body as I searched for signs of life. I tore away the layers of her uniform to place my ear above the collar of her vest. I heard the thump-thump of a heartbeat. "Oh, thank Brigid," I whispered as I watched the rise and fall of Shay's chest.

"I'm alright," Shay squeaked through gasping breaths.

"What the hell just happened?" I asked as I pulled her into my arms.

"I'm not sure, but she's got a lot of explaining to do." Shay grabbed my arms and leveraged herself forward, never taking her eyes off of Kai. "What the hell do you want from us?"

Kai's face dripped with pus, and oozing tendrils webbed from the pieces of skin hanging near her shoulders. It must have been painful, but she tore the flesh away and tossed it on the ground. I watched as the torn skin shriveled into paper, much like the cut-away slice of material we'd found tucked inside the Assistant Mayor's file. Her flesh was the same as this demon flesh, but how could she be the original combination of the Magick and the Maker?

"I want my time back!" Kai yelled, shaking the last piece of bloodied skin from her body.

"We didn't take your time from you," Shay explained.

She positioned herself between Kai and me, and I felt the heat of the Magick's fire ignite my *ignis* flame. The call of Brigid's fire was as loud now as it had been that day in the mine, and I fought the urge to run inside the darkened tunnels.

"Shay." I stepped close enough to whisper in her ear, my hand clenched tight to her shoulder. "The cave. Brigid is calling me."

Shay's hand covered my own, but her eyes never left the demon in front of us. "I feel it."

"I feel it, too." Kai laughed as she stepped closer to Dani and Amelia. "Can you feel it too, little—baby—Kota?"

Amelia twisted from the dirt, her stance strong, the demon-forged bow gripped tight in her hand. "Don't think for a second that I won't shoot you right where you stand." She pulled an arrow from the quiver on her back and nocked it against the bowstring. Dani was motionless on the ground. "You're not getting one inch closer to my wife."

I looked at Amelia, noticing for the first time the patch of red growing beneath the slash in her skirt where Kai's first arrow had found its mark. There was no time to check wounds or compare the damage caused.

"Baby Kota lost her mommy. She lost her daddy, too." The cruelty of Kai's words seemed miles removed from the kindness of Shay, the Magick. What had caused the vile fracture of Kai's soul, creating this heartless being standing before us?

"Did you take him, too?" Amelia asked. The magick stalemate was creating a powerful field of earth energy around us.

"Jacob wasn't a very smart man, and he was the least of the Makers. He didn't deserve Brigid's love, and she never called to him–even when he begged."

"You mean like you're begging now?" The words flew from my mouth, and I felt a warm palm press against my heart.

Shay wanted me to stop, to hold my tongue, but Kai's spite and misplaced hate exhausted me. We hadn't asked for Brigid's call. We didn't choose to become the Magick and the Maker. It hit me then, this truth about the goddess. Kai hadn't chosen it, either. "You chose to give up the power. You must have, or how do you explain being here?"

"Chose!" Kai laughed as she said the word. "You know how the Magick comes, don't you, Shay?"

Shay's hand fell away from my chest as she reached for the gun in her holster. She nodded, and I wasn't quite sure what she was thinking. It had been so long since the transfer of power, but I wondered if it was the sacrifice of Benton's life that my lover reflected on now.

"And you, little blacksmith. You are the special one, aren't you?" Kai stepped closer. "The Hammer of the Goddess. The power is like a drug. You can almost taste it in your mouth, can't you?"

This creature in front of me had the voice of a human, the flesh of a monster, and the kind of hatred birthed from more than one lifetime of pain. Kai, the Magick-Maker, once worthy enough to carry the power to protect this territory from pure evil, was in there.

"Why do you want to hurt us? You've already carried Brigid's Hammer. What more do you want?"

"So—damn—naïve!" Her body lunged as a hand shot forward to grab at my throat. Shay stepped in front of her.

"*No!*" Kai's body flew back against the cave entrance as the two collided, and I heard the snap of bone and flesh colliding with rock. The more we fought with the human side of our Magick-Maker ancestor, the less we could see that humanity.

Amelia loosed an arrow at Kai's demon form, embedding the tip through her and into the rock wall. Amelia fired again and again, pinning the monster's arms in place.

I grabbed Shay's shoulders, turning her toward me. "Honey?"

I felt the thick material of her bullet-proof vest and realized that my demon steel experiment had protected us again. Shay dropped to one knee and pulled the punch dagger from her boot. Without hesitation, she ran toward our attacker.

The creature pulled an arm away and swung with full force at Shay. Shay blocked the strike with her wrist cuff, and the monster tore from the wall and collapsed to the ground. Frozen in place, Shay plunged the dagger deep into the monster's neck, burying the weapon beyond the flesh of her knuckles. The flash of fire and magick was blinding, and I held my hand to cover my eyes from the light.

The vibration of Magick and the separation of demon and human echoed around us. It was impossible to know what remained as Shay pulled away from the limp creature's neck. Shay opened her hand. The blade of her dagger was gone, and all that remained were the two bone scale halves of the handle.

Shay looked at the monster slumped against the rock wall. "The demon steel. She—it's gone."

I felt the same sense of loss as if a human life had been taken. My heart was heavy as my hand fell to the Dagger of Doom fastened to my hip.

"What does it mean?" I hesitantly approached and placed a hand on her shoulder.

"It means she's gone." Dani's voice was weak as we turned to look at her. Her heels were folded, bent under her hips as she rested on her knees. She looked pale, but it was clear she was disappointed she'd missed the fight. "Gatekeeper steel, right?"

It took a second for me to process the half question. Yes, I'd made the punch daggers from Gatekeeper steel, but why would that kill Kai? And what did it mean for the lifeless creature before us?

"It *was* Gatekeeper steel," Shay explained. "Wildwood made the punch daggers from the Gatekeeper we buried in the carriage house."

"Put the pieces together; *really* think about it. Kai was bound to that monster." Dani pushed up from the ground. "And that thing, it's some breed of Gatekeeper."

I picked up the hammer, pumping my wrist to feel for Brigid's magick. "And this? What could she do with my hammer? She's not the Maker any longer."

"Some part of Kai was still inside this thing." Amelia stepped close enough to poke the tip of her bow at the lifeless remains.

"You okay, D?" Shay asked, pulling the light from her duty belt to shine it down the mine's tunnel.

Dani was rubbing the skin under her chin. The bruise was dark purple, and it was difficult to tell if she was out of breath from fighting or struggling with an injury to her windpipe. She coughed to clear her throat. "I'm good for now." She pointed at Shay's shoulder. "You need to look at that wound."

Shay rubbed at the ripped shirt and pulled a bloody hand away. "I'm good. We can manage wounds after we find Dex."

"What about that?" I pointed to the corpse resting against the rock wall of the mine entrance.

"It's not going anywhere," Shay said as she jogged to the patrol car. The back doors popped open, and she slid out our bag of weapons. "Take this." Her hands worked quickly around my waist as she fastened a belt over my hips. "And the axe." She spun me in a half-circle and threaded the axe handle into the loop.

I eyed her up and down, comparing her gear to my own. Her hair hung wild around her face; her cheek was painted with a smear of blood. It was impossible to know if it was hers, mine, or Kai's. Her shoulder wound was visible, but it didn't appear to be bleeding any longer. Her duty belt rested around her waist, loaded with her usual accessories: hand-radio, gun, handcuffs, ammunition magazines, expandable baton, and a now-empty taser holster.

Shay pulled the trigger on the taser to test the battery before inserting a new cartridge. There were no Maker forged weapons around her waist.

"Where's your cuff?"

She pulled up her sleeve to reveal the shimmering metal around her wrist. "Kai's powers were almost too much for us."

"She wasn't supposed to exist," I said without thinking.

"You're right." Shay combed her hair back and fastened it into a ponytail with an elastic band. "Hundreds of years living a half-life must have been excruciating."

I heard fast feet kicking across the gravel. "Are you going in to find Dexter?" Dani asked as her body spun around to rest against the side door of the patrol car.

"Andrea—I mean, Kai said something about the embryos and their power to control Dex. He should be out here. Something's not right."

"Do you want us to go in with you?" Dani asked, and I watched Amelia flinch.

"Danielle."

Shay shook her head. "I want the two of you to stay here." She pointed at Amelia's leg. "She hit you?"

"It's just a minor cut. Nothing to worry about." The bow was still tight in her hand, and it was clear she could take care of herself.

"Good, we don't have time for first aid. We need to find Dexter." Before anyone could say a word, Shay issued commands. "D, I want the two of you to stay here and watch that." She pointed to the combined demon remains of Andrea Peters and Kai.

"You want us to do anything with it?" Dani asked.

"Build a fire." Shay slammed the sliding drawer of the patrol car shut. "But nothing else. I want to check the magick before we destroy it."

"Roger that," Dani said as she pulled the first aid kit from the back of the SUV. "I'll take care of my wife. You hit the radio if you need help." She squawked the button on her hip radio to check the connection. "Echo ready."

Shay rotated the dial on her radio until we heard the crackle of feedback. "Roger that." Her fist bumped against Dani's shoulder, and she turned toward me. "You ready, baby?"

I wasn't ready. I would never be ready to go back inside the terrifying tunnels. Shay's flashlight clicked on, and I was two steps behind her as we entered the mine.

As we followed the single beam of light through the darkness, I realized my fairy friend was still missing. I whispered to Shay. "Where is Stout? Oh goddess, did she kill him?"

Shay stopped and rested her hand on my shoulder. Her flashlight clicked off, and she whispered words I couldn't quite hear. I felt the energy of the earth, the vibration of Brigid's Hammer as the weight lifted from my hand. The surrounding space changed as if we'd disappeared into a drifting cloud.

"Stout is okay," she said, but the magick passing between us distracted me. My hand raised to reveal the *ignis* flame burning strong.

"What is this?" I flexed my hand into a fist, and flame squeezed from the edges.

"It's the Rasavatam. An incantation to create a protective barrier, holding time for us."

"Holding time? What does that mean?" I adjusted the hammer into my sigil hand and the energy waned.

"We did it in the bar," she explained. "Well, we did it wrong in the bar, but it's meant to freeze us together. To help us if we're under attack."

"As long as we are together, we're shielded?"

She kissed me. "That's right, baby."

I closed my eyes, taking the first long, calming breath since Andrea–or, I guess, Kai–had dragged me from the carriage house. "What did she do to Stout?"

"It was terrible." Shay holstered her flashlight and held both of my hands.

"Is he dead?" My heart was heavy as I tried to read the answer in Shay's eyes. The sting of salty tears hit the slight cut on my cheek, and I pitched my shoulder up to wipe them away.

"Oh, no." Shay's hand covered my cheek. "No, Wil. He's alive, but she nearly killed him."

"She tore his wings," I explained. "It was so horrible, and I couldn't stop her."

"It's okay. He's okay. I'm not sure if he'll ever fly in a straight line again, but he'll be annoying you in no time at all." She pulled me against her, and I surrendered to the moment. There was no safer place in the universe. "I love you," she whispered in my ear before letting me go. I felt the Rasavatam barrier fall away just before the flashlight beam lit the tunnel.

"I love you, too," I whispered, and we took our first steps toward finding our dragon-dog.

The tunnels felt damp, more so than I recalled from the last trek through. The walls were slick with embryo remnants, which meant Dexter had been here.

The flashlight paused on a pool of liquid on the ground. Shay tapped the toe of her boot against it. "Looks like blood." She dropped to a knee for a closer look.

"Animal or monster?" I asked, and she turned to look at me.

"With the dirt mixed in, it's hard to know, but there's not enough for a kill, just a wound."

She pushed off from her knee, and we continued onward. The light swept side to side as we navigated through the twists and turns of the tunnels. Shay moved with caution, but Dexter's safety was her focus.

"*Reditus.*" Shay spoke the command for him to return, but I wondered if it would be that easy. Silence fell over the tunnels.

"Now what?" I asked as Shay took another step forward.

"We keep going."

I looked down at the hammer in my hand, realizing that there were few circumstances when I would ever face danger with a four-hundred-year-old shop tool in my hand. But here I was, feeling the strength of Brigid pulsing through me. My fist squeezed around the hammer handle at the same time I bumped against Shay. She stood frozen in place—her light shining bright against the limp body of a dog on the ground.

The flashlight fell, and the beam cast a long line of light as Shay rushed toward Dexter. Her hands roamed across his body, raking through his thick fur. I didn't know if he was alive, but the tears streaming down Shay's cheeks were most likely from an answer I didn't want to hear. She collapsed against the animal, and the sound of her grief echoed off the tunnel walls around us.

"Is he…?"

I couldn't form the words with my mouth, but somehow, I knew. Dexter's blood-soaked chest wasn't rising and falling. His furry legs lay still, and his fluffy tail lay motionless in the dirt.

Shay didn't say a word as she pushed her arms under the animal to scoop him off the ground. I picked up the flashlight, directing the beam in front of us as one partner carried the other down the turning tunnels toward the opening of the mine. Shay's body jerked and trembled as she stopped fighting the tears.

"Shay?"

I didn't know what to say. We'd experienced loss before, even faced the death of someone we'd called mama, but this was different. Dexter was her partner, her magickal best friend, and there was nothing I could say to lessen the depth of her pain.

She didn't respond to my call, and as much as it concerned me, I also understood. There was no plan for this loss. It took twice as long to navigate the tunnels, but Shay's pace quickened as we saw the first glimpse of daylight. Dani was standing watch as we exited the mine, and I heard Amelia's bow twang as it fell from her hand.

"What happened?" Dani asked, helping to carry the dog to the open rear door of the SUV.

Shay's silence was unbearable, so I answered for her. "He was like this when we found him."

"He's covered in blood," Amelia said, as she stopped behind us.

"What do we do?" I looked at the women in front of me. Their experience with the demon magick forces of Bannock *had* to afford them answers.

Shay wiped the tears from her face with the back of her hand and opened the drawstring on the top of our backpack. The bottle of anvil dust was the size of a salt shaker, and I wondered if it had the power to restore the life force of a dragon, a dog, or a combination of the two.

Amelia opened the water container and poured it over Dexter, searching for his wound. She worked from his head, along his torso, and down to his hind legs. "There's nothing." She made a twirling gesture with her hand, and Dani and Shay rolled the animal over. Amelia washed away the bloodstains. "I can't find a wound."

"You'll find nothing on the outside." The voice came from the mouth of the mine, and we turned to see the creature crawling to its feet.

"What the hell!" Shay yelled, and before I could stop her, she was running toward the monster. "What did you do to him?"

"I did nothing." It shook its head at the ground, directing us toward the scales of bone from Shay's punch dagger. "You killed Kai, and you killed him. You should be more careful where you stick your knives."

Shay's hands clamped around the shaft of an arrow, and she twisted it inside the creature's shoulder. "What do I do?"

"Dig a hole."

It screamed as Shay pulled out the arrow and stabbed it into the creature's shoulder again. She pulled out arrow after arrow, puncturing the demon over and over until she'd exhausted herself. She stumbled backward, aware for the first time that the Gatekeeper was standing on its own.

"Shay!" I yelled as the demon lunged at her.

Amelia reached for her bow, and I heard the dense clang of a shotgun round being racked into the chamber. Before my next breath, the demon flew backward toward the mine entrance.

Dani stood with the shotgun tucked tight to her shoulder. "Not my wife, you piece of shit."

Amelia stumbled to her feet, bow in hand, and in one seamless motion, drew an arrow from the quiver and shot the demon. The arrow's tip pierced the monster through the neck, and it fell limp against the rock wall once more.

"Shay."

She stood facing the demon, chest heaving, eyes cold and hard, her handgun drawn, but she was frozen in place. I looked to Dani, questioning how to release Shay from the disconnect. I heard the metronome cadence of a wing flutter, followed by a horrifying cry.

"*No!*"

I turned toward the open end of Shay's SUV to see my fairy friend weeping over Dexter's lifeless body. Stout disappeared into the saturated mass of fur, burrowing for what I guessed was the wound to the animal's corpse.

"There's no wound." He splashed through the puddle of diluted blood and water. "There's no wound!" he yelled again, this time getting Shay's attention as he screamed at her. "Get your Magick ass over here!"

Shay holstered her gun and sprinted to the open end of her patrol vehicle. "What do I do?"

"He's not dead." Stout hovered in front of Shay, and I got my first glimpse of the fractured wing and the bright red wound where it met his small body. Stout flew to Shay's hand. "He's poisoned by that—that—thing." He spat the words as he pointed to Andrea's demon remains.

"Poisoned?" I asked as I stood beside them, watching for the rise and fall of the animal's chest. I wasn't sure how or where to search for a pulse, but I was sure Dexter was gone. "He hasn't moved. Not once since we found him."

"It's the embryos," Shay said, barely a whisper.

"It's the embryos," I agreed, turning to watch Amelia and Dani secure the demon behind us.

Shay searched through the gear in her SUV. She tore open a kit that wasn't for medical first aid, then opened a jar and sprinkled herbs and oils into it. I didn't understand the Latin words she was saying, but I knew the Magick was about to perform a spell that required everything within her.

"Kai said her guardians would eat him back," she said.

"And that helps us, how?" I asked.

"The goddess is the source of us," Shay said as she unclipped the belt from her waist and threw it in the SUV. "The goddess is the source of us." She pulled the flaps of her shirt, tugged it off her shoulders, and removed her body armor. It was my first glimpse at her wound in the light of day, and it appeared the bleeding had stopped. "Goddess—is—the—source —of—us!" she yelled before pouring the mixture of oils and herbs into her hands.

The contents of her magick kit were rolled out, and I saw the labels: "hale and thistle," "bane and rye." But my eyes focused on two things: demon sift and fairy dust. I knew from experience how dangerous the combination was, and I stood frozen as Shay slathered it on her hands and pulled the slippery concoction through Dexter's thick coat of fur, under his eyes, and all around his snout.

"Goddess is the source of us." She repeated it, and this time, I repeated the words with her.

"Goddess is the source of us."

"Stout!" Shay yelled.

"It'll work. It has to," he said.

Shay's hands stopped in place, and I could barely make out the whispered words. "We have to surrender to the magick of the book."

"Shay!" Dani yelled as I heard the whizzing fling of an arrow leaving a bowstring and finding its target. Our demon wasn't ready to die, and I didn't understand why it was so hard to kill. We'd fought Gatekeepers many times.

The next few minutes happened in slow motion. Shay reached across her K-9 to the duty belt thrown inside and drew the handgun. Stout ran across Dexter's fur-covered belly to the canister of ammunition Shay collected. He lifted two cardboard boxes with his feet until he found the one marked *Last Resort*. Stout ripped the cover and removed two of the three shells. His wings flipped and flapped twice as loud as they had before as he balanced one shotgun shell under each arm. He landed on the barrel of Dani's gun and tried to force the ammunition inside.

Amelia released another arrow while Dani discharged the final round from her shotgun. The demon's leg buckled below the knee, and the creature fell to the ground.

"I'm not that easy to kill!" it roared as it crawled up onto the uninjured leg.

Shay stepped closer, gun drawn, and aimed at the demon. She fired once, hitting the creature in the center of its chest. The monster howled with laughter as the bullet impacted it, and I realized why: the shot hadn't penetrated the taut skin.

Dexter's body lay in front of me, and I stared at the glistening oils saturating his fur. He was our secret weapon, but here he was, already defeated. I fell back against the door of the SUV and felt the pressure of my axe. It was *the* axe, the one that never missed, the one that killed demons with a single strike. My fingers gripped the cold metal as I pulled it from my waistband.

It took five steps for me to get clear of the vehicle and be able to focus on the fight.

Shay ejected the magazine from her gun and forced another inside. Dani was pumping the action of her shotgun, loading the *last resort*. Amelia stood atop her perch, her last arrow nocked on the bowstring.

Shay looked at me, aware for the first time that I had the axe. The demon surged forward, and before I could take another breath, Dani fired, Shay fired, Amelia fired, and my axe flew through the space between us and into the demon's chest.

I'm not sure which strike made the kill, as all the blows hit close enough that the demon exploded into pieces.

"Oh, gross!" Dani yelled as she shook the guts from the end of her shotgun.

Chunks of demon landed near my feet, but I was more concerned about Shay. She let her gun fall to the ground as she raced back to her truck.

"Dex?" She called his name, but the animal lay motionless. "Dex!" Her voice was louder as she shook him.

"Shay." Dani touched her shoulder. "He's gone." The shotgun fell to her side as she looked at her wife for help.

"He's not gone!" Shay pulled away. "He can't be."

"Oh, Shay." Amelia touched her hand.

"*No!*" The scream came from the deepest part of Shay's soul. It was primal, visceral. It spoke of the pain of grief, wasteful loss, and ultimate sacrifice. "We have to get him to the circle." She picked Dexter up and carried him to the kennel area of her patrol car. The door lock released, and Shay loaded him inside.

I understood she meant our sacred circle in the carriage house, and I ran around the side of the SUV into the passenger seat. Shay steadied her hands as she started the vehicle and tore away from the scene, chanting, "Goddess is the source of us." Her right hand fell from the steering wheel as she reached for my hand. "Say it!" My body twitched from the abruptness of her command, but I understood.

"Goddess is the source of us," I chanted with her.

Shay's eyes returned to the road. The drive from the mine to the carriage house takes less than thirty minutes, but it felt like hours. The SUV lurched to a stop as Shay jammed the vehicle into park while leaping from her open door.

"Get to the carriage house," Shay said, scooping Dexter from the kennel bay.

My trembling hands fit the key into the lock of the bright orange door. She was two steps behind me as we stumbled our way to the sacred circle on the floor.

"What do you need, Shay?" I asked, ready to run in any direction.

"Everything," she whispered as her hands drifted over her partner.

I didn't know what that meant, but I ran up the stairs two at a time until I was at the top, racing to the apothecary room. I picked up our grimoire, Shay's notebooks, and the Rasavatam. My heart was pounding as I carried them down the stairs. With my free hand, I added Brigid's Hammer to the pile. Shay was lighting candles and drawing symbols on the floor around the circle.

"You don't need any of those," Stout said as he weaved and flapped to the ground in front of us.

"What do you know, Stout? Please!" Shay's cries for help cut through me as I stumbled inside the circle on the floor. The room glowed from the blue-lit runes of the carriage house walls, and Shay froze. The desperation faded as the realization hit. She reached for my hand and pulled me down beside her.

"*We* are the source, Wil."

"We are?" I asked, my eyes wide with surprise.

"You and me, like it's always been." She held her palm to mine and said, "*Ignis*." The blue flame flashed.

"*Ignis*," I said with a hoarse mumble as the orange flame exploded from my sigil beside hers.

Our hands met, palm to palm, and the stunning orb floated from us and stopped as it hovered over Dexter's body. The magick fell from the air, exploding against his furry side until his entire body took on a green glow. Shay fell forward onto him, unable to control the tears running down her face.

I didn't see a change as my hands tangled in the thick, damp fur. I didn't want to believe that the universe would be so cruel, but my head dropped, and I couldn't fight the tears any longer.

"Oh goddess, Shay. I don't want to believe this." My hand brushed against hers, and I paused when I felt the tremble beneath us. If the earth could respond with pain, that's what I'd think was happening, but it wasn't.

"Dex?" Shay whispered against his neck. Our bodies lifted again, this time with enough force that she sat upright.

"Holy shit!" My palms flamed, and I pulled them off of Dexter. I blinked hard when I saw his hind leg twitch. "Holy shit!" I yelled again.

"Dexter!" Her voice broke as she said his name.

His legs kicked, then his torso jerked, and he rolled to his feet like a wild stallion after playing in the dirt. His eyes blinked twice before his slimy nose pushed against Shay's cheek, and a giant tongue slapped against her face.

"Holy shit." I couldn't believe he was back, and I didn't know what else to say as my arms wrapped around the two of them.

"You're back." Shay kissed the side of his face as she rocked us back and forth. He relaxed against her, and we sat together for a long minute. "You're back." Shay sat upright, taking the dog's face in her hands. She was serious when she looked him in the eyes. "Naughty dog." She scolded, and his paw raised toward her lips to stop her from talking.

Dexter turned to Stout, and an exchange of information passed between them.

Shay stared at the fairy. "What did he tell you?"

"Well, he kinda said you should…" He stopped and stared at the dog.

"I should what?" She turned her attention to the sad puppy eyes in front of her.

"You should let other people take care of you."

Shay's body shook with tears as she fell against the dog, who was strong enough now to sit at full height. Relief flooded the room as my hand traveled up and down Shay's back.

He was alive. Our family was alive, and we were going to be alright.

CHAPTER XXIV

SEAMLESS

As I walked through the carriage house workshop, I tried to process the events of the day. My anvil stand sat ice cold. The forge's fire was extinguished. There was no sign of the Maker's productivity, but the Magick's presence was everywhere.

I dropped to a knee to touch the remnants of candle wax from the casting circle Shay had set only a short time before. The pooled wax was still soft. The books, our history as Brigid's children, lay strewn around me, and I couldn't recall a single spell we'd used today. The hammer lay on the floor in our circle.

I was still processing.

"Hey," Shay whispered in my ear as her arms wrapped around my hips.

I welcomed the embrace. "Hey yourself." I looked down at her hands, still bloodied from the fight.

"How are you?" she asked, tightening her hold on me.

The weight of my head felt impossible to carry, and it fell against Shay's shoulder. I didn't know how to answer the question. "I'm not sure."

Her arms fell away as she turned us face to face. Dirt and debris stained her stunning pale complexion, except for the white streaks running from her eyes, down her cheeks, and over her chin: a warrior's face.

"It's going to take a while. I understand." Her fingers touched my lips, grounding herself in our connection before pulling me in for the most tender kiss. I closed my eyes and surrendered to everything. This righted my world. Shay Pierce was alive, holding me close to her, and the solid ground created from that knowledge was what I needed at this moment.

She stepped away, taking my hand in hers as she led me toward the staircase. I followed simply because she'd never led me in the wrong direction.

"We need to take care of your shoulder," she said as we walked past the kitchen.

Dexter's head popped up long enough to see us before returning to whatever interaction was taking place between him and Stout.

My fingers fanned over my shoulder, and I felt the sting of pain. It was all I was really aware of in this moment: my pain and the shock of the unbelievable. "I guess I kinda forgot." My voice sounded fragile, unreliable to my ears.

"Don't worry, love. I didn't."

She led me through the apartment to the doorway of the bathroom. The shower was already running, and I stared at the wet paw prints on the bathroom mat. I felt her hands tug at the hem of my shirt.

"Let's get this off," she said gently.

She threaded my body through the holes of the shirt. I felt the sting of my wound as the cotton fabric pulled away from the dried blood. The shirt fell off my fingertips. Shay popped the button of my jeans and slid them, along with my briefs, down my thighs. I kicked them to the floor and tugged my bra over my head. She held my hand as she opened the shower curtain and helped me step over the side. Shay didn't move as the water pulsed against my back.

"You're coming in, aren't you?" I clutched the curtain to keep it open.

Shay smiled. "I'm going to take my clothes off first."

"Oh, right."

The fabric curtain fell from my hand, and I turned to stand in the cascade of hot water. I bent to adjust the dials and raise the temperature, and the heat pelted my skin, reminding me I was alive, affirming that we had made it through the most brutal attack we'd ever faced. I turned my shoulder into the spray and felt the stinging bite of the puncture wound.

"Shit!" I yelled just as the curtain moved to reveal Shay.

"What is it?" she asked as she stepped over the side of the porcelain basin.

"A bit more than a flesh wound." I tipped my shoulder at her.

Shay nodded, and I watched her tug the curtain aside to grab something from the shelf on the wall. "This might help, but it's going to hurt a little." She guided me out of the spray, twisted the cap off the bottle, and poured a generous pile of demon sift into her palm.

"Just do it."

My eyes clamped shut as I gripped her shoulder for support. Seconds later, I felt the slap of ice-cold flakes of demon sift hit the wound. The scorching sensation of fire replaced the cold as the puncture puckered and bubbled in response.

"Shit! That hurts," I seethed through clenched teeth, looking down to watch the sift work.

"Only for another second, and then you can do me." She winked, and I felt the lightness of her affection soften the moment as she smeared a pinch of sift across the cut on my cheek.

"Ooh, forgot about that one."

"It's just a minor cut."

Our foreheads touched, and I drew a slow, deep breath. It released across her throat, and I felt safe for the first time all day. My spirit surrendered as the trembling sobs took over.

"I was so scared." The words came out through streams of tears.

Shay turned us toward the cascade of water, washing the scale from my shoulder and face, never for a second breaking the contact I so desperately needed.

"I know, baby," she whispered in my ear. "I've got you now."

I've got you now.

Those four words hit me hard. Andrea had taken me against my will and forced me to harm Stout and bring terrible pain to my found family. My hands shoved the shower curtain as I pushed at the wall, and I wept as the truth became clear.

"Thank you," I whispered, but it felt like it wasn't enough. Part of me hoped she hadn't heard because I hated this feeling of helplessness.

"Hey." She touched my chin, and I resisted, embarrassed. She tapped my chin again."Wil, look at me." I turned around, and her wide green eyes spoke volumes. "Nothing would keep me from you. Nothing! You hear me?"

I did. I heard her words and saw every emotion in her body language. She had me, and it was all I ever wanted for the rest of my days. But today had almost been my last.

"She hurt me, Shay." I stared into brilliant green eyes. "She had me, like Dani." I touched my throat. "But she didn't stop. I fought so hard, but I could feel my life draining away, and all I could think of was you. I thought about you finding me just like you found Dexter, and that I was breaking my promise to never leave you."

"Wil." Her hand caressed cheek.

"I love you, Shay."

"I love you, too," she said, and we stood holding each other, letting the hot spray of water wash away the remnants of the day. "How would you feel about a cleansing bath?" she asked.

"I'd feel like it was an excellent idea, but first we need to take care of your shoulder."

Shay's tolerance for pain was superior to my own, and when I poured the demon sift over her wound, it puckered and bubbled, but she barely flinched. She soaped her body and washed the residue away before switching the shower stream to fill the tub. I tugged the curtain into the corner and pressed the stopper to plug the drain.

"Candle?" I asked.

"This one will work." She took it from the shelf behind us, along with lavender oil and a few pieces of rock.

The rocks were an interesting addition, and I raised my eyebrow. "Rocks?"

Her smile was sweet and patient, and I prepared for a lesson in magick. "Crystals, baby, and you know these." She raised the first one. "Rose Quartz for healing and forgiveness." She held the pink translucent hexagonal crystal up to the light. "Kinda beautiful, isn't it?" She placed it in the basket hanging from the waterspout. When the water reached the right height, the crystals would fully submerge.

"Everything in this bathtub is beautiful."

"I agree." She smiled and kissed me before holding up the second rock. "Citrine." She pinched the honey-colored lemon-drop-sized gemstone between her thumb and pointer finger. "This will help restore the earth energies we used today."

The rock was small. "That's a lot to ask from that little crystal, don't you think?"

"Don't worry. It can handle our magicks." Shay set it in the tub basin.

"I know this one," I said as I picked it up from her open hand. "This is quartz."

"Rock crystal, more specifically," Shay explained. "And why do you think we want this in the bath?" she asked.

I didn't have a clue. "More than because it's pretty?"

"Yes, love." Her laughing smile was polite as she took the crystal from my hand and set it in the water.

I offered my best guess. "The crystal is clear. So will it help with all the mess of the day?"

"That seems like the perfect explanation." Shay lowered herself into the water that had risen to mid-calf. She pulled at my wrist, and I snuggled myself between her legs. Her arm draped over the rim of the bathtub, and we relaxed in the heat of the rising water. "Spill a few drops of this."

She held the lavender oil in front of me. I twisted the top and tapped a couple of drops into the bathwater. The smell was the perfect complement as I felt her hand rest against the soft skin of my belly. Her hands had carried the scars of a warrior long before she'd battled the demons of Bannock. Her hands had also held my hammer–a hammer that had transformed.

"Can we talk about that hammer?" I played with her fingers, lifting them from the bathwater.

"Crazy, right?" She raised her hands out of the water.

"Brigid's hammer changed into a freakin' sword." I turned my body to face her. "Baby, you wielded the sword of the Goddess Brigid."

"Kinda cool, I guess."

"What?" Her lack of excitement was not going to work. I knew it was more than "kinda cool."

"Okay, yes, it was incredible," she admitted. "And the magick was everywhere, not just in my hands. I've used so many weapons in my life, but Brigid's sword is like nothing else."

"Kinda cool. I can't believe you." I shook my head and turned to lie against her again. "We're going to have to go and play with it."

"I'm not even sure how I made the blade appear," she said, relaxing her legs against me.

"Dani will be happy to help," I said.

"I'm positive she'll enjoy experimenting with an enchanted sword."

I closed my eyes and let the warmth of the bath and the heat of her skin comfort me, but mentioning Dani reminded me of being in Andrea's chokehold and of Amelia's injured leg. We'd left them behind. My body shivered at the idea of them still out at the mine.

"What is it?" Shay asked. Her arm fell from the edge of the basin to wrap me closer.

"Dani and Amelia," I said. "We left them there."

"It's okay," Shay soothed. "While you were downstairs, I sent D a text. I told her we were okay. She and Amelia are cremating the remains."

"The remains. It seems impossible."

I thought about Kai's transformation. Andrea Peters had lived a half-life, or possibly a third life. It was dizzying to consider, Andrea hiding the demon that commanded the tortured spirit of the first Magick and Maker.

"What seems impossible, love?" Her fingers caressed my chest as her palm steadied over my heart.

"How was Kai inside Andrea all this time?"

"I've been thinking about that myself." Her knee came up, and her foot tucked beneath my thigh.

"And?"

I felt her chest shake against my back as she chuckled. "And my best guess is it's your hammer and their relationship with it."

"What was their relationship, exactly?" I asked.

"Stout said something that brought it all together."

"About Brigid's Hammer or about Kai?" My finger made tiny circles around the drops of water on her knee.

"About the reason Kai couldn't manage our powers and Brigid's destiny, too."

I turned sideways in the tub so I could see Shay's face. "Destiny, huh?"

"That hammer—you and me—it didn't come to you just because you're the Maker of Bannock. It came to you because you're meant to protect me so that I can protect everyone else."

She made it sound so easy, the way we fit together all nice and neat, but this had been a sloppy mess from the start. "Kai was a demon for hundreds of years."

"It must have been a terrible struggle."

"Do you think she fought it?" My back rested against the tub wall as I tangled myself in between Shay's open legs.

"As much as anyone could."

Kai, the Magick and the Maker, had lived trapped inside the demon of all demons, and we sat there trying to figure out how. Her magick had become entangled with a great evil, and now the human being was gone. I wondered what we had to do next.

"How are we going to explain Andrea's disappearance?" I asked.

Shay tugged me into her arms. "Dani and I will meet with the Chief. The official report will read very much as Jacob's did."

"Andrea wasn't kicked by a horse." I raised a skeptical eyebrow.

"No, not the horse part, but another terrible and unavoidable accident."

"That's creative." I rested my head on her shoulder, staring at the candle flame burning beside us.

"That's Bannock." Her comment was unapologetic.

"Can you live with that?" I wondered if they used such imaginative report writing for all of their demon attacks.

"To protect this town and the people I love. We all have to live with it."

It wasn't my place to question procedures for suppressing the demon activity that generations of Bannock residents had survived. The rule of law had provided hundreds of years of protection, and functioning in the modern world was a delicate exchange. Bannock Police Department took care of their own, and I realized now, I was one of them.

Shay trembled. "Are you cold?" I asked.

"Maybe a little, I guess."

"Let's get out of here and go to bed. I think I'd like to hold you for about a million years."

"Just a million?" she teased as her toe hooked the chain connected to the drain stopper.

"That might be enough." I pushed against the side of the tub and stepped out.

Her slight smile made me pause. "Yes, I think it might."

I wrapped a towel around her shoulders, and she opened her arms to include me in the linen hug. I felt content in her embrace as she worked the cloth up and down our bodies. It wasn't efficient, but I was okay taking every bit of time to be with Shay.

We climbed naked into the bed, and the warmth of her skin touching mine was the last thought I remembered until the light on the following day broke through the open window shade.

I lay in the same position I'd fallen asleep. The absence of a morning alarm was almost as loud as the alarm itself. I felt the steady motion of two fingertips treading back and forth across my shoulder as I lay beside her.

"Good morning," she whispered over the top of my head.

I tucked myself tighter, worried she was about to leave our bed. "It wasn't a nightmare, was it?"

Her hand stilled, and I felt the rise and fall of her chest as she took a deep breath. It was clear that I was not dreaming, and that the two of us were still here.

"No, baby. It was all very real."

CHAPTER XXV

CONJURER

"Do you have to get up to answer it?" I heard the vibration of a cell phone on the bedroom floor. I knew it was Shay's because mine was somewhere downstairs, abandoned in the workshop the day before.

One day. It had been less than twenty-four hours since— since what? Since the Assistant Mayor turned into Kai, trapped inside a powerful demon. I felt the warm body beside me scoot to leave our bed.

"No." I pouted. "I have to. It might be Dani." Shay rolled over the side of the mattress, and I fell into the warm vacancy she left behind. I watched her walk naked across the room.

"Pierce," she answered in what I liked to call her sexy, just-out-of-bed voice. She was silent as the person on the other end spoke. "What time is it?"

I looked at the clock on our side table. We'd slept past 7:00 am, but it didn't feel long enough.

"Wait, what?" Shay set the phone on the table to pull a shirt over her head. She pinched the phone between her shoulder and ear as she jumped into a pair of pants. "I'll be right there." She dropped the phone on the bed. "Put on some clothes, baby. Dani and Amelia are downstairs."

"They are?" I pulled the blanket over my head and buried myself under the pillows. "I don't want to do any people today."

Shay laughed, and a few seconds later, the covers moved down my torso, and my naked body felt the cool temperature of our bedroom.

"You only have to see Amelia and Dani." She lifted the pillow covering my head and whispered. "The only person you're going to *do* today is me." She walked away, and I rolled on my back and watched her go.

I lay naked, arm over my eyes, fighting the inevitable. I wanted my morning in bed with my girlfriend, but that was obviously not part of her plan. Dani's voice was impossible to ignore, and my feet dropped to the floor one at a time. I dragged myself to the dresser for a shirt and pair of pants, fighting the need for clothes. I didn't plan to have them on for very long, so I didn't waste time with briefs or a bra. My feet were bare as I walked out, trying to comb my fingers through the tangles in my hair.

"Hello, Wildwood," Amelia said as she sat in the chair Dani was pulling out for her.

"Hello," I said, taking the hand she was reaching out to me.

She was using crutches instead of a cane, and I noticed the absence of her prosthetic leg. I remembered the stain of blood on the hem of her skirt. Each one of us had suffered during Kai's attack yesterday, and it would take us a while to recover, mentally and physically.

"How's the leg this morning?" I asked, tipping my chin at her leg.

She gave it a pat. "It'll heal. I just have to use the sticks for a couple of days." She crooked a thumb at the crutches wedged against the back of her chair.

I frowned, thinking about the wound, or lack of wound, on my shoulder. We'd been selfish last night, Shay and I, using demon sift to heal both of our injuries. Amelia needed it, too.

I looked at my girlfriend. "Shay?"

"What's up?"

I tugged my lip in my teeth, hesitant to ask, wondering if too much time had passed to use it on her injury. "Do you think it's too late to try demon sift on Amelia's wound?"

Shay hesitated. "I don't know." She looked over at Stout, who sat on the kitchen counter staring at the growler of beer from the bar. "What do you think, Stout? You have more experience than we do."

"It'll work." He jumped in the air to fly to the table. "But it's gonna hurt like hell."

"Maybe we shouldn't experiment on my wife," Dani said pointedly.

"It'll be fine, Danielle. It can't be worse than the fight that took it off." Amelia pushed up from the chair to follow Shay.

"It'll be fine," Shay echoed, knocking her fist against Dani's shoulder. "I'll take excellent care of her."

Dani held Shay's hand, giving it a squeeze. "I'm sure you will."

I watched Dani as her eyes followed Shay and Amelia out of the room. I saw a lifetime of admiration as she focused on the empty hallway. The silence was solitary and awkward.

"It only hurts for a few seconds," I said, but I wondered if the comment was for my comfort or Dani's.

I hated to watch suffering. But Dani had been there at the mine weeks ago when we'd healed Shay's wounds. She had to know what was about to happen to her wife.

"I guess that's a good thing." Her eyes kept focused on the hallway.

"It's difficult to watch the person you love suffer," I whispered, mostly to myself.

Dani turned to look at me, devotion in her eyes. "Yes, it really is."

I heard our fairy clearing his throat, and I ignored it. He was louder the second time.

"Yes, Stout?" I rolled my eyes.

I didn't turn to look at him because I already knew what he wanted. It was 7:00 in the morning, and he had a one-track mind. His desire for that first taste of beer was almost as strong as my desire for Shay. Who was I to impede a little happiness?

"Did you bring the beer for me?" he asked, and I could hear the paper tear from the end of the straw just before a puff of his breath shot the wrapper across the room.

"We brought it just for you," Dani answered with a chuckle. She pushed up on the edge of the table to stand, and I waved her off.

"Sit down. I've got it." I moved to the cabinet and pulled out a glass. The automatic coffee pot beeped twice to signal its finish. "Would you like a cup of coffee?"

"That'd be great."

"Son—of—a—motherfu—Damn!" Amelia's voice echoed from the bathroom, and Dani's head turned toward the sound. My fist clenched the cup as I relived the demon sift experience from my shower last night. Toughness didn't mean painless.

"I guess it's working," Stout said as he impaled the glass of beer with his straw and sucked a long sip.

Dani's fists were white-knuckled as I set the mug of coffee on the table. Shay and Amelia were down the hall, less than twenty-five steps away, but it might as well have been ten miles from the way Dani fought the urge to see her wife.

"Everything alright?" I yelled down the hallway.

"She's a damn trooper," Shay answered. "The wound looks fantastic."

Dani's fingers rubbed over her eyes as she struggled to listen to her wife in pain. "I can't stand this. I hate when she's hurting."

"Does it happen a lot?" I asked. Amelia was the first amputee I'd ever spent time with, and I wasn't sure if my question was appropriate, but I was concerned about my friend.

"Not much anymore." Dani's hands wrapped around the base of her mug. "That first year was tough, and we were so lucky to have Benton, but sometimes I wish it had happened to me instead of her."

"Oh, you are such a great big dummy," Amelia said, as she made her way back to the kitchen. Dani jumped up to pull out her chair. "You couldn't handle it." Dani leaned in to kiss her wife, and Amelia gave her a loving tap on the cheek. "Everything is as it should be, my love."

"So you say." Dani sat, and Shay dropped into the chair between us.

"The wound is gone, and you'd never know an arrow struck her," Shay explained as she got up to pour a cup of coffee.

"There's a two-inch dinger in her socket, and the liner is trashed," Dani said, passing her mug to her wife.

"We can replace it." Amelia sipped from the hot cup. "We're still here, and that's what's important." She reached over to pat my hand. "How are *you* doing, Wildwood?"

"I'm alive, and so is she." I grasped Shay's hand and held it in my lap. "But I don't think I'm ready to manage the reality of Kai and Andrea and that thing that was left behind."

"Yeah, that thing," Dani said with a shudder. "That Gatekeeper on steroids. I'm having a difficult time wrapping my head around it, too."

"And what Kai said about your family…" Shay said, but I could hear the hesitation in her voice.

"That was a bit of a shock." She turned her eyes on Shay. "But you already knew, didn't you?"

Shay nodded.

"You should have told me," Dani whispered.

I had to agree with Dani. No one should carry the burden of someone else's past. Keeping secrets about Dani's parents' deaths could come between the two friends and partners. Andrea's revelation was cruel, but knowing was better.

"I didn't want you to hate Reg for keeping the truth from you; I just–."

Dani interrupted. "So, you were going to carry that lie for her and protect a dead woman?"

"Until the day I died. Right or wrong." Shay reached across the table to her. "I guess it doesn't matter now. What Andrea did. That she killed your mother, that Reg knew. Reg should have been the one to tell you, but maybe she was afraid to lose you, too."

"Like she lost my father," Dani said.

Regina had lost Jacob piece by piece. First, after Mary's murder, and then when Dani came out, but losing the Maker and Magick bond had sent Jacob down that final self-destructive path.

"The call of the hammer is hard to fight," I said. "Kai and that demon inside her would have killed us all."

"They're gone now." Dani removed a bag from her back pocket and tossed it on the table in front of Shay and me. "When we raked the ash from the cremation, we found this." Dani tapped the plastic.

"What is it?" I asked, picking it up. It was less than five inches and looked like bone, but the char on the edges highlighted the jagged grooves. I remembered researching mace-style weapons, and this object was reminiscent of battle clubs. Perhaps this was some kind of spire? "Is it a weapon?" I asked. An odd whistling filtered through the room from somewhere nearby, and I turned to search for the source.

"We don't know," Dani answered. She didn't seem to notice anything odd.

"It could be a spire," Shay said as she held the bag up to the light. "I can't see through it." She fanned the plastic ripples flat and traced the four notches through the bag. "You said it was the only thing left?"

"Aside from the ash, there's nothing," Amelia confirmed. "Not a trace of that demon or Andrea."

"What about Kai?" I asked.

"You and Shay are the only ones who can answer that," Dani said.

"Do you feel different?" Amelia asked.

I looked at Shay, who was staring at the dog curled up across the room. "When we lost Dex, I felt it. The void was like being torn in two." She tossed the bag on the table. "When I buried the punch dagger in that monster's throat, I felt overwhelming relief, and I lost myself in that fight. My only thought was protecting Wildwood and avenging Dexter."

"I think the loss of the Magick and Maker bond tainted Kai's connection with the real world. I mean, there have been three Makers before me and three Magicks before Shay. The demon part of Kai must have felt those transfers of power."

Shay sat back in her chair, and I watched as she flicked at the corner of the table. "There's no way that demon's been in Bannock for four hundred years."

"What are you thinking, Pierce?" Dani turned her body toward the table, leaning in to listen.

Shay stood and reached for the leather-wrapped book on the counter. "The history of the Magick and the Maker, our grimoire, is a diary of the people who protected Bannock and carried Brigid's magick."

"Yes," I said. "We don't know half of what's inside."

"And the Rasavatam." She unfolded the cover. "Spells meant to tear us apart and bring us together."

"What are you saying, Shay?" Dani asked.

"These notes and reference books were in Benton's cellar. A solitary Magick protected all of it for years. Why?"

"There's something more," Amelia whispered.

Shay's head tipped in agreement. "There's something more."

I felt the surge of energy, perhaps the call of the earth. Or maybe it was the rush of adrenaline meant to protect me in a fight-or-flight situation. Whatever it was, my hands trembled in response.

"We're going to need access to Andrea's apartment," Dani said as she stood from the table to put her mug in the sink.

"Probably," Shay said.

"But, not today." Dani pointed to Amelia's coffee. "Done?"

"Yes."

They stood to leave. "We're going to get out of here and let the two of you rest. I'll take Amelia home and get to work on the incident report."

"That's a lot for one person, D." Shay stood beside her friend.

"I know, but strange things happen in Bannock all the time."

"To the Assistant Mayor?" I asked.

"No one is immune to demon attacks," Dani said. "We should know that by now."

Amelia reached for her crutches. "Yes." She stood and made her way around the table to hug Shay. "Take your lady back to bed and get some rest. The official paperwork can wait one more day." She patted Shay's cheek, gave a reassuring squeeze to my arm, and turned to the staircase.

"You heard the boss." Dani wrapped Shay in a hug. "I'll do the preliminary paperwork, and tomorrow, we'll secure Andrea's place."

Dani followed her wife down the stairs, and Shay was a step behind the couple. I heard them talking for a few minutes, then a loud, "Later, Wildwood," echoed up the staircase. I set our coffee mugs in the sink and picked up the plastic bag.

"Curious, isn't it?" Shay said, her arms wrapping around my waist.

I peeled the bag open and reached inside to touch the bone. "Do you hear it?" I asked as I rolled the stick in the bag.

She took it from my hands. "What do you hear?"

"You do, don't you?" I asked, comforted by the knowledge that I wasn't the only one who could hear it.

"It's like a birdsong," Shay said.

"Oh," I hesitated. "I thought it was more like a whistle, but now that you say it, I think it might be a birdsong."

"What does it mean?"

Shay carried the stick closer to the dog and nudged the animal awake. "Dex?" she whispered.

He hadn't moved since crawling into his bed after the revival spell. It took time to recover from magick that powerful. His head popped up, and he sniffed twice before his head feathered with dragon scale armor, and his body transformed so quickly he knocked Shay off balance.

"He hears it too," Stout said as he walked over Dexter's scaley shoulders. "He said that it's not a birdsong. It's a fairy whistle, and he's right."

"This bone is a fairy whistle?" I asked.

"No, the bone whistles for a fairy." Stout took the bag from me and ran his hands across the seal. "Don't take it out."

"Because it calls to you?" I asked.

"No, because whoever it calls to, they aren't here." He took the bag from Shay and flew it to the desk. His arms and legs struggled to pull the heavy grimoire over the top to smother the sound.

"Where is the fairy?" Shay asked as she picked up the bag and sealed it inside a glass jar.

"I guess only Andrea knows," Stout said.

Shay set the jar on the table and took two steps toward the dragon in the room. She whispered something in Latin, and Dex transformed back into his fur-covered self. I could see the exhaustion in Shay's eyes, and I reached to take her hand.

"Come on, baby. Let's go lay down for just a little."

I stepped backward, holding her hands as I directed her down the hallway into our bedroom. Dexter followed us, and for the first time, he climbed into bed beside Shay. I understood how he felt; I wanted to be with her, too.

The three of us snuggled in to rest.

~~~~~~~~~~~~

The whisper of the wind fell across my shoulder. It was delicate, like lace-covered silk resting on my skin. The whistle's song played over and over while countless fairies danced above me. It was divine, the way the magick filled the surrounding space, and I could see Shay twirling through the waving grass as she touched the tall white-flecked stones.

I didn't recognize the location, but it felt like the safest place in any dimension. I was glad to see my lover and to feel connected to whoever's tune had her lost in its song.

"Come and dance with me!" she sang, stretching her arms over her head to move with the whistle's tune.
~~~~~~~~~~~~

I stepped closer, and my feet stumbled on the crumbling planks of aged wood. I bent down for a closer look, and the voice whispered, "Don't touch it."

I pulled my hand to my stomach and watched as thousand-legged centipedes wriggled through the dark knotty holes.

"Come dance with me!" Shay yelled again, and my eyes volleyed back and forth between the dancing redhead and the insects squirming across the boards.

"Don't touch it."

I heard the fluttering sound of fairy wings. It was my fairy, clinging to a jagged bone. His little arms stretched to cover the holes, which were the source of the whistling sound.

Shay continued to dance until my finger trailed across the most exposed piece of wood. My hands turned charcoal white, and I tried to spark my ignis flame to halt the progression as the ashy transformation inched toward my wrist. The forged cuff caught the sunlight, and a burst of earth energy forced my hand to flex with bright orange flame. Sparks flew from my palm, dropping like cinders, and before I could stomp them out, the boards caught fire.

"Come dance with me," the soulless voice whispered, and a taloned hand reached up to grab my ankle. As the ground collapsed around me, I saw the stone marking the grave. The name was gone, hammer strikes erasing any history of the creature locked inside.

"Don't touch her, you son of a bitch!" Shay yelled as the head of Brigid's Hammer exploded with flame and torched into a massive sword. The talons skewered Shay's wrist and wrapped around to tear the weapon from her hands.

The sigil sparked in my palm and seconds later, Shay and I were standing inside the cavernous wooden box.

"Where are we?" I asked.

Shay struggled against the rooted ropes snaking from below us. I recognized it now, the tongue-and-groove planks hooked together with sanded pegs. We were inside the coffin, trapped with the whistling song of evil.

"You're in my world now."

The roots spiraled up Shay's torso and wrapped around her throat. I dug my fingers deep into the disintegrating wood, searching for the source of the snaking roots. Shay gasped for breath as her fingers clenched the root, trying to stop the suffocating hold.

"Stop!" I yelled.

My fingers scraped the tendrils as I struggled to cut Shay free. Her eyes opened wide, seconds before her head fell lifeless against the coffin's side.

A guttural scream ripped through me, and sobs wracked me as I tore through the tendrils to free her. I felt the rope-like roots climb my leg and creep around my hips and torso until I could no longer fight. There was no one to save me, and the pull of evil sucked me through the wall of rotten planks and into the soil.

My body sprang up from the bed, and I gasped for air, my hands clutching at my throat. I felt the sensation of the cotton fabric against my legs as I found myself in the safety of our bedroom. I turned to look for Shay and saw her wide, tear-filled green eyes locked on me.

Shay's body posture mirrored my own as she felt around her throat. Her body shook, and she struggled to take a breath. I reached for her, but she pulled away.

"It's me." I held my palm in front of her. *"Ignis,"* I whispered, and the orange flame rose in between us. "It's me."

Her fingers hesitated as she stretched to touch the flame.

"Baby, it's me," I said again.

I looked at Shay, and my breath caught as the bright red marks appeared around her throat.

"Your…your neck." She was struggling to speak.

I jumped from the bed and ran to the bathroom mirror. Streaks of dirt covered my neck, and I could see obvious lines where something had wrapped around my arms. Shay was reflected in the mirror behind me, and she turned her chin for a closer look at the marks around her throat.

"How is this real?" Shay whispered.

"I don't know, baby. It doesn't make sense." I ran a cloth under the cold water from the sink and held it to Shay's neck.

"You were there, weren't you?" she asked.

"I'm not sure how, but I was." Tears fell from my eyes as I watched Shay wince from the towel's touch.

"What the hell was that?" Her voice strained as she spoke.

It took me a moment to find the words. How to describe what we'd just experienced. Taking a deep, shuddering breath, I steeled myself for what I was about to say.

"Something bigger than you and me."

The silence in the room was paralyzing as the two of us considered the weight of those words.

<u>The Maker Series</u>
MARK OF THE MAKER
(BOOK 1 OF THE MAKER SERIES)

Wildwood Blackstone believed her dream of being a country blacksmith was coming true. When the town of Bannock hires her to restore their abandoned carriage house built in the 1800s, she can't wait to begin.

But there are more than ghosts in Bannock and shortly after her arrival, she discovers this truth. When a childhood friend answers a call for help, Wildwood finds a part of her past that she longed to rediscover. Together they reveal Bannock's secret and uncover the Mark of the Maker.

THE MAGICK AND THE MAKER
(BOOK 2 OF THE MAKER SERIES)

Wildwood Blackstone longed for a life as a small-town blacksmith. She didn't imagine monsters or magick, and she never expected to fall in love with Shay.

Book two of the Maker Series finds the two women tangled together in the dark secrets buried deep in Bannock's small-town history. Is their commitment strong enough to carry them through? Who is the keeper of the Magick? When will Wildwood and Shay uncover the mystery behind the Mark of the Maker?

ORIGIN OF THE MAKER
(BOOK 3 OF THE MAKER SERIES)

Wildwood and her girlfriend Shay have uncovered Brigid's secret hidden deep in the earth.

Who is the stranger in the carriage house? How are they there? What do they know about the secret and the power it holds? Can Wildwood and Shay find the answers and keep fighting the monsters hunting them night and day?

LEGACY OF THE MAKER
(BOOK 4 OF THE MAKER SERIES)

In a secret world filled with magick, Wildwood Blackstone has encountered unbelievable mysteries. As the blacksmith in her new hometown, she's survived and endured the call to wield the hammer of the goddess Brigid, but to what end?

Celebrating a year with her girlfriend, Shay, the two continue their search for answers. What lived inside Andrea Peters? How did the entity survive for hundreds of years? Who controlled her all this time?

Their call to be The Magick and The Maker of Bannock comes with more questions than ever, but it might also come with answers to their past. Wildwood and Shay are drawn into endless realms, all of which lead to the Legacy of the Maker.

BEHIND THE EYES

Theirs was a love story for the ages: Rasabel, the captain of the guard, and Isolde, the woman of the territory. In a world of swords and arrows, love could not defend against a cruel curse. For years, they searched for an end.
When the alarm bells of Acadia ring, Rasabel goes home, but she is not welcome. Her path collides with Bylyn, a young thief on the run from the executioner's axe. Their lives are forever entangled.
Can Rasabel and Isolde find hope in the hands of a girl who will do anything to keep her freedom?

DEAR KANE;
WHAT I WISH WE WOULD HAVE SAID

Do the words that we say in front of our children build them up or tear them down? This short story explores the consequences of hatred and bigotry when it applies, unknowingly, to someone that you love. There's a time in every relationship when a parent must let go of the dreams they have for their child, so the child can chase what they dream to become.

IMMORTAL HUMAN TRUTH

Immortal Human Truth is a collection of poetry written by the author as she traveled to promote her first book
Dear Kane; What I wish we would have said.
Each section explores experiences with love, injustice, loss, and triumph of the spirit.

SHE BELIEVED SHE COULD

What can you do in a single day? Why haven't you done it yet? Jump out of your comfort zone and dive into life as you follow the author on her journey to achieve 365 new experiences in 365 days.

ABOUT THE AUTHOR

 Sharon K Angelici, she/her, was born in the American Midwest, but her heart and soul belong to the mountains of Colorado.

She began writing as a child, using words to recover from trauma-induced depression. As a member of the LGBTQ+ community, she's an advocate for depression awareness and suicide prevention. In 2016 she published her first book dealing with both subjects, Dear Kane; what I wish we would have said.

Sharon is a full-time lover of life and all things Pagan and Magick. She's an artist and blacksmith, which inspired her to create her new Maker series. Book one, Mark of the Maker released in 2020, Book two, The Magick and the Maker, released in 2021, and Book three, Origin of the Maker released in May of 2022.

Origin of the Maker

Sharon K. Angelici

Copyright © 2022